THE BONE HARP

THE BONE HARP

VICTORIA GODDARD

Copyright © 2024 by Victoria Goddard

All rights reserved.

No part of this book may be reproduced in any form or by any electronic or mechanical means, including information storage and retrieval systems, without written permission from the author, except for the use of brief quotations in a book review.

For Wesley,
who was the one to point out this seemed like a story

CONTENTS

PART ONE
WEST OF THE RIVER

CHAPTER ONE
THE SPRING TIDE

Tamsin came slowly to himself.

He drifted for a long time at the lapping edges between waking and sleep, not quite dreaming, not quite thinking. Even half-asleep he knew it was an inexplicable peace. He held himself there, floating in the warmth, his soul open to the sun, listening to the song of water and wind, the coming and going of the sea.

There were birds singing. Not sea-birds, or not the sea-birds of the waking world; these sang like the memory of birds in the bright and brilliant country of Elfland, the Home Across the Sea, before everything.

The dim thought came to him that perhaps he had nearly woken before, drawn into himself by soft familiar voices, voices that sang the old songs, gentle hands that brushed his hair and stroked his face. But he could not remember: not without waking fully. And he knew even in his half-dream that he did not want to wake fully. When he woke, this dream of peace and warmth and wholeness would break as a wave upon the shore, and leave only the fragmented remnants of himself to struggle sodden and heavy to his feet. It had happened before. Many times before.

He had been very young indeed, the last time there had been peace on waking. For thousands of years he had woken to the pressure of all the curses with which he had doomed himself, the pain and the grief and the gnawing restlessness. When he woke from this dream of singing birds and sunlight there might, indeed, be singing birds and sunlight, but there would be no peace. There would be the silver sword in his hand, the shadow-woven cloak on his shoulders, the endless turning away from comfort. Even with all his enemies long since slain or gone away into their own long rests, there was no rest for him.

Nevertheless Tamsin felt as if he were floating in to shore, borne on gentle waters, the air warm and welcoming, fully embraced. He tried to stay there, one moment longer, but the more he grasped at the feeling, the less he could hold. Resignation settled in, the familiar cold comfort of the only remaining choice, how to respond to what he faced.

Perhaps he could stay another night here, wherever his feet had last taken him. Two nights were all he was granted, two nights in one place before the curse set him once more moving. Perhaps, if there were in truth birds, and sunlight, and what peace could be found Over the Waves, even he could have one day where he ... rested.

He could not remember if he had passed one night or two in this place, wherever it was that might be full of singing birds.

Had anywhere been full of singing birds? He did not remember birds singing before he wrapped himself up in his shadows, trusting in the silent weaves to keep him safe through another cold night. It had been so long since he'd been ... alive, in any true sense. His memory was starting to fail. He was beginning to lose names. Words. He could not even care.

He had thought more than once he was fraying, fading, his weary soul wearing away his body's housing at long last, nothing more, in the end, than what he had become, the ghost of long-dead vengeance still staining a world that had no need or want of him, the bright sword in his hand the star of his own much-heralded doom though there were none left to reckon it.

And yet he woke. He passed whatever point it was that would have let him sink back down into the whelming sea of oblivion. He became ineluctably more aware of himself, drawn to that shore of consciousness he had for once managed to evade a whole night through.

He flooded into his body as if poured by some kindly but irresistible hand from a jug of soul, and lay there for a long, long while, listening.

The birds were still singing. He could not fathom their song: there were too many birds, and their voices were too sweet, too liquid, too fast.

(Had he once been able to understand their words? Or had that always only been his friend, his rival, left behind so long ago?)

They were not sea birds at all.

He did not know their names. He listened, drawing their song into himself, their music into the deep wells where he kept his own music, for when he found himself once more alone in the dark and silent places.

Those were leaves in the wind, not waves on the shore. He listened, safe in his own net of shadows and silence. He did not need names. The birds were singing: there were no enemies here.

There had not been enemies for a long time. All the goblins and monsters Tamsin had fought were gone now; all the other elves were gone, too, long ago across the sea.

Tamsin's family had died long, long ago, but for a time other elves had lingered in the land Over the Waves, before it had been poisoned, before it had died, before Tamsin alone had been left. He alone had wandered the wastes, witnessing the long and deadly winters, the slow and hesitant springs.

Perhaps there had been birds, at the end, here and there. Perhaps even that land was healing after the long and dreadful wars. Tamsin did not remember. He remembered his cloak of shadows and silence, the sword in his hand no longer needing to be drawn, the ceaseless wandering through ever-stranger lands.

Scent came next: he breathed in, out, lingering in the slow

patterns of rest. The air was sweet and fresh, scented as with many growing things in the spring of the year.

Faint images came to mind, memories from long ago, of a garden full of irises, purple and gold blooms rich as ripe plums to the nose, gold-dust pollen on the nose of the one—who was it? (he had left her behind, as later all Tamsin's family had left him behind, so long ago)—she had stuck her face deep into the blooms, declaring rapturously that she would be a bee, a queen among bees, and drink deep of the nectar until she was drunk with its sweetness.

Tamsin sat up.

He sat up, because whatever was in the waking world would be better than falling into those memories. Fraying and fading he might be, but he was not yet so wholly lost to himself as that. Not yet.

His head swam, and he pushed at strange masses of silky stuff half-covering him until he could rub his face with his hands and blink crusty eyes open and—breathe.

The birds were still singing. He blinked against bright sunlight. Green, and green, and green—trees? grass?—his eyes focused: a greensward, a lawn, speckled with tiny pink and white flowers—daisies?—and those were—were golden-bells, with cups no bigger than a child's fingernail.

Tamsin stared at the green grass, which was brighter than anything he'd seen—anything he could remember seeing—(was that true? But he could barely remember the time before the Oath, before the Breaking of the Lamps, when the sun and the moon were not yet set in the sky)—he breathed.

There were grey shadows from nearby trees, gentle on his eyes. He feasted himself on the colours: the grey and the green, the graceful shapes of trunk and branch, the lawn sweeping up the small hillock upon which he sat.

At the base of the mound there were, indeed, irises, purple and gold as in his memory, and silver and wine-red too, and white touched with gold and white touched with blue and white fringed in silver-pink like the inside of a shell. Tamsin breathed in the air, which was sweet and that kind of fresh that felt cool and warm at the same time, refreshing as a draught of spring-water.

There were darker shadows puddled around him, falling over his shoulders, still draped over his back, catching in his ears, the corners of his eyes. They were a strange silky texture, sparkling with static electricity, warm and almost pleasing on his skin. Tamsin closed his eyes. He had not realized how far he had fallen, that he sat in sunlit peace and found a better comfort in the old dark shadows of his curses.

Had he not been done?

He had hoped he was done.

Why was he here, if he had not faded? He could not be home, could not be Across the Sea, could not have finally abandoned his exile and damned his brothers to the final consequences of their misbegotten Oath. Not after so long.

There had been no ship, not for him. Could have been none, after so long. The only way home for him was through the gates of death, and he could not take that road.

They had sworn themselves to the Eternal Night if they did not reclaim the holy fire bartered from the mountain with their father's soul. Tamsin and his brothers had sworn it. He was the last—the last —he bore the responsibility for fulfilling the Oath, in the faint hope that thereby he might keep his brothers' souls from the Eternal Night.

Tamsin breathed, and listened to the birds singing, and tasted the air, and remembered without detail that long-ago time when he was a mere elfling laughing with his brothers in the sweet youth of the world.

Eventually he braced himself. In the echoing spaces of his mind he focused, as if he were to sing power into the world, and he sang silently until his body resonated with the silent music of his imagination. Only then did he open his eyes again, protected as best he could make himself against the lingering traps and enchantments of the Old Enemy. They were weak after so long, but so was he, after so long.

He lifted up his hands to touch the smokey-dark shadows clinging to him—and stopped, stunned, when he realized what he touched was hair.

His own hair, tumbling in great wavy masses around him, shadow-dark in this bright sunlight. It caught in his elbows and under his hips as he shifted position, trying to make sense of its existence. He had hair—of course he remembered he had hair—of course he knew that his hair was dark. It was just that it had been so long since he'd seen a mirror that he had forgotten what it looked like.

He had kept his hair shoulder-length so he could wear mourning braids, even though there was no one to see them, no one to care. It had been long habit by then, the two braids from his temples, coiled around his head in a coronet, held in place by a length of ribbon. He had rarely unbraided it, except when it occurred to him to wash it, or when it grew enough that the braids loosened. Then he would take his belt-knife and saw six inches off the ends of each braid, and burn the leavings with a quiet wish (he had so long ago forfeited prayer) that his brothers would find rest and healing in the Halls of Rest, despite their Oath and what they had done in service of it.

Tamsin tugged this inexplicable cloud of hair free from where he was sitting on it, and wondered what it meant that he had woken in this strange, too-beautiful, too-familiar place, with his heart at a kind of peace and his hair loose and longer than he'd ever worn it.

There were strange knots in it, catching his fingers as he clumsily tried to shove the strands behind his ears, and—no, his mind was catching up with himself now, those were braids, intricate and far finer than anything he had been able to manage since his hands had been crippled—

He dropped his hands to stare at his palms, ignoring the way his hair slid back over his shoulders, pooling around him.

(He had been vain of his hair, once. Alone of his brothers he had favoured their father, Tamsin's hair dark to his brothers' red copper. He had never been the most handsome of his brothers, nor had his hair been in any way special—in colour it was very common amongst their people—but it had been his, and shown off jewels well, and its texture was lovely. Another thing he had long since forgotten.)

Tamsin's hands had been scarred by the snap of a fire-demon's whip, caught foolishly in his bare hands after he'd dropped his sword to kneel at the side of his brother who had died in the battle of Sawwalith (at the side of the third of his brothers who had died in Sawwalith, for the seven of them had entered the enchanted woods, and two only had left). That had been ... he didn't know how long it had been. But well did he remember how the wounds had never healed. He had been able to grasp his sword through the pain, able to make his fingers bend enough to wield it, because that was what he was needed to do. But little else.

Now, in this dream that was not a dream, with sunlight on his head and birds singing undisturbed all around him, the only dark shadows the false ones of his own hair, Tamsin looked at his hands. The livid white-red weal of the burn had faded to pink, and the puckered and melted flesh was only a ridge to his questioning thumbs. It was still visible, still ugly, still a marker of his folly and his grief—but there was no lingering burn, no bone-deep ache; he could move his fingers.

Tamsin had once been reckoned a great bard, before the dragon had taken his voice and the fire-demon the skill of his hands. Before the rising of the sun and moon. Before he had sworn that Oath and started down the path of becoming a monster. Before he had understood anything.

He stared at his hands, head bent, until his tears filled his cupped palms. The sun had descended in the sky: orange-pink beams streamed through the trees surrounding him, catching the tears into flame. He jerked his hands apart at the flash of beauty, and splashed himself with the tears, cringing back as if they would in truth burn. And yet they didn't.

His hands were healed. The gnawing, dreadful restlessness was gone. He—he might be able—he might be able to *speak* (he could barely think, *sing*—)—

He might be able to live.

He could not grasp it. He had thought he was fading. He had forgotten everything.

Tamsin breathed deep, deep, deep, and lay back down in the curve his body fell easily into, his hands folded beneath his cheek, knees drawn close to his chest, tucked into himself like an unborn babe within the womb, and fell once more asleep.

CHAPTER TWO

THE SWORD OF THE FIRNOI

His second waking was swifter.

The birds had fallen silent for a time, and began again to sing. Tamsin roused as the chirps and chuckles and querying notes gathered together into the complex, overlapping songs of the dawn chorus. This time he sat up easily, less dizzily, and remembered that his hair was everywhere. He brushed it out of his mouth, and wondered a little more consciously about the braids holding some of it back. When his fingers touched something hard, metallic, he was quicker to realize it must be an ornament and untangle it from his hair.

It was indeed an ornament, a hair-comb of an untarnished silver metal. Moon-silver, he recalled slowly, turning the comb in his hand so it caught the soft unfocused light of the last stars, the yet-hidden sun. One of his brothers, the smith (the second to die at Sawwalith, in those woods where the enchantments caught both the enemy and their own forces, come to aid those who dwelled there—but that was long, long ago—)—Tamsin's brother the smith, second in their tally of brothers—or was it third?—he had been the one to capture the moon's light into silver, rendering the metal untarnishing, luminous, strong and yet light.

This must be his work, or the work of those he had taught. It had the echo of a song Tamsin had once known, though it was not quite, or not only, the song of his brother the smith ...

Had he ever taught any apprentices how to make the moon-silver? Tamsin could not recall.

He could not even recall his brother's name.

And yet the comb was here, in his hands, having been tucked into his hair while he slept.

He turned the comb in his hands. It was not a design he recognized, though it was something someone who had known him when he was young might have thought he'd like: extremely simple, a curve like a wave or the wing of a bird or the neck of a harp, perfect.

He ran his fingers along the teeth, flicking his nails against the tines so they sang sweetly in the air, soft vibrations on his skin. He listened, his hair slithering around his shoulders, his tears falling silently.

The light was changing, gold flushing pink from silvery-grey. Even more birds were singing. Tamsin looked up, away from his hands, up at the circle of trees that surrounded him. Small birds were perched in the highest branches, silhouetted against the sky, so tiny for the sound pouring out of them.

He stood slowly, unsteadily, trying not to catch himself in his hair. There were no clinging shadows here, sticky as cobwebs, devouring memory and emotion alike. The birds would not have been singing like that if he were anywhere near those haunted woods; the air would not have tasted like honey-sweet sunlight; the wind would not be fragrant with plum-scented irises.

There were no shadows but the gentle ones of the twilight before dawn; it was his own dark hair in the corners of his vision.

He straightened, shoulders back, lifting his chin against the strange weight of his hair. He was clothed, in his own familiar tunic and leggings; he had been lying on his old grey cloak. His hand fell to the hilt of his sword, but touched nothing. No sword-belt, no sword.

A spark of panic caught in his chest. Tamsin forced himself to breathe, reminded himself again that the birds were singing, the irises blooming, the air was fresh and free as the barely-remembered air of his childhood, and his hands were no longer broken.

His hands, and—and it *seemed*, in these first minutes of awakening, that he was no longer burdened with ... anything.

He had fulfilled the Oath—

Had he? But he remembered fire in his hands—but there had always been fire in his hands, after the fire-demon's whip—and yet now there was no fire, holy or fell, in the curve of his scarred palms, when he stretched his fingers ...

Had he died? He did not remember. He could not remember anything, but that he had been cursed, and his hands broken, and now he was not, and they were not.

Perhaps he had died, and it was the hands of his dead family he remembered in his hair, braiding those intricate braids, tucking this comb into the mass of it. Perhaps this was what happened, this healing, this long sleep, when you died.

There were stories that elves would return from the Halls of Rest when they were healed of their mortal wounds, return into new bodies to walk the bright fields and forests of Elfland once more.

He had never seen it: those who died Over the Waves were gone, gone, and walked no more amongst the elves there. Not even Tamsin's brothers, Oathbound as they were, had come back in any form but his vain imaginings.

It had been a long, long exile for Tamsin, and the sun and the moon had not yet been set in the sky when last he had walked the meadows of home, but the air—oh, how he remembered the taste of the wind! And the birds were singing, still!

He had been silent for so very long. He did not know whether the dragon's death-curse would still coil around him, fire crackling in his lungs as soon as he tried to utter a sound.

And yet his hands were healed. The Oath was gone. He seemingly was no longer cursed with restlessness—

The sun rose, and Tamsin remembered the first time the sun had risen, so very long ago, and he opened his mouth and sang what he had sung then, a triumphant song of praise for the light in the dark.

Tamsin could not account for his hair. Even as he sang, it fell from behind his ears, fluttered into his face, whirled about him under the influence of the light breeze. Although he tried to gather it in his hands, the wind whipped it into his mouth, and at that he broke off his song. His voice was breathy, pitchy, hitching unbecomingly anyway—hardly the sound and skill for which he'd been named Tamsin Tammorath, Tamsin of the Golden Voice, long ago.

It had been at the very least several thousand years since he had been cursed by the dragon with silence: that he could sing at all was something of a miracle. He laughed at himself for immediately criticizing his own performance.

Hearing his own laugh ring out struck something awake in him. A sense of himself, perhaps—a yearning to go, to move, to find other things to laugh at, to talk about, to *sing*—

If he *was* back home, if he had managed to win his return, if he were free, if he were *healed*—

It was all too much to think about, after so long silent, alone, broken, lost. Tamsin took another breath, coughed, coughed again, cleared his throat, and resolutely finished the dawn-song despite how he sounded.

He stretched his arms over his head, fingers wide and so astonishingly free of pain. He felt more himself than he had in—he would call it recent memory. No need to dive too deep into past hurts when all was made new and bright and full of possibility.

It occurred to him he did not know anything at all about what Elfland was like, now. He did not know how long he had been asleep —save that it was long enough for his hair to grow into this ridiculous abundance—he did not even know how he had been come to be here.

He had no idea what had happened, back Home, here, in all the years he had spent Over the Waves. Was Tirn of Firn still king? Was Tamsin's mother still alive? Did the gods still live on the mountain in the west? (Had they kept his father's soul, that old bargain, for the fire that had been stolen?) Had his people come home through the Halls of Rest? Had his *brothers* returned to life, no longer Oathbound, no longer broken?

Was *anyone* still alive?

Or was this more of what had happened in his long exile, in the land Over the Waves, and Tamsin had once again outlived everyone? —No. He could not believe that. Someone had braided part of his hair, at some point; someone had left him that moon-silver comb. Surely not everyone had gone to the Halls of Rest or some land even further west and left him to face the world alone. Not again. Not here. Not *home*.

He reached for his sword-hilt again, the habit of millennia, and stopped again. He firmed his mouth against the panic washing through him. He did not need a sword here. He did not.

He breathed, and let the air hum in his mouth, his throat, singing comfort to himself at a level inaudible even to other elves, a level below the curse's snare. He could sing comfort, sing silence, sing endurance—to himself. He'd needed his sword for almost everything else.

He could sing out loud, now, again. He tried: a song of comfort, a little power pushed into it—

All the birds screeched and scattered into the sky. He stopped immediately.

Before the dragon, Tamsin had been a very powerful Singer. Before the dragon, he had long since turned his voice into a weapon. After the dragon, he had spent thousands of years attempting to guide the power of Song through subvocalizations. He had succeeded with a bare few things, slowly and excruciatingly eked out of the trickle of magic that could be wrought without audible song.

He would have to be careful, he decided, standing very still as the birds wheeled overhead before slowly and begrudgingly settling back down into their perches. His power had not dissipated, but his skill had. And—there were no enemies here. He could slay with his voice, very easily.

He had slain so many with his voice, before the dragon. He had not forgotten that.

He put his hand down to his sword, seeking comfort in its familiarity, in the one tangible thing he had left of any of his family—and this time felt a trickle of shame twining through the panic when once again his hand closed on empty air. He should not *need* his sword. He should not. He did not.

Tamsin had borne the same weapon since the first years Over the Waves, a moon-silver blade made by his brother the smith in the first year after the moon rose. He had not been more than arm's-length from it since—well, at least since Sawwalith. Probably many years before then. It was not entirely odd of him to feel off-kilter, even naked, without it.

Now all he had was his hair, and a moon-silver comb. Hopefully whatever Power had brought him here had not turned his sword into the comb—

He pulled agitatedly at said hair, trying to ground himself with the pressure, and when that failed, took up the silver comb. Perhaps running his thumb over the teeth would do, if he could not touch the pommel of his sword.

The comb was too delicate, too beautiful, too much a part of this paradise that had once been home and was not, could not now be. Running his thumb over the teeth, the elegant sweep of the curve, a shimmer of music resonated in the air. Tamsin gripped it in his hand, a hand that was no longer a claw, no longer brutal; his fingers *could* be delicate. Could learn again to be delicate.

He wanted his sword.

He tugged at his hair. It helped, a little, if only by making him feel foolish and young.

His hair really was absurdly long. Standing, it fell in glossy waves to the back of his knees. It didn't quite curl—it never had, he vaguely remembered wishing it would, when he was young, when some one or other of his brothers had had coppery curls and ringlets—but it was much healthier than he could remember it. A shining black, just a hint of red where it caught the sunlight, glorious as it twisted between his fingers, around his wrist.

He put his hand down to his sword—no, no sword—he *would* not panic, he would *not*, this was Elfland, this was safe, the Old Enemy was fallen and gone, bound away in the Eternal Nothing where his lies could not come twisting through anyone's minds again, and the weight of his death-curse was no longer crushing Tamsin—

Tamsin breathed. He was alive. He was free. The birds were singing. He did not need a sword. He had three extra feet of extremely beautiful hair instead.

And a voice, and hands that were scarred but no longer crippled.

He didn't *need* to be a warrior any longer. Not here. Not now. Not ever again. There had been many years—so many years—when the idea that one day he would be able to set down his sword had been all that kept him going. *One day*, he had told himself, when that compulsive restlessness had driven him away from yet another resting-place. *One day* it would all be over. *One day* he would be able to stop fighting. *One day* he would be free.

Now, to all appearances and what little he could remember it *was* that *one day*. It *was* over. He *was* free.

Tamsin clenched his fist in the air, and then lowered his hand and made himself open the fist again, spread his fingers wide, press them against his hip, where the tunic felt loose and unmoored without his sword-belt to cinch it. It was over. He was free.

He wished he had been able to set down his sword properly, lay it down somewhere significant, choose.

He breathed. The birds were singing, and the air was scented with irises, and the sun was shining, and the wind was fresh as a draught of water. He had bound away all his choices long, long ago, the first time he lifted up a sword, when he swore that dreadful Oath, when he lost himself. That he had come to this other side and didn't get to make the decision to be done *himself* ...

He breathed. Of course he hadn't. He had forfeited that right. Long, long ago Tamsin of the Golden Voice had become Tamsin Tamurzîn, Zîmdurdam, Korrokaith—the Thrice-Accursed, the Oathbound, the Dreadful—

Perhaps he was healed now of those curses. Perhaps he had finally fulfilled the Oath, and freed his soul from the chains with which he had strangled it. Perhaps his brothers, safe in the Halls of Rest, had also been freed, and were able to be healed by the ministrations of holy death. Perhaps they walked these lands, fair Elfland, free and fair themselves, no longer fell and strange. Perhaps Tamsin had only to pass beyond that fringe of trees to find them.

Perhaps.

Once he had felled his enemies as much with his voice as his sword. He would not do that again; he would not sing power into his voice. He had learned his lesson, facing that dragon. If he was here, he was safe, and, moreover, everyone else was safe from him.

He turned the delicate silver comb in his hands. And yet someone had given him this, as if he were not forgotten; nor unforgivable; nor unloved.

Tamsin breathed, and braided his hair back into a single plait, ignoring the intricate smaller braids, tying it off with the old ribbon he found in the pocket of his tunic. The crimson was faded brown now, the silver embroidery tarnished black, but it was familiar in his hands, beloved memory from his third brother.

One braid, to mourn his old life and all that had died with it. This was a new life, granted even to him by whatever inscrutable grace, whatever incomprehensible force. He could be ... anyone. Start over. Start small.

He did not need to be the lone last survivor, name forgotten, cursed to wander. He did not need to be the warrior who had terrified his allies as well as his enemies. He did not need to be the Butcher of Hinnúrin, the Scourge of Chirrkal, the Blade of the Firnoi.

He did not need to be Tamsin the Dreadful. He did not need to be a warlord of the House of Dâr; did not need to be a lord at all. He had never been very good at it, anyway. People had followed his voice, not him.

He did not need to be Tamsin the anything.

He picked up his cloak, and his sword and sword-belt fell out of its folds. He could not tell if this was inauspicious or not. He was far too relieved.

CHAPTER THREE

RIVER AND ROWAN
AND ASH

With his sword and his cloak, there was really no further reason to stay where he was, and his feet itched to be moving. To see this land he had all but forgotten, and which had surely forgotten him. And good riddance! Tamsin was neither bard nor butcher now.

He did not know what he was, but he could assure himself of that: he was not who he had been.

Even if a melody had started to curl through his mind, and his hand rested in its accustomed curve on his sword hilt.

—If his family *were* alive—his mother had not gone Over the Seas with them, after all—

Elves died by violence; very rarely from something like grief. Tamsin's mother had certainly grieved their going, husband and sons throwing their lives away. But somehow he couldn't imagine her giving in like that.

Perhaps this unmoored feeling was *anticipation*. It wasn't as if he'd had much call to feel that for a while. *Hope*, yes, he'd held grimly onto that idea of the *one day*. But anticipation? After he'd realized he was the last elf left Over the Waves, he'd hardly *expected* anything.

He circled the little grassy mound, and noted that the irises grew thick and vibrant all around, without gap or path. Whoever had come to braid his hair had not been by in a long time. Tamsin touched the silver comb, which he'd nestled into the top of his braid.

He imagined asking after his brothers, his mother, his ... friends. He'd had friends, hadn't he? Or perhaps not. Followers, for a time, before the dragon. A lover, once, if the long years had not coloured that memory more brightly than truth. But in truth, he'd never been very good at friends.

Tamsin could not imagine facing his family, acknowledging those horrible truths. *Yes, I am the Thrice-Accursed, the Dreadful, the Scourge. Yes, I swore an Oath of vengeance for the death of my father, and became little more than the shadow of death to everyone else. Yes, I killed the Father of Dragons with my Song, and in doing so lost my voice, which had been my joy, and what I was known for. I fought for my family, and I outlived everyone. In despair I struck the Old Enemy, and with his dying breath he bound me never to die. I lost myself in grief, in silence, in loss. And then I woke up.*

And then he woke up.

Tamsin stepped through the wide ring of irises, purple and gold, white and silver. He crushed stems under his feet no matter how lightly he tried to tread, and for a moment felt the old spite and cruel mockery of too many battles on fair fields, the inward sneer at beauty destroyed by his touch because otherwise he would do nothing but weep.

But then he remembered this was a new life, and there was no true darkness here. He turned, and knelt, his dark braid falling over his shoulder, catching on his sword, and he collected the broken stems.

He had a great sheaf of blooms by the time he waded out of the iris-moat. Past the flowers was a band of grass, which shirred pleasantly against his ankles as he stepped across it. Tamsin looked down, a little bewildered that he still wore his shoes. Like his other garments they were very, very old, acquired in the days when other elves still lived Over the Waves, and were held together now mostly by the inaudible Song Tamsin had been able to weave into them. But they served their purpose, and protected his feet against stones and thorns and cold.

And he was not the vain young Tamsin Tammorath now, was he? What matter if he wore a cloak and tunic faded grey and grim? What matter if his shoes were hardly more than the memory of leather? He did not need to sing up a glamour, even if he could.

Or—he could. He *could*. The dragon's curse was lifted, and his voice was no longer bound to fire and smoke, to burning and death. Tamsin began to gather power, the energy thrumming in his chest, his throat, his mouth—and then he remembered the screeching birds, the crack in his voice, the imprecision, and with a long, careful sigh he released it again.

Even that barely-a-tone flattened the grass before him, a gust cold and dry as the desert winter that left a scar of sere and blighted brown amidst all the green. Tamsin bent his head over the irises in his hands until he stopped trembling.

No. He could not limn himself with glamours, as once he had. He might still hide himself in the dim blur of his silent Song, a silent, deadly shadow with a sword made of pale moonlight—but he would not. He had done that for need, and there was now no need.

And yet—and yet neither could he trill the notes to set light glimmering in his eyes, his hair, shining like the stars, the golden-shimmering singer from long ago before they knew to call that golden hue *sunlight*.

This was his face, this his hair, these were his clothes, old and yet new. Until he could buy or barter or make something new, this was what he had.

He imagined learning a new craft, now that his hands were healed. He'd never liked weaving or embroidery, but perhaps he would enjoy shoemaking. It was not something Tamsin the Dreadful had ever tried.

He breathed the fruity iris-scent, and lifted his head to where the meadows were waving merrily in the spring breeze, and looked around, at the circle of trees around him.

He had never been good with plant-names, save as they came

into his songs. Might these be rowans? Fans of white flowers tossed at the ends of the branches. All those small and loud-singing birds were flittering here and there, bending the branch-tips under even their light weight. The trees had grey bark, mottled with paler grey and white lichens, and their many leaflets rustled pleasingly in the breeze. They were set so close together Tamsin had to turn sideways to squeeze between the boles. Fortunately he *was* wearing his old clothes, so imbued with the virtues of his Song that they would not tear; so old and faded a smear of lichen and moss mattered not at all.

He blinked in the bright sunlight of the other side of the circle of trees. The land sloped a little away from him, down to what seemed a stream or small river, hidden in a fold of the meads. It was all meadows here, meadows and little thickets of trees and shrubs all in flower. Tamsin stood at the edge of his copse, taking in the view: the blue sky dotted with white clouds, larks overhead, and an eagle circling high above the songbirds. He listened to the larks.

Mountains in the distance, blue and white, like something out of a dream. A pale splotch a little nearer: might it be a city? It was no more than a blur to Tamsin's eyes from this distance, but the idea of people made his heart beat faster. Other people—*his* people—?

It could not be *his* city. Those were not the peaks he knew, and they were angling off away from him, fading into the dim purple distance, in a way his mountains had not. But yet ... a city.

Nearer to him were green meadows, impossibly green, except where they were streaked and stippled with flowers—red and white, purple and gold, blue and pink, and some fine silvery thing like the glimmer of moonlight caught in his sword.

Tamsin breathed.

The air was sweet, cool, springlike indeed. He had his sword, and his cloak, and very little else. The small knife he'd long used for everything that the sword could not serve him for was in its sheath at his belt, opposite the sword. There was the silver comb in his hair, and the old ribbon, and in one pocket he found an oval grey pebble, water-smoothed, of no particular value except that he'd found it comforting, sometimes, to hold it. It fit well into the crooked curve of his broken hand.

Tamsin shifted the irises in his hands, and breathed, and listened to the birds singing in the sunlight. He set the irises down, in thanksgiving for the healing, for the peace, for the new beginning. He did not know to whom he should address such a prayer, he who had long since forgotten how to pray ...

And yet, someone had brought him home, despite everything.

For want of any better idea, he set off in the general direction of the distant city.

He followed the meadows to the edge of the river, which ran peaty-brown and sweet-sounding between the grassy leas. There was a game-trail along the bank, winding between clumps of rushes and the odd willow. Tamsin followed the trail, wondering idly what sort of animal would create such a route. Elfland had many strange and wonderful creatures never to be found Over the Waves, many he barely remembered or had never known.

Perhaps it was a unicorn—did he recall aright that they were solitary beings?—that paced along this brown water, dipping its pearly horn to touch the golden nectar at the heart of the water-lilies in the backwaters.

It was a pleasing image, white unicorn with moon-shining horn, eyes dark and liquid as the stream. Tamsin found the curl of melody in his mind had grown another tendril or two, and he played with the music silently for several hours as he swung along at his so-long-accustomed pace, unaccustomedly content.

And then he came around a bend of the river, through a small grove of ash trees, and discovered that he had forgotten that the animals that liked to walk along riverbanks were people.

He stopped, very startled: almost as much as the elves in front of him were startled.

He knew why he was startled, but even as he stared, utterly

confounded, he could not stop himself from wondering why *they* were so surprised to see him.

After a moment it occurred to him that he might have lost the skill of reading expressions.

There were two elves, standing under a tree as if deciding whether to sit down in the shade. They wore tunics and leggings not so very dissimilar from Tamsin's own, though their tunics were shorter—falling mid-thigh rather than to their knees—and they wore wide sashes about their waists.

One wore green and yellow, bright as the meadows and almost as strange-familiar to Tamsin's eyes: green tunic, blue leggings, yellow sash, blue and green and yellow ribbons braided into their—(her?) red-gold hair, which all clashed terribly. The other, taller and broader in the shoulder, a sword at their hip, had hair almost as dark as Tamsin's, though it was scandalously short, not even to their shoulders. She—Tamsin was fairly sure she was an elf-maid as well—wore two shades of purple, grape and lavender, and pale orange for her sash.

Tamsin had not seen another elf for countless years. He had not been able to speak for several hundred years before that. He stared.

They seemed so very young.

It was always hard to tell age with elves—once fully grown, it was mostly behaviour and language and garments and ornaments that told age, as well as something indefinable in the face, as if all the time that did not touch their bodies pooled in their eyes.

These two elves were young by every measure Tamsin could remember. They held themselves uncertainly; their clothes were pleasing to the eye, well-made, but not *fine*; the one wore ribbons in her hair, and the other had a necklace of intricately carved wooden beads. They might not be Firnoi, and thus not drawn towards gold and silver and gemstones as were Tamsin's people—but their features suggested they were.

Perhaps styles had changed. Tamsin had travelled and fought his way through the elf-kingdoms Over the Waves, watching the tides of fashion come and go. The Wood-Elves of Sawwalith had never ceased to dress themselves in leaves and berries and flowers; the Firnoi had never ceased to wear as much jewellery as possible. But it was possible that things were different, in Elfland.

The two young elves exchanged wide-eyed looks, and then the one with red-gold hair cleared her throat. "Well met, fellow traveller! I offer you no harm and would take none of you," she said, the old traditional words, if in a very strange accent, and held out her hand, fingers extended.

It turned out that ancient habit could overmaster even several thousand years of solitude, for Tamsin found himself touching her offered fingertips with her own and replying, "Well met indeed, fair travellers! No harm will I offer you save to harm given first," just as if he'd stepped out of his great-grandmother's stories of the earliest journeys of the elves.

The formal greeting was ancient magic, power sparking in the deliberate touch, fingers to fingers. An offering of vulnerability, of self, of intention, of a kind of promise.

It felt very strange to feel the tingle of warmth that flooded in the wake of the touch, half static shock, half a draught of some health-some cordial. No harm intended either way, evidently.

The red-blond elf-maid smiled, though Tamsin did not think he could name the emotions chasing themselves across her face— intrigue? curiosity? surprise? Her dark-haired friend removed her hand from the hilt of her plain, serviceable sword and offered her fingers to Tamsin for the same ritual. Another flood of warmth, of magic.

He dropped his hand and stared at the two elves, entirely at a loss for what to do next.

The last elf he'd touched had been his eldest brother, the last to die, when he had begged Tamsin to give him the mercy cut.

But they could hardly want to know that. Tamsin didn't want to remember that. And ancient customary magical ritual to establish a basic degree of safety or not—and it was hardly *binding*, except insofar as freely-given promises usually were binding, in Elfland— Tamsin had no desire to test it with his full history and identity. He had no idea how long he had been asleep, or if his reputation had possibly survived the years—or, if survived, grown somehow even worse.

The dark-haired one had a sword and the stance of one with some training, but Tamsin had been the most feared elf Over the Waves, once. He could easily be the monster of their cradle-songs.

The red-haired one was smiling happily, thumbs hooked into her sash, entirely at her ease. Her friend said something in a language Tamsin did not know, and waited expectantly, eyebrows rising higher the longer Tamsin regarded her without comprehension.

Tamsin smiled, hoping it didn't come across as one of the expressions that had once terrified his foes, and was pleasantly surprised when neither of them showed any fear. But then they had just established he meant no harm to them. Nor could they have any idea who he was, could they? Even if they had ever heard of him, they surely could not have been expecting Tamsin Korrokaith to come striding around the bend of a river here in some distant corner of Elfland!

He said, "I do apologize, but I don't speak your language." That had come out in the Firnoian of his youth, before the Exile. He pondered a moment, and added: "I speak Sawwalithian and Exilic Firnoian and the Chirrtal creole, if any of those help? And I understand Gharluish and Chirrian." He shrugged, trying to seem harmless, not giddy with the taste of speech in his mouth, words on his tongue. "I'm ... new here, I suppose."

The two elves looked at each other again, and then the one who had greeted him said, haltingly, in formal old Firnoian, rather bookish in mode: "My knowledge of this tongue is not full, for it is long indeed and indeed since the tongue has been heard even in this land." She paused, evidently rallying her thoughts together; Tamsin rather thought he recognized the efforts of someone trying to translate words in their mind. "If it be not too importunate, may I ask if you be one who has returned from the Halls of Rest?"

Tamsin hesitated. "I believe so, but do not know," he said at last, unwilling to begin this new life with an outright lie—and he did not know what was the truth.

What *had* happened, there at the end? He remembered the feel of the Oath snapping, unbinding his soul: and nothing clear after that, but for the relief surging through him in great overwhelming waves. But perhaps he had thrown himself into the sea, or fallen, in the end, delirious with his impossible freedom, and those were the waves he recalled. Perhaps it had all been delirium, his fading memory stealing even the burden of the Oath. And yet he was here.

The young elves whispered urgently to each other. Tamsin tilted his head, listening intently, connecting this new language to sounds and rhythms he did know—was that a cognate of the old Wood-Elf tongue from Over the Waves? Overall it sounded like Firnoian, though much faster in pace, lilting and running, some sounds sharpened, others elided, grammatical forms clearly having shifted. He caught a few words, fragments of meaning:

"... *No questions* ..." That was the elf-maid with the red-gold hair. Tamsin's mother and brothers all had—had had?—red hair, dark and shining as copper. Tamsin liked this paler version, like watered silk in the sunlight.

"... *No one ... Who ... they said ... but who could it be?*" That was the young warrior, with a spear-wielder's shoulders and a straight sword at her hip, a hunting bow and quiver on her back. Tamsin regarded the way she held herself, calculating threat and skill. She balanced well, and even as she argued with her friend she kept one eye on Tamsin. Skilled, perhaps, but not war-ready. Well, this was not the land Over the Waves under the Old Enemy.

"*No questions,*" the scholar insisted again, talking right over the young warrior, and with a huff the latter subsided. The scholar smiled, triumphant, and turned with her chin high and her eyes flashing to Tamsin, who—laughed.

He couldn't help himself. He laughed, delighted with their youth, the way the ribbons clashed with the elf-maid's hair, the sound of their voices on the air, their solidity, the familiarity of familial squabbling, their very existence.

And he laughed because once upon a time Tamsin had been the one to so royally declare *no questions!* And none of his brothers or cousins had been inclined to listen, either. Tamsin laughed, and though his hand was on the hilt of his sword, of course (of course), he felt no concern at all. He carefully shifted his posture away from offering any hint of threat. The warrior's eyebrows went up again, but she relaxed.

Perhaps she had not realized Tamsin was armed? His shadow-woven cloak was quite enveloping, and even if this young elf bore a weapon, she did not hold herself as one *anticipating* threat. So had Tamsin's brothers worn swords, in the youth of the world, when it had been little more than affectation.

The scholarly elf-maid was still trying to work through what she wanted to say.

"We welcome you back to the world of the living," she said at length. "We do not remember all the customs. It has been long." She shook her head. "We have not—we have never—never have we two met one come returning, yet nevertheless have we heard the stories of what we are to perform. Might thus we—" she bit her lip, frowning hard. "Will we—no—will you seek—no—" She stopped, but before Tamsin could come up with any words himself, her friend said something in their quick and flowing speech, and she, just a little doubtful, said: "We two welcome you to walk with us, traveller, and learn the new words?"

Tamsin was still parsing what she'd said. There were customs for meeting those who came back from the dead? Were those stories, then, *true*?

If he had, he Tamsin Korrokaith, the Dreadful, then—

If he had, then his brothers—

If he had—

Even if he had not, he might as well have. It wasn't as if *he* knew anything but that he had been in exile, and alone, and cursed, and now he was not.

It was nevertheless incredible that they would simply offer such an invitation. They had no idea *at all* who he was. Neither did he, perhaps, but he knew who he had been, and that was a person no one two such young elves should have been so comfortable with.

Even with the greeting-ritual Tamsin was not sure *he* was at all comfortable—with them, with the situation, with himself—

But it had been so long. He had been so lonely, so alone, for so very long.

"Yes," he said, and: "thank you."

The elf-maid looked at her friend, and then said, "I am called River, and my friend is Ash."

Tamsin felt greatly relieved that apparently false names were part of the customs. Had Ash chosen hers because they stood under a little grove of ash-trees? Tamsin tried to think of a name for himself—something simple and natural, apparently—a tree?—he could not use *ash*, obviously, and he'd not been particularly keen on oaks or elms, not after Sawwalith—

The tossing branches full of singing birds of the grove where he'd awoken came to mind. He smiled at River and Ash, these young elves struggling with a very old tongue, meeting one who might as well have come back from the dead—

"You may call me Rowan," he said, firmly. "And I should be glad indeed to walk with you for a time."

CHAPTER FOUR
FROM THE HALLS

River had been the one to argue that they should walk on the *other* side of the river that formed the border between Elfland proper and the Perilous Lands, and therefore this was entirely her fault.

Ash kept lowering her eyebrows in a very telling manner. River lifted her chin up and said nothing. She had promised Ash an adventure, and an adventure she had found! It was hardly *her* fault if it wasn't the sort of adventure her friend had been anticipating.

It wasn't the sort of adventure *River* had been anticipating, admittedly. In all her daydreams, she had never imagined finding someone returned from the dead might be a thing that *actually* happened.

She looked sidelong at their new travelling companion, who was walking along with a small smile on his face. She probably didn't need to look so circumspectly, given the bright interest with which he was regarding everything, including the two of them.

It wasn't that she really thought it was rude to look on someone who was looking so frankly back. It was more that—

She looked sidelong at the so-called Rowan again, and tried to smile when he caught her eye. He didn't say anything. He hadn't said very much, actually. It must have been several hours since they'd encountered him, and apart from their initial exchange, none of them had said anything.

River was considered odd for loving the stories of the ancient days, especially the Golden Age before the rising of the Sun and Moon, and the Shadowed Age when three-quarters of the Firnoi had gone Over the Waves to doomed Kheir. Most people did not care to ferret out the truth behind the songs even for the Age of Homecoming, when all the elves who had gone Over the Waves had come back, either by the short sea-road or the longer way of the Halls.

Or ... not *all* the elves. There were whispers that there were some elves, mostly those born in Kheir, who had refused to be returned to life, and others who had refused to go to the Halls at all, and instead faded to evil wights or houseless nature-spirits.

River was sure that if she had access to her books (small as her library was), she might be able to figure out who this elf was. There couldn't be *that* many Shadowed-Age Firnoi left to come back at this late date, deep into what people liked to call the Sunlit Age.

But she did not have access to her books, because she and Ash were heading to the Tourney, and River had brought only notebooks and a book of tales she was working on translating.

She'd hoped that in the great crush of elves competing in the Tourney she might manage to snag an interview or two with someone who might conceivably remember something from before her grandparents' stories of the ships coming home from Over the Waves.

And now she had met ... this one.

She looked sidelong at Rowan again. He had the classic Firnoian look, dark-haired and pale-skinned, with arched eyebrows that winged up a little at the outside corners, and lovely long eyelashes. His eyes were very, very dark, and yet brilliant, like a starlit lake. River felt a little uneasy every time she caught a direct glimpse of those eyes. They were too deep, even for what the old stories said of those who'd died under the Shadow of the Great Enemy.

River wished she could remember more than a few of the injunctions for what to do with someone who came back from the Halls of Rest. She was sure you weren't supposed to interrogate them, because the newly-returned-to-life often had uncertain memories. You couldn't, for example, ask someone why he'd chosen *Rowan*, of all trees, for his use-name. It was clearly not his own: apart from his expression while very obviously coming up with it, Old Firnoian names were supposed to be much more complex.

Ash was no help at all, of course. She hadn't wanted River to come with her in the first place—she'd been eloquent that she wouldn't be able to properly attend her (as if River *needed* her to!), and that Ash didn't need her support (hah!), and that River was never going to be able to persuade any of the great and distant ancient elves to speak to her, and all sorts of other pessimistic opinions River had taken leave to blithely ignore. *Her* parents thought it was a fine thing for her to go see more of the world, and Ash had only been able to stand her sauntering along half an hour behind her for all of a morning before giving up on her stubborn isolation.

River glanced once again at Rowan. It was hard to focus on him: he was strangely shadowy, almost ... blurred, around the edges. He had an old-fashioned cloak fastened at his neck with a clasp whose star device was conceivably in one of those reference books River didn't have.

He looked at her, grave as one of the village elders, and said, "Will you speak with me, *miradë* River? Teach me the way of things now? It has been long indeed since I walked these lands!" He had a rich, slightly husky voice. In his mouth the Firnoian words were *speech*, not simply sounds River tried to make into sense.

He looked out over the river chuckling quietly beside them, visibly full of wonder at a pair of white swans that were dabbling in amongst the waterlilies near them. "Ai, it is so beautiful under the Sun!" he added, tipping back his head to smile up at the celestial body in question. His hair was so long that the end of his braid nearly touched the ground when he did that. "Never dared I imagine seeing it thus!"

River giggled nervously. That suggested he was not simply a Shadowed-Age elf, born in Exile and lingering long in the Halls before coming out to this land he'd never known. He might be a *Golden Age* elf.

(If he was, he was *certainly* in one of those reference books. There were lists of names for those who had gone Over the Waves from Elfland, noting how each had died—and they had almost all died—and when they had come back.)

"Certainly," she said, trying not to squeak too unbecomingly. "Um —I—I'll start with vocabulary, shall I?"

Some yards ahead of them, Ash made a scoffing noise. River blushed, realizing she'd slipped into modern Firnish, but Rowan nodded encouragingly. He gestured at the stream. "River—" he grinned at her, the sense of infinite grief suddenly lifting with the expression, and he gestured at her. "And River again. Ash," gesturing at Ash ahead of them, and then, after casting his eyes around, pointed triumphantly at a tree on the other side of the river. "And ash, tree of *dirilan*."

She wanted to ask what *miradë* and *dirilan* meant, wanted to *talk* with him in Old Firnoian, but—well, his need to learn the modern language was a lot greater than her desire to improve her knowledge of the old.

Besides, a practical part of her said, if she helped him then he would probably be more inclined to help her. *That* surely hadn't changed, no matter how long it had been since he'd last been alive. There were barely even rumours about what the price of studying under the *old* old elves was, but even the merest hint at least suggested that one *could* make the exchange.

Not that River wanted to promise her as-yet-unconceived (in any sense) first child or a hundred years of servitude or something for the sake of learning Old Firnoian fluently.

She'd require *at least* a first-hand account of Rowan's first life for anything like that.

It was possibly a good thing that her parents had drilled the old stranger-meeting ritual into her head. She'd probably have invited Rowan along regardless, and that would have been foolish indeed if she hadn't been clever enough to trap him into a promise first. At least now she and Ash both could be sure he had reasonably good intentions.

"This is the path," River said, tapping the narrow trail with her foot. "Which we are walking along ..."

Ash could scoff all she liked. River had promised her an adventure, and an adventure they were having. It wasn't her fault if it were so apparently perfectly tailored to *her* interests, was it? If Ash had wanted this to be for her, she should have gone across the haunted bridge by the godswood *first*.

CHAPTER FIVE
SPIRIT AND BONE

Travelling with other people was strange.

Very, very strange.

Tamsin had been wandering for millennia. Curse-driven, admittedly, which certainly had had an effect on his behaviour. He had not cared where he went, only that it was somewhere other than where he'd been. He had long ago ceased to worry about where precisely he set up camp for the night, for instance, save that it was reasonably safe. For many centuries he had hardly bothered to camp at all; he would sleep for an hour or two in the middle of the day, cloaked in his shadows, and then continue on his relentless, restless, endless trek.

River and Ash took breaks. They stopped to look at flowers. Late in that first afternoon, they spent a full hour sitting by a particularly lovely stretch of water so they could ... enjoy the ambience, apparently.

Ash lay down on the grass and smiled up at the sky, fingers playing with her sword-hilt as she imagined something invigorating, if Tamsin was at all capable of reading her expression. Probably he wasn't. He felt he shouldn't be, anyway.

It was proving surprisingly easy to be around other people.

Extremely strange, but not *hard*. Tamsin wondered if there had been some sort of emotional healing happening while he was asleep, too, or if all that murderous misanthropy had *also* been a result of his idiotic Oath. He was pretty sure he hadn't *actively* wanted to murder anyone before then, not even his older brothers or their friends. Not even—

Certainly he'd never acted on such an impulse.

River pulled a notebook out of the pack she had on her back, and an inkwell with a quill (had there been no developments in writing in all these years? Tamsin was surprised and disappointed in his people —were they not the *crafty* elves?), and appeared to disappear into her own thoughts.

Tamsin watched the water flow past him for a while and wished for something to do with his hands that was not practicing fighting forms.

He flexed his fingers, astonished again to remember his dexterity. He wanted—

Oh, how he wanted a *harp*.

His first harp had been a gift from his mother when he was very young. She was a wood-carver of great skill, and she had been delighted to make for the young Tamsin all the instruments he could desire. Viol and sackbut and flute, mandola and mandolin and lute, and harps from tiny ones fit for an elfling's hands to a great standing harp as tall as his shoulder.

Tamsin had not been particularly drawn to the material arts, but he had loved his mother, and she had insisted he learn the basics of her craft.

"You should know how to make your own instruments, my love," she had said (or he imagined she had said; he had gone over this memory so many times he had rubbed it as smooth as that one grey pebble in his pocket, all that was left of shadowed Chirr). "You never know when you will need to repair one, at the very least."

At the time they had imagined nothing more dire than an outdoor performance far from a workshop, or a trip far from any other artisan. Once he and his rival had dreamed of travelling together, exploring

Elfland and its music. But she had not come with him, Over the Waves. He had learned Chirr's music on his own, yearning for her company and having nightmares of her swallowed by freezing shadows.

Later events had led him towards making and repairing any number of harps, right up till the fire-demon's whip broke his hands. Which Tamsin did not need to think about right now, did he? He rubbed his thumbs along the ridged scars. His hands were healed, and he did, theoretically, have the technical skill and experience to make a harp. He just needed the materials.

There was a tangle of wood, left from some highwater flood no doubt, a little downstream. Tamsin rose and stepped around the intent River, the daydreaming Ash, and examined what he might find.

It was not the seasoned wood his mother had used. Most of it was poplar, rotten with long immersion. There was a tangle of something harder, whiter—he crouched down so he might pull at the branches, only to pause, discomfited, when he realized that the white branches were not wood at all, but bone. A ribcage, shoulder-blades, a skull ... for a moment, seeing a pearly flash, Tamsin worried he had found the unicorn of his imagination. But then he realized the iridescence was the shell of a snail the size of his hand, clinging limpet-like to the skull of some sort of large deer or elk.

He tapped his finger on the wide ribs, humming low, deep in the back of his throat, and startled when the bones resonated.

He had a sudden flash of a vision, of a great elk, taller than a warhorse, with wide palmate antlers, running through the woods with an elf-lord's hounds baying after it. Fierce and free had the elk been, and glad of its own strength. It had not been sorry to escape the hunter by leaping off a cliff, dead instantly when it landed on its neck, free to the end.

Tamsin swallowed, and then hummed again more deliberately, holding a question in his mind, wordless: the image of a harp, the memory of how he had been free in his music; how he wanted more than anything to find that freedom again.

The spirit of the great elk, disturbed from its rest in its remnant bones, was ready to run again, but it tarried a moment to listen to the echo of music in his mind, the flash of Tamsin's long wilderness life.

He sang softly, no power in his voice, nothing like what it had once been. But yet the lament rushed forth, dark as the river running below where he crouched on the bank, hands on the resonating bones. He sang for the great elk, free to the last, and for all his brothers, who had bound themselves and were unfree even in death.

He sang, because he was, after everything, once more Tamsin Tammorath.

He sang until the first grief had poured out of him, and then he crouched silently until his heart ceased thundering, his breath crackling. But though his breath caught it was not with the fire and smoke of the dragon's death-curse, simply with the disuse of lungs and throat for such work.

He had had such laments behind his teeth, silent, thrumming only in his own bones, for so very long.

A cold touch on his forehead, as if the elk nuzzled him. Gave him its blessing. Tamsin shuddered.

The elk-spirit paced out of the tangle of bones and wood, a wisp of silver-grey, barely an echo even to itself, but still holding its great crowned head high, spectral eyes bright, as it ran away from the river and into the lands behind them, where meadows turned to woods in the west.

Tamsin bent his head. He had forgotten that there was death even in fair Elfland, and pride, and shattering gifts.

He blinked back his tears, and when he felt a little composed, he gathered up the elk's bones.

He had forgotten the young elves, who stared, wide-eyed, tears still running down their faces, when Tamsin turned around with his arms full, ribs and antlers and shoulder-blades clacking against each other, knocking at his cheek.

He had no idea what to say. River had screwed the lid back on her inkpot, and Ash had sat up, half a daisy crown formed in her hands. Tamsin met their eyes solemnly. The echo of his lamentations hovered in the air.

The tips of Ash's ears slowly flushed pink, and she turned her gaze to the flowers in her lap.

River wiped her face and said, voice wobbling only a bit, "What are you doing?"

"I intend to make a harp," Tamsin replied, in Firnoian. "I was thanking the elk for granting me the use of its bones."

Said bones were very white against the grass.

Tamsin pictured a travelling harp, and the likelihood he would make a mistake or two, remembering how to carve, and looked at River, who was visibly equally fascinated and disturbed. "Are we staying here?" he asked carefully, in his best attempt at the new language. "Or do we continue?"

River looked at Ash, who was frowning even more severely at the daisies. She cleared her throat. "I think we thought to travel a little longer before we camp."

Tamsin nodded, and unclasped his cloak for want of a better bag. Ash looked sharply up at the flash of his sword-hilt, and grunted sharply.

"I—we two had not seen your sword," River said in Firnoian, faltering. The accusation in her voice was clear.

What *were* people supposed to possess, coming back from the dead? Nothing, presumably. The more this day went on the clearer Tamsin's mind was, and the more questions he had for his own situation. But he could not answer any of them. All he knew was that he had woken up in that iris-moated hillock, in the centre of a circle of rowan trees, with his old cloak and clothes, his very ancient sword, and that hair-comb he did not know, made by an art he dared not hope he recognized.

Tamsin shrugged, removed his hand from his sword-hilt, and checked the balance of his bundle of bones, wrapped in his cloak of shadow. It was an image worthy of a ballad, he thought idly. *Tamsin Tammorath and the Bone Harp*. But of course people would think first of Tamsin Tamurzîn.

"I," he said, "was long a warrior. But I mean you no harm. Nor anyone, who does not attack me first. Come, then, if we continue. Will you tell me more of where we travel?"

They walked for another couple of hours. The sun was bright but not too hot, the birds were singing, and behind them clouds were building up—and staying behind them. Tamsin felt (a little begrudgingly) refreshed by the break—by the prospect of having a *harp*—by having *sung*—and he was pleased to focus on River's quick pattering conversation.

This new language, Firnish as she called it, was not so very different in its basic grammar from the Firnoian Tamsin knew. Firnish had dropped many of the inflections that were so notable a feature of Firnoian—but that had been in the process of happening even when Tamsin was young, before the rising of the Sun; his grandmother's language had been more complex yet—so the general trend was comprehensible. The simpler forms made for a sinewy and flexible language, and Tamsin could already begin to imagine how he could write new melodies to take advantage of Firnish's particular virtues.

The biggest difference was vocabulary. There, too, he found himself surprisingly well-equipped, for the words were drawn mostly from the tongues of Over the Waves. It would take him time, he knew, to figure out *which* words had come from where, which were calques and which loanwords taken up entire, but his ability to understand would not lag so far behind as he feared.

River expressed astonishment at his linguistic aptitude. Tamsin laughed. "I have learned, ah, six languages of elves already," he explained, "and my father, long ago, was a great linguist and lover of words, once."

He fell silent, thinking about Dâr of the Mountain, who had been a weaver by craft but who had loved words as Tamsin loved music, or his mother the curls of wood under her knife. Dâr had loved words, and used them to weave an Oath that would damn his seven sons and doom his people.

"Perhaps you might find him again, now that you are back," River said encouragingly.

Tamsin shook his head, but he had not the words or the heart to explain his father's dread bargain, which had seemed so inconsequential, once.

Once upon a time, when Dâr was courting the elf-maid who would become his wife, Tamsin's mother Alina of the Shining Wood, Dâr had taken it upon himself to find her the greatest courting-gift anyone had ever given or received. After various adventures and trials, he had in the end gone to the uttermost west, to the mountain where the gods were said to dwell, and bargained there for a branch of the flame imperishable.

In return for the flame, Dâr had promised the gods his spirit, should ever he die. In those days no elves had yet died in Elfland, or at least not to their knowledge, and it had seemed a negligible price. But that was before the Old Enemy stole the flame, and Dâr swore himself and his sons to recovering it, whatever the cost.

It had cost them everything, in the end, including their father's soul.

Possibly even elves as young as River and Ash could have heard tales of Dâr and the Flame of the Mountain. Tamsin had written songs about it: songs to stir the blood, in the first days after the theft of the flame; and laments to sear the heart, later on. Once upon a time.

Yet the chain of the Oath was gone, and the blood was washed away by the clean rains of all those centuries after the last of the monsters had fallen under Tamsin's sword, and Tamsin was here, at last, back home.

"Perhaps," he said, and smiled at River. "Have you any siblings? Brothers or sisters?"

"Two sisters, both older," River replied. "And Ash is the middle of five! Not so many as the Seven Damned Sons of Dâr, of course, but then that *is* an unlucky number!"

"Indeed," said Tamsin. He supposed it was justice, of a sort. They'd wanted to be remembered.

"We're not damned, just doomed," Ash said, so deadpan it took Tamsin several moments to realize that *doom* must have lightened in meaning, and that Ash meant it as a joke. By then it was too late to laugh, which was embarrassing.

At least they thought he'd come back from the dead that morning. Surely that granted him a little leeway when it came to morbid jokes.

~

They walked until the sun turned rich gold, flooding the westward land with a light so close to the gods' lamps of old that Tamsin could not resist singing one of the hymns he'd written for the gold-gleaming Light of Day.

His voice was still rough, but each time he opened his mouth and sound came forth it sounded sweeter. It would likely never be what it had once been, before the dragon and before the battles where he had sung death to his foes ... but then Tamsin himself could not go back before then, either. He could only be who he was now, after the long silence and the long solitude and the long sleep.

Each song helped him knit a ravelled piece of himself back into the whole. He could not sing for long—even speaking too many sentences at a time had left him hoarse and dry-mouthed—but he *could* speak, he *could* sing, and soon he would have a harp in his hand as well.

For a given value of soon, that was.

Tamsin left off his singing and turned to find that River and Ash were listening to him, their packs on the ground. Their eyes caught the sun, golden as the dragon when it had stared Tamsin down. He refused to shudder, and instead gestured at their packs. "Did you wish to rest?"

"We thought we'd camp," River replied. "This seems like a pleasant spot."

Tamsin glanced around. It was a pleasant spot. The river-bank was very low just here, and the grass grew rich and lush. There was an old willow tree with long silver leaves and yellow-green twigs, and the river—grown greater with the addition of smaller streams that afternoon—was golden in the light and a deep brown in the shade. Behind them the clouds had grown massive and black. Unless the weather in Elfland was *entirely* different from Over the Waves—or what it had been in Tamsin's youth—there would be rain over the southern hills that night, and lots of it.

"Do you disagree?" Ash said, a hint of challenge in her words.

It was exactly the sort of place two very young elves on their first adventure would choose.

Tamsin had given up on *most* considerations for camping over the years, but even he tried to avoid obvious danger.

"Let me teach you a better way," he said, and headed inland to where they might find firewood, and food, and perhaps even shelter, and avoid the sort of flash floods that had given him the tangle of elk bones.

CHAPTER SIX

THE WET AND THE DRY

The younglings were not incompetent—not that Tamsin expected them to be: they had reached this isolated stretch of land safely enough, after all. From River's brief explanations, they were from a small town or village tucked into the southern hills, near the Black Lake. That was not a name Tamsin knew, but then he'd been a child of the city, once upon a time, and the geography of Elfland was notoriously hard to map.

He chose the lee of a large boulder for their camp. The stone was warm from the sun, and provided them a windbreak from the wind blowing down the river-valley. He tasted the air, and considered the clouds.

"We shall greet the rain ere morning," he declared. "Have you a tent?"

"Of course," said Ash, a little offended. "We'll set it up, then, shall we?"

"I'll lay the fire, if you'd like to collect some wood, Rowan," River interjected.

It took Tamsin a moment to remember that was his new name. "As you will." He was glad to have the time to himself: no matter how pleasant the company, or surprisingly easy the conversation, it was still true that he was woefully unaccustomed to people.

He took his time gathering wood. The game was abundant, he'd noticed that over the afternoon. Not only the birdlife, but rabbits and deer, and many other small creatures he'd have eaten, had he needed to. How long had it been since he'd had any meat that wasn't carrion crow or vermin!

He brought his first armload of wood to River, who was placing small stones into a circle. She jumped as he stepped out of the shadows. "Oh! You startled me! No wood-gathering song?"

He blinked at her. "It is unnecessary when there are no enemies about."

He'd left his cloak bundled around the elk bones, but he probably didn't need it, with how long he had spent weaving shadows and inconspicuousness around him. His inaudible humming was ... probably unnecessary, too. Just a habit. Like the sword.

It was probably immoral how easy all this made it for Tamsin to catch a brace of rabbits. But if that had been the worst of his crimes, he'd have come home long ago.

It turned out the Firnoi had not entirely forgotten they were the *crafty* Elves. After they'd eaten a meal of Tamsin's rabbits, waybread Ash had been carrying, and dried berries courtesy of River, they settled down around the fire with their crafts. River had a splendid crystal light that shone with a clear, warm radiance, just right for reading— or woodcarving—or embroidery, which turned out to be Ash's handicraft of choice.

"The lights were invented a *long* time ago," Ash said, when Tamsin expressed his fascination.

"Maybe before the Sun rose?" River said. "When it was dark all the time."

"It wasn't dark under the Lamps," Tamsin murmured. "It was beautiful." He set the crystal down on the rock they were using for a stand with a soft clink. He had spread the bones out beside him, and was pondering the basic construction of a harp. He'd start with the soundboard, he decided, as it was the largest piece and would determine the rest of the harp's dimensions.

The great elk's antlers were huge—not the eighteen-foot spread he'd seen in a majestic trophy mounted in the king's palace, once upon a time, but the great rack must have been at least twelve feet across when it was intact. Either the impact of landing or the subsequent action of the river in spate had snapped the right half off entirely near the base, and broken a few of the tines from the left.

He considered the palmate antler. The usable area was perhaps three and a half feet long and nearly a foot and a half wide at its greatest breadth. In depth—he peered at the antler side-on, imagining what his mother would do. If he could split the thing—he started to hum, low in his throat, trying to catch the resonance—

"Will you tell us of the time of the Lamps?" River asked. Tamsin started, his voice lashing out. The antler fell apart in two neat halves, and he set them down as if he'd entirely intended that result.

"Certainly," he said. That was quite enough song-craft for now.

The rain started around midnight.

Tamsin was sitting by the fire's embers, restful but not sleepy. He had shooed River and Ash into their tent, which was a cunning little thing with interlocking poles that folded down to fit Ash's pack. It was much easier to carry than the big campaign tents he remembered from the wars Over the Waves, and Ash said that they could have used osiers or other pliable young shoots in place of their folding poles.

They'd nearly invited him to share the space, but even if it had not clearly been too small an interior to house three happily, Tamsin did not think he could bear being so close to them. He might trust them—and they him—enough to travel together, but he could not trust enough to be enclosed in a small space with them. Nor could he quite trust in Elfland without setting a watch of some form. His subvocalized protections, wound about their little encampment before he settled down, would wake him if necessary.

He was glad they would be continuing on in the morning. He was glad he had his sword at his side. He was glad for his old cloak. The bones would be fine for the night.

He watched the burning stars until the dark clouds hid them, and then he flicked up his hood, the old songs in the back of his throat, and let himself fall into a reverie with the sound and feel of the rain on the tent beside him.

He had new songs in his mind when the dawn turned the rain silver. What a gift, he kept thinking. What a gift!

He had to stop thinking *how long it had been*. It had been very, very long: and so? Here he was, travelling with two splendid young elves of barely two centuries, learning a new language as tripping and fast and fun as a cantering horse. Here he was, with hands that obeyed him and a tongue that could sound forth. Here he was, in this strange land that was *home*. Here he was, with a new name that had nothing of doom or damnation about it.

What a gift!

The wind picked up just after dawn, shredding the clouds and sending golden light slantwise through the lingering rainshowers. Tamsin built up the fire anew. He sang his cloak dry and then, discovering the long tail of his braid was utterly sopping wet from where it had lain unnoticed outside the shelter of his cloak, unbound it so he could sing it dry too.

This turned out to be a mistake.

He was still regarding the snarling cloud of knots that had been wet but orderly an ill-timed note or two before when the tent flap opened and Ash crawled out.

"Good morning," Tamsin said, catching his fingers experimentally somewhere in the mass of hair.

Ash merely nodded, straight-faced (but then she had siblings, and with four that was surely enough to have had one as vain as Tamsin had once been), and disappeared around the boulder. Half-suppressed laughter floated back the moment she was out of sight. Tamsin sighed and put another piece of wood on the fire. He should have whittled himself a comb last night, rather than getting so excited about the prospect of a harp. The silver hair-comb was beautiful but was not designed for practical detangling.

Bone was probably a better material for a comb than the remnant firewood, he decided after examining what he'd found the night before. It was all ash and poplar, quick-burning even in the damp, and a couple of pieces of gnarled chestnut. In his youth he could have sung the wood into shape—the part of his mother's craft Tamsin had naturally been the best at—but as it was, he contented himself with a quiet but sharp sequence of notes that cracked the rib he was holding into half a dozen pieces.

Ash ran around the boulder as a muffled cry came from the tent, and Tamsin caught himself at this reminder that he was not alone.

"What *happened*?" River said, scrambling upright. Her hair was half-braided, too, but significantly sleeker than Tamsin's mess. "Rowan, what—what happened?"

Tamsin considered what he could say. He could feel himself blushing. He hadn't blushed since—he had no idea when. Tamsin Korrokaith had hardly been known for being *bashful*.

But he wasn't Tamsin Korrokaith here. He was Rowan, recently returned from the Halls of Rest and understandably—or at least plausibly—a little out-of-sorts as a result. He shrugged, a little self-deprecating, honestly embarrassed at the state of his once-greatest skill. "My Song has had a few unexpected results since I've ... come back to myself."

River nodded, as if this did indeed make sense, but Ash was more persistent. Or possibly more awake. "But what about the cracking noise?" she said suspiciously. "Something broke?"

"Oh, that was on purpose," Tamsin said, gesturing at the neatly segmented rib. "I spoke of my hair. Now I must shape a comb."

The two young elves exchanged glances. "I've got a comb you can borrow," River said after a moment, her gaze lingering on Tamsin's cloud. Bush? It probably looked more like a bush. But Tamsin was a bard. He was going to go with *cloud. A snarl of tangled shadows.* Something like that.

A comb was, or would have been, back when Tamsin was young, a very intimate offer indeed. But from River's expression she did not think of it that way, and even Ash did not look disturbed. Tamsin had lost most of such niceties long ago—he wouldn't want anyone not close to him *touching* his hair, but borrowing a comb was not so bad. He'd done as much with his cousins, when he was young.

"Thank you," Tamsin replied gravely. "I would appreciate that."

"I'm going to practice, then," Ash declared. "Pass me my sword, River, will you?"

River went for water from a stream that had been a much smaller rill the night before, and proceeded to make both tea and a kind of oat porridge involving such unexpected delights as hazelnuts and *cinnamon.*

Tamsin had not been in the habit of eating more than once a day, if that. Yet he had not so much as smelled cinnamon since the last Elves had passed over the sea. His stomach still felt full from the previous evening's meal, but ... *cinnamon.*

River smiled at him from time to time and sang in a light, pleasing voice *new* songs. Tamsin's grasp on the new language was not quite good enough to be able to follow all the lyrics, but the melodies and harmonies—new, new, new, and so glorious to his ear.

He listened, humming along as he began to understand the patterns of rhythm and mode. It was slow work, the porridge River was making—clearly she and Ash were in no hurry whatsoever for whatever journey they'd undertaken—and even slower to wrestle his hair from its static snarl.

On the meadow a little downhill from where they'd set the tent, Ash had drawn her one-handed sword and a long knife, and was going through forms. Tamsin watched with mild curiosity at first, and then increasing respect, and then with a growing question in his mind.

Ash was driving herself to improve. That much Tamsin could see, from the care with which she sought precision and the force when she was satisfied with her own form. She was already at a very high level of skill, of the sort that suggested she had spent decades if not most of her few centuries (how old were they, anyway? Tamsin was assuming a couple of centuries, but he had no real idea) practicing with focused intent.

The question was *why*. What could possibly be driving a child of peaceful Elfland to master the sword?

He was still only halfway through his hair when Ash finished. Seriously, it was *so much hair*, what was Tamsin supposed to *do* with it all—especially if it was going to respond to humidity and being dried by turning into a bush?—but yet the idea of *giving up*, of just cutting it off—

There were reasons why Tamsin was the lingering last survivor of all the elves who'd lived Over the Waves, and part of it was simply that once decided on a course he was stubborn. Deciding to chop off all that beautiful hair the second day he had it, simply because he was unaccustomed to caring for it, didn't sit right with him.

"Would you like some porridge, Rowan?" River asked, and Tamsin realized he'd started brooding about his hair to the extent he'd entirely lost track of his surroundings. He sighed to himself. And to think he'd managed to keep himself alive all that time alone.

"Yes, thank you," he said, and added *utensils* to the list of things he should probably make before a harp. A bowl, too; this was almost certainly River's own dish. A bowl would be easier if he had a gouge, so he decided to look for potentially useful stones as they travelled as well.

At least the night's reverie seemed to have settled the new language in his mind. It was much easier than learning Sawwalith had been—that had not had very many connections with Firnoian at all—and certainly easier than learning Ghairluish, which had come from the east, behind the Old Enemy's lands, and was foreign indeed to any of the other tongues of the Elves.

Tamsin finished his porridge quickly and left the younglings to their own breakfast so he could wash his hands and the bowl in the stream. The rain had blown entirely away now, and the land falling away from their boulder was fair and glittering in the low sunlight. Tamsin sang a few lines of his morning-song as he returned to their little campsite.

"Oh, I know that one!" River exclaimed, and joined in on the chorus.

Tamsin stopped singing abruptly and stared at her.

"No, don't stop!" she cried. "You have such a beautiful voice! I've never heard that song sound so fine."

"Like it's *really* the first dawn," Ash muttered, then went red when Tamsin looked at her.

"I wrote it for the first dawn," Tamsin said, and then bit his tongue. *Surely* that would give him away.

But River and Ash did not stare at him with the fear and dread Tamsin associated with his reputation. "I'm sorry," River said blankly. "Did you say *you* wrote the Dawnsong?"

"You know I was there for its first rising. I was telling you about the Lamps before the sun and moon last night," Tamsin pointed out cautiously.

"You wrote the *Dawnsong*?" River said again. "*You*?"

"I thought you said you were a warrior," Ash put in.

Tamsin's hand drifted down to his sword-hilt. "A bard first, and then a war-bard, and then when my hands and voice were damaged in battle—"

No sense in being even more obvious and mentioning the dragon, Tamsin decided (probably futilely, given that it had taken less than a full day for him to mention this)—but if anything was left of his reputation, singing a dragon to death was probably it.

"After that a warrior alone." He touched his half-untangled hair ruefully. "I am relearning my voice now." He glanced down at his hands, the puckered pink scars that had once been such a constant fire, and spread them out, palms up, before the young elves. "My hands also."

"You wrote the Dawnsong," River said, and shook her head. "It never occurred to me that a real person wrote that. I thought it had just ... sprung into being. The old stories talk about how the Sun rose and its Golden Voice sang out, like it was the voice of the Sun itself singing for joy."

Tamsin felt himself blushing again. He'd been so vain, and yet even he had not imagined that he'd be remembered as the voice of the Sun itself singing in the first morning of the world! "They used to call me *Tammorath*," he said, and stabbed at his hair with River's comb again in the hopes that *that* didn't reveal him. Except that of course it was not as Tamsin of the Golden Voice that he had come to be remembered. He coughed. "As you can see, I am much less impressive than the Sun."

Ash had grimaced at the sight of Tamsin's scarred palms. (Well, she was hardly the first one.) She hesitated, and then looked at River, and back at Tamsin. "You are a warrior."

"I *was*," Tamsin corrected firmly. "I will fight no more, save in great need."

To defend, first of all. Against the forces of evil ... ai, if he had to. He was so tired of killing, of violence, of the bloodlust that had flooded through him in the channels carved by that damnable Oath.

Ash frowned, and nibbled at her lip. "We are going to the Tourney," she said abruptly. "Games—River?"

"A tournament?" she said in Firnoian. "That is, warriors for to compete?"

"I understand."

"I wish to win," Ash said, blunt and firm.

Tamsin nodded. His brothers had been *very* competitive.

So had he been, once upon a time. In music, not in the art of the sword. He wondered suddenly what had ever happened to his—his rival—his friend—his—his lover?—

"You have skill," Tamsin said, when it was clear Ash was waiting for some other response. "I watched."

Ash nodded once, sharply, pleased. "At the Tourney I will meet with many elves of old. It is held by Daerleon Son of Dâr, and none has ever beaten the Stonehand."

Tamsin felt a shock go through him at this mention of his older brother.

His older brother, who was not lost in the Halls of Rest, or the Eternal Night, or a houseless spirit never to come to Elfland again. His beloved oldest brother, for whom Tamsin had once damned himself.

"Oh," he said, entirely focused on Ash, as a splendid idea blossomed in his mind. "I have a quarrel with the Sons of Dâr, and he most of all."

His brothers had left him alone to carry their Oath, left him to that silent, terrible, relentless wandering. And Daerleon had been—well, without Tamsin there, who *was* there to rein in his pride?

"May it be that I help you? To defeat him?"

Ash met Tamsin's (possibly, *slightly*) feral grin with one of her own. "Yes," she said. "Yes *please*."

CHAPTER SEVEN

TALES OF THE GOLDEN AGE

If anyone had asked River what an elf born before the rising of the Sun and the Moon was like, she would have had an answer. Such an elf, she would have said confidently, would be grave, and rich with wisdom and beauty.

They would be powerful—perhaps even overwhelmingly so—their arts refined to the point of utter incomprehensibility to younger and lesser elves. Such ancient elves would be distant, their minds bent on grand concerns, walking in memories of the long ages of the world more than the present. They might even be so spiritually advanced that they were starting to lose their physical form altogether. They would be thoroughly ensconced in, even bound to their homes—or in the case of certain of the Firnoi, their works.

(It was said that the King of the Firnoi *was* the city he had made so long ago, his spirit so thoroughly sunk into its stones he could no longer confine himself to his elven body. No one had been able to answer River's curiosity as to whether his elven body was still around somewhere or whether—and if so, how—he could communicate. Her village was a very long way away from the City, and no one had had reason to go there since Ash's grandfather had competed at the Tourney, centuries before River and Ash's births.)

River had composed this mental image out of stories and songs told around their village bonfires, their family hearths. There were minstrels' songs and travellers' stories of the King of Elfland, golden and glorious as the sun in the sky. There were the handful of encounters her village had with the Wild Hunt, who were fey even in the very oldest of tales. There was the time River's uncle had encountered one of the great Ladies in the hills, dancing without music under the sky until the very stars fell down around her in sheets of of flashing silver arrows. He had danced with the Lady for a night, and come home to discover a century had passed, and he himself had been gifted with a crystal blossom that held the hint of a song in its heart, in the very quietest moments of the night.

And then there was Rowan.

On the one hand, Rowan sang with a beauty and purity that had grasped River's heart just as firmly as her uncle had said the Lady's dancing had caught him. When he had sung the lament for the bones, the stag's very spirit had come forth to listen. River could not have prevented herself from weeping any more than she could will her blood to stop circulating.

On the other hand, he was quite possibly the *ungainliest* person River had ever met.

And he seemed endearingly determined to teach them. River had learned more about how rivers worked in his explanation of why their initial camping spot was a bad idea than she'd ever absorbed from her parents. And her father was a miller!

Rowan sang a note, and all the water steamed off their tent. He watched with obvious satisfaction. "Much better than my hair," he said. "The material, I presume."

He was still fighting with the wild frizz that had taken the place of his long braid. River was trying not to laugh, she really was, but it was very hard. He had so much hair, and it was now crackling wildly around his body.

"At least it's dry?" she offered.

Rowan rolled his eyes and attacked the next section with her comb. "I should have just left it wet, and sung my clothes dry as necessary," he grumbled. His Firnish was improving greatly, uncannily so. But then River had had no one to teach her Old Firnoian.

That reminded her of a phrase she'd gotten stuck on the night before. "May I ask you a question of the old tongue?" she asked in her self-conscious best attempt at the formal High Speech.

"As you will," he replied, with a nuance she didn't quite understand. (Teacher to student? Friend to younger friend? Stranger to friendly stranger? There were so many options!)

"I have been working through this book of tales," she explained, pulling out her book. He regarded it with keen interest. He was even more alert this morning than yesterday: his eyes were very bright and intent. "I do not quite understand the final line here." She read the line slowly, trying to shape her tongue around the modulations that meant this was formal *written* High Speech. She had only recently switched to trying to read it at all in the old alphabet, and it was slow going.

She set herself to the slow, ponderous syllables. "'And the king shouted, and the queen blessed by his love sang out, and the city that had been full of merriment was quiet'. It's *blessed by his love* that I don't understand."

Rowan blinked. "Perhaps you need to start earlier in the story, for context."

"They're short tales, with moral lessons."

"How salutary," he murmured, tugging at a knot and gazing mournfully at the snarl. "Why must my hair be like this," he muttered more lowly, still in the formal High Speech. River giggled, because if she'd thought about it of course Old Firnoian was a *language*, one which real people had spoken, but yet she'd never imagined people speaking *normally* in it.

"It is a tale from the days of the Lamps," she said, by way of introduction.

Ash came up from where she'd gone to wash in the stream, realized what River was doing, and set about taking down the tent without comment. River smirked at her friend. Ash couldn't have everything her own way, could she? Yet River's small adventure had not only been very interesting but was going to be educational for both of them, *and* they'd managed to find someone who seemed immensely excited about helping Ash beat the best swordsman in all of Elfland.

River felt very smug about it. Even if Ash was still reluctant to trust Rowan more than the minimum. Well, that was probably sensible.

Rowan set down the comb and began to braid the one section of hair he'd managed to disentangle, presumably to keep the wind from immediately undoing all his hard work. River watched him for a moment, amazed as he began an intricate fish-tail braid at his temple, and then dropped her eyes to the book.

"'Long ago, before the rising of the Sun and the Moon, in the great city of the Artisans, there were two sisters who loved each other with a love so fierce it might have mended the world, had things been other than they were. One sister had seven daughters, each fairer and more accomplished than the next; the other had seven sons, each handsomer and more skilled than the last.'"

Rowan nodded and corrected her pronunciations. "If I do not offend?" he added hastily in near-Firnish.

"Please!"

"You have no idea how she has yearned for someone to correct her pronunciations of Old Firnoian," Ash said from where she was organizing her pack. "It is the greatest desire of her life."

"I am most pleased to be of assistance, in that case," said Rowan, getting up with the end of his braid still in his fingers so he could offer her a fluid and courtly bow. His hair was so long he could put that hand over his heart without tugging.

It was very, very hard not to laugh at the contrast between the elegant fishtail braid and the gesture and the thundercloud of snarls that was the other half of his hair.

Then River caught Rowan's eye, saw the wry glint in his expression, and she lost the fight. River had a nice laugh, she'd always privately thought, if perhaps a bit abrupt; it was very much the same laugh her mother's mother had. Rowan laughed too, but his laugh rang like silver bells. And that *was* straight out of the stories.

Quite literally, straight out of the stories.

The Tale of the Breaking of the Lamps was a terrible one, but it ended in hope, as that dark period had ended in the first sunrise. River had loved it since she was a very young elfling indeed, listening to the village choir sing for the Festival of the Lights.

For then it was the Sun rose, and all those gathered there in the dark heard the golden voice laugh in silver joy as the song of the morning sounded forth for the first time.

Rowan had written the song of the morning, the Dawnsong. That was *his* silver laugh in the story.

"Well now, do then go on with these seven beautiful elf-maids and their seven handsome cousins," Rowan said, still grinning in an easy and wholly ordinary manner. He finished off his braid by simply tying a knot in the end of it, which River supposed was a method.

She cleared her throat and returned her attention to the text. "'These cousins were beloved to each other, rejoicing in their strength and beauty and wit, and all the people of the City of Those Who Make rejoiced in them also.'"

"What appallingly swollen heads they must have had," Rowan murmured cheerfully, this time in Firnish. Ash snickered. By virtue of her friendship with River she knew a *little* Old Firnoian, and she had certainly heard River's opinions of the characters in this particular book of tales.

River wrinkled her nose at her friend. It wasn't her fault that there were so few books to be had in the market-town of the Black Lake. She'd had to take what she could get.

Rowan ran his hand down his first plait with satisfaction, and then sighed as he picked up River's comb again to tackle the other half of his hair. "Roll your *r*s more, River," he said. "It should be almost a trill." He spoke a few lines with his beautiful pronunciation, the sounds falling like birdsong.

He was *much* better at languages than River was. It was deeply irritating.

"'One day, if the light of the Lamp of Gold might be said to be *day*'—"

"We used the same word," Rowan said. "*Dawn* was new. Not day."

River filed that particular piece of information away to be considered later. She was struggling *mightily* with the idea that Rowan literally remembered the first sunrise. She wondered how old he actually was—how long had he lived after the Breaking of the Lamps? Clearly long enough to have gone Over the Waves and died in Shadowed Kheir ...

"'One day, if the light of the Lamp of Gold might be said to be *day*, the cousins met under the trees that border the great river that runs through the City of Those Who Make, that they might make merry together, as was meet for those so fine and free in the youth of the world.'"

Rowan snorted. Ash said, "This is *much* more entertaining than listening to her Old Firnoian practice usually is."

"Hush, you. Where was I?"

"They were having a *teska*," Rowan said helpfully. "In the park."

"Teska?"

The old elf made a vague gesture. "When you take inside food outside?"

"A picnic," Ash said.

River looked down at the text, reading over the fine old words and suddenly realizing this was a much simpler story than it had ever sounded before.

"'They sang and they danced, for amongst their number were two greatly gifted in music. Indeed, so great was their love of the art that they danced long into the gloaming, into the dusk when the stars shone over the Lamp of Copper'—"

"Bronze, rather," Rowan interjected. "You couldn't see the Lamp of Copper in the city."

River blinked. She'd always assumed the Lamps were like the sun and moon, visible everywhere. Even though the stories *said* they were spread across Elfland to shine into every corner, which suggested they were very much like ordinary lamps, and had limited reach.

"The text says *Copper*. Anyway: 'They danced long and long, and drew many of the city into their dances, for the music of those who played was as the wine of the gods to those who heard it, and no one could resist the call. Loud were the merrymakers, and loudest of all were the cousins dancing to the music of those who played, until the sound of their merriment rose to the heights of the palace of the king upon the hill, and lo! They woke even the King of the Makers, the king and his wife who was blessed with his love, and much wroth was he, for'—"

The story did not continue much past this point, but River didn't get even that far, since Rowan had started to laugh. He was laughing so hard, in fact, he let go of his tangled hair (River noted numbly that her comb was caught by its teeth somewhere near his ear) and tipped back from where he had been squatting on his heels to sit splay-legged on the ground.

"I remember this!" he cried eventually.

"What? I mean, I beg your pardon?"

Rowan waved off her interjection. "Oh, we were in so much trouble!" He wiped his eyes with his hand. "We were so drunk. So very, very drunk."

He bent over the book River still held open to the page. He hummed, finger trailing across the letters, snickering as he read the conclusion. "What is this? *Be not too merry, nor too lusty for noise, for even kings cherish their sleep!*"

"They are moral lessons," River said, apologetic. Not that it was *her* writing.

Rowan laughed again, silver-chiming joy like the sound of the Sun laughing in the first morning of the world. And yet: he was still fighting with his hair. He shook his head, fished out the comb from the tangles, and began to work at the knots again. "Ai, what a way to be remembered! It was not the king who cherished his sleep so, but his fair queen—and *their* newborn babe, the crown prince. Blessed by the king's love, indeed! He was the one who was lusty for noise. We were punished well for disturbing him, let me tell you."

"How so?" River asked, after translating quickly for Ash. Rowan listened attentively, nodding as he understood the parallels from his words to hers, and went on in modern Firnish.

"We—my brothers and our friends and I—were set to cleaning the whole palace, top to bottom. My—the other musician and I were the sensible ones," he added, smug, his eyes warm and faraway with memory. "We volunteered to do the—hmm, I do not know the word? The cisterns? Where the water comes from, and where it goes."

"The plumbing?" Ash guessed. "Pipes and privies and so on?"

Rowan hummed. "Perhaps. When we come to a house you may show me. I shall learn. As it was, then, my—that is, we Sang them clean long before anyone else was finished."

"It's a good memory, I hope," River said quietly.

Rowan had finally gotten the comb through the last portion of his hair. His eyes were still faraway as he set down the comb and began to plait another fishtail braid down that side. "I wonder what became of her, my ... the other musician," he murmured softly.

"The Tourney is in the City," Ash said awkwardly. "You can ask after your family when we arrive. We can help you." She looked at River expectantly.

"There are supposed to be records, in the City," River said. "Of all those who went Over the Waves, what happened to them, and when they came home, by the sea or the Halls."

Rowan smiled wryly. "She did not go with us. My—my—my rival —not my cousin. Those seven sons and seven daughters are all too convenient! But some of us were siblings, and some cousins, and some friends." He chuckled again, in a much more ordinary fashion. "And some rivals. I wonder who it was who decided to write down our youthful follies like that? Is the tale of the Three Sovereign Cranes in there? Or the Water from a Stone game? I hope not the one about the bears! I do not come off well in that one!"

River looked down at the book. Despite her better intentions, she could not stop herself from flipping to the page with the story of the Minstrel and the Bears.

One day in those days that came before the Sun, a Minstrel went travelling through the woods on the flanks of the mountains, where dwell the bears who are the children of the Great Bear of the Skies, seeking a new song to sing.

Rowan had written the *Dawnsong*, she reminded herself. River herself had witnessed him singing a lament so poignant an animal-spirit had come prancing out of its bones to hear him.

"Were they really the children of the sky-bear?" River asked him.

Rowan wrinkled his nose. "What a question!" he said, laughing. "If they were, they never told me so! But I think I know who told *that* story, then, even if she was not the one to set down these tales like this. It was always her favourite. She liked anytime I made a great fool of myself." He twisted his lips. "At least that kind of folly. I had worse ones later in my life."

He tied off his second braid with another knot, then spiralled both long plaits around his head so they formed a crown. He wove an old and discoloured brown ribbon from out of his pocket around and through the circlet, anchoring the braids into place.

"There," he said, tipping his head experimentally. "River, you had a pleasant voice singing the morning-song with me. Ash, do you sing? What songs are there of your people? I am behind-hand in all the music!"

"When—" River elbowed Ash, and she coughed. "Right." Ash offered a sheepish smile to Rowan, who did not seem to have noticed; his eyes were on the far distance, no doubt remembering his family and friends from long ago. "Shall we sing as we walk? We'll need to make the Grey Bridge by the full moon to cross in safety, or so 'tis said."

"Is that in a song?" Rowan demanded eagerly. "If it isn't, I shall set it in one. Tell me more."

Ash looked helplessly at River. She hefted her pack even as Rowan hummed a vague, distracted note that immediately quenched the fire. "There's a ballad about this side of the river," she said. "I think I know all the words ..."

The moral of The Minstrel and the Bears was *Beware coming between the musician and his harp as between the bear and her den, and never stand between both!*

River had never thought it would be particularly relevant to her life. She looked sidelong at Rowan. It was hard to see that he'd go after a bear in his den to get his harp back. And yet he'd said he'd been a war-bard ...

That was why no one sang the way Rowan did now, after the dreadful deeds and even more dreadful ends of the Twelve War-Bards of Kheir in the Shadowed Age. But presumably there were—had been—*other* war-bards? Less famous ones? Less *dreadful* ones? Ones who hadn't warped the very song of their own souls in order to kill with the power of their voices?

Ones who ... might have had other reasons for staying in the Halls of Rest for a full thousand years longer than *even the Seven Damned Sons of Dâr*?

River cleared her throat and began to sing *The Ballad of the Knight of the Mists*. At least she knew how that song ended.

CHAPTER EIGHT

THE PERILOUS HILLS

Tamsin was coming to the conclusion that it was possible that he had not hitherto been enjoying the healthiest of all lifestyles. What with the multiple meals and the multiple rest-stops that River and Ash insisted upon he had a great deal more energy than was usual.

Perhaps a little of it was this land, fair Elfland. The land Over the Waves had been beautiful, always, even in its ruin; even in the long, slow return to life after the devastation of the wars against the Old Enemy. Beautiful, and deadly, and full of a kind of brilliance stark against the desolation.

Elfland was beautiful, and deadly too, but it was also full of magic.

Tamsin hummed as he walked, now beside River, now beside Ash, now alone in a line. The air moved curiously in response, trees and rushes rustling their leaves to investigate this stranger whose utterance was not theirs but not entirely foreign. The land unfolded its Song to him, hesitantly, when River's questions or lessons fell into silence and Tamsin could let his attention slide away to *listen*.

Over the Waves had had its Song, of course—all the world was part of the Great Song, and no matter the Old Enemy's efforts with shadowed Chirr, not even his twisted monsters had lost all connection to the deeper themes. But Over the Waves the Song was buried deep, deep, so deep that Tamsin's song had been as much a matter of mining and making as it was of echo and response.

Here he hummed, or sang a note or two, and the little green-and-yellow warblers of the river-bank came tumbling through the willows to peer at him and sing back, and the swallows dipped low over his head, forked tails whispering across his brow, their twitters falling into the spaces of his song.

The river was larger today, swollen with the night's rain. Midmorning their way was blocked by a large subsidiary, and had to track quite far up the new stream to find a safe ford.

"We shouldn't go too deep into these hills," River said, looking uneasily at the steep forest-clad slopes rising up above them. "Not if we want to make the Tourney this year."

"When does it begin?" Tamsin asked. The idea that they might have anything like a required arrival time was rather incomprehensible. He turned the thought in his mind. They were in Elfland: they were immortal elves: there was, as far as he knew, no reason they could not spend a year or a hundred years exploring those fascinating folds of stream and stone, waterfall and moss, and trees each of them older than the next.

It was an oak wood here, carpeted thickly with bluebells. The stones were a ruddy-gold sandstone, striated with charcoal-grey lines. Some sort of vine with extravagant festoons of rosy-white almond-scented flowers—Tamsin had never been all that good with flower-names—clambered all over the rocks and up into the trees, where it draped down in vast curtains like a stage set.

"The Tourney starts at Midsummer," Ash said. She looked rather perturbed. Tamsin ignored her expression, leaning into the wind singing down the valley cleft. This was just the sort of landscape that would have caves ... cascades ... *secrets*. Tamsin hummed, the song curling in his throat, just above the place to which it had been so tightly constrained. The stone thrummed, and the water moved faster over the boulders in its bed. It was very clear, silver where it foamed, deep brown in the shadowed pools.

"They say that those who go into *these* hills never come back," River said, and there was almost a note of desperation in her voice. "Rowan—"

That was him, Tamsin recalled vaguely. "Mm," he said, harmonizing with the stone. He could *feel* the magic ahead of them, sleeping deep, deep, deep as he himself had slept. Behind the curtains of cascading flowers, behind the sweet almond-scented air, behind the wind through the bluebells ... There was something almost familiar back there, something calling him, a fire like the holy fire for which he and his brothers had damned themselves, and yet sweeter, easier, *wilder*—

Something touched his shoulder, and he whirled, sword instantly in hand, to stop with the edge across River's throat.

Tamsin refocused sharply. River stood very still. Her eyes were ... wide.

He swallowed, and sheathed his sword with deliberate motions. "My apologies," he said gruffly. And then: "I thank you." He cut his glance to Ash, who was unsurprisingly frowning, but also standing protectively next to their bags. Tamsin cleared his throat. "We should cross and return downstream, I take it."

"Yes." River shuddered, and hastily turned to pick up her pack. "Rowan ... Will you come with us?"

It was unfathomable that they *wanted* him to stay; that they did not simply let the strange old elf wander off under the song of the wild hills. But then Ash's desire to win the Tourney was striking, and Rowan had not yet taught her a thing.

Once Tamsin had himself collected his bundle, they helped each other across the boulders littering the stream. He kept his head turned away from the hills, the wind, the whispering song of the water. If he listened ...

It would be far too easy to disappear back into the hills and come nevermore amongst his people. He would have already, without River and Ash.

He smiled at them, grateful beyond measure. There would be a cost to this grace—but no matter that. It could hardly be worse than the death-curses. He cleared his throat from the song that wanted to come forth. If he started trying to sing to the wind he would follow it.

And—

Best keep to a subject that would not cause Tamsin's mind to wander. "Will you tell me of how you learned the art of the sword, then, Ash?"

Thus they passed back down the small river, out of the hills and down into the sloping meadows of the larger river-valley. After they came out of the oak-wood, there was a place where the bluebells mingled with pale yellow and white jonquils. Their scent was heavier than the bluebells', and if Tamsin had not been focused on Ash's explanation of how she idolized her grandfather he might have been inclined to sit down amongst the flowers and, no doubt, fall deep asleep.

"This is a perilous country," he observed, stepping over a dappled fawn curled up amongst the jonquils. "Be careful where you step, bretha."

"Bretha!" River exclaimed, laughing, as she tugged Ash around the fawn. "We are not so young as that, surely. We are both of age!"

"Ah, but I am a very old elf indeed," Tamsin replied. "Born before the rising of the sun and all!"

River wrinkled her nose at him. "I will see my first hún next year, O Ancient One! We are not *elflings*."

"I never said you were. But that is a word I do not know. How many years is a hún, River?"

"One hundred and sixty."

Tamsin choked, and nearly stumbled on a stone half-hidden in the grass. "You haven't even reached two centuries? Bretha indeed!"

He caught River's sharp, exasperated look at Ash and was sent back in his memory to when he had finally grown as tall as his father, and he'd tried to insist to his older brothers—all of whom had inherited their mother's substantial height—that he was *grown*, he was not an *elfling*.

"Bretha means 'youth', or it did in my day," he said. "I mean you no insult. I was surprised! I took you for at least two centuries, if not more." He recalled his long isolation. "But it has been very long since I was last amongst elves at all, and there were few so young as you amongst the armies of Chirr. None in my companies."

Not that Tamsin had had much in the way of a company, even before the end. He had fought at Daerleon's side after all their brothers had died, the Sword of the Firnoi at the right hand of the last Lord of the Firnoi, though they had naught but a captain's twenty-five to stand with them for that last desperate assault upon the Old Enemy.

Ash clearly wanted to ask questions, but at River's quelling glance she refrained. Tamsin was grateful for this courtesy, this grace. They *could* have left him to follow the wind ... Tamsin had lifted his sword to River's throat, and she had looked only ... sad. He had to offer them something in return.

He said, softly, "I fought to the end. Do not ask me for the details; not yet." He met Ash's startled, curious eyes. "I fought at Dumloth, and at the Fords of the Ghaur, and at Halen. I faced the dragon upon the plains of Anquielle." He swallowed. But he could speak, he could. "I fought at Sawwalith, where my brothers fell." He rubbed his right thumb along the ridged scar of his left hand. "I fought the Long Retreat to the sea. I was there when the waters rose, and when they ebbed away, I was still there. I was there to the end. I assailed the iron gates of the Old Enemy's stronghold, and I was one of those who followed Daerleon the Stonehand within."

He stopped there, lips twisting. Even that was almost certainly too much. But they had no histories bar River's book of tales, and he had already claimed himself as the foolish minstrel who had followed a bear into her den, the singer who had cried paeans to the Sun.

"That sounds as if it was very hard," River said quietly.

Tamsin glanced sidelong at her, grateful beyond all words for her kindness and innocence. "It was."

He did not want them to look upon him as a monster, Tamsin Tamurzîn, Tamsin Zîmdurdam, Tamsin Korrokaith—but even oath-bound, accursed, dreadful, he had survived. And he was still Tamsin despite all that.

Well, right now he was *Rowan*, but they knew that was not his true name, and one day he'd tell them the rest of it. Already he knew that. So long as these young elves wanted his company, he would give it to them.

He'd fallen in love with the land Over the Waves just as quickly as this, immediately determined to protect it, cherish it, nourish it. It had taken him one breath of the wind, one sight of the sun rising over the mountains, one glimpse of a green valley full of deer, and Tamsin had been willing to die for it—been willing to kill for it—been willing to *endure* for it.

He and his brothers had left Elfland for the Oath, but always Tamsin had wanted to plumb the land deep, find the Song that hid deep in the roots of those mountains, deep in those valleys, caught like his shadows in the trees that grew even under the Old Enemy's blighted winds.

Once he and Daerleon had ridden out together, after the rising of the waters, when they were the last. They'd climbed a headland, and looked out over the sea that sundered them from Elfland. *We shall never find what we seek*, Daerleon had said, and turned again to look at the black walls of the Old Enemy's stronghold, his back to the sun and the west and home.

Tamsin had not been able to say anything, of course. But he had thought, *We already have.*

He had thought it was true, then. He had long since learned to ignore the ache of his missing mother, his lost father, his rival who had not accompanied him Over the Waves. Learned to ignore the loss of his voice, his hands, his music. Learned to ignore the loss of his brothers. Learned to hold himself to the moment before him, ready always for the fight in which he could lose himself. In that moment, Oathbound and Accursed and Dreadful, he had thought they had found everything.

That sunset had been as bright as the holy fire for which they had damned themselves.

For which they had *thought* they had damned themselves.

For if Tamsin were here, and Daerleon was said to be, could the rest of his brothers not be? Might they not have come again to life, as in the old, old stories that these young elf-maids knew as true?

What could Tamsin's brothers be like, after passing the gates of death and the Halls of Rest? Tamsin had been changed by the curses and again by his long exile and again by the long sleep. He felt much closer to that youthful minstrel than to what he had become.

Yet Daerleon had decided to hold a tournament instead of seeking peace.

Tamsin's older brother had been an artist like their parents, a sculptor in stone: *Stonehand* had originally been a family joke for a party trick Leon had where he pretended to shape a (previously prepared) stone with his bare fingers. It had become a name to conjure fear, Over the Waves.

He hadn't thought of him as *Leon* in—

"Even if we were not counting years," Tamsin managed almost lightly, recalling his present surroundings, "I'm afraid that you seem very young to me."

They walked lightly through the grass, studded now with orange pompom-like flowers Tamsin did not know the name of. He bent, hiding his face for a moment, to snag a stem. The flower didn't have a scent; at closer view each overlapping petal had a crimped edge. The stream chuckled beside them, white in the sunlight. Ahead of them a cluster of willows marked the edge of the river. A flight of white-bellied ducks whirred overhead, heading north. Tamsin clutched at the bundle of bones in his cloak, trying not to hum himself into invisibility. Those shadows were only full of memory.

River started to sing another song from her village, some sort of harvest-song, and Tamsin gratefully turned his thoughts to learning it.

They stopped for a midday meal on a knoll around which the river bent, silver-green in the noon sunlight. Tamsin could not manage more than a few mouthfuls of the waybread River and Ash offered him. He sat instead with the small pieces of bone and his old belt-knife, trying to remember old skills. A wide-toothed comb could not be so hard, could it?

(It could. It was a great piece of fortune that he needed a comb before he attempted the harp.)

After they'd finished eating, River lay on the grass to watch the clouds, and Ash looked thoughtfully at Tamsin. He had managed to rough out a shape before deciding he might as well take a break. His hair was under control for the moment, at least.

He felt jittery, too full of energy. The wind had shifted and was no longer coming down from the dangerous hills: it blew from the north, ahead of them, with strange and alluring scents twined in its touch.

He wished he hadn't thought of his mother. Or his old rival. *They* were very likely still in the city where he had abandoned them.

"I don't suppose you'd be interested in a spar, Rowan?" Ash asked.

Tamsin sheathed his knife and was standing before she'd finished the question. Ash laughed and followed, down the knoll to the flatter ground by the river proper.

"I haven't *sparred* in a long time," Tamsin warned her, drawing his sword. He moved through a few sequences, slow and calm, easing his muscles into readiness since there was no danger. "I'll follow your lead, to begin with."

Ash nodded, her eyes intent. "That's a beautiful sword."

"My brother made it."

That was enough chit-chat: with a quick step-lunge Ash was suddenly in Tamsin's space, and the old familiar dance took him. *Here* an opening—there a feint—there a step, a lunge, a dodge—parry and thrust—the sweet sound of two elvish blades upon each other. A dance for which Tamsin had written a hundred songs, once upon a time, to the drumming of boots or hooves, the songs of warriors riding with their banners held high.

It was an endless song, but each stanza had its point of rest, and this one came in its time. Tamsin caught Ash's sword and disarmed her, his own sword sliding forward in the same move to touch the young elf's breast. And—there.

He stepped back, smiling. Ash was breathing hard, sweat in her hair, eyes alight.

"You shall be my better one day," Tamsin said, sheathing his sword and bending to collect Ash's blade from the grass.

The words fell like prophecy.

It was strange to have the gift of speech, when the sword had been singing in his hand.

He breathed in deeply. Green grass, bruised underfoot; the wind, sharp with those northern flowers; another flight of waterfowl, swans this time, a heavy creamy-white in the sky, their yellow throats sounding trumpet-calls.

"You'll teach me?" said Ash, taking her sword. "Please. I've never ..."

She trailed off. Tamsin remembered when he had sought out teacher after teacher of the harp, too good for most of them even as an elfling, a brethan, until at last he had followed rumours to the strange harpist who lived behind the city, in the woods beyond the walls.

They had played a duet, Tamsin and the harpist, Tamsin chasing the harpist's melody with his own.

You shall be my better one day, the harpist had told him, and sent him away.

It had been incomprehensible to Tamsin. *Teach me*, he had begged. *Teach me*. But the harpist had refused, then and always.

Tamsin had returned to the harpist's door over and over again, chasing greatness in that little hut in the woods where the greatest musician of all the Firnoi lived. He had studied in the city, studied in the country, practiced: and each year (those endless long years of bliss before the Breaking of the Lamps) he had returned to the woods to match his skill in the duet.

Teach me, he had begged the harpist each time. *Teach me*. But each time the harpist had refused.

(Each year Tamsin's skill had grown, always seeking after the great harpist's approbation, always dreaming that one day he'd win the harpist's instruction. It was not until he'd faced the dragon on the plains of Anquielle, its eyes as fire-golden as the sun, that he'd had the thought *what the Old Enemy taught us is war*, and *let me make my teacher proud*, meaning at once the Old Enemy who had sent the dragon, and the old harpist, who had never granted Tamsin more than a night's music-making together, and yet taught him well.)

"I shall," he said to Ash, a promise, already proud of her.

CHAPTER NINE
THE SWANLANDS

Time was difficult for Tamsin to grasp, to hold in his mind. Over the next few weeks—months?—he and River and Ash settled into their travels together, sometimes speaking, sometimes singing, sometimes pausing to look at the small beauties of riverside and mead as spring unfurled, sometimes—often—taking the opportunity to tell a story or spar.

The river grew ever wider and deeper, running silver and smooth through increasingly rich and verdant pastures. The walking was easy: the narrow trail they had been following continued, a footpath trod by whose feet they did not know, here on what River called the *uncertain bank*.

Tamsin felt as if he wandered half in memory, half in dream, and entirely in hope. The sunlight was familiar. The zing and the richness in the air, the wealth of power and virtue in everything around him was, too—but never hitherto had he known them together. The silver sword in his hand, clashing against Ash's darker steel—the songs in his mouth, there to be uttered at his will, no longer bound by curse and fire—the laughter and quick-running speech of River, whether in Tamsin's mother-tongue or hers—

The ease with which they made their campfires of an evening, watching the sun set over the perilous hills, the mist rising over the river, the stars burning above them—

Tamsin did not know how to accept these gifts, except with humble delight. Or at least delight. He had never been particularly humble, and did not really know how to start now. He could not say he *deserved* these gifts, or had earned them—he had certainly lived long enough to know that the sun shone on the wicked and the good alike, and fellowship, apparently, came even to the Accursed and Dreadful—but he was quite certain that if the gifts were given, if he were granted this second chance, then he would do his best to offer his gratitude and joy in return.

Admittedly, ever and again Tamsin would start, and come back to himself, seeking the familiarity of his silence, his shadows, the pain in his hands and his lungs anchoring him to his body and the need to fulfil the Oath.

He would start, hand falling to his sword-hilt, until his fingers curved without pain or struggle.

He would look at River, trailing her hand in the air, humming one of the songs of her young village, or one of the songs Tamsin was teaching her of his old life, and think: *never did I dream of such a thing, in all those years alone.*

He had imagined his brothers crowding around him, watching him with stern, star-bright eyes, the bloody chains of their Oath heavy on their shoulders. He had imagined them in all moods. Sometimes they chastised him, mocked him, castigated him for his many failures, were the voice of all his doubts and fears and darkest memories given hideous face.

But all too often they were kind, his wraithly brothers: sometimes they whispered to him to eat or find water, to call up his shadows, to light a fire. Sometimes they cried warnings. Sometimes they told over stories of their youth, or sang his own songs back to him. Sometimes they simply sat beside him and wept.

He had never imagined anything like River or Ash, and he was glad for it. When he caught his memory wandering—and sometimes his feet went after it—they were there to call him back to himself, to the present, to this fair Elfland.

He stuffed the new language into his mind, relishing the feeling of stretching his intellect. He had not *thought* in so long. He had not dared to, for a long time, knowing at some level that if he looked upon his actions he would quail; and then his mind had started to fail, and he could not think of anything but survival.

He did not know, at the end of each day, if he had truly sung so much as he imagined. Certainly his throat was sore from the laughter and the speaking, as his hands were not from the fencing but from the attempt to relearn the fine detail work of carving.

After ten days or so he had a comb in his pocket (the fruit of his second attempt), and a spoon, and several two-pronged items that served as hair-pins (from the pieces of his first attempt at a comb), and a shallow dish sufficient to hold a serving of oatmeal.

Most importantly, the pillar of his harp was starting to take shape. His fingers ached to be so close to having an instrument in his hands again, but he was taking care with the gift of the great elk's bones.

He could, now. And that too was a gift.

Gradually the land fell away from the rolling meadows of the uplands to a lower country where the river split into many branches and formed many pools, full of purplish reeds and yellow flags and pink-and-white waterlilies. Here they found innumerable swans and other waterfowl, white against the silver water, the green banks.

"The Swanlands," River said when they stopped with one accord to look out at the wide marsh ahead of them.

"I remember hearing of these," Tamsin murmured, and sang a snatch of an old song about the river-maids who had once dwelled here. "Does the River-King still demand a toll, I wonder?" He examined the landscape doubtfully. "We shall have difficulty crossing this afoot, if our way leads thither."

"There's supposed to be a causeway," Ash said.

"And a bridge," River added.

"This is the one with the Knight of the Mists?" Tamsin asked, humming the melody of the ballad River had taught him. "Fighting all who would pass his way, bound for his ill deeds, and so on?"

"In the ballad," River protested. "Those sorts of curses are only in stories."

Tamsin rubbed his throat thoughtfully. "Not only." But then he shook his head, focusing back on the present. "No matter—we shall find the truth of it soon enough! Let us bear along the edge of the marshes, as we have neither boat nor, I deem, the skill to cross without one."

"I had hoped you might be able to guide us," Ash said, with apparent disappointment.

Tamsin had started to grasp the young elf's sense of humour, and he smiled reluctantly back. "I can teach you a song against the midges, but I have never loved swamps, and my times in them were with others to guide me."

"The Fords of the Ghaur?"

"Halen, more," he corrected, and began to pick his way along the damp, spongy ground to a low rise some dozen yards away. "The Ghaur ran through a rocky country—where the battle was, two canyons met. It was a place for an ambush, had we made it before the enemy could set up his! Halen was in the lowlands, near the sea, and the people there had built a system of dikes and sluices to claim land. Long ago they had been overrun, and though their aboiteaux, as they called them, still worked to drain the land, many had been broken by the burrowing goblins under the Old Enemy's command."

He described the land, which had been full of cranes and grey geese and eels: good food, which they had needed badly at that point. It was before Tamsin had lost his voice, before the loss of two-thirds of their forces at Sawwalith, when the war had still seemed winnable.

"You were a war-bard," Ash said a little uncertainly.

Tamsin recalled that it was considered impolite (or dangerous?) to ask the returned-dead too many questions, especially about things that might have been their deaths. More and more he wondered about what exactly *had* happened to him. His memories of the end of his time Over the Waves had not cleared. But surely he would remember dying?

All that had come was an image of his brothers, standing around him with their eyes bright, while the fire burned in his hands. And that could have been a dream as easily as memory.

"I sang storms," he murmured, remembering power in his throat and fell purpose in his heart. "Sang floods. Sang fire. I sang the wind full of ice, and the earth into mud. Sang madness and death upon my foes." He looked out at the silver-threaded marshes, gauzy with the soft grey mists of a clement day, clamorous with all those tens of thousands of swans, the folded layers of frog and insect and bird and wind and water all singing together.

He sang a note, soft as a whimper, and the wind bent all the rushes away from him. In the distance the yellow-throated swans trumpeted harshly.

He looked wryly at River and Ash, who had not yet learned to fear him. "I lost my voice, later. It was very hard for me. Better for others."

"People don't sing like that any more," River said quietly. "I think they're afraid."

"They should be," Tamsin said grimly. "I wrought much evil with my song."

"But you wrote the Dawnsong, Rowan."

"I wrote many songs, River." He sang another note, one he had rarely had cause to sing Over the Waves: a song of life, of joy. High above them a wind cleft the clouds, and sunlight glittered down like a thousand spears upon the marshes, piercing the mists with green and gold.

It was easy, so easy, to weave that note into a song. Not a true Song of Power—he raised no storm, no flood; he dared not reach so high— but a song that called to the nameless singers of the marshes, and answered their returning calls. Swan and cygnet and egg, rush and frog and dragonfly, the small creatures that burrowed in the mud or built homes on the dry edges.

He opened his eyes, to see the water nearest him white with silver-bellied fish drawn by his song. A white-tailed fish eagle dropped down out of the sky, yellow talons striking, the splash reaching their ears a moment before the ripples ran up to their feet. They could have scooped up a basket-full of fish, had they had a net to hand.

Tamsin let the song trail off, holding the last note, letting his body resonate with the marshes. The fish hesitated, then darted away, a hundred thousand flickers of silver in the dark water.

Something shifted, in the marshes, in himself. He plucked a chord in his heart, let it sound in his mind, resound in the heavy, humid air. The midges swirled in dewdrop-bright clouds, grey as they faded again into the mist. A light gleamed here and there on grass, like a green thread unspooling before his eyes.

If he'd been by himself he probably would have taken his chances with the path the marshes offered to him, that green thread winding ... somewhere. But he had been listening to River's ballads, and this was Elfland, after all, where tales became truth just as much as the converse. He was still too inclined to sleep, his soul yearning after it: and in the marshes there could be a quiet drowning, sinking deeper and deeper into the peat, clear water over his face.

Or there could be a hall under some hidden islet where the River-King held court, and had put out this invitation for a musician. Once upon a time Tamsin would have thought that a fine adventure for a spring morning. If he did not come back for a year or a century, what then? Who would miss him?

(His brothers, perhaps, depending on when exactly this hypothet-ical adventure took place. His rival, his lover, his love ... ah, but *she* would have come with him, flute in hand, and challenged him for the honour of playing at the court of a king under-the-hill!)

Here and now, whenever exactly that was, Tamsin's brothers were long lost to him, and his rival (best to name her that; she had still been that, in the dark, after the love had surged and broken upon that terrible and foolish Oath Dâr had woven around his sons and Tamsin had sung them all into taking) ... longer lost to him yet.

Besides, Tamsin still had much to teach Ash. Even thrice-daily sparring matches and stories of ancient battle techniques needed time to be assimilated and understood, body and mind. Ash would give the Stonehand Tamsin remembered a good bout, but not yet a true challenge. Not *yet*.

River said, "I think it's a pity that people are so afraid of what happened long ago that they cut themselves off from something like *that*. Don't you, Ash?"

Ash shrugged, but she had a curious smile on her solemn face. Tamsin wondered what she was looking at, or for, as she stared out at the marshes. She had a quiet voice, light: Ash was no singer, but there could be power there, as Tamsin's middle brother had once had persuasion curling silver through his words. "You know the tales better than me, River."

River nodded, determined. "It's not as if *every* great bard was Tamurzîn the Death-Singer. Isn't that so, Rowan?"

"Right you are, River," Tamsin replied, wondering where in his list of awful epithets that particular one belonged. (Before or after *Butcher of Hinnúrin*?) He could only laugh, if more than a touch ironically, at his proper name being replaced by *Thrice-Accursed*. "Fortunately for everyone, I suspect. Onwards?"

The Swanlands were vast. The three elves picked their way along the marshes' western edge for several days. They didn't want to drift too far westward, for the perilous hills pressed once more close in, and Tamsin was well aware of the danger on the wind.

He taught River and Ash the keep-away songs for insects. They learned quickly, for all that songcraft had been a matter of legend to them before meeting him. Tamsin did not understand it; when he'd been young, Song had been taught with speech.

"We still learn songs," River told him, defending her people.

"And I have been learning them, have I not?" Tamsin returned. "Yet to ignore our heritage ... we are elves: songcraft is in our blood, our bones, our souls, our hearts! How can you love music as you do, and yet know so little of the virtues?"

River didn't know. All she could say was that she'd never heard of such works after the Breaking of the Lamps. "Did all those who knew the art leave with the hosts?"

Tamsin's rival (lover, beloved, friend) had been his match, and she had not crossed Over the Waves with him.

"Perhaps the magic is gone," River suggested, but to that Tamsin could only laugh. If Chirr had had anything like the sheer power he felt here in Elfland!

"Or perhaps they still sing the way you do in the city," Ash said, "and I shall find myself overmastered by those who wield both song and sword."

"It's extremely difficult to wield both at once," Tamsin could confidently tell her. There were reasons he'd been feared as he had! "And certainly Daerleon was no great bard. You need not fear him raising Songs of Power against you."

"Unless he fights with his brother beside him, as in all the old stories," River said.

Tamsin only shook his head. "He won't. But even so."

They camped on what higher ground they could find. The first night, it was in a thicket of swamp-laurel, magenta-pink and pale rose, with bees sleeping away the coolth in the cupped blossoms. As the sun rose Tamsin sang his morning-song. Both River and Ash now sang along, grinning at him when they caught his eye.

The second night they found a tall menhir standing on the highest point for what was clearly many miles around. Tamsin sang softly to the stone, querying its nature and purpose. Protection, far-seeing, warning ... He laid his hand on the rough grey stone, voice wreathing them, listening intently to the answering song.

"I can see the causeway, look!" Ash said, breaking his concentration.

Off in the distance was a dark line of trees or shrubs: to the east, the gleam of the setting sun reflecting off something.

The menhir offered a sense of sturdy endurance, acknowledging Tamsin's own long persistence. He had been restless, rootless, a tumbleweed; the stone offered him welcome.

"We shall be safe here tonight," he declared, wondering at who might have set this stone here. Long ago—longer perhaps even than his memory went.

They set up a camp. River practised singing flame to their little campfire, and Ash went for water, while Tamsin tickled fish out of the streams with his hands rather than his song. They were being careful to boil the water, for though to all Tamsin's knowledge it was clean, he much preferred swift-flowing water to this slow circulation.

It was good to be able to sing life and merriment, not death and urgent necessity. He cleaned the fish and packed them with wild herbs he and River had collected during the afternoon. Sorrel and salad burnet, wild fennel, what Tamsin knew as smallage and River called soup celery. He made a kind of salad out of the crunchy bases of the cattails, digging them up with his bare toes in the shallows. After ten days of upland food—rabbit and oat porridge, mostly—it was a delicious change.

River and Ash murmured that they were sorry they had not brought supplies enough for three, but what with the regular meals and the much slower pace Tamsin was certain he was putting on weight, and was glad.

His harp was starting to take form, though he wasn't yet able to manage the interlocking teeth to join the pieces together. He was quite pleased at how the pillar was shaped, and the curve of the neck was as satisfying as that in his silver hair-comb, which he'd taken as the model. It was possible his brother—if his brother *had* been the one to make the comb (but who else?)—had chosen to echo the curve of a harp's neck in the ornament.

The sound-box would be antler and bone, very carefully fitted together indeed; the pillar and neck bone. He'd use the smaller tines from the antler for at least some of the pegs. And then it would be a matter of figuring out what he could possibly use for the strings ... Well, and polishing the harp. He did not have the carving skills to do proper ornamentation, so he'd need something he could use as a polishing medium.

What had his mother used? Sandpaper, which required glue or wax he did not have and did not know how to make. Sharkskin, imported from the coast—not a luxury Tamsin could command, here and now!

What Tamsin had was mud. He didn't even have any cloth he was willing to spare, so he did his best with layers of tough leaves. Properly polished, the bone should be ivory-smooth, if whiter than ivory-pale. He was getting there with some of the hair-pins.

The third night they rested under a stand of tall alders. Their catkins dropped golden pollen all over them, which made Tamsin sneeze sufficiently that the next morning, after he and Ash had sparred, he undid his braids so he could comb out the pollen.

"Your hair looks beautiful like that, like you've sprinkled gold-dust all over it," River told him. "Surely the court ladies would swoon!"

"With desire, or with envy?" Tamsin returned, laughing, running his fingers through the long strands until they were stained with the pollen. He sneezed again. Once upon a time he'd worn perfumes and make-up—it had been the fashion amongst the artistic set, when he was a young minstrel seeking fame—and as often been taken for an elf-maid as not. He'd never minded, in fact enjoyed the doubleness, the freedom, the fluidity.

For a long time he and his rival had danced around each other, swapping clothes and jewels and instruments from party to competition to concert to wedding, the two great bards of the Firnoi. They'd been so well-matched that they'd been able to fool their siblings if they took care not to sing too much like themselves.

Tamsin dropped his hand to his sword-hilt, and felt the long strands of his hair, silky again, brush over his knuckles. Once Over the Waves it had been different. He had been different. He'd never felt the desire to play like that.

But he was not Over the Waves, now, and he did not know what to do about his brothers, what he could say to them or what he wanted them to say to *him*, or if he could even let himself begin to believe they could be there to be found, no longer dead and bound, no longer grim and dreadful, and ...

It was not very practical, admittedly, having loose hair down to his knees. He compromised by braiding it into many smaller plaits as they walked towards the bridge.

CHAPTER TEN

MIST AND MEMORY

As they walked northwards, a mist rose up from the marshes. It was thin at first, light scudding filaments like cobwebs, glinting palely as the sun climbed in the sky. As they walked, it grew thicker, denser, whiter, and the temperature dropped. River and Ash drew hoods out of their packs. The garments did not seem quite as useful as full cloaks, but Tamsin did acknowledge they looked good. Though Ash's choice of orange to go over her purple tunic was a little brighter a contrast than Tamsin, personally, would have preferred.

"Where does the causeway lead?" he asked once they'd started forward again.

"West to the mountains of the gods and the Halls of Rest, or so they say," River answered. She hopped from one tussock to the next, trying to avoid a squelchy green patch. "East to the City."

"Surely there is more than one city in Elfland now? Even when I was young there was Firlond—the city of the Firnoi—and to the southeast the Sea-Elves had their city. We used to trade north to the Dwarrow, and with the people of the Great Forest in the south. And then there were many cities of Elves in Chirr, at one time."

Before the Old Enemy had destroyed three-quarters of them, and Tamsin and his brothers most of the remainder. But still.

"Chirr—oh, Kheir, that's how we say the name now." River shrugged. "They say that the Sea-Elves went under the sea when the Lamp of Silver came crashing down upon them, and come no more to sing to the stars, but I don't know. No one has gone further than this City from our village."

"Or has come back, at any rate," Ash put in.

For there was death, and danger, even in fair Elfland.

"This city is Firlond, yes?"

River overbalanced on the next tussock and grabbed at Tamsin's arm to right herself. He smiled at her and lifted her easily over the next boggy patch. "It's the King's City. I've never heard another name,"

"It's the great city, they say," Ash added.

Whether it was Firlond or not, Daerleon was said to be there, and —and Tamsin did want to see his brother again. He did.

It was hard to remember Daerleon as he was before the end. Hard to remember that Daerleon had passed through the Halls of Rest, and would no longer be the broken warrior dying of crushed ribs who had begged his last remaining brother to put a swift end to his suffering.

"Once we reach the road the travel should be easier," Ash said pragmatically. She seemed to mean to assuage his concern, which suggested she'd much mistaken his expression, but at least her words shifted the direction of his thoughts.

In Tamsin's experience roads could provide as many problems as they solved, since it was not only those with wholesome business who found the going congenial, but he decided for once not to borrow trouble in advance of it arriving.

He thought it strange that there had never been a great road west, when he grew up in the city. But then they had not had kin in the Halls of Rest whom they might expect to come home, not in those days.

By the time they reached the causeway proper, the mist had become thick indeed. Tamsin was singing softly to keep it moving enough to permit them to pick their cautious way. He found the constant exercise of his power rather more fatiguing than he would have imagined. He was a long way from the heights of his strength, he who had called down storms upon the mountains and sung the dragon to death!

But now he was not maddened with Oath and grief and fear and rage.

Tamsin shivered in the damp air, because he was growing soft, after a fortnight of gentle weather.

River suddenly exclaimed, the sound reverberating oddly in the mist, and Tamsin looked up sharply.

"There's a wall," Ash said, one of her flat statements of the obvious.

Tamsin grinned. "So there is." He brushed his fingers down the dressed limestone, a dull grey in the mist, streaked with darker patches of mould and moss. There were tiny worlds in the crevices between stones, green cushions of moss nestled against red-cupped lichens, where insects crept through their miniature forests.

The stones sang of age, though they were younger than him: they had always known the Sun, rejoicing in the long length of their bed in the warmth of the day, and turned and twisted in their courses under the cold and mysterious light of the Moon. Tamsin offered them one of his songs of the Lamps, but the stones did not understand of what he sang.

The embankment was much more of a raised road at this stage: the stone wall rose a good twenty feet above them. They probably could have climbed it, if it had been necessary, but since it was yet early in the afternoon, they decided to turn west and seek an easier point of access.

"I knew I should have brought a rope with me," Ash muttered.

"Can you sing one?" River asked Tamsin curiously, turning her head to peer at him. Her green hood was all netted with silver beads of moisture. It was a fine effect: Tamsin found himself wanting to tell his brother about it, that Forro might create something similarly beautiful out of his moon-silver.

The name settled sweetly into place, as if Tamsin had never forgotten it. He swallowed. He had not let himself remember that he had forgotten his brother's names, that time had stolen them from him.

"Rowan? Are you all right?"

"No," he said, mind whirling as he heard his brother laugh, holding up some splendid trifle. ("Sing me a new song, Tamsin, and you can have it!") His voice was shaking. "I—my brother—"

River stopped, turned, and took him by the shoulders. "Breathe," she said, looking into his eyes. Hers were bright, and so young: so unshadowed, even as she frowned at him in concern. Tamsin breathed. The air was very still, clammy, and smelled strongly of mint. Ash must have walked into a patch of it.

"Your brother?" River asked gently. "Would you like to talk about him?"

"He died in Sawwalith," Tamsin answered. "He was a smith." He forced the words out one at a time. He was not silent now, not silenced. He could sing the laments for his brothers he had never been able to voice. He could *name* them—

He could name them. If he remembered their names.

River knew them. Or of them.

The Seven Cursed Sons of Dâr, still remembered for their cruelty and violence and folly.

"He ... he was a smith." His hand dropped to his sword-hilt. "He forged my sword." He bent his head, so the handful of braids he hadn't tied back with the rest slid forward over his face. He lifted his hand in what had become an easy gesture, pushing back the hair that always came loose out of anything but the tightest war-braids he could devise. His fingers found the cool metal of the comb. "I think he made this," he said, pulling it free. The moon-silver shone even in the pale, directionless light of the mist. He rubbed his thumb along the elegant curve, the simple lines.

"It's beautiful," River said, looking carefully at the ornament, though she must have seen it already. Ash crowded close to look at it as well. Tamsin was far too comforted by the warmth of their bodies close to him.

He closed his hand around the metal so that the tines pricked at his palm. "He was a jewel-smith, before we left. He used to tease me for making songs instead of something real ..."

"Songs are real," River said indignantly.

"They were all crafters, my family. My oldest brother was a sculptor ..."

River closed her small warm hand over Tamsin's cold scarred one. "We'll help you find them, when we get to the City."

Daerleon Stonehand, Tamsin said to himself, letting the name ring solidly in his mind. He could not picture him, not truly. He could imagine Daerleon's red hair flying, his red banner flying—not his face.

Forro of the Silver Hammer. That was what they'd called him, Over the Waves. He'd had another byname before ... Tamsin could not remember it.

He could see Forro's banner held high, the silver hammer on the red field—

He could see it singed and torn, trampled and bloody. There had been no sign of what had taken Forro else, but by then they knew that the fire-demons were accompanied by strange creatures of slinking shadow that absorbed the fallen. There had been no bodies to recover out of Sawwalith.

He breathed. He was leaning against the cold, damp stone of a road that led from the Halls of Rest to the City. If his brothers had not been lost to the Eternal Night, if Tamsin's long watch and endurance was worth anything, if that strange fulfillment of the Oath had released them—

He knew Daerleon lived again. The Stonehand, still fighting.

None of River's stories or Ash's rumours of the Tourney suggested he had taken up chisel and stone again.

Tamsin pressed the silver comb against his forehead. He knew nothing, in truth. The scant information the children of a remote village had heard from a far-distant city: what did that mean? The Tourney was not every year, or even every ten years. A century passed between trials, so Ash told him. That was enough time to sculpt as well as train.

A fortnight or a month ago, Tamsin had been dead, or as good as. And here he was now, with two bretha fast becoming *friends*, and songs in his mouth, and a harp slowly taking shape, night by night, under his hands.

"Yes," he said, and straightened, blinking the damp out of his eyes. "I would appreciate that."

They started walking again, and soon found that the land was rising underfoot. The mist thinned, swirling silver-gold as the sun slowly sank ahead of them. Soon the stone embankment was only high; and then it was at Tamsin's head-height; and then their waists; and then they came to a place where the green grass met the closely set cobbles of the road proper.

"Wait," said Tamsin, before Ash could step on the stone.

He could not say why, a moment later. A trickle of cold down his neck, some ancient instinct, even more ancient caution? But he had spent too long in the wilds not to listen to such instinct.

He hummed, deep in the back of his throat, a seeking song. Questioning, probing, querying—

To step *off* the road, west of the bridge, was a matter of grave peril. That was immediately clear.

To step *onto* the road, west of the bridge ...?

He sang another note, soft as the mist, which formed a cool white wall behind them, back the way they wished to go.

You did not take the green path, the mist told him, curling and coiling with a deep and alien mind. *You must therefore take the stone road.*

Nothing else would it tell him. Mist or marsh, road or bridge: it was silent and obdurate.

"I think I offended it by refusing the earlier path," Tamsin murmured, rather incredulously. Had the River-King truly thought he'd blithely follow that uncertain invitation?

(He would have, had he not had River and Ash to think of.)

"Once we stand upon the road, we may not leave it again," he told them.

"What happens if we do?" River said nervously.

Tamsin looked at her, even more incredulously. "Nothing good," he said at last. *Surely* her stories had taught her that.

"We could hardly leave it safely in the middle of the marshes," Ash pointed out. "It's the causeway, the marshes, or going back and swimming across the river."

"No," said River, clutching at her bag defensively. "My books!"

Tamsin could not say he much wanted to swim across that cold water, either. It had not been friendly, guardian of the western edges of Elfland as it was. "I follow you," he said politely to them. "My advice is to hazard the Road, and take what adventures we find." They would hardly be so perilous as what he'd met facing the Old Enemy, at any rate.

Ash shrugged. "I wouldn't have hesitated, but for your warning, Rowan." And without any further comment, she stepped onto the cobbles. They followed, Tamsin a moment behind River. He looked west, where the sun shone in a blue sky, dim purple hills rising up into distant white mountains.

Somewhere in that direction was the Mountain from whence his father had brought the holy fire, the flame imperishable, source of such great inspiration, and such great sorrow.

Tamsin turned to face east, into a wall of white mist. He could not help himself, and snorted.

River's voice was sharply anxious. "What?"

"Oh, nothing," he assured her, settling the sling of bones he'd made from his cloak better on his shoulder. "I was merely reflecting on the clouded way before us."

Ash hid her guffaw almost immediately, but not quite fast enough. Tamsin grinned at her. "Come, bretha, will you sing with me? To pierce the mist—literal—is not so different from piercing the mist—metaphorical."

"Can we use a similar Song to the shoo-fly one?" River asked, placing herself between the two of them. "And can we please walk abreast? The Road is wide enough for that."

It was wide enough for six horses to ride abreast. Tamsin wondered if there had ever been a great procession of the dead down its length. Or if the making of the Road and causeway had been for some other reason. Such a large project would occupy even the most restless of elves for some time.

Tamsin had rarely had much occasion to teach. His older brothers had had very different interests to him—they sang, but did not *Sing*—and by the time he had grown enough in his own skill to teach others, he was too proud to think to. He and his rival had danced around each other, daring each other to ever greater feats of musicianship and Song.

They had been shining and dazzling and adored, and had had many followers, and many imitators, but no *students*. Not even Tamsin's rival had thought to share her knowledge that way with anyone besides him. *They* had goaded each other, criticized each other, taught each other by example and critique, each pushing the other on a relentless quest to *be better*. They had not looked at those coming up below them as anything but an audience at best.

Over the Waves Tamsin had been one of his brothers as he had not been in Firlond before the Breaking of the Lamps. He was still admired (if no longer adored), but ever increasingly, feared. At first he had hated that fear, but the longer the Oath burned in his mind, the more he had sought it. Craved it, even. To be feared was to be powerful: and he could not bear to admit how powerless he was, truly, under the chains of that Oath.

He had been, he could reflect now, so very stupid.

There was nothing much to see: the wet cobbles of the road, slick underfoot; the low parapet bordering each side, which meant they were unlikely to wander off the Road proper without realizing it; and the white mist filling the Swanlands and everything but their immediate vicinity. They could hear the swans and other denizens of the marshes in their vast multitudes, but at a distance, remote, removed.

Teaching River and Ash came so naturally that Tamsin wondered at how blind he'd been before. Why had it required thousands of years of solitude for him to realize company was good? Why had it taken him losing everything to learn that it was a joy to share his knowledge?

It did not feel strange to teach Ash swordplay. Perhaps that was because even as the feared Tamsin Tamurzîn he had practiced with his soldiers and his brothers. Perhaps it was just that no matter how skilled a warrior he was, it had never been the same as music.

Perhaps it was because he was still as petty and competitive as he'd ever been that the thought of teaching this young elf-maid to beat his oldest brother Daerleon Stonehand was so delicious.

"Hold that note a little longer, and raise the pitch a trifle—like this—" Tamsin sang the note, and felt a small unfurling of pride as River grinned and gamely followed suit. Her voice was improving under the practice, and even Ash was starting to sing more often with them.

He fell silent, letting River carry the Song. The mist ebbed and flowed around them, a curtain close at their backs, their sides, variably before them. River frowned as the visibility dropped, lapping ever closer to them. Her voice wobbled, wavered, and then grew in strength, steadied: and the mist dissolved back.

"Well done!" Tamsin said, clapping her on the arm.

Her eyes were sparkling with the achievement. Despite her use-name, it was clear her skills were much stronger with fire than with water or air—she'd been able to call flames almost as soon as she started to listen to the kindling and tinder before her. The flies had been annoying enough to provide sufficient motivation, but the mist did not listen well to her.

Not that it was listening all that well to Tamsin, who *was* much more inclined to air as an element. But then he had insulted the River-King, or whatever spirit inhabited the Swanlands.

River's stamina was low, as was to be expected from such a new Singer. It was easier for both of them if he sang along with her, letting his voice hold the majority of the Song. Even if he was more tired than he thought he should be, there was nothing he knew better than endurance.

Well—there was one thing. Before he'd even finished registering the noise of something scraping across stone, he'd lifted his voice to cleave the mist and drawn his sword to meet—

"Wait!" cried River, but Tamsin had already stopped to stare at what faced them.

CHAPTER ELEVEN

THE BRIDGE

Three great swans stood before them. Even as they blinked, the swans turned into three proud elven-queens, tall and fair.

River's singing faltered, but the mist only swirled whiter at their feet, forming a wall around the two parties. Tamsin hummed thoughtfully as he sheathed his sword.

The three swan-maidens were pale blonde, their straight hair falling to their waists, long strands of white feathers braided into the golden tresses. They wore golden circlets, too, set with pale green jewels. He glanced down at their gowns, but it had been a long time since he had last thought much of fabric, and he could not discern more than that it was beautiful, pearly-white, glimmering, overlaid with lace worked into the form of more feathers.

The River-King's daughters, he guessed. The central swan-maiden regarded him with eyes that were deep and black like a bird's, like the secret pools of the Swanlands.

"Well met, O fair ladies!" River cried. It sounded much the same in her Firnish as it would in Tamsin's own Firnoian.

The three swan-maids had nearly identical faces; their voices, too, when they spoke, were high and breathy and eerily the same even to

Tamsin's well-trained ears. Three silver flutes could not have sounded so similar.

The first said, "Well met, or ill, strange travellers, is yet to be seen."

The second said, "Strangers they are, that come from the west upon the road that leads only behind them."

The third said, "Travellers they are, who seek to cross the bridge that carries only the dead."

Tamsin regarded them solemnly, silently. He might or might not have passed through the Halls of Rest, but his companions certainly had not. They were young, and untried, and yet ... so fearlessly kind.

So fearless, in general. And yet Tamsin did not think it was only innocence and naïveté that girded their hearts.

River lifted her chin. "We crossed the river upon the bridge by the godswood, high in the hills to the south, and have followed the river to this bridge, the last before the Northern Sea, that we might travel to the city of our people."

"Those who wish to cross this bridge," one of the swan-maidens said, "must prove themselves."

"How so?" said Ash, stepping up beside Tamsin, so he was bracketed between the two of them. "What will you have of us?"

"They come from the West, where dwell the dead," said the second swan-maid.

"They seek the East, the land of the Ever-living," said the third.

The first was still staring at Tamsin, her black eyes boring deep into him. He said nothing. What, really, was there to say? All his years seemed to weigh on him, heavier than the death-curses of the Old Enemy, the dragon, his own father—

But he had endured those curses, and all else that had come to him. He held the swan-maiden's eyes, patient and silent as he had learned so hard to be.

She smiled suddenly, very coldly. "This is the bridge of the dead," she said. "Those who pass from the east seeking the westward road must face their death. For you who come from the west and seek the eastward way, it shall then be the opposite."

"Do you mean we die if we continue?" River asked, a slight quaver in her voice.

"No," said the swan-maiden. Tamsin did not notice which one: he thought he knew what she meant, what they intended, and his eyes were already turning without his conscious desire to the mist behind them.

"If you would cross against the way the dead take," one of the swan-maidens said, in her high, breathy, fluting voice.

"If you would cross the bridge that leads between the living and the dead," said the second.

"If you would find your way back," said the third.

"Then you will find," said the first, "that you will face your dead coming to meet you."

River and Ash stirred. Tamsin rather thought they were looking at him, but he could not shift his eyes from the cold black gaze of the swan-maiden before him. Pale gold was her hair, and white the feathers in it, he thought, the words not quite right for a ballad, a song.

"Speak not, once you begin," said the maiden on the left, and turned back into a swan, the green-gemmed crown a sudden collar about her throat.

"Stop not, once you begin," said the one on the right, and she too, was a swan.

The third said nothing, but her cold, dreadful smile seemed to linger long in Tamsin's mind after she too returned to her swan-form, and the three swan-maidens flew over their heads in a heavy whistle of wings.

One white feather drifted down, to land on the bridge before them.

"Do we pick it up?" River whispered urgently to Tamsin, not moving.

He swallowed hard. He could not think of stories, tales, legends, lore. He could think only of all the death his hands and voice had brought. "Perhaps you should go without me," he said hoarsely, his voice cracking. He, he, he, Tamsin of the Golden Voice—

Tamsin Zîmzurdam, Tamurzîn, Korrokaith, the Death-Singer.

"We know you were a warrior and war-bard," Ash said, and took Tamsin's left arm in her own.

"You don't know what that means," Tamsin said, shuddering. "River—"

For River had taken his other arm, linking their elbows, so that he was held between the two young elves. "We will learn," she said, fearless and in this case, he feared, naïve.

"But I am—"

"Tell us on the other side," Ash said. "It doesn't matter now."

It did matter. "It *does*," he said, trying to govern his voice, though fear shook through him.

"Tell us on the other side," River echoed Ash, squeezing his arm tightly. "You can tell us everything on the other side."

They did not *know*. They could not know. Even Tamsin himself did not know how many he had killed, over all the long years of his life.

"Take the feather," Ash said to River, her voice unbothered as ever, "and then we will go in silence and without stopping, until we have passed this test."

Tamsin shook his head, but then he said, "I said I would follow you," quietly, honestly, fearfully. He had followed his father and his brothers to ruin, and on and on following no path but that forced by the curses at his back, pricking his feet, his soul, until he had at last woken in that strange iris- and rowan-girded mound, with the sun shining and the birds singing.

He had chosen to go towards people, as best he could.

"There's the spirit," River said encouragingly, nudging Tamsin with her shoulder so that his bundle of elk-bones rattled and clattered behind him. But somehow the noise was comforting. The elk had welcomed death so gladly—

He closed his eyes against the mist, but he had never been a coward, Tamsin the Thrice-Cursed. He took a deep breath, and felt the two elf-maids squeeze his arms, one on each side. River bent down to collect the feather with her free hand, and they stepped forward together.

~

The mist swirled about them, white and clammy, close as their breath. Tamsin breathed. River and Ash were comforting warm bodies bracketing him, alive, holding tight as the mist darkened, grew greyer, thickened.

He blinked and shook his head, but the dimness persisted, as if they'd walked into a cloud of gnats.

He blinked again. His eyes could not focus.

You will face your dead coming to meet you.

Tamsin wanted to laugh, laugh and never stop laughing, because his dead—*their* dead, *these* lives were not on his hands alone—included all the insects he had ever unthinkingly swatted.

They walked, slow and steady, through the endless fog of gnats and flies.

And then, some dark, some silver, at waist level were the fish they had caught: and then there were rabbits, hares, pheasants and pigeons and snipe, ducks and geese, the cranes—

And still the insects came, and the fish, and there were rats and mice (mice?), and a flash of a falcon that made Ash grip Tamsin's elbow tightly, some old grief spiking through her fingers, jumping like a static shock across the spaces between their souls, so for a moment Tamsin felt her grief and horror and regret—

Deer; many. Some met his eyes as they ran past, and Tamsin remembered the times he had used his Song to draw them towards him, taking their wills with his own, a crime grievous and fell, but not so grievous and fell as what would yet come to meet them. Him. Them.

Them, because these two young elf-maids had lifted their chins and refused to let him walk this bridge alone.

Fox-cubs, which Tamsin had once killed in an attempt at mercy.

More fish. Eels, thousands of them, from that long period when

Tamsin had wandered the marshlands of a dying continent and found nothing to eat but them. Grubs, and some sort of cricket-creature, and a bear, no longer rabid—

They came, and came, and came. How long had Tamsin lived, Over the Waves? How long after everyone else had left? All he had had to eat was what he could forage or hunt, and there had been precious little foraging.

The air was cool, clammy, damp. His brow was pearled with sweat, cold; one of his braids came unravelled, and the tendrils stuck to his face. Tamsin wanted to close his eyes, and dared not, for this was a kindness, that it was the insects and the game he had hunted for survival that came first.

Then came the goblins and the wolves, the twisted rodents, the screaming eagle-kindred with their steel-tipped talons.

So many, many goblins.

Tamsin kept walking as they loomed out of the fog before him, running and loping with the strange scuttling movement they had, as often a hand on the ground as their feet. Their eyes were bright and malicious, full of blood-lust.

(Tamsin's eyes had also been bright and malicious, full of blood-lust, in those days.)

They wore armour, some of them; others were in the ragged clothes they had stolen from the elven dead. They moved utterly silently, but he could hear in his mind their chittering and cackling, the clicking of their nails, the rough bellowing.

They came in singletons and packs and companies, goblins small as a cat or large as a troll.

There were trolls, too. Ogres. Nameless monsters. And always, always, always, the goblins.

(Always, always, always, until Tamsin had ferreted out the last of their holes, killed the last of their hives, and then it was him alone, wandering the dead land.)

They came, and came, and came, as they had come in the land Over the Waves under the command of the Old Enemy.

They bred in darkness and despair, did goblins, in abandoned homes and desolate cellars. Some were ghouls, before the elves had learned to burn their dead. Some were shadows given substance by blood. Some were ...

Tamsin did not know what they were. He looked at those bright, malicious, bloodthirsty eyes, those fanged grins, as the goblins he had killed ran at him out of the mist and disappeared again behind him.

His hands were aching, yearning for his sword. River's fingers were digging deep into his elbow, her nails gouging into his flesh. He dared not look at her, dared not look at what expression this child of peaceful Elfland bore on her face.

And still the goblins came.

And still too did the fish and the rabbits and the hares, the deer and the ducks and the geese; and the pigs and sheep and cattle; and the horses who had died under him in battle, or under his hand when their injuries precluded healing.

Tamsin bent his head into the charnel-house wind. All he could smell was fire, now, burning wood, burning flesh, burning air. He knew what was coming next.

But still the goblins came.

He had walked, one foot in front of the other, all across the land Over the Waves, goaded by the death-curses at his back, the Oath chaining his soul. He could walk forward now, face what his hands had wrought, his voice had wrought, over all those long years.

Tamsin the Dreadful. Tamsin the Thrice-Cursed. Tamsin the Butcher.

(They had not yet come to the elves who had died by his voice, by his hand.)

And still the goblins came.

The scent of fire grew stronger, ashes in the wind, the mist, stinging at his eyes. Tamsin's fingers were very cold. Ash's hand was slipping on his arm, and he shifted carefully, bringing up his hand, seizing her wrist in his. The ridged scars on his palm rested on her fluttering pulse-point.

Even if they had been permitted to speak, it was not as if there was anything Tamsin could say.

A horse ran by in a great crowd of goblins—a proud gelding, high-crowned—his first war-horse, which had died from his Song, the first time he had used his voice to kill.

He knew what was coming after this, with the fire behind them.

The elves of Dumloth did not look at him. They had not known what death had struck them, whose had been the voice twisting itself out of the Song of the world until it could cut even the bond between body and soul.

Tamsin drew in a deep shuddering breath, and another, and another. His hand was tight on Ash's wrist. River's fingers were digging ever deeper into his arm; that hand was starting to tingle.

The elves of Dumloth did not look at him, but he looked at them. He had been their death. He had murdered them, these elves, who had done nothing wrong but be on the wrong side of a river when the war came upon them.

The elves of Hinnúrin looked at him. Their eyes were starlit, sad, accusing. The silver sword at his side had been their deaths, for by then he had lost his voice and his hands, and he had lost himself in the work of death.

There were not so many elves as goblins, but then there had never been as many elves as goblins.

Dumloth, Hinnúrin ... Sawwalith. The air was thick, unbreathable. But yet they must breathe, and walk, though the dead walked silently past them, elves and goblins and the strange unnamed monsters of the Old Enemy's workings.

More goblins, as there had always been more goblins. So many goblins.

And then—

Tamsin could not help himself. He flinched, and stumbled, would have stopped if River and Ash had not dragged him forward.

It was not the dragon. (Not *yet* the dragon.) He repeated that to himself silently, silently, chanting it loudly in his head. It was not the dragon. It was not the Old Enemy. (Not *yet* the Old Enemy.) It was not even the fire-demon. (Had he ever killed one of those?)

It was only his brother, his eldest brother, the last but Tamsin to live, who had begged Tamsin to give him the mercy cut. Who had forced Tamsin to give him the mercy cut.

It was *not* Daerleon, he told himself, panicked, pulling at River and Ash now, desperate to pass by this apparition. Daerleon had died under his hand, yes, that knife which Tamsin had been using to carve combs and bowls and harp had cut also his brother's throat, one last swift cut before Tamsin had been the last of all his brothers, before the fell doom of their Oath had fallen solely upon his shoulders.

Daerleon—but not Daerleon—walked not as Tamsin had last seen him in the flesh, nor as he had seen him in some of his wilder hallucinations, when his brothers comforted him, told him to eat, told him to move on, whispered they loved him, that he would survive—

This was the Leon of their youth, with his hair like a banner and his face fair and free, laughing as he had not laughed after they swore that impossible Oath and gone Over the Waves.

Daerleon—but not Daerleon—smiled at Tamsin as if there was nothing between them but the love the eldest of seven brothers might bear the youngest.

Daerleon was in Firlond, setting up a great Tourney, still fighting. Daerleon was alive again, free from the Oath, free from all the dark deeds. Free.

Tamsin could not stop himself from looking after his brother. His feet might have turned to follow him, as Tamsin had always followed him, had River and Ash not silently gripped him and kept him from straying.

He turned his head: and there in front of them, taking up the entirety of the bridge, a black shadow where in life it had been bronze-green as verdigris—there was the dragon.

Tamsin's breath hitched. It was his turn to pull his companions forward, to keep them walking, to grip Ash's wrist and hold River's hand tucked tight against his side. His to remind them silently that they must stay silent, even as the glowing eyes—white-gold as reflected sunlight—stared hard at them.

The air was so thick. Tamsin could feel his throat closing again, rough as sharkskin as he swallowed the furnace-dry air, as he spun forth chains of Song out of his own soul. Chains to bind, to hold this huge creature, this monster with the fire in its belly and the sun in its eyes, this monster whose teeth had killed more elves than even Tamsin's hands.

He had Sung for three days, they told him afterwards, while all around him the world burned.

Three days he had Sung, standing alone before the dragon, its eyes burning into his so that for weeks afterwards he had thought himself blinded as well as voiceless. He had not been able to bear strong light for months longer than that; had become a creature of the shadows, of dusk and night, silent and deadly as the strange inky shades of Sawwalith, which swallowed anything that entered whole.

They walked, step by slow step, straight at the great body of the dragon. Tamsin did not know if it was bigger in his imagination: if Daerleon had not been real, surely this too was not real. It was ... a ghost, a true ghost, the last thing he had killed with his Song.

Just as they were about to touch it, it rippled and dissolved into the mist, leaving only the afterimages of its burning eyes in his vision.

He heard first Ash, and then River, take a deep, relieved breath. Tamsin simply walked, his head down, the steady relentless pace of his long wanderings. He knew what must be next.

The mist faded into grey, and then into charcoal, and then they walked into the inky lightless dark that was the Old Enemy.

CHAPTER TWELVE
THE DEAD

River had never killed anything larger than a rabbit, and that only once. She fished. She had sat beside many generations of dogs when their time came, and she had wept with Ash when her friend had accidentally shot a falcon, first learning archery. She had helped butcher goats, cattle, deer, sheep; they did not eat pigs in her village.

There was death even in Elfland, this was to say, and River was not entirely unfamiliar with it. Had thought herself not entirely unfamiliar with it. Had thought that when Rowan paled and hesitated that she understood what he meant by *I was a warrior, once* and *I will fight no more, save against evil and at great need.*

The dispassionate ease with which he had taken on hunting for their meals had been a little disconcerting, until River recalled accounts of the hardships of life Over the Waves. She had guessed that squeamishness had not been something that was countenanced, in his life there.

She had thought she understood why people spoke of the greatest warriors of Shadowed Kheir with horror and fear; why Tamurzîn the Death-Singer had single-handedly destroyed the use of Songs of Power. Why even wanting to fight in the Tourney was considered a bit strange and suspect. And why there was a hint of reluctance in the acknowledgement that it was good that some people chose to keep up those old skills, just in case.

She had known she would be horrified, and gripped hard onto Rowan's arm so that she did not spurn him immediately and after she had said she wouldn't. River might be young, and not near so much a fighter as Ash, but she had her principles.

If she wanted to be an historian, she had to know the truth. To know the truth, she had to be willing to face it.

So it was she gripped his arm hard, and looked forward, bit her tongue to keep from speaking, and did not let her feet stop.

She waited for the horror, but as those ghostly forms shaped themselves out of the mist, shades of grey and silver and black, their eyes looking at and through Rowan (always at and through Rowan: only the falcon had looked at Ash, and the one rabbit River had killed; the fish swam past them, and the insects, and she could not see if they looked, if they saw)—all River felt was an intolerable great wave of grief.

Rowan had apparently spent most of his long life killing everything that moved. River thought of the kindly, ungainly, funny elf who told her stories about the youth of the world and sang so joyously of the morning that the memory of his voice had come down as the sound of the Sun rejoicing in its first rising. She dug her fingers into his arm as he stumbled forward, always forward, facing the endless waves of creatures she guessed were the goblins of the stories.

There were so many of them. River caught herself over and over again from whimpering at what it must have been like to face these fierce and clever-faced foes in the numbers that thronged the bridge.

They were not injured, these shades. They bore no signs of their deaths, save that they were grey and black and silver, no colour to them. They were silent, but she could imagine the clicking of their nails, the high laughter of their voices, the guttural shouts they surely also made.

And still they came.

Dozens, first. Then scores. Then they came in hundreds. And then in numbers utterly beyond counting, beyond comprehension.

She should have been horrified at what Rowan had done. Instead she gripped his arm in grief at what he'd faced, at what he'd become. Whatever reason he'd had for going Over the Waves—

She dared not look at Ash, or at Rowan's face. She could only face forward, into the mist with the dark shapes looming always suddenly out of it. And still they came.

The stories of the Shadowed Age spoke of the *numberless goblins of the Great Enemy*, how they had swarmed the elven armies, how they had never stopped coming, driven always by the relentless will of the Great Enemy. How they had cared for nothing but destruction and devastation: how they had sought to tear, to rend, to eat, to deface, to destroy. How the great warriors of the elves had faced them until they fell one by one, picked off by the sheer overwhelming numbers of the goblins or by the greater weapons and foes of the Great Enemy's devising.

Here, on this bridge, they came and came and came and *still* they came.

Rowan had, apparently, never fallen.

How long had the Shadowed Age lasted? A thousand years? Two? The texts were unclear: those few who had survived had left confused reports that time seemed to work differently there than at home. They had dates in the archives of the City, River had heard, and hoped to see for herself.

(A thousand years for the Shadowed Age. Two and a half millennia for the Age of Homecoming. A thousand years again in the Sunlit Age.)

A thousand years was a long time, even if you weren't facing endless waves of goblins.

She gripped Rowan's arm harder. She must be hurting him, but she needed to feel his warmth under her hands, that he was alive, that he was not trying to draw his silver sword with the incredible reflexes that had been ingrained in him by these endless waves of foes.

But he had stopped, both times he had drawn. Once with the sword at her throat; once angled before her, facing the swan-queens. He had not let the sword land without seeing what he was striking, first.

This did not help, when there was a break in the goblins and scuttling monsters and instead she saw the dozens of elves who walked past them.

Rowan's step stuttered, and he jerked his arm in River's grasp. But Ash was walking forward, Ash was not stopping, Ash had said nothing. She must have already realized that Rowan could not be one of the innocent. Not after all those goblins.

Not after what he'd said; not after the skill with which he pushed Ash in their sparring lessons. Even River had wondered who he could possibly be, coming back a thousand years after the Seven Damned Sons of Dâr.

Could any of them truly have slain more than Rowan? Could even Tamurzîn the Death-Singer have killed more than Rowan had?

River did not want to make the next logical step. She shied away from it. Even in their village they had heard the stories of the Sons of Dâr, of Tamurzîn who had killed a dragon with his voice—

But there it was, of course.

There were dragons in Elfland, in the northern mountains. Serpentine graceful things, winged, elegant, deadly. Riddle-masters. They had treaties with the giants who held the borders. Legends said that sometimes adventurers would go seek them out, challenging a dragon to a riddle for some treasure out of their hoards.

Sometimes Ash had dreamily suggested she might go to the dragons, if she did not do well at the Tourney and needed to make her fortune and her name in another way. River had said she'd have to go with her, then, to help her answer the riddles, for those were not Ash's strength.

This dragon was not that kind of dragon. This was the Father of Dragons, or so a dozen tales said. This was the dragon large as a mountain—certainly larger than the wide bridge—whose breath was fire and poison, whose eyes could hypnotize any who met it, who had eaten half of Shadowed Kheir before meeting Tamurzîn the Death-Singer on the field of battle.

Three days did the Singer face against death, went the story. *Three days did the dragon breathe death, and three days did the Singer sing. When the smoke cleared from the field on the fourth day, the dragon lay dead, the fires of its eyes dark and cold. But never again did Tamurzîn the Death-Singer sing, on battlefield or off.*

No one else had ever killed a dragon, in any tale she had heard. Those who failed in their riddling did not return.

I am relearning my voice, Rowan had said, that first morning, and laughed at himself for drying his hair into a tangled snarl.

River dug her fingers into Rowan's—into *Tamurzîn's*—arm.

Tamurzîn the Death-Singer had been teaching her—*her*—how to use her voice for small, useful, reasonable things. How to shoo away midges (so they did not join those great clouds of dead spirits still streaming behind them). How to stir the mist, real and metaphorical. How to light a fire with damp wood.

He had sung the elk-spirit out of its bones, and said, *I am thanking it for its gift.*

He had sung the Dawnsong on the first morning of the world.

He had sung this huge monster to death, with its mouth that could swallow all three of them at once.

He had sung for three days, the story went, and never again after.

(He had killed goblins and elves and small scuttling things and huge fang-mouthed monsters and goblins and goblins *and goblins* with his sword instead.)

The dragon slunk around them, a huge shadow that went on seemingly forever, as they walked steadily forward.

Had Rowan died then?

But no: he'd told them that he had accompanied Daerleon Stone-hand into the Great Enemy's fortress. He'd said ... he'd lived. Fought every battle, all those endless waves of goblins.

A blackness hung over the bridge ahead of them, as if night itself had cast its curtain down here, just here, and nowhere else.

River gripped Rowan's arm even harder.

No, she knew he hadn't died to the dragon. There was the story they told at the winter festival each year, to celebrate the turning of the seasons and the return of the Sun after the longest night. Daerleon Stonehand and his youngest brother Tamurzîn (no longer the Death-Singer) had fought together, side-by-side as they had fought for so long through the Age: had forced their way into the Enemy's fortress: and then, as Daerleon reached for the thing the Enemy had stolen from the Sons of Dâr, Tamurzîn had struck the Enemy a mortal blow in the neck.

It was only *then* that he went out of the stories.

River swallowed hard. Surely facing Death, coming the other way, would be harder than this.

If she'd been by herself she would have faced a rabbit and some fish and a cloud of flies. If it had been simply her and Ash there would have been rabbits and waterfowl and a handful of deer and that poor falcon.

River gripped Rowan's arm and walked steadily forward. The Great Enemy was *gone*, because Tamurzîn had faced him already, had *felled* him already. This was no more the Enemy's true darkness than that dragon's shade had been the Father of Dragons that had eaten whole cities.

It was tremendously, terrifyingly *dark*.

River did not like the dark. Not *real* dark. Starlight—she was an elf! Of course she loved the stars! Moonlit nights, of a certainty. The warm coziness of a house at night, just the lingering glow of a banked fire, starlight or moonlight coming in through the windows ... and for those nights when the clouds were heavy and the moon and stars were hidden, there were lampstones.

It had not occurred to her to bring one of hers out of her pack, walking down even a misty bridge in full daylight. She could not let go of Rowan's arm—not now—and her pack was too awkward to sling off one handed, not if she couldn't stop—and they *couldn't* stop —no matter how dark it was.

Ash stumbled, and Rowan jerked and tilted as he caught her.

River nearly fell herself, and had to bite her tongue hard against crying out.

No stopping. No sounds. The only way out of this was through.

Rowan had *lived* this, she reminded herself. Or died from this. She wasn't sure. That wasn't a good thought—he had lived, he had lived, he had lived. He *must* have lived. He and his brother Daerleon Stone-hand had dared assault the Enemy's own fortress, and Tamurzîn the Death-Singer had struck the Enemy *in the neck*.

Had *killed* the Enemy. It seemed. Since they were walking through this heavy, clammy, suffocating darkness, the darkness of the Enemy who had sent all those thousands of goblins in their waves upon waves, like the endless strength of the sea in the tales.

Rowan had killed the Great Enemy, with the silver sword with which he was teaching Ash.

Ash stumbled again, and River realized with a horrifying suddenness that she had no idea what direction was the right one. She could see *nothing*. If they got turned around—

She could not bear to face her own death, not after facing all Rowan's dead. She couldn't. She *couldn't*.

They were on a bridge, she reminded herself. They had been doing their best to walk down the middle, facing always into the steady stream of the dead coming towards them, into a wind they could not otherwise feel. There was no wind now, no sense of anything but the soft scuffing of their feet on the cobblestones. She could smell something old, rotten, coppery—dried blood?—and she could feel Rowan shaking against her side, his arm rigid under her tight grip. Ash was breathing loudly. She didn't like the dark, either.

They were on a bridge, and she didn't *think* they had turned, not yet. Not all the way. They were still pushing forward, in a slightly staggered line, River a little ahead of Rowan a little ahead of Ash.

If she angled towards the side, very slowly, very carefully, keeping her feet well planted, she should ... eventually ... come to the side of the bridge or the causeway or the road, however far they'd reached.

(There had been *so many* goblins. And that was without the

strange scuttling creatures, and the *big* loping creatures, and the giant wolves and the tiny clattering things and the *dragon*—)

No panicking, River told herself sternly. Rowan was, quite understandably, struggling. It must have been terrible enough to have to kill all those beings without facing them in one great overwhelming flood like this.

Perhaps later she would grieve with him for those dead elves. Ask for his side of the story, whom the history-tales called a villain. The Butcher, the Death-Singer, the most feared warrior in all of Shadowed Kheir.

There had to be a reason why he had become what he had been; and why he was now sufficiently healed that he could laugh at himself fumbling a tune, at Ash managing to slip his guard, at River's stories. Why, when they had touched fingertips in the ancient ritual, there had been nothing but a spark of friendship.

River's questing foot suddenly dipped into nothingness, and it was only her death-grip on Rowan's arm that stopped her tipping off the bridge.

He twisted to catch her, and Ash tripped, but they didn't *quite* stop, they didn't quite cry out—River's breath stuttered in her throat, panic-driven, but she didn't speak, she didn't, she didn't, and she didn't stop—she caught her balance using Rowan's suddenly-steady arm, as if her near-fall had been enough to make him calm and strong.

There was no parapet or kerb on this part of the bridge.

They walked a few steps, slowly, Ash's breathing coming fast, Rowan's now steady, so steady he must have been counting. River focused on the sound of it, wondering if *this* then was Tamurzîn the warrior, who had faced all those monsters and people without flinching.

Or perhaps he had flinched. Perhaps he had been sick before every battle, or after them. Perhaps he had wept while he fought. None of that was in the stories—only that *for three days he Sang, until Death itself fell dead upon the blasted land.*

As if the great dragon was Death, and not the Old Enemy whom Tamurzîn had killed.

(As if there had been no death after the Old Enemy had fallen to his sword.)

As if he were not called Death in the songs he had not written; as if he had taken onto himself, or into himself, the attributes of those he had killed.

One day she would write the full history of Tamurzîn the Death-Singer, River told herself, as she carefully dropped her right foot to run along the edge of the road, keeping them always moving forward in the dark, refusing to tip and fall into the yawning emptiness beside her.

She would write of the young minstrel who had followed a bear into her den so he could retrieve his mislaid harp.

She would write of the proud young bard who had played for all his drunken brothers and cousins until the king and queen ordered them to stop being so loud.

She would write, too, of all these his dead, and how he had returned past them.

And she would ask him how he had gone from the Dawnsong to the Death-Singer to the smiling, shy elf they had met on the other side of the river.

Her mind sank into the routine. Step, scrape, careful, careful, listening to Rowan's steady breathing, his now rock-steady bearing, the light clatter of Ash's shoes on the stone.

She would—

She blinked. But no—the darkness was not so complete.

She could not *see* anything. But now there was a sense of depth, of deeper darkness and lighter, as if the blackness was becoming the strange red non-colour of eyes closed too tightly against the sun. Then there were the sort of flecks and specks of light and warped vision of opening them again, and then—

She wanted to sob, or cry, or sing one of Rowan's mist-piercing songs at the top of her voice. But she didn't.

The blackness faded step by step, black to not-red to red to a glittering silver, like sunlight passing through rain, and then they were all almost running, except that River was cognizant of the edge right at her side, so close she could still drop her foot over it, and so she tugged at Rowan who tugged at Ash, and so they walked on, trying to be steady, into the light.

There was no more death on this side. Only sunlight, and clearing mist, and the cobbled bridge arcing down under the feet to a roadway stretching into green fields, fair and free.

Even Tamurzîn had eventually run out of things to kill.

Rowan didn't look set and stern and terrifying. He looked … sad.

"I'm sorry," he said, the moment their feet touched the earth. There were so many shades of grief in his voice that River wished she were a musician herself in truth, to capture the layers of lamentation.

(But she had heard him sing a lament; even with his voice rough and unpracticed, as it had been that first day, it had been true enough, *deep* enough, to call forth that elk-spirit.)

"You're Tamurzîn the Death-Singer," she said.

He flinched, but nodded. "Yes. Though … it's Tamsin. Tamsin Tamurzîn, if you … prefer that name."

On his tongue *Tamurzîn* no longer sounded like a meaningless sound, but a word. *Thrice-cursed*, in fact.

Something in her twisted, that that word had become his name.

"Tamsin," she tried, tasting it.

"Tamsin Tammorath, once," he said, his lips quirking as he tilted his head to look at the sun. *The Golden-Voiced*. "Tamurzîn, apparently, to history. Korrokaith, at the end." *The Dreadful*.

He made a gesture behind them, indicating the darkness they had walked so slowly through. The curtain had disappeared, and the grey bridge stretched straight and clear into the green marshes. The sound of the tens of thousands of swans was very loud again in the air; the wind was blowing out of the west, behind them. It caught the loose tendril of hair that had fallen out of Rowan's braids until he grabbed at it with his hand and tangled the tresses around his fingers.

"Not the very end," Ash said, looking sidelong at River. A small smile was tugging at her lips.

Ash had been River's best friend for *decades*.

River took a long breath, drawing the fresh, clean, lovely, *lively* air deep into her lungs.

What did Rowan—Tamsin—*think* they were going to do? He knew perfectly well that Ash wanted to be the best fighter at the Tourney and that River wanted to write a history of the early days! Even if they hadn't enjoyed his company over the past month, who was possibly going to be a better resource than *him*?

"Not the end, no," said River, and she looped her hand once more through the crook of Rowan's elbow. Tamsin's. His expression was deeply flummoxed. She smiled sunnily at him. "Clearly your story's begun a new chapter, at the very least."

"Come on," Ash said, and though she did not like touching quite as much as River did, she too took Rowan's other arm. She pointed ahead with her free hand to a dark mass in the distance. "Let's see if that copse of trees will make a good campsite."

PART TWO
THE OLD CITY

CHAPTER THIRTEEN
THE BREAKING OF THE LAMPS

Klara hung up her last gown on the line, and picked up the empty laundry basket with mild satisfaction. It was quite dim: the sun hadn't yet cleared the mountains east of the city. The courtyard between her small house and the next was stone-flagged and caught the morning sunlight magnificently. The pots of flowers, vegetables, and herbs her neighbour Minyana grew relished the light and heat. So did Klara, who sometimes felt untowardly chilled.

She danced back into her house, spinning the basket around on her hip as she went, a song on her lips to greet the rising sun.

Minyana, up earlier than usual, yawned as she joined in the chorus. Klara let her voice rise up a little more loudly, no power in it but joy, and heard other voices pick up the song from beyond the walls of the old city.

It was an old, old song, the Dawnsong, and not very many people even in this part of the city remembered now who had written it. For most people it was a song of joy and triumph, the light over the dark, hope over fear, the morning over the great Darkness that had fallen over Elfland after the Breaking of the Lamps—

It was for Klara, too, of course. She was one of those who remembered what it had been like, that first sunrise, that first dawn, after the terrible Darkness that was not a night as they would come to know them.

But she had been standing next to the one who had lifted up his voice in that joy, that triumph, that hope. She had not sung it first; that was one of the griefs of her life.

Klara had been silent, struck by a shard of something icy-cold in her heart, unable to do anything but stand there awash in terror and fear at the light rising over the mountains.

Tammorath, Klara called her friend, if she ever named the one who had sung that first Dawnsong. She didn't; it had been a long time since she had met anyone who cared to hear tales from before the rising of the Sun and did not already know that one. But she held the name in her heart, sharp as the shard that had wounded her.

Tammorath, the Golden-Voiced, as if that was his name.

It was not the sort of name younger elves chose for their children, in this Sunlit Age that stretched out as indefinitely pleasant as the Golden Age of the Lamps. Nowadays they called their children simple names, fit for simple desires and simple lives. Minyana was a name from the Age of Homecoming—it meant 'She Who Has Returned in Joy' in the old Firnoian that had become a language for scholars only—but Minyana's daughter was named Juniper, plain and simple.

Klara set her basket inside, and rubbed at her chest. Thinking about Tammorath was never a good idea. She let the song trail off as she shut the door behind her. This was the problem with being immortal. You never really got over loss.

And no one was as lost as Tammorath. Even that name no longer fit anything but a very distant memory.

When the Lamps had been destroyed by the Old Enemy, Klara and Tammorath—call them that, though *Klara* had not been her only name, then, either—had been practicing together. They had been a short distance outside the city, in a grove of ancient birches near the river, their leaves golden with the coming winter.

(For they had had winter, then, and spring too. Tammorath had always liked spring best, singing glimmers of gold and copper so his dark hair shone almost as red as that of his mother and his brothers in the light of the Lamps. Klara had always loved winter best; her favoured colours were silver and white.)

They had been so close in those days, Tammorath and Klara. Their other names—no. Klara had put hers away with the other gifts Tammorath had once given her, as Tammorath had thrown away all his names and loves but one. The person who had gone Over the Waves with his brothers was not the one Klara had loved.

No one could say in truth which of them was the greater bard, not in those days. No one could say even *which* of them was performing, oftentimes: they dressed alike, sometimes in the lordly garb Tammorath had earned with his skill, sometimes in the queenly robes Klara had earned with hers. Their songs brought them gifts and tribute and the ability to barter for whatever beauty of craft and skill and material their eyes and hearts desired.

They wore gold and silver and shining jewels from the jewellers and smiths of the city, and long strands of pearls traded from the Sea-Elves to the south such as not even the queen wore. Tammorath favoured gold, and Klara silver, but they were mirror-images of each other when they chose to be.

No one had been as fashionable as they, or as daring: everyone followed them, amazed at their clothes, their adornments, their complementary excellences, their rivalry.

For no one *had* known that Klara and Tammorath had taught each other their voices, so in the parts of their ranges they shared each could sing exactly as the other, their powers glossing over the differences.

No one had known that their great rivalry was a game they played with each other, a courtship of daring and skill, challenging one in the other's voice, a wooing by music and performance and nerve.

They had meant nothing by it. They had not thought anything

much of consequences, in those golden days of the Golden Age of the elves, before the Breaking of the Lamps. They had laughed with each other at each successful impersonation, and met in that copse of yellow birches or green beeches or under some silver-leaved willow or in a snowy glade to laugh and kiss and sing and Sing, for magic ran in their voices as it did for no one else at all.

They let their courtship take its time. They had all the ages of the world before them: why should they rush, when the rivalry was so sweet, and the music sweeter? The stolen kisses were as honey on their lips, laughter hiding behind painted eyelids, painted fans, the long gauzy veils of those who had given themselves to their arts.

On the stages and streets of the city they were the great rivals, fierce and proud, their songs and their instruments raised up against each other.

Tammorath loved the country, and Klara the city. That was what they said, what they sang, though in truth it was always Klara who ranged afield, and always Tammorath who planted himself in the central square before the holy fire his father had brought back from the west.

Or it had been. Before the Breaking of the Lamps. Before Klara had fallen, struck by a shard in her heart; before Tammorath had run, struck by his father's words.

It had been Klara who stayed, bound to the city Tammorath had loved more truly, and Tammorath who had gone, gone, gone, farther even than Klara had ever dreamed of going.

Not Tammorath. Tamsin.

Not Klara. They had called her by other names, in the Shadowed Age, in the city of the Firnoi who had not gone Over the Waves. It was not only Tammorath—Tamsin—who had lost himself.

When they were themselves, and only themselves, Klara played the flute, and Tammorath ... *Tamsin* the harp.

Yet it had been Tamsin whose flute-playing had called down all the swifts of the north to foul the roofs of the upper city, and Klara whose harping had flooded the lower city.

When they were called before the king, each played their own selves and accepted the punishment meted out for the other's skill, and afterwards met again in one of their secret places to laugh and kiss and spin their songs together again.

They were so rarely themselves, and only themselves. Later Klara wondered what they had been thinking, what they had ever expected to happen. But of course they had been thinking of nothing but the next song, the next challenge, the next dare: the next smile in Tamsin's eye, the next kiss on Klara's mouth, the next gleeful, exhilarating step in the mad dance they had begun and had no idea how to stop.

They did not want to stop it. Klara had not; she still believed Tamsin had not.

They had played together for a ball one night, one of those magical nights where their music never faltered. They had played the reels ever faster, letting no one escape their music, the laughter and the wheeling, the whirling, their songs and their Singing. They had *been* the dance, the music, the song and the singers—

That was all they had ever wanted, the golden voice and the silver. They had wanted never to stop.

They hadn't, until that day under the yellow birches, when the Lamp of Bronze was extinguished, and in the sudden darkness something struck Klara in the heart.

Her cry split the world, just for a moment. Later she had wondered if it had split Tamsin's heart, too, and that was why he had become what he had.

But then he had cried out, too, the same note, two voices sounding in perfect unison, and perhaps that was why she had become what she had.

No one actually remembered what happened, that day.

Or—no one *admitted* they remembered what happened.

Or—no one *wanted* to remember what had happened.

Klara had written songs of this. To ensure this.

She had fallen to the ground when the Lamps were broken, a cold shard in her heart and the cry still bloody on her lips, in her ears. Tamsin had not fallen, but he had run off, the coward. He had fallen into the river, and that had jarred him back to himself.

He had come back for her, songs of light in his mouth, wavering glimmers hardly more than the glamours with which they were accustomed to gild themselves. In the strange unnatural dark he looked ghostly, like the unhoused spirits of those who had forgone their bodies and still wandered the hills and vales of Elfland.

For a moment Klara had not been able to recognize him, her other half. He had looked so strange, sopping wet, pale light crawling over his skin. His hair had dripped shadows down his back and into his eyes.

Her heart had been struck cold, but everything was cold in that moment. She saw with savage clarity: the broken Lamps, the cries rising up from the terrified city like huge flocks of alarmed crows, their cawing and their black wings deafening. She saw Tamsin, still Tammorath, but with the shadow of his coming Doom falling already over him.

His eyes were so dark, so wild, so fey. The Song was still on his lips, golden light creeping across his skin like ivy, blossoming into silver when he reached out to grasp her hands and lift her upright.

Klara let him, her mind already calculating. Her cry was still in her throat, locked behind her teeth, the power reverberating in a silent chord.

Tamsin surely heard it, for he was her mirror, and her cry had cracked him also.

She could not, at that moment, sing. Tamsin sang for her, his hand wet in hers, the river-water flowing in his footsteps long after he should have ceased dripping. Would he drown? she remembered thinking. Was that the fate she saw spiralling inwards, the cloak of shadows given bare form by his faint glimmering light?

He sang, the Golden Voice of the Firnoi: and she was never quite certain, afterwards, if he had not sung the stars back into being. It was that sort of night, and they had had that sort of power, Tamsin Tammorath and Klara the Silver.

The Song in her throat grew and grew, but she could utter no sound.

She and Tamsin followed the river into the city, past all the people crying and screaming or hiding in silence. She did not know what drew him, save that it was not what lay in her heart.

There was no wound, no blood, nothing she could feel with her hand. All she knew was that something had struck her, something cold and sharp, and now she looked at her rival, her friend, her lover, her beloved, and saw a stranger.

His eyes were black, but light came from his voice as they walked through the winding streets up the hill towards the king's palace. People followed behind them, drawn by those glimmers of gold and silver, the barest illumination shining bright as the coming moon in that utter dark.

The glimmers streamed up around him, around them, as if Klara were singing as she ought to have been, as they all thought she was. Tamsin was shifting between their voices, seamless as a call-and-response duet, concealing her silence.

No one else sang, but the terrible cries began to fade and diminish as they wound up the great processional route. Behind them crowded all the people of the city, the most attentive audience Klara had ever known, they the greatest bards of the Firnoi, perhaps the greatest of all the Elves, who could command any stage.

At the square in front of the palace they found Tamsin's brothers.

All six stood in an arc, the closed doors of the palace behind them, their father Dâr in the centre facing them. In front of Dâr was the basin that usually held the great triumph of the Firnoi, the symbol of their art and cunning and strength and might, the holy fire Dâr had taken from the mountain of the gods.

The flame imperishable was gone, the stone basin cracked in half. The Song still growing in Klara's mouth tasted of the ashes, the acid stone. The broken stone.

Tamsin and Klara walked hand in hand to stand in the small open space left for them by the crowding silent throngs of the people. They stood facing Dâr and the other sons of Dâr over the broken basin. The only light in all that square came from the song Tamsin was singing.

Tamsin's brothers were red-haired and tall as their mother, the carver; Tamsin dark and slight, most like his father. Yet it was Dâr the weaver who had gone to the uttermost west for a courting-gift worthy of his love, and Alina who had gone in faith of his return to the north, and from some secret valley to the back of the North Wind had found her own reciprocal gift. A great spherical stone, rough grey on the outside, the hollow interior full of perfect crystals the colour of summertime.

In Tamsin's soft light the crystals glittered darkly, their hearts no longer honey-gold but black.

They stopped there. Tamsin sang—Sang—and Klara watched.

Klara had never been one to *watch*. She acted: it was her idea to play Tamsin, to play the rival, to switch their places and their voices and their instruments and their lives.

Tamsin, it was said, loved the country, and Klara the city. Yet it was Tamsin who had never gone out of sight of the city walls but once, and Klara who had once told him that she would only stay in the city if she could rule it.

All the songs of the city that the people thought were hers were his in truth. He loved people, company, community, the buildings and the gardens and the markets and the streets.

Hers were the songs of the mountains and the fields, the rivers and the forests.

Hers were the songs of trade and war; his were of home and peace.

But no one knew that bar themselves, for it had been the great game of theirs since their youth, when they had first met, their cousins friends with each other, and realized that for the first time each had met an equal.

Already the silver light had taken the familiar golden tinge that said *Tamsin* to everyone else, though there was still enough silver for everyone to assume that Klara was, or had been, singing.

The Song in her throat was so thick. She dared not open her mouth, because she knew not what would come forth.

This next moment everyone remembered, or thought they remembered, or imagined they remembered. Klara had written the songs to ensure that, too.

What she remembered was this:

Six sons of Dâr standing in an arc behind their father, looking at their seventh brother. (Who was not, always, their brother; but they did not know that.) Dâr looking at his son the great bard, the one singing light in the darkness, the one *everyone knew* loved chivalry and adventure and the romance of war.

Tamsin let his voice fall into quiet, a doubled echo, as if Klara herself had been singing with him and now was not. He was very powerful, was Tamsin Tammorath: the lights took a very long time to fade after he had stopped singing them into being. The very last glimmers clustered along the sharp edges of the crystals in the broken stone basin.

The Old Enemy has awoken again, cried Dâr into the silence, the desolation of a city that had always known light and music. *He has broken the Lamps and stolen the Fire and cast us all into Darkness, but he shall not prevail! My sons and I swear to you that we shall cast down the Old Enemy and regain our fire, or be damned into the Eternal Night!*

And then had followed the great and terrible Oath, the greatest work of Dâr the great word-weaver, and each of the seven sons had stepped forward and cried out the words, binding themselves in a net of words that would never let them go.

In the dark, with the spirit of Dâr as bright as the holy fire that had been stolen, the Lamps that had been broken and cast down, it was hard not to be moved. Tamsin certainly was reeled in, crying forth the words in a voice that burned in the air long after he had been gathered into the embrace of his brothers.

He was the last to stand forth, Tamsin: the youngest, the most like

Dâr in feature, the least like him in heart. But Tamsin did not even look at Klara when he stepped forth to doom himself.

The city poured after them, all those people who followed Tamsin's song, his light, his voice.

Klara wrote the songs to make it the work of Dâr, that it was his Oath-weaving that had caught them, that it had been inevitable: that once the words were begun, they could not be taken back or stopped. But yet she knew the truth.

It had been Tamsin's call that had brought the people there, Tamsin's song that had heartened them, Tamsin's voice that had bewitched them.

If Klara had sung out, said a word, let out even a breath of that Song in her throat, she could have broken the spell. She could have freed Tamsin and his brothers; could have freed the people from the Doom they all so gladly called down upon themselves; could have saved everyone.

So she thought then, but with the coldness in her heart she did not care to do it. She could see the shadows of the future falling ever more heavily upon the people around her, family and friends and fellow citizens alike, binding them to a fate of terror and terrible death across the sea.

She could have saved them all, with the Song in her throat that was a match for anything Tamsin Tammorath could sing.

She did not. As Tamsin of the Golden Voice sang a people into an army, Klara listened to the silences and the shadows, and let her voice rest. She followed along beside Tamsin until that first sunrise, when he sang the Dawnsong and brought a false and terrible hope to himself and all those who followed him, and left her cold.

She could not bear the brightness of the sun, so much stronger and harsher than the beloved Lamps. She could not bear the song Tamsin was singing, could not bear the light he had turned to so gladly, could not bear the Doom that had nearly drowned him and which only she could see.

She had not said anything since the breaking of the Lamps. The Song was still too strong in her throat, burgeoning, unsingable. At first Tamsin had been concerned, but every time she shook her head in denial, dismissal, refusal, he stepped back.

By the time the army of the Firnoi left for the strange and terrible land across the sea, Over the Waves, where their deaths would come upon them, Tamsin and Klara were no longer mirror-matches, but true opposites. Tamsin strode forth shining in golden armour, gleaming with his glamours, the new sunlight, his voice always sounding bright and beautiful through the air.

Klara stayed in shadows and the harsh light of the moon, silent, cold.

Tamsin never asked if she would come with him Over the Waves. She could not tell if this was because he knew her answer already, or because she had not volunteered herself, or because he could hear the Song still growing in her throat, and he was afraid.

(They had never been afraid of each other.)

She felt no fear: not of him, not of herself; not for him, nor herself. She felt nothing, in fact. She merely watched, and waited, until the army left.

CHAPTER FOURTEEN

THE SHADOWED AGE

The army left, and most of the Firnoi with them. They marched off singing to the sea, to the ships they had built or bought or stolen, with Tamsin's voice floating always over all the rest. Already they were giving him new names, Tammorath too innocent, too tame for the fire now always in his voice.

Indorath, the Great-Voiced, was such a truism Klara might have sneered, but for how she could see the jaws of despair and disaster into which they were walking. She knew that Indorath would not be Tamsin's name for long.

She walked through the empty city in the new dark nights, running her fingers along the old familiar stone walls and balustrades.

Klara walked through the nights, the sleeping city, listening to the hollows and emptinesses that so recently had been full of people and life.

No one really knew what had happened to the king and queen; the prince, young and hot-blooded, followed Dâr and the Sons of Dâr to build a new kingdom for himself Over the Waves.

Or so said the later stories, the songs Klara would write.

The wife of Dâr, the mother of the seven brothers, the one who had brought from the farthest north a stone worthy of holding the holy fire from the mountain of the gods—Alina of the Shining Wood —she did not go Over the Waves, either. She did not enter into the songs; did not, for a long time, see anyone.

Klara wrapped herself in silence and darkness and ice, and the city grew still and frigid around her.

The palace doors stayed closed, as they had been closed when Klara and Tamsin returned to the city after the Breaking of the Lamps. The few people who remained avoided the great square with the broken basin that had once contained a holy fire, where Dâr and his sons had sworn their great Oath, where the people had followed the only light that was left, that sung out of memory and imagination by Tamsin Tammorath.

Klara did not avoid the square. She walked it, night after night, the Song in her throat growing and growing, the coldness in her heart radiating out. She avoided even the moonlight now, though when she slept the daylit hours away she dreamed of light and song, the voice of her friend (her lover, her beloved, her rival, herself) singing out over the shining sea, the strange and beautiful and terrible land Over the Waves.

The shadows came to her instead, gathering at her footsteps, folding themselves into her clothes, her eyes, her hair. Klara let them swirl around her, ever thicker, ever richer, ever colder. She walked alone through the silent city in the dark hours after the sun was gone, listening, watching, waiting. She pricked her fingers on the crystals of the basin, their colours bleached out, singed, honey become coal, dead embers, extinguished, extinct.

She dreamed of sunlight and blood and song.

Over the Waves *he* dreamed of shadows and silence and ice.

They were the greatest bards of the Firnoi, and they had grown into their powers handing off their identities to each other until no one but themselves knew which was which. They were sundered now, their souls torn from their gradual blending, their hearts separated by sea and Oath and song and silence. Or—so she would have said.

Klara dreamed of Tamsin's days, and he of her nights.

She walked through the city he had loved and left, in the nights that had once been full of music, radiant with their Song, with the Lamp of Bronze and the Lamp of Gold taking turns to shine. They had never known true night before, not in the city. It had been something you travelled to, darkness.

The shadows followed the unsong in her throat, the power growing with every unuttered heartbeat. She walked through a perpetual winter's night, ice in her footsteps, following her fingers trailing on stone wall and balustrade. She traced out a spiderweb of shadows, each night pacing the streets of the city, touching every wall, gathering all the warmth and light of the day into her keeping.

They said later that the king of the Firnoi had become the city he had built, his body fading as his soul entered its stones, until its slow heartbeat became his own. They said later that the queen had turned into a serpent, into the river, and coiled deep into its waters until its currents became her own.

Klara wrote those songs, too.

Klara walked the night, alone in the empty city. Those who remained cowered in their houses, next to their hearths, candles and lanterns lit against the cold darkness that surged against their windows.

It was true that elves who lived in one place for a long time, who *ruled* a place for a long time, became entwined with their place.

It was also true that the elves of the Firnoi were crafters, and their souls did enter their creations.

Over the Waves, Tamsin shaped himself into a death-dealer, a creature of violence and fear. Klara's daylit dreams were still full of sunlight and song, but now she woke with blood in her mouth, and the light burned and blinded those who dared look upon her dream-self. Over the Waves, a continent rolled onto its back at Tamsin's feet, and he glutted himself on its weaknesses. He sang of death in the sunlight, and sang himself into legend.

This side of the sea, in what had once been the only home either of them knew, Klara shaped herself in silence. It was ice and darkness she gave his dreams, shadows so dark even Klara's hungry eyes could absorb no light from them.

She was so very hungry, was Klara in those nights. She walked the city, enveloping it with the shadows that came crowding to her. Still silent, still with that Song thick in her throat. She had uttered no sound since the shard had struck her heart, and walked in no light since Tamsin had gone Over the Waves.

She too was a songwright, and she too became what she sang.

The king in his palace let his soul settle into the stones, but his authority never went past that square where Dâr had called on the people, and the people had followed. Klara let him be, the ancient king in his ancient palace, let his beating heart beat a steady drumbeat behind the closed doors. His shadows came to her, whispering of dust.

The queen became a serpent, a river, a moat, the moat of the palace, guarding her king, her heart, her home. Klara let her be, the queen in the river that moated what had once been a palace on a high hill, let her twist and twine in sinuous curves whose currents were slow, slumbrous thoughts. Ice rimed the water, when Klara brushed her hand across the surface.

The king ensouled his palace, and slept behind the shadow-barred doors.

The queen became a moat around her king, her thoughts the fish blurred beneath the ice.

Each night the city drifted farther from the palace, the hills and valleys rippling under Klara's feet, her touch, the shadows that thronged around her, the Song still caught unsung in her throat. She gathered the light and warmth from the stones, swallowing them down past the Song that would not sound forth. The ice grew each night, caging the houses with the long spikes growing down from rooflines, the ferneries taking form on each window.

The city shifted around its new centre, the streets moving to follow her wanderings, taking new shapes as she listened to the shadows, shaped herself into the hollows and silences left behind.

Each day Klara drew back as she felt the sun nearing, as Tamsin's sleeping mind tilted towards wakefulness, as his voice started to rumble in her lungs and chest.

There were people behind the closed doors, eking out a life in her abandoned city. Sometimes they muttered in her ears like crows.

At first the ice melted each morning when the sun crested the mountains, and the people were able to come out in their ones and twos to do what they would during the daylight hours.

But there was little and less food, and with the king in his palace and the queen deep in her moat, and winter growing ever stronger, there was little hope of more.

Klara did not know why so few left. Those who had not followed Dâr and the high-hearted prince had already been bound to their crafts and their homes, perhaps, had already been too attached, too rooted, already shifting into the spirits of crossroads and hearth.

Or perhaps it was fear that bound them here, rather than love. She did not know. She did not cross the thresholds of any home but her own, the one whose windows showed no lights by day or night. She lay in a nest of shadows, hidden deep from any touch of sun, and dreamed of all the things that burned, Over the Waves.

On moonlit nights Klara walked in the deepest shade, where the cold was bitter, sharp in her lungs and on her bare skin. Ice spread out under every footfall, pulsing in rings of symmetric crystals, brilliant once she stepped onwards, the night shadows tugging free of their casting objects to follow her. There was no warmth to the moonlight for her to swallow, to appease the aching hollow in her heart, but she could gather the light, and she did.

Over the Waves, armies fell under Tamsin's voice, his spells of hope and courage and folly and death. He spun sunlight into his voice, until even in her dreams Klara could not tell where light became sound. His voice was a spear, a sword, a slash of lightning: a weapon. As she dreamed his days she knew he could no longer sing anything but death; that his voice could no longer bring spring to barren ground.

He dreamed her nights, ever darker, ever colder. She could feel him sometimes, a pressure in the back of her throat as if she were about to open her mouth and sing. His dream-self was the glimmer of starlight on the crest of her shadows, the brief warmth blooming on her fingertips, her lips, as she swallowed the day's offerings. She felt his heart beat not quite in time with hers, the tug of his confusion when a street he had known all his life bent away from its familiar destination.

She drew him deeper into her nights as the city, his city, gave itself up to her. Let him swallow blood and sunlight and song, far away with the curse of his Doom binding his soul away from hers. She would let the darkness lap ever thicker about her, build her own walls of ice to sheath the old stones, sink into the silence and emptiness until the Song in her throat was ready.

They had bound themselves to each other, whirled and wheeled around and around each other, two great bards Singing themselves into the other's life. They had made themselves mirrors, the golden and the silver, perfectly balanced, so that no one could tell which was which unless they wished to be known. Of course when one suddenly flew in one direction the other would have to counterbalance, leaning further and further into the difference as they had leaned into the similarities, until Tamsin had become a white fire of singing death and Klara—

They had not been thinking. They had never thought what would happen, if they bound themselves like that. They had not meant it as anything but a game. It had been a game, a courtship, a strange wooing, each of them wishing to be the splendid peacock showing off his greatness, each the humble peahen making her choice.

Klara dreamed of Tamsin's bloody hands and bloodied mouth, and the sunlight beating down pitilessly upon the strange and terrible land where he waged war.

Tamsin dreamed of the ice under Klara's feet and the shadows that swarmed around her, and the way she caged the few who still lived in the city safe from the increasingly hungry dark.

Her Song had grown to fill her body and her mind, until she could do nothing but listen to it reverberate silently in her bones. The ice sheathed her now, beautiful as the gowns she and Tamsin had once worn, armour strong as Tamsin's steel corselets.

He wore cloaks fire-red, and her silver on his brow. His song gilded him, illuminated him from within, as if he were sunlight shaped into elven form.

She walked in shadows, ice crystals in her wake.

Some evenings she woke with her throat bleeding from his voice.

One day Klara fell into a deeper, heavier sleep than she had known thereto, deep as the sleep that had dissolved the king into his palace, the queen into her serpentine moat. Deep she fell into her shadows, into the blizzard that was how Tamsin met her nights, until the lightning crackled into light, and the silence on her tongue became his voice singing.

Klara had never felt afraid, either of or for Tamsin, even after all the innumerable years spent dreaming his battles. She had never doubted his power or his skill or his will. They both knew that what was sung—even more, what was Sung—became what was: and Tamsin had Sung himself into the greatest and most terrible warrior-bard there had ever been or would ever be or could ever be.

None of the creatures he had faced had ever felt real to her, not the goblins nor the elves. They had been dream-stuff, their blood on his sword, on his hands, in his mouth, unreal. They had not looked at her, not felt her, not heard her, even when Tamsin felt her in the cold breeze on his neck, the sudden shiver when a cloud passed over the sun, the way his own shadow moved according to her whim and not his motion.

What he faced now was the Dragon, greatest of all the Old Enemy's allies, old as fire, old as death, old as the dark.

It saw her.

Tamsin was singing—Singing—pouring himself into his voice, reverberating like a plucked harpstring, his voice against the Dragon, his fire against the very spirit of death by fire.

The Dragon looked at him, and Klara—moved by what she could not say, for had she not lost her heart when that cold shard struck her, when Tamsin led her to the city and left her there, when she had found her Song sticking in her throat?—Klara summoned all her shadows and her ice and stepped in front of him.

Three days Tamsin sang against the Dragon.

Three days: and three nights.

In the day Tamsin was the greatest bard of all the Firnoi, the greatest perhaps of all the elves. He had shaped himself into the greatest warrior-bard of all—that was a reputation no one ever contested—his voice an instrument of certain death. Even facing the spirit of death by fire, his voice rose up, clear and golden and perfect and strong.

But in the nights Tamsin had walked with Klara, dreamed her darkness and her ice, been the warmth she swallowed, the light she fled. If he woke in the dark nights Over the Waves his voice was silver and shadow, cages of coldness and silence, empty streets and hollow homes.

Facing the Dragon, Klara felt the tug of the shadows waking in the city, felt Tamsin's mind turning to follow hers back across the water, falling into the strange tether between their souls.

It was not her throat that moved, but it was Klara who stood fast, who refused to return to her night, and who *Sang*.

All that night she Sang in Tamsin's voice, and he with her.

She became him singing—Singing. They sang of ice, of cold, of the long frigid nights, of the shard in her heart that had never melted. They sang of ice, and the Dragon sang of fire, and when the sun rose on the second morning, Tamsin stood singing in a great billow of steam.

He sang through the day, sunlight and death, his voice a blade, white as the light upon a sword. He sang, Sang, *Sang*. Klara's shadows curled in his dark hair, in the shadows splintering around his body, in the dark pupils of his eyes.

(So bright, his eyes were so bright; reflected in the Dragon's eyes his were white with his power, with the light he had summoned into himself, like fragments of the sun, impossible.)

Tamsin Sang, fire against fire, sunlight against the fire that was older than the stars.

The second night, Klara sang of darkness. Before the stars there might have been fire, but there had certainly been the dark, and she *knew* the dark.

Tamsin sang in the hungry glint of her eyes, her sharp white teeth, the ice cladding her skin, the warmth that blossomed on her fingertips when she called the day's light to her, when she swallowed all the meagre warmth the stones of the city had gathered. When she slept in the dark, Tamsin's dreams of sunlight caught on the ice and reflected that refracted sunlight into all the corners, made of her city a thing of crystalline glory.

She sang her shadows to the Dragon that had eaten half the world before the rising of the sun, and when the sun rose on the third morning the shadows still lingered in Tamsin's brilliant eyes, his glowing skin.

The third day, Tamsin sang: his golden voice thick with blood, raised yet like the red-and-gold banner of the Sons of Dâr against their Enemy, raised like the holy fire that had once burned in the centre of his city. Tamsin sang, and Klara's shadows clustered at his feet, a cloak around his gleaming armour, his shining face, the glamours of centuries become part of his being.

He sang, and Klara sang with him, rendering up to him all the hoarded warmth and light she had swallowed. The Dragon laughed, for it was older than the sun, older than the stars, older than the very concept of light.

But Klara and Tamsin were older than the sun, and had not Tamsin Sung the stars into being? Had he not been the only one who had been able to hold light in his mind when all else had gone dark?

Had she not swallowed the dark?

~

The third night, they Sang of silence, until Tamsin's voice became hers.

~

On the fourth morning the Dragon lay dead at Tamsin's feet, but his voice was still Klara's.

CHAPTER FIFTEEN
THE CITY OF ICE

Klara awoke from dreams of ash and fire with the Song in her throat no longer choking her.

It was morning. Over the Waves Tamsin was crumpled insensate, silent, at the feet of the great Dragon he had slain.

Klara raised her hand to her throat. The ice had melted from where it had sheathed her so closely: her skin was paler than it had once been, milk-white. Her hair spilled down in an inky river over her shoulders, blacker than coal, blacker than the shadows cast by a full moon.

It was morning. Over the Waves Tamsin was dreaming himself into the light filtering in through the ice-covered windows, all the rainbow glitters that had been tied into the war-banners of his songs.

Klara brushed her hand across the rainbow refractions, gathering them into her palm. Tamsin slipped away from her hand into a thread of air curling through the shadowy nest at her feet.

She felt the power resonating in her, echoing in her ears. Tamsin's voice in her throat, nestling there into hers, as if he had fled the Dragon's fall to safety.

She stood, the handful of rainbows melting in her hand, sweet on her tongue when she raised them to her lips. Klara hummed (Tamsin hummed), a thread of the song of the nights that had passed, the days she had dreamed into his song.

The shadows formed themselves into a gown such as she had worn (they had worn) on stage, black as her hair, as her eyes, as the cold hunger in her heart. Tamsin rested wearily upon her shoulders in a skiff of sunshine, his voice in her throat, dreaming that he only dreamed of her.

It was morning. Over the Waves Tamsin dreamed he dreamed of her, and fell ever deeper into silence.

Klara went out into the city.

In the morning the city was a dream of light. Rainbows everywhere, cast by the ice sculpted through the endless winter's night of Klara's silence.

It was all utterly, perfectly empty.

Klara walked the streets she knew in the darkness. Tamsin dreamed of strange labyrinths made of familiar houses; Klara ran her fingers upon the ice sheathing the houses, caging the windows, casting everything into a crystalline confection. Her shadows were stranger in the daylight, their black shapeliness less a shade cast upon the world than holes cut into it.

The moat around the palace was thickly iced. The fish were deep below the surface, in the murky water of the queen's serpentine mind, slow flashes of silver and gold. The palace doors were closed, looped in shadowy bonds; the king's heartbeat was slow and steady in his deep slumber.

Klara turned to the city Tamsin had loved. From here she could feel the faint flashes of life in the houses where the people had not left, cradled by ice and shadow in a semblance of safety. They slept, too, those who were left, curled close together.

Tamsin had been the one who had sung light and hope, and led all the rest to their Doom.

Klara had been silent, her heart struck by that shard, and the city she had claimed was cold and clear as her own mind.

It was morning. Over the Waves Tamsin had sung the Dragon to death.

Klara stood where they had stood, Tamsin's hand in hers, facing Dâr and the sons of Dâr across the broken stone basin that had once held a holy fire. At her feet the stone basin glittered with a thin film of ice, the sharp-tipped crystals sleek and almost soft under her questing fingertips. Her hands drew warmth and light into them: her touch melted nothing.

Tamsin had cried out that Oath. Klara had listened and said nothing as her friend, her rival, her lover, her beloved had damned himself.

She was so cold, and so hungry, in this city that had listened to her silence and huddled close to her shadows as if for comfort. She was so cold, and so hungry, and so alone, in this city where those who yet lived slept because they dared not face her silent conquest of the streets.

She was so cold, and so hungry, and so alone, and she was tired of being silent while Tamsin sang.

He had destroyed his voice with the power running through it. Three days and three nights! It was unheard of. It would make a song beyond all others.

He would not make of it a song. His voice was gone, fled to her throat.

It was morning. Over the Waves Tamsin dreamed she was singing, and was comforted.

Klara lifted up her voice.

She filled the city with starlight; with mist that rose from icy gardens in the golden twilight, and hoarfrost that silvered every edge. She unwound the ice caging in the houses, drew back the darker shadows to veil the emptinesses, and called awake those sleeping.

This was the city of the crafters, and those who had remained were those who loved the city and their works beyond any call of prince or vengeance or glory. They heard her song as they had heard her silence, and heeded both with cautious steps and curious eyes.

This was the city of the Firnoi, the city of those who made, and though Klara was now the only great songwright, she was not alone in her love of stone and street.

That first day was the only day she walked in the morning. Let Tamsin have the bright hours, the blazing noons, the pitiless afternoons. She would have her deepest shades, the moonless hours, the fiercest, coldest midnights.

They shared the twilights of dawn and dusk, when neither quite slept and neither quite woke, but instead walked together in radiant daydreams of growing shadows, gathering light.

Now it was Klara who sang, and Tamsin who was silent.

She still dreamed his sunlit days, the blood in his mouth and the sword in his hand. She was still the shadow at the corners of his eyes.

He still dreamed her nights, the cold under her touch and the shadows thick on her skin. He was still the glint of light in her smile.

Over the Waves, Tamsin shaped himself ever more perfectly into death. This side of the sea, Klara slowly thawed.

Klara sang the City, and the City sang back.

Those who were left found crafts that fit with the place they now knew, with the place they now were. There were weavers who learned to capture the sky into impossible fabrics, so the people went garbed in sunsets and moonrises, in the blue of a mountain morning, the starry field of a winter midnight. There were glassblowers who created bells and bellflowers as delicate as Klara's hoarfrost, gardens of glittering jewels where there had never been aught before but stone.

Someone caught the winds in jewelled nets, and created symphonies of storms over the mountains. Someone sang the city into hills and towers, plunging pools and hanging gardens, and then spun bridges at dizzying heights between them.

Someone—and Klara knew that someone, though she never met her, kept their paths always apart—someone left gifts for her at every corner. Wooden bells with silver clappers; tiny ivory hedgehogs which ran into her cupped palms when she knelt before them to drink the starlight puddling there; fragrant oils burning in terracotta and bronze, always the scents Tamsin and Klara had worn.

Klara walked the city as the sun fell into the western mists, her shadows running at her feet, trailing ice across all her people's inventions, limning them with silver and shade, making them her own. She drank in the day's warmth, but she sang back the light, now, filling the basins of fountain and pool with foaming starlight.

She walked the city in the glimmering nights, delving into the deep wells of darkness where her people tossed their fears and doubts. Klara gathered them up, swallowed them into herself, into that endless hunger that was still insatiable, that cold heart of hers that never warmed more than an instant at a scent or a bell-sound or the snuffling huff of an ivory hedgehog's curious snout.

The stars wheeled overhead. The moon waxed, waned, waxed again. The sun rolled through the sky, shining on Tamsin's silent wars, Klara's singing city.

Tamsin played the harp, until in a mazy wood so full of shadows even Klara was lost he lost his hands to fire.

Klara screamed for him; but he could not hear her, and the part of her voice that was his was his no longer.

His days grew darker, as fumes rose out of the dying land Over the Waves and clouded the sun. Her nights grew brighter, as she captured ever more starlight and bound it into her ice-crystal city.

In the twilight before dawn she started to Sing birds into existence. Ice-birds, clear as glass, casting rainbows even as they sang like the chinking of windchimes, the leap and laughter of a meltwater stream. She sang flocks of them: tiny wren-like creatures with flicking tails, titmice tumbling through the hanging vines of crystal frost, translucent swans for the starlit pools. Snow-white doves to coo and murmur from the cornices and corbels; sparrows to flutter in the frosted outlines of the ivy that still clad some of the older buildings.

The crows came next, white-eyed and white-pinioned, sitting high in the trees with their white and silver leaves, their crystal branches. They followed Klara as she walked through the city, the night darkness no hindrance to their ghostly flight, to their watching, wary eyes.

After the crows, the starlings, rainbow-speckled shadows in their winter flocks, murmurations wheeling ever larger in the endless winter afternoons.

Over the Waves, Tamsin looked with uninterested eyes at the starlings that billowed over the wide, desolate marshlands where he fought endless waves of twisted monsters. Even when Klara sang in his dreams he no longer seemed to hear her; it was almost as if he had ceased to imagine anything at all. She still felt his voice tucked deep into her throat, but he never reached for it even when he slept.

Klara dreamed of white egrets and spoonbilled cranes, of grey herons and endless ducks, of marsh harriers quartering the salt meadows, sandpipers running after the waves. In her inland city at the foot of the mountains she Sang them too, and the streets opened up around the lakes that looped around the moat the queen had made.

The palace was an island now, snow-clad and shining, in a ring of black water edged with frost. The city shouldered away from it, centred still on the broken stone basin that had once held the holy fire that Dâr had won from the mountain of the gods. Klara tucked the basin into a secret garden deep in the heart of her city, in a place where the frozen shadows never stirred and not even the white crows flew.

Klara filled her city with light and flight and birdsong, until the encircling mountains shivered with the songs rising up, the symphonies of storms, the ever-rising pinnacles of ice and song.

She walked, restless, eyes seeing sometimes the glittering battle-fields where Tamsin was the shadow of death, his sword a slash of moonlight, no longer catching the sun. Klara offered him her city, his city, the birds and the songs and the gardens of ice and glass, the people dressed in the sky, their hands creating marvels. But though she could feel his dreaming mind resting on hers, he no longer borrowed her eyes.

She remembered the shadow that he had walked so hopefully into, the jaws of the Oath opened wider than the great Dragon's to swallow him and his brothers and all his people, the trap she had not sprung when she could.

The white-eyed white crows followed her, their cawing the panicked noises of the people in the first dark after the Breaking of the Lamps, when Tamsin had sung light and Klara had been silent in the dark.

Her heart was still cold, the wound of that shard unhealed. She sang—she *Sang*—out of the silence the dark, and out of the darkness song, and out of the song light—

But Tamsin was no longer listening, could no longer listen. He had made himself only an instrument of death, and there was no death in her city of ice, this side of the sea.

Klara walked the streets of the city, and the city shaped itself to her song, curled in a protective spiral around the broken basin where once the flame imperishable had burned, and now all the shadows dwelled.

Over the Waves Tamsin cut his way into a fortress of stone and iron.

In the twilight, Klara walked through the mists, white as breath in the cold, clear air. Candles burned in the windows where the other elves dwelled, thousands of flames in chimneys of coloured glass. Her city was silver and shadow, the distillation of a deepest winter night, but the people within it had found colour, and beyond the thresholds she never crossed were all the brilliant hues of summer.

Someone had made an avenue of silver-branching trees, their leaves each of them a wafer of frosted glass, each of them unique in the shaping. They had time, here in this city of endless winter: time enough to forge silver into trees; time enough to shape a million leaves with individual care. The white crows hopped from branch to branch, gathering in their thousands, watching her.

Klara walked down the avenue, gathering all the shadows into her train. She breathed deeply, pulling the frigid air deep into her lungs, tasting the scents of snow and ice and lightning and the living flowers that someone had convinced to grow. Wooden bells lipped with silver chimed softly as she passed, quiet as the clink of crystal leaves against each other.

It was a moonless night. The stars overhead were thick in the crushed-velvet sky. Klara hummed in the back of her throat, where Tamsin should have rested. But he was wide-awake in the twilight on his side of the sea, the blood hot in his veins, on his hands.

Overhead, the crows followed her from branch to branch, their white claws clicking on the silver trees. A gentle wind rose at her hum, setting all the glass leaves to ringing. Klara sang the notes to the trees, catching their chime with her voice, throwing it back again.

Over the Waves, Tamsin's sword cut through goblins and strange monsters, deeper and deeper into the maze of stone and fire.

Klara Sang all the shadows out of the night, gathering them into her gown, her voluminous cloak, her hair, her eyes. She walked the curving avenue of silver trees until she came to a stair of white marble, climbing up and up in a spiral around a frozen waterfall.

Over the Waves, fire burned in Tamsin's eyes, his hands, his heart, his mind.

Klara climbed up and up, the marble extending itself under her feet, stone becoming snow becoming ice, the fountain casting ice ever higher. Under her Song the city turned and shifted, humped its shoulders, lifted the land so this fountain, this stair, rose up upon a hillock, a hill, a mountain.

A tower of diamond-bright crystal, spearing up into the night. Klara climbed, crystal tears freezing on her cheeks, falling down into the glittering cascades of her impossible art. She sang—she *Sang*—

Over the Waves, Tamsin cut his way into a cavern lit by holy fire, and he *burned*.

He burned, and Klara sang, Sang, *Sang*: sang ice and darkness and the cold, Sang winter, *Sang* the night—

Over the Waves, Tamsin and his fire-haired brother—the last of his fire-haired brothers—together they stepped up to the Old Enemy in his elven-fair form, with the crown of holy fire bound burning upon his brow, and Tamsin was burning, and Klara was *Singing*—

She called up all the birds she had formed out of ice and shade, and they swarmed out of their roosts, out of the silent city she had filled with their enchanted song: all the wrens and titmice and doves, the cranes and swans and starlings and crows in their thousands.

She Sang; but Tamsin was burning.

She called up her shadows, all the shadows she had so resolutely gathered, cold and thick and dark and deeper than the fire that the Dragon had breathed forth upon the field.

Over the Waves, Tamsin met the laughing eyes of the Old Enemy.

Klara could see the Doom of the oath Tamsin had sworn: a great serpent of dark flame, circling ever closer around Tamsin and his fire-haired brother, looping in heavy links about their souls, their hearts, their minds, their hands.

She had seen the distant shadow of this Doom when he had stood beside her, hand-in-hand, singing light and hope to her silence and doubt. She had felt the cold clarity of the shard in her heart, even as he had let the fire catch in his, his father's words lighting each son's heart in turn like torches lit from a taper.

Klara lifted up her shadows, and her birds flew around her in a blizzard like the blizzards that had once filled Tamsin's dreams, long ago now when he had been the one singing sunlight, but he had no voice left to him now, no Song she could enter. He had the sword in his hand, and the fire in his blood, his eyes, his mind, his heart, his soul.

In the city of ice and shadow, the city that Tamsin had once loved, Klara stood on a tower spearing itself into the sky in a spray of frozen light, all the shadows of the centuries and all the birds of the endless days flaring out across the burning stars: but though her voice rang out high and clear and full of might, Over the Waves no one could hear.

She could only watch as the last two sons of Dâr turned to face their final foe, the Old Enemy of all the elves, the one who had broken the Lamps and stolen the holy fire and slain their father: the one who bore on his brow the holy fire they had sworn themselves to the Eternal Night to reclaim.

Over the Waves, Daerleon the Fire-Haired lifted his sword, and Tamsin once the Golden-Voiced lifted his; and as Klara watched— witnessed—in the instant they moved forward, the Oath barely an instant from being fulfilled, the two brothers not even a breath away from being free—the Doom *struck*.

Death came, went the song Klara heard on the winds bearing the elves home, after the end of the Age.

Death came
Crowned in moonlight and blood
Death came

Even to the greatest of Dragons
Even to the fell fire-demons
Even to the Old Enemy
Death came

Crowned in moonlight and blood

His sword of moonlight red with blood
Death came

Merciless the mighty-voiced singer
Merciless the silent swordsman
Merciless the Son of Dâr

Even to himself, last of all his brothers
Death came

But songs were not always true. He was thrice-cursed, was Tamsin once called Tammorath, and though he had made himself the instrument of death, he himself lived on.

CHAPTER SIXTEEN
THE KING OF THE EXILES

Klara did not weep, for her heart was frozen.

She descended the spiral stair of her tower, the shadows flowing at her feet, foaming darkly about her ankles.

Down the delicate helical marble tracery, the ice of her impossible fountain glowing with the blazing starlight of this impossible night in which the Old Enemy had met his death, and Tamsin his Doom.

Down she walked, her feet white on the white marble, her hair black as the shadows at her back, steady and straight-backed, no tears but falling hailstones rattling down the stairs before her.

Down she walked, until she reached the peak of the mountain that had once been the square of a city's marketplace, and was now a great sheaf of stone and ice and metalwork trees.

She followed the mountain down, and the city rippled and shifted under her as the shadows followed and the birds wheeled overhead, crying.

The streets led her—

Not home. The city was her home, her place, halfway to her being. Since she had reclaimed her voice she rarely found herself in the inner room that had once been her sanctuary; she walked instead, and in those drifting noontide dreams she let herself dissolve into the breathing life of the streets and stones, the ice and birds, the bloodied sunlight Over the Waves.

She did not flee herself. She sought no crowds of elves or enchanted ice; she sought no valleys of singing silver or starlight. She walked instead, drawing all the shadows of a city of shades with her, until she found herself in the dark garden where the broken halves of the stone basin sat empty and alone.

Over the Waves, Tamsin's Doom fell upon him, and he wandered.

This side of the sea, Klara crawled into a nest of shadows, curled around her cold heart and the silence that should have been the singing voice of her friend, her rival, her lover, her beloved, and there, for a long time, she stayed.

Later, Klara learned that the elves Over the Waves had kept count of the years, and could number them. They could pin moments to dates: could say that this battle had happened on such-and-such a day, in this year of the reign of the great King of the Exiles.

No one who had stayed in the City of the Firnoi could comprehend the point.

They agreed that the first age of the Elves, the Age of the Lamps— the Golden Age, someone decided, and Klara later sang—that age had ended with the Breaking of the Lamps.

The second age began with the rising of the sun, and ended with the death of the Old Enemy, but for all that it was marked by light and the search for light, it was called the Shadowed Age for both those who had left—the Exiles, they came to be called—and those who had stayed behind.

The third age began with the first return of the elves from Over the Waves, in blue ships with sails of gold, and the triumphant march of the King of the Exiles back to the city of which he had once been the prince.

He found the city where he had left it, but not as he had left it at all.

Klara shaped herself a seat of curving ice, in her garden of shadows, with the broken basin at her feet, at the heart of her city of ice and starlight and mist. A thousand white crows attended her on the silver trees, the stone towers. The elves who lived there, the artists and crafters of strange beauty, wore their clothes of sky-stuff, their jewels like stars.

The King of the Exiles came to her alone, for the city was hers, and she bade the streets let him alone through. One by one his entourage faltered and turned aside, caught by an open door, a beckoning way, a marvel of art or the call of a bird or the face of one long left behind.

The King looked neither to the right nor the left, not up to the spire nor down to the valleys; every door he came to opened to him, every gate swung out of his way, every stair and every step led him where he wished, which was where Klara wished, for she had felt his coming and found in her cold heart a seed of curiosity.

She remembered the prince who had gone, fair-haired and fair-faced, singing of the glory he would win Over the Waves, the kingdom he would build for himself. The King who returned was broad-shouldered and tall, stern of face and steady of eye. His hair was gold as the sun on a field of wheat, and he wore it loose but for a circlet of gold set with jewels blue as his eyes. He wore gold-washed chainmail, and white was his surcoat; blue was his cloak, and gold the hilt of the sword at his waist.

Klara watched him come before her seat, watching him hide the uneasiness he felt at the touch of her swirling shadows, her humming winds, the power threaded through the air.

She wondered if Tamsin's shoulders had grown so broad, under the long years of war. In her dreams she had felt the strength in his arms, the way the Song had buzzed beneath his skin even after he had lost his voice to the Dragon. She had never seen the King of the Exiles fight in any of Tamsin's battles: the Sons of Dâr had taken their swords far from the lands the King had claimed.

Overhead, the white crows called to each other, and at her feet, the shadows swirled.

The King of the Exiles said, "I am the King of the Firnoi, and yet the city of the Firnoi knows me no longer."

Klara said, "You are the King of the Exiles, and this is the city of those who stayed."

It was the first time someone had spoken directly to Klara, or she to another, in all the years since Tamsin had spoken the Oath and gone away from her. But if Tamsin had made himself an instrument of death, Klara had made herself into an instrument of Song, and even soft and speaking, her voice was full of power.

The King of the Exiles had not always been unversed in such things: once upon a time Klara and Tamsin had been bid to teach the young prince how to Sing, though even then he had loved the bow and the spear of the hunt more than any instrument they could teach him.

Over the Waves he had foregone such subtleties. Though he put his hand to his sword, there was nothing he could fight here: he had not the skill, nor the cunning, to match her words. He did not even fully comprehend that he had lost the challenge. He merely found himself turning at the cry of some bird of prey in the distance, and when he thought to turn back to her, the path no longer led anywhere but away.

～

Over the Waves, Tamsin wandered alone and silent, still killing monsters.

In her city of ice and shadows, Klara felt the sap slowly rising.

～

The King of the Exiles built a wall, sturdy and strong, around what he called *the old city*. Klara shifted its position until she had all the land she desired within its circuit. She left him the palace the old king his father ensouled and the moat that had once been the queen his mother, for they still remembered their son even if he could no longer hear them.

The Firnoi who had left had changed as much as those who had stayed, though in perhaps the opposite direction. Those who had stayed dedicated themselves to their arts and the wonders they could devise in a city of increasing airiness and mystery; those who had left had found a land of hard edges and solid shapes and elves who preferred arms to magic, and learned their ways.

The King of the Exiles built a new city around the perimeter of the old, where all those he had brought back from Over the Waves could shape new homes for themselves. Over the long years which only the Exiles counted he had become the king of all who survived between the hammer of the Old Enemy and the anvil of the sea: Firnoi and Sawwalithians and the kingless elves alike, people of wood and water and mountain and plain.

They sang, these newcomers, in a new language wrought out of many tongues, but they did not Sing. They told tales of the Old City behind the high wall their king had bade them raise, and some went in to explore that place of magic and learn from those who still dwelled there. Klara let them come, for her people welcomed them, though she rarely permitted any to see her, and spoke to none.

In the age before the Breaking of the Lamps, when the old king had been king of the Firnoi, the city had been known for its crafts, wealthy in the creations of hand and voice. Elves had come from other places, from the city of the Sea-Elves to the south or the lands of the shepherds in the west, and traded as seemed good. But the old king had not sought to rule past the sight of his own city, the hinterland of field and forest where the hunters rode: he had been, in the parlance the King of the Exiles had learned Over the Waves, merely a petty king.

His son had greater ambitions, and if no sense of the subtle arts, a far greater understanding of other forms of power. He had all the people he had brought singing from Over the Waves: those of the Firnoi who had followed the blazons of the Sons of Dâr, their hearts held by the voice of Tamsin Tammorath, and who had left the banners with the dead and the Songs of power with the one they now called the Death-Singer. But they had brought with them swords and shields, and ploughs and chisels and axes too, and new ideas that had never been needed before the rising of the Sun.

The King of the Exiles built his wall, and a city around that wall. He had more under his banner who wished to settle but who were not elves of cities, and so he settled the hinterlands out of sight of the old palace.

Out of sight of the old palace, but at first not out of sight of the Old City that was Klara's great work, viewed from the spire of ice and white marble that shone in the darkest night with all the gathered radiance of the day.

He settled the hinterlands with shepherds and hunters and farmers and miners, and the wealth of his city grew great with jewels and furs and precious metals as well as the spoils he had brought back from Over the Waves. Some of the new city-dwellers traded with what they came to call the enchanters of the Old City, Klara's city, who were glad to have new materials for their workings: the King and his lords came to wear sky-cloth and shining crystals along with their gold and silver, their sable and ermine and mink.

As his city waxed, the King of the Exiles came to see her again.

This time he brought no attendants through the gates: and though he still wore his sword at his belt, he wore the sky-cloth her people wove instead of mail. He had chosen the blue of a cloudless day, which brightened his eyes to match, and his cloak was the gold of dawn-lit mist, lined with white ermine.

The King looked on her, and he said: "My people beg me to take a queen, and though I could choose any of the maidens of the Elves, it is my thought that none are so lovely nor so powerful nor so desirable as the Enchantress of the Old City."

Klara looked on him and found him fair; but yet she wondered whether Tamsin's eyes were as bright as they had once been, as he wandered the dying lands this king had abandoned, and she said: "Your realm grows great indeed, but still you are only King of the Exiles, and I am not."

Perhaps he wanted her, or perhaps it was that he wanted to swallow the shadows and the ice and the starlight of the old city, of which he had once been the prince but which no longer knew his voice.

She did not know. She knew, instead, what it was to stand before the broken basin that had once held the flame imperishable, and find only ice and darkness.

~

The King of the Exiles settled all the people who had come with him in ships from Over the Waves in a great circle around his new city, but yet he turned his gaze ever outwards. He had a hunger in him as greedy and insatiable as that in Klara's heart, though his was for treasure and acclaim and power.

Klara sent out her birds of ice and shadow in their hundreds and thousands, and they brought her on her seat of ice, in the garden of shadows, the news of all the lands this side of the sea.

They told her how the King reached out long arms of trade and settlement and war. He had taken possession of the shorelands when he had returned from Over the Waves: no longer did those who had been the Firnoi need to trade to the Sea-Elves in the distant south for the products of the sea. Perhaps there were no pearls as fine as the pearls that Tamsin and Klara had once worn in their hair, but very few were those who remembered the days before the Breaking of the Lights, or cared to.

From the great harbour the King had built for his returning Exiles, the ships ranged out, north and south along the coasts, until all who lived there bowed their heads to the King with his banner of gold and blue, and took his chosen knights to be their lords.

In the south the meadows and woods of Elfland stretched fair and free forever, or so the old tales had told. The King of the Exiles did not at first send his armies there: even he only had so many people to settle, and there were few of the treasures he sought in those hills and dells. Instead he looked north, until his armies met the frost-giants of the northern border, and could go no further.

Perhaps the King of the Exiles feared the ice and the long nights of the north, or perhaps he wished to test his strength there before he confronted Klara in the heart of what he thought of as his own city. Or perhaps he had heard the rumours that beyond the North Wind there were lands of plenty and richness where the dragons kept their hoards, and his desire for their treasure would not let him rest. Or perhaps it was simply that he, too, had shaped himself with his craft over the years, and his was the craft of conquest.

The giants allied with dragons, lured from their own distant caves in the land beyond the North Wind by the jewels and gold the King of the Exiles piled up in his city: and if none of these dragons was anywhere near so great or powerful as the Dragon Tamsin had once Sung to death, none of the King's knights were Tamsin Tammorath either.

The white crows ate well, in those days.

Over the Waves, Tamsin wandered, his thoughts dark and fell. There were fewer and fewer monsters left for him to fight, in that land that had withered under the poison of the Old Enemy, under the fire and blight of the Dragon, under the blood of all the Elves who had killed and been killed there.

On this side, the King of the Exiles set his border at the edge of the frozen mountains he named the Impassible, and began instead to think of the west.

Klara listened to her birds.

It had always been the legend that the dead could come again out of the Halls of Rest, and return to life. Before the Breaking of the Lamps, none ever had, or at least Klara had never heard of any who had. There had not been many who died, in any case; not in the city of the Firnoi.

There had been many who died Over the Waves, before and after the going of the Firnoi, but they had never come out of the Halls of Rest, either, not for all those long years in which those who remained in the city delved ever deeper into their own arts.

The King of the Exiles built castles to guard against the dragons and the giants, set mighty lords to hold those lands under him, and then he brought his armies back into the heartland of his kingdom, and set them to building a road that led due west.

Klara walked her streets, her gardens and her towers, weaving shadows like ivy and cobwebs to hang from the stone walls the King had built around her, singing the starlight into the fountains, and slowly, slowly, she began to Sing the transmogrification of ice into crystal.

After the road was built, and the birds had brought her the rumours of an assault on the very doors of the Halls of Rest, and Klara was beginning to feel the weight of his strength beating against the walls of her city like a hand plucking at a harp string, the King of the Exiles came a third time.

Again he wore sky-blue and gold, albeit now his cloak was as rich as the light before sunset, and the blue had just a hint of purple in it. His eyes were blue, though they were sharper now; and his golden hair was bound with many strands of jewels. He shoulders were still broad, and the sword still rested at his waist, though now its golden hilt was dressed with sapphires, and Klara guessed he rarely drew it himself. He wore many rings on his fingers, and many necklaces upon his breast, and his crown was heavy as a helm.

Klara waited for him in her garden of shadows, in a gown of deepest midnight, and she wore stars in her long dark hair.

He came before her, as he had twice before, and they stood with the cracked basin between them.

Perhaps he had learned something, when he crossed the river that had always been the boundary between the lands of the living and the haunts of the dead, for this time he asked her a question.

"O Lady of Shadows and Starlight, will you not lead me to the top of your high tower, that I might show you the kingdom that is mine?"

Over the Waves, Tamsin wandered in a fog, silent and alone. If his eyes were still bright there was no one to see, or to know if his hands still burned. If he still had hope in his heart that he might yet find the holy fire that the Old Enemy had cast into the depths of the earth, only he knew.

Klara looked at the King of the Exiles in the beauty of his might, and though she said nothing, at length she stood from her seat, and took him by the hand.

CHAPTER SEVENTEEN

THE AGE OF HOMECOMING

The King followed her up the paths that unfurled under her feet alone: up out of the shadowed garden, and up the great spiralling avenue of silver trees, up and up that mountain that had not been there, when he had been only a prince, and his voice heeded.

She sang as she climbed up the spiral stair in the tall narrow tower, the King pressing close behind her, sheltering in her trailing shadows from the cold clear winds that blew through the openwork walls. He was solid, hard-edged, his boots ringing on the marble. He had enough of the Song left in him that his footsteps fell into the rhythm of her song, but not enough to lift his voice against the wind, nor to hear the birds that called news of his kingdom to him.

Klara called the starlight to her, and the winds that did not pierce her, and the shadows that garbed her; her voice was falling silver. When she turned to face him at the top of the spire the King looked on her with eyes that burned like the Dragon facing Tamsin.

"What then would you show me, O King?" she challenged him.

He smiled at her, proud and in easy command, and if she thought again of the Dragon, that was perhaps unfair.

She did not resist when he took her hand and led her to the edge of the high platform, where the ice of her frozen fountain hung glittering in the air around them.

"Look," he cried, and with his other hand he gestured at the wide green country falling away from their height. "Look, Lady of Starlight, Lady of Shadows, Lady of Song, upon my fair realm! See how my kingdom prospers! See how it stretches from the Impassible Mountains in the north to the Endless Woods of the south, from the Shoreless Sea in the east to the Uninhabitable Hills to the west!"

Klara looked. "I see the northern mountains, where the frost-giants and the dragons defeated your armies," she said. "I see the eastern sea, over which you yourself sailed to the farther shore. I see the southern woods stretching beyond your strength to swallow it. And I see the Perilous Hills of the west, where even you dare not leave the Road you wrought."

His face darkened, and his eyes flashed, but he mastered his words. "Look, Lady of Starlight, Lady of Shadows, Lady of Song, upon my people! See how I have found the wandering and granted them homes! See how I have brought forth the dead and granted them new lives! See how I have brought all Elfland under my banner, and granted them a share in my glory!"

Klara looked. "I see a fair kingdom," she acknowledged, for she did. "And I see also that at its heart is a garden you cannot conquer."

The King set one hand upon his sword, and his other hand tightened on hers. Klara felt the hard bands of his rings pressing on her fingers, and with a twist of her wrist and a trill of her voice freed herself.

"You dare?" he said, low and fierce. "I, who have conquered all the lands you can see?"

"Not all," Klara reminded him, and she sang.

She Sang the gold from his cloak and his rings and his necklaces and his sword-hilt and his hair; she Sang the blue from his tabard and his sapphires and his eyes; Sang the warmth the metals had borrowed from his body, and him from the shelter of her power. She stopped only when his eyes were grey as mist, his hair white as snow, and his shadow quivered in the palm of her hand where she had torn it from his feet, and he himself had fallen to his knees.

"I will build up the walls and close the gates against you," he cried, furious, when she released him.

"You cannot," she said, in her voice of molten silver.

His eyes glittered, snow-white, unbearable. "I will bring my armies against you, and destroy you."

"Again I say: you cannot."

She spoke the truth, there where her word was power, and made it so. For he was indeed King of a wide realm, whose word was law everywhere outside the walls built to hide the city he could not seize: but he had named her Lady of Starlight, Lady of Shadows, Lady of Song, and this was *hers*.

His face was ugly, twisted with his rage, his thwarted lust, his pride. She stepped towards him, and despite himself the King scrambled back, until he teetered at the edge of the stairs spiralling down. He stopped then, his skin blistering under the biting cold of his rings, the frosted thing that had been his crown. Power broke through his voice then, the fire that had been his birthright rearing up through his pain and anger. "I swear never shall I rest until I have made you mine."

Too late he realized the trap he had made for himself.

Klara smiled at him, cold and dark. "So be it."

For each step he took away from her she let him have a tint of his colours back: the blue of his eyes by the time he reached the bottom of the tower, the gold of his hair when he arrived at the gate. When he stepped across the threshold of the city, she let him have his shadow.

Though he stood tall and proud when once again on the streets that were his, it still shivered at his feet, his shadow, and it was lighter than it had been, greyer, as if the King was not quite so solid as he had been before he entered the Old City and challenged her there.

Over the Waves, Tamsin wandered in and out of dreams. Sometimes when Klara walked in his mind his brothers were there, taking turns anchoring him to life. Tamsin regarded them with disbelief; but when they warned him of dangers, or encouraged him to eat, he listened.

This side of the sea, Klara listened to the rumours and news her birds of snow and shadow brought her, and smiled that the King continued to order them shot, as if they were not notes of a song he could not hear and could not silence.

Those who had returned from the dead were changed.

They remembered who they had been, the returned dead, their deeds and their crafts and their families. But they had lost something in the passage through the Halls of Rest, or so the birds reported, repeating to her whispers and rumours and scraps of song.

Those who had been dead lived again indeed, and their wills and their bodies were free as they had ever been.

But yet—

It took Klara a long time to piece together the whispers and rumours and scraps of song, for the elves under the King's banner of gold and blue were not the Firnoi of her youth, and few of them were songwrights, or interested even in the related crafts of enchantment. They sang: she heard their voices rising up, brought on the winds to her side of the wall. But no one *Sang*.

It took her a long, long time to realize that *none* of them were songwrights. Not even those who had been great in that craft in the time before the Breaking of the Lamps. She could understand why those who had turned their voices to death might hesitate before Singing again, come once again to life as they were, even if she deplored their cowardice.

And yet, though they sang, none of them Sang.

Those who had gone Over the Waves and returned again by ship had long since ceased to Sing, but that, she understood, was because they feared what had been done with Song, in the wars against the Old Enemy. They feared Tamsin now called Korrokaith, whose voice had come to be death.

The King did not dissuade them from first dismissing and then shunning and then outright rejecting the power that had once been theirs. His was a might of arms first and gold second and words third, and if his people would set aside the best weapon they might use against him, who was he to stop them? He had no need of bards, if he did not care to cross the mountains he called Impassible or leave the road into the hills he called Uninhabitable.

Klara could have Sung the dragons of the north out of the sky, tamed them as she tamed the shadows at her feet, but he wanted her his subordinate, not his rival.

Those who came from the Halls of Rest either would not, for much the same reasons, or else they could not. Though it was not clear what it was, exactly, something *was* lost with death, with the passage through the Halls of Rest.

Those who had passed that way could come into the Old City, could seek out those they had known, those they had loved, the homes in which they had once dwelled. But they could not bear to stay there: not for long. They whispered to their kin that the city was too loud for them now, the captured starlight too bright, the shadows too dark. They stumbled where no one intended them to falter, and were lost on streets that no one thought labyrinthine.

They came to visit, those who had been dead, in ones and twos and small companies, and most drifted away again into the wide lands not yet settled by that those who had come from Over the Waves. They dwelled simply, close to nature, and many rarely picked up the tools they had once used, the instruments they had once played. Most faded quickly again into spirits of water and wood, field and glade, tangible only to those they had loved or hated in life.

Over the Waves, Tamsin was losing himself. He saw his brothers constantly now, and in the dreams Klara shared they crowded close in their concern.

The King could not defeat a Singer such as Klara was, or Tamsin had been: not with all the force of arms and armies, not with all his gold and his jewels, not with all his vassals and subjects and servants. He could not bar the gates to her city from her, nor wall her in entirely, nor find his way to her if she did not permit the paths to lead his feet.

And yet. Klara sat in her garden of shadows, and though she felt the sap rising, yet the ice still held her in its grip.

They called it *the Age of Homecoming*. When all the remnant Firnoi had come home in the ships, and brought with them to new homes all the elves who had once lived Over the Waves. When all the dead had marched together out of the Halls of Rest under the gold-and-blue banner of the King they were now calling the King of Elfland.

The great waves of return had swelled and crested in festivals and great orgies of settlement, and slowly ebbed away again. There was a wave then of births, the old lullabies rising up to the ears of the birds of ice and shadow, the winds that caressed the shoulders of Klara's mountain. And yet, Klara walked in her garden of shadows, ice under her fingertips as she trailed her hands across stone and fountain, silver tree and glass flower.

The city, her city, drew close and comforting around her, and one day stair and street led one of those who had stayed to Klara's garden.

Alina was a sculptor: her hand and spirit and song had wrought many of the finest pieces in the city. She was the wife of Dâr, the mother of Tamsin and his brothers, and though Klara had not spoken with her since before the Breaking of the Lamps, it had been a comfort to her to know the other too had stayed.

Like six of her sons, Alina had hair like copper threaded through with gold, and she wore a gown of early evening, spangled with golden stars. She wore copper and gold bracelets on her arms, and golden ribbons woven through her hair to bind it back from her face. She entered Klara's garden like the setting sun.

A murmur of Song, and Klara's seat grew wide enough for the other elf to sit beside her.

Alina took her place, and together they sat in silence. The shadows moved gently at their feet, like the ripples in a lake or the movement of grasses in a breeze. After a time Alina sighed, and put her arm around Klara's shoulder.

"It has been a long time, daughter," she said.

"It has," said Klara, for it had been for so many things. A long time since they had last sat together; since they had last spoken; since Alina's sons had gone into Exile under the red banner of Dâr and the golden song of Tamsin Tammorath; since the Breaking of the Lamps.

"Tell me, daughter," Alina said, and her voice was soft and sad as the white doves that cooed on the corbels of their city, "have we not grieved enough?"

Klara looked at the broken basin, rimed with ice where it had once been filled with fire, and said nothing. Her heart was hard and cold, like a marble sphere, a hailstone, foreign in her breast.

The broken stone basin rested before them, each half of a once-beautiful whole dull, the shining crystals opaque, black, dead.

Alina said, "My sons did not come out of the Halls when the King summoned forth the dead. They will not be returning to us, I fear."

"Tamsin lives yet," Klara said, soft as one of the shadows moving at her feet. "His brothers stand with him, for though the Oath has swallowed them, while he lives there is yet hope."

"Is there?"

Klara folded her hands together in her lap. They were very pale against the midnight fabric. She wore no jewels, no rings or bracelets, no necklaces or crowns. Only the stars in her hair and the silver of her voice.

"If we had exchanged these places," she said quietly, "he would have hope."

They had never told anyone, never admitted to anyone, how often each had taken up the other's instrument, clothing, voice. They had fooled their siblings—Tamsin's brothers, clustering in their worry and fear to the last of their number; Klara's sisters, who had gone Over the Waves and come back through the Halls, and lived quiet lives now far from her towers and streets. They had not been able to make it to the heart of her garden before they had fled her Song.

Klara and Tamsin had fooled their audiences, their patrons, their would-be apprentices. They had fooled Klara's parents, who were shepherds in the western hills and had rarely come to the city even after their daughters had chosen to dwell there. They had fooled Dâr much of the time, when Tamsin's father was preoccupied with his own craft and could spare little attention for theirs.

"I did wonder," said Tamsin's mother, with a low laugh.

Klara moved her mouth. Her face was stiff. The stone in her chest was very heavy. She wished she could set it down, or find the cold satisfaction she'd felt facing down the King, or something.

"It has been winter a long time in this city," Alina said presently. Her hand was warm on Klara's arm, her body warm at Klara's side.

Alina tilted her head so their temples rested together. Klara could feel Alina's pulse throbbing. It felt as if it had been thousands of years since she had last felt such a thing.

It had been thousands of years since she had last felt such a thing. Not since Tamsin had let go of her hand, after he had clutched it so tightly all the way up from that grove of yellow birches by the river.

"Tamsin was always the one who sang spring," said Klara.

"Was he?" Alina said mildly.

Klara had no answer.

Over the Waves Tamsin sat on the edge of the sea, staring west at a sun setting over the home he had left so long ago and could not imagine seeing again.

This side of the sea, mother and near-daughter sat together in the garden of shadows while the birds Klara had once Sung out of ice sang around them. Klara thought of the sap rising through the depths of winter, readying the woods for the coming spring, and felt a new song beginning to sound in her throat.

CHAPTER EIGHTEEN
THE FLAME IMPERISHABLE

When the sun rose the next morning, Klara slipped out of Alina's loose embrace and sang, first, the lament for his brothers that Tamsin had been unable to sing.

She walked the city, all its streets and stairs, touching every wall and balustrade, every silver tree and every crystal sculpture. Every wooden bell, every ivory creature, every fragrant lantern.

This time she did not leave a trail of ice; this time she released the warmth she had been swallowing for so long, and water ran behind her.

She walked the city, all its streets and stairs, from the gate where the subjects of the King of Elfland trembled at the song of grief to the top of that highest tower of marble and ice.

The city wept as it thawed.

Klara sang for those who had died and found their way from the Halls, and for those who had not died, and for those who had stayed, and for those six brothers who lingered still with the ghosts of the Old Enemy's monsters, unable to leave the one who had not yet failed.

Klara sang: and if her heart had been struck by a shard when the Lamps were broken, and if she had rolled ice around that frozen wound to form a hailstone like a pearl, still she had not lost her art, not in all the long years of frozen grief and shadow. She Sang.

Klara sang forth all the warmth of sunlight and candlelight and long-lost Lamplight she had hoarded deep in the hollow of her hunger. She sang of the ageless years she had known long ago, when she and Tamsin had danced around each other like courting eagles, daring each other to ever greater heights of skill and craft and musicianship.

She sang up the spring of the year, the spring of all the years, out of the deep winter of grief.

So long had she sung shadows, sung ice, swallowed all the light and the warmth. So long had she curled around that shard in her heart, and refused to touch it for fear of—what?

For fear of the grief that would swallow her, and which she had swallowed instead, until the hole in her heart was deep as the long ages of loneliness.

Klara sang.

She sang of the sap, starting to rise long before the sun grew warm and the days grew long, as the trees took the deep season-long inhale that they would sing forth in their silent shout of leaves, blossoms, seed.

She sang of her birds, her birds of ice and her birds of shadow, and how over the long years they had grown feathers and blood and beating hearts: that they brooded their eggs now in nests of woven shadows and light in the corners of buildings made of stone and crystal and memory, and their chicks hatched into life.

She sang of all those who had stayed, who had curled deep in the houses when she had crusted all the city over with ice, whose hearts had wept their own griefs as she froze hers into stone: how they had come out with curiosity and renewing life when once the light had shone again through the windows, casting rainbows upon their dusty floors: how they had picked up their tools and their imaginations, and wrought out of all the loss something new, something great, something grand.

Klara sang.

The ice shivered around her, glittering and then gleaming and then shining as the sunlight she had captured returned its warmth— all the warmth of all those days she had swallowed—and the ice melted and ran, until the city that had been a city of shadows and ice became a city of sunlight and fountains.

High above the city, on the highest tower, Klara stood and sang, her hands uplifted to the sky her people had learned to weave into cloth, the airs whose winds circled to her Song. The marble stair spiralled around the spray of water that flung itself up higher than ever the ice had gone, and Klara tilted her head back so that the sunlit water fell upon her face, and at last, at last, she wept.

Over the Waves, Tamsin lifted his head, where he sat upon the shore still looking westward, and felt an earthquake roll under him.

Klara sang all the songs of spring and growth and new life that Tamsin had once sung, in the voice that she had never forgotten, long though it had rested silent in her throat.

These were the songs that had made him renowned as the herald of spring, the voice of the living countryside: why Klara was thought the lover of the city, with her songs of market and workshop, of artist and crafter, of home and hearth and kitchen garden.

They had not traded those places, save insofar as they had taught each other the beauties of the worlds they knew, the ones they had grown up loving. It was Tamsin's father who was the weaver and his mother the wood-carver, his brothers the sculptor and baker and merchant and glassblower and painter and smith. It was Klara's parents who were the shepherds, whose sisters were the gardener and bee-keeper, who taught Tamsin the signs of stirring life, the names of plant and bird and animal and bee.

Tamsin had loved the things Klara had taught him to see, as she had rejoiced in the crafts he placed in her hands. They turned every-thing to the service of their songs, perhaps, as they pushed them-selves and each other: but that did not ruin the beauty of the crown of flowers Klara had once placed upon Tamsin's head after a concert in which he had sung the city into riotous bloom, nor the circlet of silver with which he had once crowned her after she had tuned all the rain-chains of the city's houses to play symphonies of each rainfall.

And so she sang, as once Tamsin had sung, though she wept as she sang, as he never had.

Over the Waves, Tamsin's dead brothers crowded close as he stood on shaking feet to look at what had broken with this latest tremor. Cliffs had fallen, and the beach upon which he stood was crumbling. Yet they did not urge him to move to safety, as they customarily did: they did not pluck at his sleeves, half unravelling as they were into song-stuff even the dead might touch, nor whisper in his ears in voices that his fading spirit had begun to hear.

For not far from where Tamsin stood, under the surface where the murky water deepened into blue even after all the land had crashed into it, there was a familiar, long-lost glow.

Over the Waves, Tamsin did not weep. He had not wept for a long, long time; not since the last ship had sailed back to Elfland across the sea, and he stood truly alone on the farther shore.

This side of the sea, Klara wept, and her tears washed away the ice in her heart, and the hurt in her heart. She descended the tall stair of her tall tower with the water glittering and dancing around her, down and down with the water running white and gold under her feet, with her song catching her feet, catching the light, catching the droplets until the rainbows were flung everywhere through the Old City of those who stayed.

Down she went and down, with the water and the sunlight and the spring following her, spiralling down her high mountain into the secret garden of shadows, and then, there, at the last, she came to the broken basin of stone that had once held the flame imperishable.

Alina still sat on the crystal bench, her head tilted back, her eyes closed, as she listened.

All the shadows were thick and cold at Klara's feet, at the intangible boundary between winter and spring. Klara sang, more softly now, grief thick in her throat, Tamsin's voice sweet in hers. Alina straightened and opened her eyes to look levelly across the space between the two of them.

If Klara let herself look through his eyes, she could see what Tamsin saw, Over the Waves. He stood now at the boundary between sea and sky and shore, with the cold sea frothing up about his feet as the deep shadows frothed up in starlight about Klara's.

She looked at the broken basin. He looked at the glow in the water.

For all the sharing of voice and eyes and body and soul, they had never been able to speak across the long distance between them. Waking mind and sleeping whispered to each other, but Klara had not felt more than the ghost of his touch, and she did not know what was going through his mind as he looked into the sea that had been the barrier between him and home for so long, and saw the light to which he had sworn his soul.

If he broke first, or she, Klara could not tell. He flung himself forward into the water in a clumsy dive, the breath in his lungs like the breath before an aria. Down and down he plunged, a kingfisher after its prey.

Klara fell to her knees, his song in her mouth, and bent her head over the broken basin.

They had not seen what had broken it, when the Old Enemy had in one fell swoop somehow stolen all the lights at once: broken all the Lamps, silver and bronze and copper and gold, and when Elfland was cast thus into shadow he had plunged down, as Tamsin was now plunging, out of the darkness between the stars to the one light left shining in all the lands this side of the sea.

Dâr had been the one to bring that light to the city: had been the one to weave himself a ladder to climb up the highest mountain, far to the west of the Halls of Rest which none of them had thought much of, not in those days. Dâr had been insatiable, restless in his curiosity, and he had yearned to capture light in his weaving, light in his words, light, at last, in his hands.

It had burned him, the flame imperishable: he had never woven after he had come down from the high mountain where it was said the gods lived, and where certainly the fire had burned.

It had burned him, but he had not cared, not with the flame in his hands, not with the flame in his care, in his keeping, in his heart and mind and eyes and mouth. Dâr had been fell and fierce and almost irresistible, with that fire in his possession.

When the Old Enemy had stolen it, broken the basin that Alina had brought from beyond the North Wind, and had fled like a comet into the deep night that had come before the first dawn—oh, something had broken in Dâr then, and he had sworn that terrible Oath to retrieve the holy fire, come what may, and doomed his people and damned himself and his sons.

The last living son of Dâr and his six dead brothers plunged down through the water towards the light: down and down, Tamsin's breath tight in his lungs as he kicked and pushed himself down. Long ago he had learned to swim with Klara and her sisters, with his brothers and their cousins, in the river that ran now through the new city. Long ago they had dared each other to dive to the river-bottom to see if they could find the river-spirit's treasures.

Klara and Tamsin had never found anything but mud and sticks and stones and songs, but Tamsin's brother Bedellin had once found a strange stone egg. It had hatched into an emerald-green serpent with amethyst eyes, which lived with Bedellin for seven seasons until a great eagle with pure black feathers came flying out of the south and called for it by name.

They had not found anything, but they had tried, diving again and again until they were dizzy and laughing and full of songs bubbling out of their mouths.

Klara knelt before the broken basin and sang those diving-songs: songs of ducks and swans and cormorants, of kingfishers and the swift strength of river-otters, for they had loved them all in those days, all those creatures of the wild and the river-bank that Tamsin had loved for the sound of their names in his mouth and the sight of them in her eyes.

Over the Waves, Tamsin dove far deeper than the river-bed had ever been beneath them, with the waves pushing him to shore as the current had once pushed them towards the meadows where the swift river slowed to a meander. The water was dark, murky with sediment: all he could see was the glow ever below him, ever out of reach.

Klara paused a moment, needing a breath herself, and looked at Alina sitting there on the crystal bench, in the garden of shadows, where the ice rimed the ground and every stone and crystal leaf or stem. She looked up, past her high white tower where the water was laughing in the sunlight: up to the sky bluer than the King of Elfland's eyes, to the sunlight bright as the voice of Tamsin Tammorath in the springtime of the world.

Then she reached forward through her shadows, even as Tamsin reached forward through the mirk, his broken hands outstretched, her pale fingers wide to cup each half of the broken basin.

Klara felt the ice and heavy stone and the cool power of her shadows: she felt the wound in her heart, where the shard had long ago struck it: she felt the grief puddling around her, and the spring pouring down upon her back with the sun.

She blinked against the rainbow dazzle in her eyes, the stinging blurriness in Tamsin's, and even as his throat caught fire with the need for air, the crushing pain of the Oath nigh-strangling him, she breathed deep.

Deep, deep as he had dived: and then, as his hands reached out to the fire, Klara sang it.

~

She sang the songs she and Tamsin had sung so often.

The songs with which they had challenged each other on stage, a gleam in their eyes, a quirk in their mouths, daring the other not to laugh. The songs which they had sung to each other, with each other, soft and secret in their private places, when they made each other crowns of flowers, and sang the flowers to bloom in great waves rushing out from where they sat.

And she sang the song that had been so fell and fey in Tamsin's mouth when he sang of the death of his father, but shifted, transposed, turning that bloody and broken chord into the song of love and radiant hope it might have been, if Klara had not been silent when that Oath was sworn.

She sang, and she wept, and the cold stone under her hands, in her heart, warmed and flushed with music, with her grief, with the love she had always held for him, her friend, her rival, her lover, her love—

Under her hands, starlight and tears joined together the stone that had been broken for so long, and the crystals caught the sunlight.

Over the Waves, Tamsin dove deep under them. The water was cold and dark, tugging fiercely on his tattered garments. His eyes stung with the salt, and he was burning.

He was burning, burning, his heart a brand, the fire of his father lighting their souls, the songs he had once sung, the sun for which he had cried forth the first great greeting.

There was blood in his mouth and iron in his lungs and the numbing cold of the water on his face.

Down he went and down, into the dark waters where the land had slid into the sea.

Down he went and down, to where the silt of an age had slid off the twisted ropes of stone, the black ripples that had once been a chasm of fire under the feet of the Old Enemy, where caught in frozen stone was the circle of fire that had once been a crown.

Klara sang of sunlight and spring and the love she had held in her heart, deep below the crust of ice and stone and pain, and between her palms the stone grew warm and whole.

Over the Waves, Tamsin kicked once, twice, a desperate thrice—

This side of the sea, Klara took a breath for him, and sang in Tamsin's voice the song that had once made flowers bloom through all the great city of the Firnoi.

Tamsin closed his eyes, but he could still see the light; could not see anything but the light, as he closed his reaching hands upon the fire, the branch of the flame imperishable his father had once brought down from the holy mountain, and with it finally in his broken grasp, released himself and all his brothers from the chains of the Oath with which they had bound themselves.

This side of the sea, Klara felt the flame catch in the space between her cupped palms.

CHAPTER NINETEEN

THE SEVEN SONS OF DÂR

K lara knelt before the basin, the fading echoes of her song buzzing in her teeth, her brain. All her bones were resonating with the last long note, what could have been a cry or a scream but was instead a song as great as that which had once slain a Dragon.

There between her hands was the flame, glowing behind her eyelids, lovelier than the sun, more brilliant than the moon, like all the stars she had ever sung gathered together.

It burned her hands, as it was burning Tamsin's, but as Dâr had found before her, before him, it was a burn like a burgeoning song, and at first Klara could not bear to relinquish it.

But then Alina cried out a wild cry, like the voice of the North Wind sweeping down from the treasure-lands of the dragons, and Klara opened her eyes.

The shadows were blooming gold.

In the repaired basin, the flame burned.

Around her stood six fire-haired elves in the strange pale robes with which their spirits had clothed themselves, their silver-grey eyes reflecting all the light in the world.

Alina said, "O my sons! Look how you have returned to me, beyond all hope!" And she wept.

Klara looked at the staring eyes of Daerleon until the Stonehand looked down, and then, with her back very straight and her head held high, she stood and walked out of her garden of shimmering lights, up the path winding through the avenue of silver trees blossoming now with hundreds of thousands of stars, up and up the mountain until she came to the foot of the stair that wound through the waterfall.

Up she climbed, one foot after another, her gown of midnight flowing behind her, her face turned ever upwards to the arches of white marble, the whirling winds, the great dome of the night sky.

Up she climbed, steady as the rising sap, the rising sun, the heartbeat of hope.

At the narrow platform at the highest point, she stood upon a spear of white marble and diamond crystal, with the living water laughing and glimmering about her as it rose up and fell again in patterns more complex than any of her songs.

There she stood, and looked for a long time east, in silence.

For after so long enduring past everything but hope, far Over the Waves Tamsin let himself slide irretrievably out of her grasp as he gave himself over at last to the welcoming embrace of the sea.

She waited until she could feel no hint of him, no sense of breath or beating heart or steadily treading step. And then she waited a while longer, in case he wandered her wakeful vigil in his dreams, and watched the sun rise into her eyes and climb over her head before sinking down again in the uttermost west where lay the Halls of Rest.

Three days she stood there, silent and still.

On the third night Alina walked up the long, long stair, and stood beside Klara.

When the fourth morning broke, a great black bird flew out of the west towards them. An eagle, Klara thought at first, for its size, but when it came closer she saw that it was instead a raven with wise, sorrowful eyes.

It flew three times around the tower, that great black raven, and then it came to a perch upon the uppermost curve of the water, as if the arc of spray were the branch of a crystalline tree.

"Will my seventh son come home?" Alina asked, her voice steady.

The raven's voice was very deep when it replied. "He has gone to his rest. He will waken only when the song of his soul is ready."

Klara said nothing, but she thought of the King of Elfland sounding out his golden trumpets at the gates of the Halls of Rest, and how none of those who had returned to life after their sojourn there had been able to Sing.

Tamsin had not been able to sing or speak since he had faced the Dragon. Klara did not know if his heart could bear being unable to sing at home; or if there was even enough left of him to make such a calculation, after so long alone, so long silent, so long under the captivities of oath and curse and utter loneliness.

Alina reached up into her glorious red hair and pulled out a silver hair-comb. She held it out on the flat of her hand to the raven's huge beak.

"This is for him, where he sleeps, and when he wakes. Long have I worn it in memory of him and his brother who wrought it. Let it be a memory of our love to him as he sleeps, and bring him sweet dreams, if dreams there are where he lies."

The raven turned its head. The fire burning far below glimmered in its eye, turning it a rich warm gold, soft-edged and lovely like the old Lamp of Day.

Klara reached out her hand and brushed her fingers across the simple beauty of the hair-comb, which was shaped like the curve of the neck of a harp. She hummed an old, old melody in Tamsin's voice. Starlight glimmered around her fingertips, sank into the silver.

She met the solemn eye of the great raven. "Thus do I return his voice to him, which I have been keeping safe since he slew the Dragon. When he wakes let him remember what it is to sing, and to Sing, and let him sound forth his voice with the joy and the merriment and the love with which we once sang together."

"So be it," said the raven, and delicately it plucked the hair-comb from their hands.

The wind from its wingbeats tossed their hair, fire-red and shadow-black, sunlight and starlight tangling in their long loose tresses.

Klara looked at Alina, and Alina looked at her.

"Ah, my daughter," said Alina at last, "we have grieved long enough. The spring is come again, and the fire burns once more: let us descend from this high tower of yours, and learn again to live. Six of my sons have come home, and the seventh is at rest: let the six be as brothers to you, as once they were, for I do not think it was ever only Tamsin who loved them."

Klara bent her head, half in resignation and half in acceptance, and took Alina's hand to lead her back down the stair to the city.

No one understood how it was that the Sons of Dâr had returned unlooked-for with the flame imperishable, but they knew the flame was true by the fire it lit in their hearts.

Klara did not disabuse anyone of the assumption that the dark-haired singer who could sometimes be found at the side of Daerleon the Stonehand was Tamsin called Korrokaith. No one who had been Over the Waves wished to run afoul of either the eldest of the brothers or the youngest, who had once sung the great Dragon to death.

Softly, gently, spreading out from the Old City in lapping waves, something of the old strength of spirit came again to the elves. Those who had stayed felt it first: the Old City blossomed with life, living plants twining up the silver and crystal trees, the glass flowers, the stone walls.

Those who had sailed home from Over the Waves felt it next; the King of Elfland, mindful of the way his shadow never quite matched his motions, gave polite credit for the great blossoming of culture in his kingdom to the Enchantress of the Old City, and publicly rejoiced to hear of the return of the Sons of Dâr.

Those who had passed through the Halls of Rest found themselves more anchored to the living world. Some returned from the fields and trees and mountainsides where they had drifted into incorporeality; others picked up their crafts for the first time since their deaths.

Still no one Sang. But everywhere there were children.

The scholars of the King declared the *Age of Homecoming* complete with the return of the Sons of Dâr and the recovery of the holy fire. The people themselves named what came after the *Sunlit Age* almost immediately, for it was, they said, a time of flourishing in the light.

Klara opened the gates of the Old City wide, and though there were still those who found the concentrated power within its walls too strong to bear for long, there were many who came to trade or study with the enchanters, or to see for themselves the light of the flame in its stone basin. Soon it was no longer strange to see the enchanters walk in the streets of the King's city or even farther afield, to the new towns and villages of his realm.

The years passed, swift and fair. Once those who had sought darkness had had to travel, away from the illumination of the great Lamps. Now those of the Old City who sought summer or autumn or winter had to travel away from the spring that lingered around the garden of Klara's shadows.

Klara herself found herself slowly folded into the noisy and creative family of Alina and her sons. She still walked her city in the soft night airs, singing starlight and the evanescent flowers of earliest morning, greeting the birds descended from her creations of ice and shadow. The white crows still nested in the silver trees, and with the shadowy starlings flew wide and far across Elfland to bring her news of all the realm.

But now she told their gossip to Tamsin's brothers, and so it was that Daerleon heard that there was unrest amongst some of his old followers, who wondered why it was that their great lord lived a humble, quiet life, and did not wear the crown claimed by the King.

"I never claimed kingship," Daerleon the Stonehand protested to his mother, but his brothers laughed and told her how her eldest son had been uncrowned king of half of the lands of what had come to be called Shadowed Kheir, with tens of thousands under his banner.

"I will not bring war to Elfland," Daerleon said, and set up a meeting with the King that ended up with him organizing a great tournament of arms.

Daerleon might not have wanted to claim a crown, or begin a war, but he was pleased enough to see himself the decisive victor. The King of Elfland declined to lift his gold-hilted sword to challenge him.

The years passed, swift and fair.

Tamsin's brother Forro the smith made Klara a silver flute, and Klara relearned what had once been her favourite instrument. If sometimes she wept, playing certain pieces, no one questioned why.

Daerleon's tournament was so great a success that the restless warriors campaigned for another, and then another, and then it was a recurrent event, with festivals arranged around its schedule. If Daerleon put as much effort into his Tourneys as he had once put into the war against the Old Enemy, only his brothers laughed at him for it.

The years passed, swift and fair.

Klara learned smithing and woodcarving and baking and even a bit of glassblowing from Tamsin's brothers, and began to find herself smiling at strangers and chatting with people at the market.

Sometimes she still walked in Tamsin's dreams, or what she hoped were his dreams. He slumbered deep in warmth and light and love, the flame he had seized cradling him in turn.

Often he dreamed of music, and on those mornings Klara woke weeping with the same tears that had once brought spring to her city.

∼

The years passed, swift and fair.

∼

The years passed.

∼

One day the King of Elfland came to the gates of the Old City, and with only a small hesitation passed through. It was long since Klara had closed them to him, and long since she had bade the streets forbid him to pass.

He brought with him an entourage, courtiers in brilliant garb and guards in gilded mail, and on his arm was a beautiful elf-maid dressed all in green.

Klara received them in her garden, with the shadows all blooming layer upon layer of gossamer light. She wore the palest silver of dawn, and along with the stars in her long dark hair were long strands of the fine pearls she and Tamsin had once received from the Sea-Elves in the south.

The King wore his blue and gold, though the blue was deeper now, darker, and the gold was ruddy. In the clement spring day of the Old City, he wore no cloak of ermine or sable. His sleeves were long and the lining shone like the last light of sunset, as if he wore a bank of clouds hiding the descending sun.

He wore even more jewels than before, sapphires and diamonds set in the red gold his miners had found far in the south. He bore heavy rings on every finger, and a dozen necklaces that looped across his broad chest; his robes were long and stately, embroidered, gilded, bejwelled, and though he wore only a simple circlet, his golden hair fell to his waist in long plaits braided with gold wire and studded with gems that blazed in the light of the holy fire in the basin between them.

Klara met his gaze steadily. His shadow moved restlessly. She smiled.

He no longer wore a sword, did the King of Elfland, save when he opened Daerleon's Tourney or knighted his lords. Though his shoulders were broad and his arms strong, she could see in his eyes and in his stance that he was no longer a warrior.

But she knew that. Though his border-lords still held the north against the frost-giants and the dragons, and his ships still patrolled the coast, and his armies still pushed ever further south, he himself had come to care first for his people and second for his laws and third for his treasure.

"Well met, O King of Elfland," she said, for it had been long since any contested his rule.

"Well met, O Great Enchantress," he replied, for that was indeed what she had made of herself.

It had been a long time since the King had last tried to break down the walls of the Old City or assail the gate. And a long time, too, since she had thrice refused his suit.

"O Lady of Starlight, Lady of Shadows, Lady of Song," the King said, "I have come to beg a boon of you. For it is said in my kingdom that the Great Enchantress of the Old City is as good as she is powerful, and as wise as she is ancient, and that her voice is as fair as the holy flame that burns eternally in her garden."

He never had found rest, had the King of Elfland, until he gave it to be spoken, and Klara let it be said, that the Old City was his in the way the sky or the earth or the bounding sea was his. Which was to say, as much his as any other elf's, and not at all.

Klara had let him unbind the curse he had laid upon himself in memory of that one whose restlessness could not so easily be lifted.

"I will hear your request, O King," she said now.

The King turned to the lady in green at his side, who was looking wide-eyed at the flame. "This is the lady I have chosen to be my queen," the King told Klara. "I would ask of you your blessing upon our marriage, that it might thrive as does my realm."

Klara looked away from him to his bride. "And you, O Lady who would be a Queen? Is there a boon you would ask of me?"

The lady in green lifted her eyes from the flame. She was beautiful, her skin and hair both a rich honey-brown, her large eyes a soft sea-green. She wore jade in a hundred shades of green and white, carved into translucent leaves and flowers that glowed softly with reflected light: jade lilies and woodbine twined into a crown and trailing down her hair, jade ivy and jasmine at her throat.

She blushed a little when she met Klara's eyes. "I would ask of you your blessing upon our marriage, that it might be fruitful and full of joy."

The King took his lady's hand in his and kissed her knuckles until she blushed a fine deep rose, and Klara could not keep herself from laughing.

"I will give you your blessings," she said, and then she met the King's eyes. For he had reshaped himself from one whose craft was conquest to one whose craft was rule, and perhaps he was no longer entirely unwise. "And I shall give you a third gift," she said; "I shall sing at your wedding."

She sang for the King and his bride—Sang for them, indeed, a song of peace and fruitfulness and joy that wove together the King's marriage with the strength of his kingdom. He called her *my lady* and *the Great Enchantress* and *the Keeper of the Holy Fire*, and no one thought it unbecoming that she came attended by Daerleon the Stonehand.

If she thought once or twice of what it might have been if Tamsin had been standing beside her, or if they had been singing a duet that would hold the whole kingdom and its future in their thrall, or if it had been them coming together in the ancient rite of marriage ...

She was the Great Enchantress, the Lady of Starlight and Shadow and Song, the Keeper of the Holy Fire. No one ever asked her any personal questions but Alina, and Alina understood all too well the lingering ache of the what-might-have-been.

Klara was not immune to the effects of her own Song. After the King's marriage she, too, felt her heart stirring in her, a longing for community and connection and craft, for new life and new relationships.

In the Old City, the spring blossomed, and Klara made the resolute attempt to live.

PART THREE
FAIR ELFLAND

CHAPTER TWENTY
SKYLARKS AND HARPSTRINGS

Tamsin woke slowly, the morning after the bridge.

He lay there for a leisurely long while, floating on the incoming tide of sleep to the shore of wakefulness, his heart full of peace and the heavy weight of summer sunlight.

The larks were singing above him, all their voices layered upon each other like the thousand shades of green he would see when he opened his eyes. He listened to them, tucking their songs into his heart, the deep well of his soul, which was already so well-stocked with wonders, and yet nowhere near full.

Oh, the songs that he would sing, once his harp was made!

He could feel the irresistible tug of the world upon his senses. His ears twitched at a sound running counter to the birdsong, a scuff and a trill of notes and a crackle. River, setting a fire alight with the swift melody Tamsin had taught her. She laughed softly, satisfied. The light patter of feet on the ground, Ash returning from the stream they had found the night before, or from an early practice, for today Tamsin was the last to rise.

His cheek was resting on something soft: moss, deep and plush, scented with green vigour and fungal life. The fronds of the moss brushed across his nose when he breathed, tickling his skin with the fine hair-like growths, until at last the sun and the scent and the touch made him sneeze.

He sat up, reluctant to face River and Ash after the dreadful revelations of the day before. The two young elf-maids looked over as he sat up. Their smiles were tentative, but they were there.

Tamsin smiled back, fingers tangling nervously in the ends of his long braids. They had said they would not leave him, or ask him to go; had said they still had things to learn from him, sword-craft for Ash and song-craft for River.

Not to mention the stories he had to tell her of what he had seen and done over the long years of his life.

There were things other than killing to speak of. There were.

"Good morning," said River, cheerful as she had been every day since that first rain-drenched morning. "You missed singing the Dawnsong today!"

Tamsin discovered he had wrapped some of the braids around his wrist. He untangled them impatiently and began to plait the narrow braids back and out of his way. "I was tired," he said, as if that were an explanation for the way he had thrown his cloak over his face and slept immediately, heavily, as one dead.

"That was very difficult, the bridge," River agreed sympathetically. Tamsin braced himself for the inevitable questions, but she just nodded to herself and offered him some porridge.

After they had eaten, Tamsin sparred with Ash, and they decided to continue on their way, with the intention of stopping early if there seemed to be a nice spot.

"Where we won't be swept away by a flash flood," Ash said solemnly.

Tamsin felt he might not be supposed to laugh, after the day before—but then River elbowed him. "Oh, don't look so serious, Rowan! Nothing will break if you laugh—not even Ash's straight face!"

He did laugh at that, and felt better for it. "Do you not have questions?" he asked after they had extinguished the fire—Ash, proving herself not inept with at least the simpler aspects of Song.

River swung her pack up on her shoulders. "Not at the moment. Of course, I will later on. You're far too good a resource to pass up, you know, O Tamsin Son of Dâr! If I am to write the definitive history of the Shadowed Age—"

"Oh, is that the new plan?" Ash asked innocently. "Very modest of you!"

"Hush, you're the one who wants to beat Daerleon the Stonehand and every warrior in the kingdom."

Tamsin had gathered all the components of his harp back into his cloak by this point, and he smiled as the two young elves bickered pleasantly with each other about their ambitions. Perhaps he should have curbed them, so they did not court disappointment—

But why? River and Ash *did* have him there as their tutor and resource, and Tamsin had been fighting for several times longer than the span of years Daerleon had lived. Ash might not beat his brother this tournament, but she would certainly place well. River was wise as well as winsome, and even if there was no one else who would speak to Tamsin, his brothers surely would be willing to speak to her …

He hoped. He looked up at the sky, which was covered in long rippling clouds high up. A pair of eagles were circling on a rising thermal some distance ahead of them.

"Come on, Rowan!" River cried. "There's a hill before us—perhaps on the other side we'll be able to see the city!"

He followed after, striding long and sure-footed on the road. It was well-made, and again he wondered who had decided there needed to be a road driven westward to the Halls of Rest, and why. The king of Tamsin's youth would never have cared, nor would his people have obeyed such a command.

But then so many had died, Over the Waves. Perhaps those who had returned home had yearned for their dead, and built the road to welcome them home.

It pleased him to be striding eastward to meet the morning, alive after all.

The road passed out of the small wood in which they had spent the night as it climbed in wide zig-zags up a long slope. After the trees were thickets of elder in full heavy-scented bloom, and then where the hill grew steeper yet, wide brakes of still-unfurling bracken. He caught up with River and Ash before the first bend, where the two young elves had stopped to wait for him. His heart warmed.

Tamsin sang as they climbed, songs to lighten their feet and lift their hearts—not though they needed much in the way of encouragement, in comparison to the bridge of the day before—and slowly, as they walked, as he sang, he found himself able to let go of the heaviest weights of his guilt.

He imagined dropping stones as he climbed back and forth across the face of the steep, tall ridge. High above them it reared green against the milky sky, with the road a slash of white.

"This must be the beginning of the Western Downs," River said, when they stopped for a break, far above the trees below but still nowhere near the top of the ridge. She broke a pebble between her fingers, the dust bright on her fingers. "Look how white the chalk is!"

"The shepherds used to sell the chalk to the city," Tamsin said, examining a small round stone that seemed as if it might hold together a little better. "It was useful to have something that marked white, as well as charcoal. My brother Armion was an artist—he used to do beautiful drawings in what they called chalk pastels. Chalk ground fine, mixed with various pigments, and bound together again with ... oil, I think it was, or some sort of gum."

He looked behind them, down the green hill to the brighter green of the bracken, the band of white-flowered elder, the trees in all their tender early-summer greens. The Swanlands spread in great pools and ribbons of silver and green far to the north and south, and farther yet into the misty west. The causeway was a stern grey line drawn taut against the soft and undifferentiated landscape.

The wind was blowing from the northeast, over the crest of the ridge. For the first time in what seemed like weeks Tamsin could not hear the swans. Instead he heard the grass, and the deep croaking call of a raven. He looked up, and saw the bird slanting overhead and over the ridge, out of sight.

Armion, he thought to himself, the name lovely on his tongue. Armion, his fingers always smudged with colour, his eyes always weighing light and shade and shape and line. He was Tamsin's next-oldest brother, and before Tamsin had shown himself a musician, it had been Armion who had been the odd one out of their practical brothers.

Tamsin touched the silver comb he'd nestled into the top of his braids. Forro was the smith—he wore his hair shoulder-length, usually up in a messy bun with various strange bits of metal stuck into it. Armion was the artist, always sketching small and oft-disregarded things: a pair of shoes left untidily in the hall, a squirrel with a nut, an abandoned bird's nest, a still life of spoons.

Forro the smith, and Armion the artist. Daerleon the sculptor, proud of his strength and his skill. Sometimes he sculpted in the courtyard, hefty blocks of stone under his chisel, his muscles rippling, his hair left half-loose to be a banner to his admirers.

Forro. Armion. Daerleon. The other names would come. Three had, and three more would there be before he reached the city.

Tamsin turned away from the misty west. He looked up the great crest of the ridge rising above them. His brothers were not behind him, or Daerleon at least was not: he was at the other end of this road, at the great Tourney where Ash would raise her sword against the other contenders.

River brushed off her hands. Tamsin tucked the pebble into his pocket, next to the grey stone he'd brought from Over the Waves. "Shall we?" he said, and River, with a small smile, took his arm.

At the top of the ridge the Downs fell away before them in great undulations, green shading to misty blue, with the white road leaping across the grass. There were sheep here and there, grazing fearlessly, and in the grass were hundreds of thousands of tiny flowers whose names Tamsin could only guess at.

River did not know more than a handful, and though Ash knew more, they were still left ignorant of the majority. Corn cockle and cuckoo-flower and lady's-smock Ash could name, and ragged robin and cowslip and thyme were known to Tamsin from the meadows adjacent to the city of his youth. Larks sang above, and sparrows and goldfinches darted away from them: but though he knew the names of redstart and whitecap and goldeye and bunting, he did not know what birds went with them.

Still he knew a thousand songs of spring and summer, and as he and River and Ash walked eastwards through the western marches of Elfland, now on the firm white road, now on the springy green turf, he sang them. He was glad how often River and Ash came to sing with him, their sweet voices improving under the practice and instruction he could offer. When they sat by their small campfire of an evening, looking up at the blazing stars, the variable moon as it waxed and waned and waxed again, they told stories.

"Bedellin is the second-eldest," he told River and Ash one night, getting chalk dust all over himself as he used it to sand the pillar of his harp into silken polish. "He was a baker, a cook. He loved making bread, particularly, and whenever we had a special occasion—or whenever he felt like it, which *made* it a special occasion—he'd make these elaborate complicated sculptures of dough. I'd write him songs about the strange figures he created ..."

And he sang of the Ivy-Bearded Man, a song from his own long-ago childhood, one of the first he ever remembered writing, and it was as if the long years were peeling off from his skin.

Bedellin had traded him bread for songs, and Forro ornaments. Daerleon had only ever offered either money or advice, but Tamsin had been happy enough for both—even if he rarely took the advice!

Daerleon. Bedellin. Armion. Forro.

Day by day Tamsin's memory was coming back to him, as if with each step he was shedding the weight of the years and regaining all their delights instead. Not that it was entirely delight; but he did not mind that the years Over the Waves were dimmer, softer, less immediate. They were not gone, not lost; when River asked a question that broached those periods he could answer. But he had not been able to think so easily of the time before the Breaking of the Lamps, not for so very long.

They were travelling across the grain of the Downs, so their days were spent on long slow climbs, wide prospects of green hills and white sheep, larks overhead and sparrows below, and long slow descents into valleys where as often as not they found clear, fresh streams and cairns marking good sites to rest.

The days were growing longer as the year wore on. They walked long into the evenings, when the golden light kindled the ridges and the valleys were soft with blue shadows.

Day by day his voice grew stronger, more beautiful, more joyous. And evening by evening after he had given Ash her lesson in swordcraft, Tamsin worked on his harp. His carving had come along far enough that he braved the soundboard, joining the flat pieces of the palmate antler and wedges of white rib-bone with the finest pattern of interlocking teeth he could manage. Simple as it was, he liked the zig-zag effect along the edges.

After several weeks they came at last to the edge of the Downs. When they had reached the top of the previous ridge they had had the sense that the world ended after the next, which meant, if Tamsin remembered his geography correctly—which was by no means certain—that they were coming to the edge of the flatlands between the Downs and the mountains on the other side of the city.

They camped that night in the hollow between the great curving shoulders of the Downs, leaving the last ridge to the morrow.

Tamsin fenced with Ash, who was now regularly beating him in their bouts. She seemed to feel he was going soft on her; he did not contest this, though he smiled whenever she indicated as much. River, he thought, understood better. Ash truly was talented, and driven, and Tamsin rejoiced in teaching her to surpass her own estimations of herself.

He would be the better choice in any true fight or battle. But a tourney was not a battle by definition. Tamsin's razor edges, his unflinching willingness to strike the mortal blow, his ruthless skill—all of that made Ash his superior in a bout.

After their supper—rabbit and wild herbs, sage and thyme, and a few white puffball mushrooms River had found while he and Ash sparred—Tamsin took out the frame of his harp, and examined it carefully.

"It seems nearly done," said Ash, watching him.

"It is," Tamsin replied. He ran his hand over the curving neck, the pillar he'd carved with just the faintest hint of a spiral like the spiral of a unicorn horn, the pale-brown and white soundboard. Under his fingers the bone was satiny, glossy with all that patient sanding. He smiled at the memory of his mother's exasperation at him getting bored with the drudgery of sanding after barely beginning, though he could spend hours happily practicing the same scales over and over.

"What are you going to use for the strings?" River asked. She looked around, as if harp strings might emerge suddenly out the twilight. She caught Tamsin smiling at her, and laughed merrily. "I suppose there will be villages soon, or certainly there will be some-where to get strings in the city."

"Or there's always your hair," Ash murmured.

That was certainly a joke, and Tamsin laughed appreciatively—how much had he laughed in their company! More than in the previous two ages of his life, surely—but then he wrapped the end of his braid around his hand and tugged it experimentally.

"The elves of Sawwalith used to use their hair to string bows," he said, thinking of the pale-eyed and pale-haired elves in their dark woods, their bowstrings shining like faint starlight. "They said it meant their arrows never flew against their own folk, no matter how they were aimed in the thick woods."

There had been no paths in Sawwalith save the tree-road high above the ground, which few not born to the woods could use. Strangers had to make their way on the ground past the monsters and layered enchantments the elves had spent centuries weaving against them.

"I'd like to hear what your hair sounds like," River said, all encouragement.

"It's so wilful," Ash added, deadpan.

Tamsin wrinkled his nose at her, which made the dour warrior grin, River-like, at him, and set down the frame of his harp so he could begin the slow process of picking out his braids.

Single hairs did not work. They either snapped or were far too quiet before they snapped. Undeterred, Tamsin tried to imagine the Sawwalithian bows he had seen, and eventually determined that they must have been strung with either twined or braided hair. He would try braids first, he decided; despite his father's efforts, Tamsin had never really mastered spinning.

Three strands were too flat; four were better, but he needed thicker strands for the bass strings, and so he experimented, four-fold and six-fold braids, too loose or so tight he could not tighten them far before they snapped ... he wished he'd paid more attention to the Sawwalithian bows, but his weapons had been voice and harp and sword, and he'd never cared for archery.

River and Ash had long since gone to sleep, and the fire was nearly out, when at last Tamsin had twenty-six lengths of narrow braid that did not feel entirely unlike string. They were not the silver or gut harp strings he had been accustomed to use; nor had he been able to form them without whispering an echo of Song into them; but there they were.

The spacing between the strings was something he well remembered. He hummed another faint melody over the strings to mark the octaves, washing the dark hair with a faint golden glow.

It was a beautiful, somewhat eerie effect. Tamsin wondered what he'd looked like—had he been so beautiful, so eerie?—long ago when he'd sung that glamour upon himself.

He strung the harp as the sky behind the last ridge lightened to a steely grey and then grew silvery, then pale gold, then flushed a soft peachy rose. How the act of tying each string to the pins reminded him of days long ago.

His mother had made him his first harp, after he had started singing so the little birds that came to feed on the crumbs Bedellin scattered for them would come to his hand. Forro had made him his second out of silver: that was the harp that he and his rival had passed to each other. His rival, his friend—his lover, he dared think, remembering now kisses snatched behind stage curtains, behind city walls, in groves along the riverbank.

A mist rose up in languid streamers from bourne and grassy slope alike. High overhead a single lark was out early, his voice falling down into their quiet, lingering night.

Twenty-seven strings, already starting to sound as he moved his hands around them, testing the strength of his work. The harp was so white, gleaming under his hands; his hair was black, slashes darker than the shadows running down the hill from where the sky grew ever lighter.

Day by day his voice had grown stronger, more beautiful. It was deeper than it had been, resonating darkly in his chest, as if the long silence had created a hollow soundbox of his heart. But it was coming close to the voice for which he'd been named Tammorath, long ago in the youth of the world.

The mist rose up around Tamsin and his young friends, a cool grey here in the shadows of the ridge. Tamsin tied off the last string, the highest, and then plucked each softly to see how they sounded.

He had not, perhaps, believed that it would work. But even not quite in tune it was a harp worthy of a song.

He tuned the strings, shadow-black and limned with gold, and then for the first time since that first morning, Tamsin Tammorath played the Dawnsong upon the harp in fair Elfland.

CHAPTER TWENTY-ONE

THE EDGE OF THE DOWNS

He was still playing, fingers rolling off the strings, stroking them into music, when he blinked wet eyes—when had he begun weeping?—to see that River and Ash had woken.

"Oh, Tamsin, Tamsin," said River when he looked at her. She had her hands to her mouth, as if to cover her expression, but her eyes were wide, catching the golden sunlight that should not have filled their valley yet.

Tamsin, she named him, though usually she called him Rowan. *Tamsin*. Tamsin.

His fingers stilled, and he rested his chin gently on the smooth cool curve of the harp's shoulder. So had he done so often when he was young, stopping a song at the call of a brother or a parent or his friend.

Ash said nothing, but in the space when Tamsin had lost track entirely of the world outside his hands and his voice and his song, she had woven together a flower-crown for him, cowslips and some purple pincushion-like flower and something frothy and white he thought might be feverfew.

So had his friend crowned him, when he sang her a song of the gardens and meadows she had loved. So had he crowned her, when she sang him songs of the rivers and woods of park and countryside. How often they had laughed, running fleet-footed through the early-morning streets after a long night's performing, hand-in-hand with their instruments on their backs, their hair and robes streaming behind them, running until they laughed too hard to sing conceal-ment and speed and had to tumble into shadows and thickets to hide from their admirers, who thought them the fiercest of rivals.

He imagined finding her in the City, her face lighting with joyous surprise at hearing him sing, hearing him play—

But it wouldn't, would it? She would have heard of his terrible deeds, all those deaths on his hands. Even River and Ash had heard of him, in their tiny village far in the south. Perhaps she might have heard from Daerleon that Tamsin had lost his voice and then his hands ...

If it was hard to imagine being able to speak to his brothers, it was impossible to imagine speaking to *her*.

He thought of that endless grey company upon the mist-shrouded bridge, the fish and the fowl, the game and the goblins and the unnamed monsters of the Old Enemy, and all those elves who had had names and lives and families, from the first one from whom his voice had stolen the life to Daerleon himself, begging for Tamsin to give him a clean end—

And yet was that the worst of it? Would *she* think that the worst of it? Or would the first betrayal always be the worst?

For at the very worst moment, he had left her. In the Darkness none of them had understood, he had let go of her hand and gone, gone away Over the Waves, lifted up his voice as a weapon of death, until death ran at his feet and crowded close at his heels and taunted him with the rest he could not have—

Until he had been granted it. ·

He took a deep, shaky breath. He had been granted it. Whatever had happened there at the end, after that endless incomprehensible restlessness under the death-curse of the Old Enemy—whatever had happened that had led him to those dreams of water and fire, and the burning in his hands as he seized the holy fire (for he *must* have seized the holy fire, must he not?)—whatever it was, it had burned away the Oath, scoured his soul clean.

And then he had woken up, curled in a ring of irises and rowans, healed beyond his imagination.

"What are you thinking of, Rowan?" River asked, kindly.

She also was beyond his imagination—she and Ash both, strange young elf-maids of this new Elfland under the sun.

Perhaps he needed to imagine something new.

Something new. Which might, in music, be something very old, brought forth out of memory into life again.

Once he'd been a bard worthy of the name.

He set his harp down on the grass beside him, and tucked the loose strands of his hair behind his ear. Ash's crown was a little big, and slid down until it rested on the silver comb whose origin he still could not imagine.

He smiled at them. "I was thinking of a friend of mine from long ago," he said.

River perked up immediately. "A friend?"

He had not mentioned any friends, he knew. He had not remembered any—and truthfully he still was uncertain whether he had ever *had* any, besides his brothers and their cousins and this one friend, rival, lover, love.

"She was my peer," he said. "The only one, as we grew in skill. She was the one to call me Tammorath for the first time. It was a bit of a joke," he explained, lying back upon the springy grass, breathing deep of the sweet fragrance of the cowslips in his hair, the sharp astringent tang of the feverfew, if feverfew it was. "She played the flute, a silver flute, and Forro my brother made her a torc of silver to go about her neck when she played, so everyone called her Kanorath."

"The Silver-Voiced," River said, working it out.

Tamsin hummed. The sky above was a pale blue, delicate as the bloom on the wings of the azure-winged butterflies new-hatched that morning. "Klara Kanorath. Tamsin Tammorath." He laughed, remembering their glee in the rhyming names, their decision to dress ever more definitively in their colours, until they barely needed to hum a glamour if only they traded their jewellery first. See a dark-haired harpist in gold, and it was Tamsin; a silver flautist and it must be Klara.

"I loved her," he said, and it was the first time he had ever said that aloud.

River hummed a note that harmonized with the song at the back of Tamsin's throat. Ash, unexpectedly, said, "*Loved*?"

"Well."

River laughed, bright as the larks overhead; Tamsin blushed.

"I used to dream of her, Over the Waves."

They broke camp and climbed swiftly over the last ridge, all three of them eager to see what lay on the farther side. The white chalk powdered their feet and legs, and was gritty in their eyes and mouths. Tamsin hoped there would be a spring at the top, or a stream to guide them down to the plains. There would be wells or fountains once they reached the wide valley that lay between the Downs and the City, he was sure: the road-builders had been careful to ensure that travellers would not want for water as well as firewood.

He walked a little ahead of the two elf-maids, cradling his harp in his arms since he was unwilling to cut his sturdy cloak into a makeshift harp-case. River and Ash were talking about the prospect of villages or even towns, where there might be places they could bathe and restock their food-stores with items not gleaned from the wild, and perhaps find new clothes, or at least the opportunity to do a thorough wash of what they had brought.

Tamsin was a little uncertain whether his ancient clothes would stand up to being washed, but even he could dream a little of the fine cloth he'd once worn. Silk from the south—the Sea-Elves' near neighbours had raised silk-moths in their foothills, and traded to the city of the Firnoi for metalwork and gems. He and Klara (ah, how her name sang in his mind, on his lips!) had sung freely, and those who had recognized their skill had bestowed all sorts of gifts upon them.

As they grew older in their crafts they had come to dress like great lords or ladies of the court, in their silver and their gold, their silks of many colours, long strings of pearls from the Sea-Elves or carved ivory beads from farther south yet. How vain they had been, Tammorath and Kanorath, in the spring of the world!

How vain, how beautiful, how grand!

He strummed the harp as he walked, pulling old songs, old memories, out from deep in his mind. River sang snatches of the ones she remembered, words that were never the ones he knew, even translated into the new Firnish. She sang ballads of adventures that were ancient to her ears, and yet had taken place—if they had in truth ever happened—long after Tamsin had left Elfland. Sometimes he recognized the blurred outline of a story he knew, his own histories made tales by later minstrels.

They reached the eastern side of the ridge mid-morning, and found a tall cairn there.

"The edge of Elfland?" Tamsin suggested, though even as he spoke he took soundings of the stones and heard their solid assurance that they marked a district, not a kingdom.

"No," River said, surprise in her voice. "The King rules from the northern mountains to the southern wastes, from the western river to the eastern sea."

The stones of the cairn were smug, or as smug as stones might be; they considered themselves well-travelled, and liked their high position. Tamsin released the trickle of power in his voice and patted the stones in thanks before turning to regard the prospect stretching before them.

The sun was high enough not to be full in their eyes, though he had to squint against its light more than did River or Ash: a difference they had noted even in Chirr between those born under the Lamps and those born under the sun. Those who had known the soft and gentle radiance of the Lamps found the full brightness of the sun a little difficult to bear, and could not look directly upon it as the younger elves could.

Behind them the Downs undulated in their green ridges and blue-shadowed valleys, the white road a ribbon flung carelessly across their waves. The mist was still rising from some of the deeper vales, white as the clouds above. North and south swept the ridge upon which they stood, its eastern face longer and gentler than the steep western. In the distant north Tamsin could see a dim blur that might have been the barrier mountains, or might have been the thick forests that clad the hills before them. Far to the south the Downs dipped down to a wide plain before rising up again into the much-folded hill country that extended south out of his knowledge.

East, though, his gaze lingered.

The road went in three lazy arcs down the green slope before it reached the plains, obvious by the way the white road straightened out. Tamsin followed the line of it, past the silver-glinting rivers and lakes of the gently rolling valley, the darker clusters of trees and what he guessed must be villages from the blue smoke spiralling up. Past ragged-edged woodlands and neatly hedged fields to the pale stone of the City.

Now he understood why River and Ash spoke of *the City*, and one city alone. He had seen a blur from the edge of the high country where he had woken, and taken it to be a city of his people from the memory of the cities the elves had made in Chirr. He had not thought it *his* city, the city of his youth, which had been small.

It could not have been his city. They had walked far to the north from that distant blur. This was a different place altogether.

It felt a different place from his city.

They were far from it yet, days of walking away, but already he could see the hazy spill of it, generous and fair in the bowl of a great vale.

And yet this great City that glittered in the sunlight was cradled in the arms of the same mountains Tamsin remembered, their names singing through so many of his songs—white-browed Dilirat, broad-shouldered Auquiel, and the curving cliffs of Irzond.

This was his country, or the outermost edges of it—and yet it had been a wild land, always, in his memory, a place for hunts and adventuring, not this clear cultivated plain.

"We're so close," River said, taking him by the elbow and squeezing excitedly. "Look, Tamsin! The City!"

"It's different than I remember it," he said, and hated how his voice was small and lost.

"There are stories that the Old City is full of magic," River told him, squeezing again, more sympathetically this time. "That's probably the part you knew. There were a lot of people who came back in the Age of Homecoming, the elders said."

All the elves who had died Over the Waves, Tamsin thought, and those who had sailed west over the sea when the poisoned continent started to crumble underfoot.

"Looks like there's a village at the bottom of the hill," Ash said, pointing almost directly below them.

"Imagine," River said dreamily, "other people!" Ash raised her eyebrows, and River hastily backtracked. "I mean—not that I don't love you both—"

An utterly impossible inclusion, that *both*. River was so free with words. So free.

Tamsin was old, old, so long bound. He had fallen—

He struck a chord, because he could not say a truth, nor a pleasing fib, and then they were all laughing. River linked arms with each of them, and they matched strides as they set off down the hill.

Tamsin did not say it, but he was nervous.

He knew how to interact with River and Ash, after their weeks of journeying together. He could trade his skill with sword and voice for their company, his teaching for their reciprocal gifts. He knew how to journey in the wild, and with his knife and his knowledge, he had been able to keep them well-stocked in game and wild herbs.

He made sure to give his thanks to each rabbit and hare, grouse and snipe, trout and bream, and did not know if he hoped their spirits would join that great parade of the dead or no.

Not that it was real, he reminded himself often as he cleaned his kills. His brother lived again in the City, still fighting; probably the elves of Dumloth and Hinnúrin and the Ghaur lived again.

That vision of Daerleon in silver and shade was not really his brother, any more than those had really been the goblins, the dragon, the Old Enemy.

He hoped someone had walked beside Daerleon when he crossed that bridge over the Swanlands. Perhaps no one had ever killed as many as Tamsin Korrokaith, but Daerleon Stonehand had come close.

(He was not sure he could bear hoping his other brothers had walked with the eldest. They had died before the worst of it, before Daerleon and Tamsin had thrown away every consideration but the Oath in the fight against the Old Enemy.)

He hoped none of the elves he had killed lived in this village tucked into the edge of the Downs. How could he ever apologize?

He must imagine better, he reminded himself. He was a bard— once the greatest bard of the Firnoi (he and Klara, handing off harp and flute, alto and tenor, crown of flowers and crown of gold)—he was finding his new voice as he walked across this land that had once been untamed.

He could find the words he needed. He would find them. He had his voice, and now he had a harp in his hand.

River and Ash were used to his occasional fits of abstraction by now, and when he attended to them he found they were having a lively conversation across him. Or River was—Ash was, as usual, more punctuation than words.

"Does it make sense to see if they have an inn?" River was saying thoughtfully.

"It's not even noon," said Ash.

"But a bath, Ash."

"We don't have so much money we can waste it."

"But a *bath* ..."

Tamsin had not thought of money. That was an invention of Chirr —it might have been the elves of Hinnúrin who had devised the idea, in fact, traders at the crossroads of the continent as they had been before the Old Enemy attacked from one direction and Tamsin from the other.

His brother Harlom had been the merchant, best at haggling and barter. He had thought the idea of using set weights of gold or silver or copper to smooth out all the complexities of barter both brilliant and a travesty of his ancient art.

Tamsin had never cared one way or the other, really. Before the dragon his voice had won him whatever he needed or wanted; afterwards his sword had done the same.

Perhaps, he mused, drifting in and out of River and Ash's discussion, perhaps he could still exchange his music for whatever coin this King of Elfland had minted.

More and more he doubted that it was the old king, Tirn of Firn. With his luck it would be the former prince, who had become the King of the Free Elves Over the Waves—or so he had styled himself —*free*, in that context, meaning those who lived far behind the fronts guarded by Daerleon and Tamsin and his brothers. That king had sneered terribly when Daerleon declared he would make one final assault on the Old Enemy's fortress: sneered, and refused aid, and mocked them for their presumption and folly.

The last time Tamsin had encountered the other elf, he had thrown the severed head of the Old Enemy at his feet. The whole devastating war had almost been worth it for the expression on the king's face.

"What do you think, Rowan?" River suddenly asked. "About a bath, I mean."

Tamsin blinked himself back to the present. He tried to be sensible, and failed dismally. "While Ash is probably right about the practical arguments, I have not had a hot bath since about halfway through the Shadowed Age. I don't think I could say no to one."

"See," said River. "You know our parents would say we should listen to our teacher, Ash."

Tamsin shouldn't have been so proud of the appellation. He shouldn't. But he couldn't stop himself from grinning as they continued the long descent from the Downs.

When they reached the village, it turned out there *was* a small inn complete with the kind of bathhouse that the Sawwalithians had once perfected. Even better, the proprietor refused to accept any money. "Oh, it's been a long long time since I last heard a harpist," she said, eyeing Tamsin's harp with something like awe. "Never met a musician unwilling to trade a song instead of a coin, eh?"

Now that he faced a stranger after so long with River and Ash alone, Tamsin felt strangely shy. "I'd be delighted, lady," he said softly.

"Not much of a lady," the matron said, though from the pink in her cheeks she was pleased enough with the compliment. She bustled them down a flagged passage to a courtyard where several elflings were hanging out laundry, and a freestanding wooden building with a smoking chimney. "There you are," she said, pointing the way. "There's a place for your things, never you fret. That's a lovely harp, dear." The matron shook her head and patted him fondly on the shoulder. "It's nice to see some younglings taking up the old arts. You girls enjoy your bath, now!"

River looked surprised, but Ash merely shook her head with a small smile. Tamsin thought of all those nights exchanging places with Klara, and laughed.

CHAPTER TWENTY-TWO

THE ROAD

That River was undoubtedly a romantic was not a great surprise. For all that there had been no mention of any love-interests on either her or Ash's part (whether left behind in their village or hoped-for in the city to come), as soon as Tamsin had mentioned Klara he could see the scheming interest in the young scholar's eyes.

That his new harp was equally romantic was a bit more of a shock.

All harps had their dispositions: their timbres might be melancholy or merry, gorgeous or clear, given to laments or to reels. Insofar as Tamsin had contemplated the matter as he shaped the harp, he rather assumed this one would be tuned to sorrow. It was made out of the bones of a dead elk and the hair of an elf who had spent the better part of two ages deeply melancholic indeed; the idea that it would be anything but equally sad was unthinkable.

That was before he struck a tentative chord in the small taproom of the inn in the village of Underdown, and found his fingers and his voice falling into a song of blithe summer.

The inhabitants of Underdown were a mixture of the elven shepherds who had always lived in these parts and newcomers—or newer-come, anyway, for they had been living there for centuries by this point—from the midlands of Chirr. None of them were from Hinnúrin itself, he was glad to determine. They had come from the small villages along the river Linwair.

Tamsin had been voracious in learning the music of Chirr, when first he and his brothers had swept across the continent after the forces of the Old Enemy, before the war had settled into fortifications and slow attrition. He had been quick to learn the sword, which at first had seemed merely another instrument whose properties he might master, and quicker to speak to the local elves to learn their languages and, above all, their songs.

The valley of the Linwair had been known for its sheep—no doubt the attraction of the edge of the Downs to the resettlers—and for a music trending to either complicated moody laments or equally complicated dancing songs, which the shepherds composed on their watches and then played in the many village festivals.

Once upon a time Tamsin had rejoiced in the complex—the more complicated the better, in fact—but he had, regretfully, to allow for the fact that he had picked up the harp that morning for the first time in two and a half Ages. At least he had recovered his voice enough to cover any failures and faltering of his hands.

The innkeeper invited them to stay for the rest of the day and overnight, so they could wash their clothes and replenish at least some of their food supplies. She saw the hesitation with which they'd looked at each other, and added that along with Tamsin's music for the bathhouse and meals she'd accept a bit of help in the garden for the afternoon in return for a bed for the night.

"It's a slow time," she told them. "Most everyone's headed to the City for the Tourney, and the sheep are up on the high pastures. Those of us left will be glad for a few stories and songs, this evening."

And so Ash and Tamsin weeded, dressed in borrowed clothes while River washed theirs, and after a supper of melted cheese on toast that had made Tamsin nearly start to weep (so long had it been since he'd had either; they were foods of civilization, and after the last ship had sailed away from Chirr there had been none), Tamsin had washed his hands and settled near the hearth with his harp.

He played scales and simple songs to warm up as the villagers slowly assembled, greeting each other and accepting tankards of ale from the innkeeper. He did not mind their conversations continuing as he explored the sounds of his harp, testing the tuning. The hair-strings had an odd texture under his fingers, springier than metal or gut, but sounding richly forth.

He found himself half-listening to the villagers, some of whom were chatting curiously to River and Ash. He was glad not not to have to talk to them himself. There were perhaps a dozen people in the room, hardly a crowd, but they felt a huge throng to him. River, at least, seemed to be thriving under the company. Ash excused herself to come sit next to Tamsin when the innkeeper gave her ale.

By this point Tamsin had picked out the Linwairi names and preponderance of Linwairi words in their dialect of Firnish, and was trying to draw out of his memory the songs from those early days in their valley.

A lament came to mind first, as was only natural, but even as he struck the first notes, he seemed to feel the harp sigh, and he could only describe the feeling of it under his hands as *sulky*.

He took a drink of the ale Ash had brought, grimacing a bit at the bitterness before he remembered he had once enjoyed the taste, and hummed a softly enquiring note.

The harp was very new to have such decided opinions—something that usually emerged after years if not decades of playing—but then Tamsin *had* made it out of bones and hair and hope.

The elk-spirit was long gone to wherever the dead went when they did not follow the white road east, but its bones remembered its pride and joy and verve for life.

The great elk had been mighty and free and glad. Its bones were entirely uninterested in lamentations.

Tamsin had braided his hair thinking of River and Ash and Klara, his brothers alive again, his mother still in the city, his music in the youth of the world, and the very first thing he had played had been the triumphant song of the first sunrise. His hair remembered the lonely dreary wanderings, but had grown so long and strong as it was in his long healing sleep under the care of iris and rowan and the small singing birds of Elfland.

He got the strong impression, from his fingers and his ears, that the harp he had crafted over the evenings of laughter and conversation and learning had learned more from the hearts of River and Ash than his own.

The matron was looking at him, her brow furrowed. Tamsin released his querying hum. Ash said, "Is everything all right?"

"Just thinking of what to play," said Tamsin, and struck a chord that led into a song he'd once heard played on a village green in Chirr, when the dancers had welcomed the summer to their lands.

He saw immediately that the villagers knew the song: conversations halted and heads turned to him, hands frozen midair, expressions shifting from mild interest to sudden focus.

He finished the song, and hesitated a moment, but no one asked him the obvious question, and so he smiled at them, sly as when he and Klara had shocked their audiences with their brilliance, and played on.

The harp liked the dancing-songs, as well it might, so graceful and swift had been the great elk in his prime. Tamsin put no power in his words—his hands did not have their old skill and he dared not risk accidentally laying a curse of stumbling on the room—but as the evening went on, the music flowed deeper and deeper into the hearts of those listening to him. He could see the memories surfacing in the villagers, as ancient sorrow was softened by the bright joy in his hands.

Someone laughed suddenly when he shifted from a reel to a jig, and launched herself into the middle of the room to perform one of the solo foot-patterned dances of the upper Linwair. Tamsin followed her, shifting his songs north in his mind, the words coming so easily, his hands transposing pieces meant for pipes and fiddle and drum.

But there were others, later in the evening: first someone thumping on the table with his fists, and then someone came running in with a round skin drum, and someone else lifted up a fife, and then first River and then Ash and then the villagers picked up the chorus of first one song and then another, and then Tamsin's music had filled not only his heart and the hearts of his audience but also the heart of the room.

Perhaps it was the Linwairi songs, or perhaps it was the harp, or perhaps it was Tamsin himself, but the evening blurred into a night of music and merriment, and no one seemed to want to stop, or need to.

They played till the dawn lit the room, and one by one the musicians stopped: the drummer, the fifer, a fiddler who'd joined later, Tamsin on the harp. One last lingering repetition of a round, and then the singers faded to a silence filled by the strong-voiced roosters of the village.

Tamsin looked down at River and Ash, who had wearied at some point and curled up in their cloaks next to him. He smiled at them, setting aside his harp so he could tug his cloak a little higher over Ash's shoulders.

His sword was at his side. He brushed his fingers over the hilt, glad for its familiarity. He'd managed to set it near the door of the bathhouse: not out of sight, but with the towels, certainly the farthest from his hand he'd managed since Sawwalith.

When he looked up, the room was empty, bar the innkeeper picking up the dirty dishes. She spoke abruptly. "I'll ask you no questions, traveller, nor thank you."

Those were Linwairi customs: elves of Chirr did not give thanks for gifts, for those were obligations that might bind one more tightly than expected or desired. And questions could very easily ensnare. There had been many years before the arrival of the Firnoi where the Old Enemy's malignancy spread across the lands Over the Waves, and not all the monsters were so obvious as the goblins.

Tamsin smiled at her. His face was stiff; as were his hands, now that he'd stopped playing. He should certainly not have played like that, but there had been power in the air, in his harp, in the hearts of these villagers. He was not tired, though he ought to have been, having walked all day and played all night. The music was still coursing through him, the festival-music of a people who had once been known for them.

"We'll have a festival, here," the innkeeper said, stopping with a tray of tankards in front of him. She worried her lip a little. "A year from now. If you'd like to play for us again."

He inclined his head carefully, neither accepting nor rejecting the offer. Had they been so lacking in music, that they would create a festival to commemorate an evening's merriment?

Perhaps when he was young he might have believed that having had Tamsin Tammorath to play one evening was worth commemorating with a festival, but it had been a long time since then. His hands did not have their old skill, and the village musicians were certainly not so mediocre as that.

Perhaps it was that the memories had been buried too deep, were still too painful, for those who had left their homeland long behind to bring them to light. Had they needed an outsider to do so?

The Linwair had been choked with mud and corpses, at the end of the great wars against the Old Enemy. These elves would mostly have long fled to the coast and the protection of the King of the Free Elves, or died and come to Underdown along the same road as Tamsin and River and Ash. Either way, they would have long grieved the death of their home and the fine river that had once been its lifeblood.

Tamsin had spent a long time mourning the death of Chirr. He might be still, if River and Ash had not called him forth into their Elfland. If he had followed the call of the Perilous Hills—

He smiled again at the innkeeper. "I would be glad of a bite to eat, mistress," he said softly, "if you would spare it."

Her lips quirked, half-sour, half-amused, but she busied herself cleaning up the room, and presently brought bread and soft sheep's milk cheese flecked with herbs, and a pot of a rich floral tea. Tamsin ate hungrily, gratefully, careful now not to thank her.

He asked no questions either.

~

They left the village mid-morning. River's and Ash's packs were heavy with oats and hard cheeses and dried fruit and waybread, and the innkeeper had pressed a serviceable canvas sack on Tamsin, which turned out to contain more food, as well as several long ribbons embroidered in the Linwairi style in red and silver and gold.

He traced the interlinked flames and stars figured on the red cloth. The style was Linwairi but the sigils belonged to the Sons of Dâr and their forces. Such ribbons had been common trade items across Chirr, valued for their delicate lines and bold colours, and the Linwairi had made ones specifically for trade using the emblems of other peoples.

It would be rude to thank them. Tamsin had plaited his hair into one braid after the bath, and now selected the red and silver ribbons to bind it up into a crown. That made him look much more himself, if any of the villagers had ever seen him outside of armour—and if they had been in one of the village festivals he had attended, they might well remember him from his voice and the crown of red and silver.

Death came crowned in moonlight and blood, said one of the songs of Tamsin Korrokaith. But Tamsin had worn red for his brothers and silver for Klara Kanorath, and he had faced his dead on the bridge over the Swanlands. He would not put away his colours now.

"May the winds be kind to you," the innkeeper said roughly, though she must have guessed *something*, to have given him those ribbons.

"And the river bring good news to your door," Tamsin replied quietly in Linwairi.

"Go safe now, girls," the innkeeper said, with a sharp nod, and on they went.

~

"They thought you were your own daughter," River told him later that morning.

"I beg your pardon?"

"They thought you must be Tamsin Indorath's daughter," she elaborated. "'The Great-Voiced.' I hadn't heard that name before."

"It didn't last long," Tamsin said, dryly. "'Scourge of Chirrkal' was more popular."

A fortnight of walking and half a dozen villages later, Tamsin had learned three things: his harp had a romantic disposition to rival his brother Bedellin's; River had managed to wheedle the entire story of Tamsin's relationship with Klara out of him; and somehow, everyone had *forgotten* all the songs of Chirr.

That the great elk with its huge spread of antlers had had a bone-deep sense of what constituted satisfactory courtship was amusing. That Tamsin, having spent a fortnight playing songs of merriment and joy, found himself ever more agreeable to rhapsodizing on the subject of Klara Kanorath was not entirely inexplicable.

But the situation with his audiences was *strange*.

After Underdown came a place called Sticklebrush, apparently well known for the quality of its fuller's teasels and thus its fullers. Tamsin was vaguely reminded of lectures his weaver-father had given his sons on the subject of cloth production, and in a fit of mild nostalgia acquired one of the teasel-heads in question from someone all too pleased to describe how to card wool with it.

He was more careful that evening, or at least he paid more attention to the shape of the powers moving around him as he played. There was no hint of an enchantment or a curse on the people, and yet—and yet it was clear that until he started to play the old songs, there had been something missing.

Not their memories, exactly. When he cautiously enquired, the elf he'd spoken to had agreed he'd come from the Linwair valley, face placid, almost indifferent. He'd patted Tamsin on the shoulder, "Oh, long ago, long ago. It's all gone, you know, dear. No sense in worrying about it now that we've a new life here."

So Tamsin was cautious, essaying a song from a sheep-shearing festival—surely that would not raise bad memories, for a people still following their flocks on the Downs, still preparing wool the way they always had.

(Once again he had to ask himself what his people, the *crafty* elves, had been doing, that there were no new tools or techniques?)

The elf who had given him the teasel was sitting halfway back in the room, having laughed when Tamsin had said he'd trade a song for the seedhead.

He watched the elf, who sat watching him with that same placid, indifferent expression, only vaguely curious. A few measures of the festival song, a catchy melody that had filled the upper valley of the Linwair in its season, and the elf's face sharpened and—and *caught*, like a taper lit by another.

Tamsin looked around the room, and saw the same thing happening, this music that had no power behind it—nothing but the power inherent to his voice, tuned more and more towards joy and merriment to counteract the ancient force of his death-singing—

The harp rejoiced in his hands, strength and vigour pouring out of it, renewed and regained life crackling across the strings of Tamsin's hair, the lust for life the great elk had felt deep in its bones.

The people seemed to waken out of a deep dream, shake off a skiff of … not quite grief, not quite melancholy, not quite boredom … *something*, anyway, like dust that had settled on an unused instrument.

What could Tamsin do, but keep playing?

River and Ash said he needed to sleep, too, but Tamsin felt nothing but awake and alive through those nights in which his music woke the villagers' hearts to life.

"I can rest in the afternoons after I spar with Ash, along the way," he said to River, and so he did.

Though perhaps it was not sleep, exactly, that he sought, that he found, when he lay under a tree and watched the leaves fluttering against the sky.

He had slept a long, long time, while all these people tried to make new lives for themselves, and the only thanks he could give to the two young elf-maids who had woken his heart to life was to pass the favour on.

CHAPTER TWENTY-THREE

THE GREAT BARD

River had thought she understood the difference between a
bard and a minstrel.

A bard, she thought, composed songs as well as played
them, and usually had a definite role in society, sometimes even a
formalized one. Bards kept the histories and much other secret
knowledge, and were responsible for passing on what was necessary.
They were excellently skilled, and the greatest, such as Tamurzîn the
Death-Singer—so the histories and legends she'd read claimed—had
been able to affect the world around them with the power of their
song. They played for kings and courts and their own secret
conclaves. Very rarely at festivals where the common people might
hear them.

Minstrels performed in inns for food or a bed or coin, for enter-
tainment and enjoyment, and were a copper penny a dozen even in
River and Ash's remote village.

Tamsin was, indisputably, a *bard*. He was the greatest bard of the
Firnoi; the greatest and most terrible of the war-bards of Shadowed
Kheir; his was the name everyone used as an example.

(Or rather, names. She had come to wonder if there actually *were*
Twelve War-Bards, as the histories had it. When she'd asked about

others, Tamsin had named five and then drifted off into the vague abstraction she recognized as him trying to winkle out a faded or buried memory. It was possible that the other war-bards were simply him under different names.)

Each night, Tamsin played for a different gathering of villagers or travellers, none of them grander than a prosperous farmer or innkeeper. Sometimes he played in inns, sometimes on the village greens. In the inns he would eat a meal and talk with the villagers, as one of them, quite without pretence or snobbery. On the greens he called up a handful of lights with the first notes of his song before settling into the rhythm of the evening.

That was not so different from the minstrels back home. Except that the minstrels never *sang* the lights into existence. Nor did the minstrels ever play more than a handful of local songs, if they were local themselves or had been through the village before.

Tamsin tailored his music for each village, plucking songs out of the apparently endless store he had of them in his memory after he'd asked where the people were from.

The days afterwards he spent telling River and Ash about the correlating homelands in Shadowed Kheir. Then, since he took teaching Ash swordcraft most seriously, he added descriptions of the fighting techniques or traditions of each place. Descriptions, and demonstrations, insisting that Ash learn the tricks associated with each style.

In the same way Ash had learned a smattering of Old Firnoian by frequent and prolonged exposure to River's enthusiasm, so River had learned at least an aesthetic appreciation for watching Ash practice. They were the two in their village with interests that took them outside the usual, who did not find art and craft and absorption enough in their local environment. There had been many, many afternoons when River had taken her books to a tree near Ash's practice-ground to keep her friend company.

When Ash practiced now, River still had her notebook open on her lap, quill and inkpot by her knee. But apart from making note of any historical commentary Rowan provided about people and places he'd known Over the Waves, in Shadowed Kheir, mostly she watched.

Ash's form was familiar. Sturdy, compact, swift and concise in movement as Ash was in speech; increasingly precise, increasingly clean-lined, under Rowan's bright-eyed instruction. Day by day Ash seemed to lose self-consciousness and a certain rawness or roughness, as if the hours of practice with Rowan were the equivalent to Rowan's handfuls of sand or chalk, rubbed with endless patience onto the bones of his harp.

River mostly paid attention to Ash. But she could not stop herself from watching Rowan.

River only had metaphors for what he looked like, sword in hand. Before the bridge he had been clearly excellent, better than Ash, but indefinably ... holding back. After the bridge, when they knew who he was—when he knew that they knew who he was—when he knew, too, that Ash had faced what he had done with that shining moon-bright sword—after the bridge, Rowan moved with a kind of inevitability, as if each strike or parry was an ineluctable law of magic.

Rowan could sing the sun from behind a cloud or a spirit from a pile of bones. Perhaps he had sung himself into the world as that sort of fighter. River did not have the words to ask if he had, did not dare to ask what she half-intuited might be true. But yet ... he kept telling her that a great bard, one who Sang power, could shape the world with his voice. Surely, if anyone could, he might have Sung himself into a certain kind of thing, a certain kind of warrior ...

If he had, then he was singing himself anew, with each step, each breath, each song.

Fighting, Rowan moved like the shadows did when he sang them into a nest of protection of an evening. He moved like the wind did, when he sang a note and called a passing breeze like a falcon to his wrist. He moved like water always downhill, like fire always upward.

And yet, somehow, Ash began to find the spaces between his movements. Where River saw only a net of light and shadow, a blur of motion, Ash found specific things to imitate, to counter, to parry, to strike.

Ash confided to River that she thought Rowan was going easy on her. River had no words to describe what she saw when they sparred together, the way that Ash moved like the fish in the river, the bird in the sky, the twist in the flame.

And yet each time he plucked the strings of his harp, lifted his voice, it was clear once again that he inhabited the world differently than other people. His voice, singing, touched something deeper and truer than anyone else's.

Listening to him now, River understood why his voice lifted in the first morning of the world had been remembered as the voice of the new Sun itself.

For despite all his skill at the sword, was he not a bard? Was he not, perhaps, *the* bard?

(It was so obvious how much he preferred the harp to the sword.)

River had long since filled her notebook, and was glad to be able to replace it in one of the villages. She and Ash had barely had to dip into their coin-purses after Rowan started playing, for he was so incontrovertibly excellent that the villages extended the traditional bargain of songs for supper and hearth-space to his companions.

The road was easy. They passed other travellers now and then, a bare handful going westwards, mostly others heading east at a slower pace than theirs. River often hailed them, and Rowan sometimes. If their paths or rest-halts coincided, Rowan came always around soon enough to asking them for their own musical traditions.

They sang, as River had sang for him, the ballads and songs of their villages. Tamsin would listen, head tilted, eyes intent, watching them sing, hands plucking an accompaniment almost immediately. He never criticized or offered advice unless the strangers asked him. They laughed, usually, at this seeming-young elf-maid, so serious about learning their songs, until he started to sing.

When River asked him tentatively if he minded being taken for an elf-maid, Rowan laughed at her and said he'd learned the modern patterns of speech and behaviour from two young elf-maids, so it was entirely to be expected that he would be taken for such. And then he told them stories about how he and his dear friend

Klara had been so equally skilled they could, and did, play each other.

Which didn't really answer the question, except that Ash pointed out that he was capable of singing a dragon to death and must therefore be at least as indifferent as he appeared, or else he would do something about it.

River found this a little perplexing. But perhaps it was something elves in the City did, or had done. There were those in her village who might prefer to be maid when they'd been born man, or the other way around, but she'd never met anyone who honestly seemed not to mind, or even enjoyed shifting from one to the other as the mood took them.

Tentatively she'd asked him about whether he wanted to be addressed differently, but he'd only laughed again and said he was himself, however other people took him.

Ash also pointed out that this Klara seemed to be of the same disposition, so River began to wonder if it was perhaps something to do with being a bard. Or perhaps being exceptionally gifted in what she'd come to know as Songs of power.

For when Rowan took up his harp each evening and played—even when he played the same songs he'd learned that day from travellers upon the road, before he shifted into the older ones he knew by heart—the music came forth with such feeling River could not fathom it.

She'd never seen the sea, but she'd often lain on her back and looked at the sky until she felt she was falling upwards into it, into the sunlit blue or the starlit black, and so it was when she listened to Tamsin Tammorath.

Perhaps it was his voice, no longer half-ungoverned, but fully under his control, his skill. Or perhaps it was the harp.

Now that it was made River was aware it was an object of great power. She did not know what to make of that, either. She had *watched* Rowan make it, struggling at first with his knife and the fragments of bone he carved into hair-pins and comb. Gradually the dexterity had returned to him, and he had shaped the curve of neck and pillar, the pieces of soundboard and pegs. And then the strings out of his own hair ...

Leaving home, River had only wanted to find someone willing to speak to her of the ancient days, and to see a bit more of wide Elfland, keep Ash company as she sought to test her own skill and strength against the warriors of the Tourney.

And then they had met Rowan.

Rowan. Tamsin. Tammorath. Tamurzîn. The Thrice-Cursed, the Oathbound, the Dreadful.

One afternoon when Rowan had fallen asleep under a tree and the two of them were collecting honeysuckle and ivy in a hedgerow for crowns, River confessed to Ash that she hardly dared imagine what Tamsin's long-lost love Klara could be like.

Ash considered the trailing vines in her hand. "She'll have the other half of the story."

River blinked at her friend. "What do you mean?"

Ash nudged her shoulder gently. "He went to Shadowed Kheir. She stayed here. Both halves."

River peered at a bird's nest deep in the hedge. The wagtail sitting deep in the nest gave her a displeased look, and she apologized quietly before stepping back. "She would, wouldn't she," she murmured, more to the bird than to Ash. An objection occurred to her. "He hasn't seen her for a long time. She probably thinks he's dead—certainly that he did all those dreadful things."

"We know what he's like now," said Ash, and picked some sweet-scented violets to add to the mix.

They were a fortnight walking from the Downs to the wide fields in front of the City where the Tourney was being held. They knew they were close, that last day, from the sharp increase in people around them. The hilly country they had been traversing flattened out into a wide plain, dense with clustered villages set in a patchwork of fields and well-managed woodlands. The road had curved to follow a river out of the hills, and soon they saw boats amongst the reeds and waterfowl.

River had been named by her parents for their love of the water—her mother was a fisher from the Black Lake, her father a miller—and she eyed the elegant grey boats wistfully.

"We could buy one," she suggested. "Or hire."

Ash did not like boats, and said, "No."

Rowan had drifted off, as he did sometimes when they fell into bickering. River had learned the correct tone to address him to regain his attention, but when appealed to on the question of a boat he merely shrugged. His eyes were on the City, or at least the hints of rooflines and towers, still hazy with the distance. A white spire rose above them, which caught the light like it was made of crystal. From here it seemed almost as high as the mountains standing behind the City.

Closer to hand was a great spread of brightly coloured pavilions and tents of all descriptions. That was where all the knights of the realm had come for the Tourney.

River—River had no cause to be nervous. *She* wasn't the one facing all of them. She'd already found her source of knowledge for the early ages of the world, and he was literally the most feared elf there had ever been. At the side of Tamsin Korrokaith, River had nothing to fear.

Really, she should be *excited* to meet the other six of the infamous Sons of Dâr. Not to mention their mother.

"No boats," said Ash.

Rowan was singing something low, quiet, deep in his throat, and very sad. His eyes were locked on the spire. River and Ash looked at each other. Since he had started playing for the villagers he had been generally much brighter in mood, as if he was playing happiness not only for the villagers but for himself.

"Tamsin," River said cautiously. She knew better, by now, than to listen too closely to what he was singing. She had learned to feel the extra quality that meant his power was stirring, and did not want such a sad and sorrowful piece aimed at her.

Ash shook her head and took him by the elbow. He followed easily enough, at least.

River thought back to that first day, when she had startled him and his sword had leaped so immediately to her throat, and despite the grief in his voice could only smile. Now he barely touched his sword except when he sparred with Ash.

Despite herself, River caught herself listening to his words, snagged like a fish by his skillful hook. He was singing in Old Firnoian—another thing he had mostly set aside, save for when he practiced with River. The words were slow, majestic. The melody ... not entirely unfamiliar.

Eventually she recognized it as the Great Lament of the Exiles, which she had only heard sung once, at the centennial festival of the Homecoming. First one of the visiting minstrels had sung the Great Lament, and then there had been a silent procession, and then the party. There had been songs of rejoicing at the party, of course, but nothing that stuck in the young River's memory the way the Great Lament had.

Probably, she realized now, because they hadn't been written by the greatest bard of the Firnoi.

She had fallen a few steps behind. She made herself catch up and take Rowan's free arm in hers. They had helped him face his dead. They could help him face his living, too.

"I think," Ash said once he had finished the Great Lament and they had waited a decent interval in silence, "that maybe you need to sleep tonight, Tamsin."

CHAPTER TWENTY-FOUR
THE HOUSELESS

It was not, and yet it was, the city Tamsin had once known.

(He was not, and yet he was, the Tamsin the city had once known.)

There had been no high mountain within the walls—there had been no walls—no crystalline tower spearing up into the sky, no such curves to the river on whose banks he and Klara had once wandered singing.

And yet—he recognized the king's palace, shifted outside the walls onto an island created by a wide and deep moat. The mountains behind the city were certainly the same; they rumbled quiet welcome to him on a cool wind when he sang their naming-song. The river had split and shifted its course, but he knew the song of its waters still.

He kept looking at the high tower, which glittered superbly in the sunlight. It was new—new to him—as its foundational mountain was new to him, and yet ... and yet he thought he knew the voice of this mountain, its secret name; and he kept looking at the high tower expecting it to be ... *something*.

He knew, and did not know, the voice that had sung it so high.

He dared not sing a query to the tower, not from so far away. If it was she—if it wasn't—

Tamsin was not ready to see Klara Kanorath. He was not sure he was ready to see his mother, or his brothers, or anyone he had once known. And yet ... and yet ... Every time he caught a glimpse of walls, roofs, that high tower, pennants familiar and not, his heart quickened in his breast and his breath caught in his throat.

Oh, it was hard, hard, to imagine facing the living. He had faced the dead, his own dead, on that bridge, all so that he might indeed walk through the gates in those new walls, walk up the streets of that new mountain-sloping city, walk up to the door of the house that might or might not be the one he had grown up in, long ago before the rising of the sun.

"I'm sure your family will be pleased to see you," River assured him, each time she caught him staring anxiously at the slowly nearing city, one hand on his sword, the other curled about the pillar of his harp.

Each time she said it, Tamsin looked at the scars on his palms and remembered all the blood he had shed, Over the Waves. Those he had left behind here at home would have heard the stories, know what he had become. What he was.

What he had been. For he had followed River and Ash, young as they were, out of the perilous hills and over the dreadful bridge and all the way across the whelming Downs.

The third time River reassured him, Ash dropped back so she could nudge her shoulder against his. "I'm going to beat your brother," she said.

"You are," said Tamsin, far too earnestly.

"You're not actually very frightening," Ash went on, completely, utterly, brilliantly straight-faced. "In case you were worried about that."

River giggled. "Oh, is *that* the problem?"

"His reputation, you know."

River laughed loudly. "Ach, that old thing! Come now, Tamsin, it's been *three Ages* since you were here last! I'm pretty sure the only thing anyone is going to comment on is that you've *still* got your same sword."

"And tunic," said Ash.

"Thank goodness the ornaments are new, at least!" said River.

Tamsin could not stop himself from lifting his scarred hand (his no-longer-crippled hand) to the thick braids into which he'd woven the silver and scarlet ribbons. The last village, someone had asked for a song of Sawwalith. Tamsin had played the night away with songs from the enchanted woods, and in the morning the elf had pressed on him a long strand of tiny silver bells in the flanged goblet-shape of snowdrops. They chimed very softly with each step.

River grinned at him. Tentatively, Tamsin smiled back. On his back his harp (now anchored by a brightly-coloured woven strap, gift of the last village but one) hummed softly in his ears.

Once again he was drowning, but this time it was in fondness for them, these two young elf-maids from the south, his friends.

The night before they reached the city proper they camped at the edge of a grove of ancient yews. None of the many other travellers had chosen it for their shelter, which puzzled Tamsin at first, until he felt the unmistakable presence of unhoused spirits.

River felt them as well. She hesitated in the act of laying the fire to look at him. "What—what is that, Tamsin? Do we need to be concerned?"

Her trust in him was astonishing. Tamsin said, "There are spirits here. Why don't you ask them?"

River would probably never be a master Singer, as she simply didn't care enough to put in the requisite practice, but she had proven herself a more than able apprentice. She closed her eyes for a moment, centring herself, before essaying the soft querying tune she had devised out of his teachings. Each Singer had to find her own way into her voice, once past the common songs most anyone might learn to wield.

She had to repeat the tune three times before the spirits came forth. There were two of them when they emerged from the shadows in the hollow trunks of the yews. They had clearly been a long time in the grove, for they had taken on the attributes of their trees, cinnamon-tinted skin and dark green and branch-like hair. They were nearly identical, though one wore a crown of red yew-berries, and the other a necklace.

"Who calls us?" the crowned one asked, in a voice like the cooing of mourning doves.

"We are three travellers," River said carefully, "who seek a place to rest this night in safety."

The second spirit sidled around the fire to run ghostly fingers along Tamsin's harp. He was not particularly surprised to hear the strings sound forth, if very faintly. Even without the connection to the Unseen that came of his musical studies, he had come very near to fading into spirit himself.

"You may stay if you play for us," the second spirit said, in a voice like rustling needles.

"Gladly," said Tamsin, before there could be any more binding requests or promises. He caught River's eye, and when she nodded he spread out his cloak upon the prickly ground before unshipping his harp from his back. Ash moved quietly to sort out their supper ingredients while River finished lighting the fire.

This close to the City, Tamsin guessed that the spirits had been of his own people before they had relinquished their physical forms. He started therefore with his own songs from before the Breaking of the Lamps. Once more he was astonished by how easily they flowed, out of his memory and into his fingers, his voice. The harp was happy with these songs written in his own happy youth.

The spirits hovered, blurred smudges of cinnamon and green daubed with red, until he started in on a cycle of pieces alternating praises of country and city which he and Klara had once spent several years composing. He shifted his voice as he went, higher for the songs that had been Klara's, deeper for those that had been his, timbre first silver and then golden as he played the long sequence.

Out of the corner of his eye he saw that the spirits were gradually coalescing into more elvish form. When he finished the sequence two elf-maids sat there, only a translucency about their outlines hinting at their ghostliness. Their faces were still blurred, and they still had much more in the way of branches than hair, but their eyes were no longer empty.

Tamsin let the last notes of the song linger in the air as he set down the harp. The spirits turned immediately to him, dark eyes fierce and hungry. He smiled at them, calm and reassuring, and hummed a note of power, binding them to their own freely given offer. The spirits settled, if with a slightly petulant air.

River silently offered him a bowl of oat porridge with an egg and some cheese on it. Tamsin felt slightly guilty at how much he was looking forward to being able to have more varied food once they were situated in the sea of tents around the City. Whatever slackness of creativity affected the music seemed to affect also the cooking, or perhaps the villages they had passed were between festivals and the first harvest, or ... or perhaps Tamsin was a bit over-fond in his reminiscences of what the food had been like at home.

If Bedellin were back, alive, did he still cook? Would he still make the complicated and beautifully composed plates of delicious food? Or would he, too, have lost ... whatever it was?

(Would he listen to Tamsin's singing? Would he *dare*? Bedellin would know what death had come from his voice, Over the Waves. He might not want to hear him now.)

With the spirits present, River and Ash did not seem inclined to idle conversation. Tamsin had taught them that much, at least. Even if these had once been elves, they were no longer bound by memory and culture in the same way as the living. Unless Tamsin could call their memories alive as he had done for the elves in the villages along the road ...

He hummed his own query of the grove, and felt the wistfulness and yearning bound into the yews by the spirits that had taken shelter there. Unhoused spirits that found no dwelling-place grew mad and dangerous, their hunger for form insatiable. Those that found a grove or a fountain or the like retained more intellect and will, sometimes memory as well, and were able to draw nourishment from their symbiotic home.

These had stayed close to the city for love of one within, but had been unable to sustain their second lives without ... whatever it was. Not power. The air of Elfland was so full of power, thrumming with it.

He let the grove guide his music, following the melodies of yearning and desire, unknotting the tangled threads of memory, fitting their songs into the ones the self-aware parts of the spirits responded to most.

Just before midnight he fell into the songs he'd written as a gift for Klara's sisters, and realized at almost the same moment as the two spirits that he had found them.

They had forgotten their names, but Tamsin's music held his memory, and he remembered them: slow-smiling Danaë the beekeeper and swift-dancing Zoria the tree-speaker, who had taken up spear and bow Over the Waves, and died in the failed ambush in the canyons of the Ghaur.

They had returned with the great crowd of the dead, their voices whispered over the soft notes of his harp, his wordless song. They had found their sister in the city, but it had been too bright, too lively for them, too dense with concentrated layers of power. They had fled to the countryside, but there they had found too *little* power, and it was if their spirits had forgotten how to be alive, and so they had faded.

Tamsin thought of what had been missing from the villagers until his song called it forth, and wondered very much what he was supposed to make of this.

(Daerleon fought. That was all he knew. Daerleon fought, and Klara sang. Everything else was speculation.)

He must make a song, he supposed. Or raise his sword. That was what he had always done, faced with a tangle of enchantment or spirit.

He was Tamsin Tammorath, Tamsin Korrokaith, and either he killed or sang. He would no longer kill: but he could once again sing.

It was midnight in a haunted grove: the land was full of power. He let his voice catch the currents, his harp untwisting the dark grief into bright starlit possibility.

He had once been the Death-singer. But that was long ago now, and the only death he would sing was the death that could be the gate to a new life, the desolate darkness before the new lights of the Sun and Moon, the night that now heralded the dawn whose song he knew best.

He sang of the elf-maids he had known, when he and Klara had by turns deceived and delighted them with their songs. He sang of the warriors he had known later, Danaë with her spear like the stings of her beloved bees, Zoria with her bow of yew-wood whose arrows always flew true. He sang of the spirits of the yew-grove outside the city, lingering as close as they could to the sister they could not approach but did not wish to leave. And he sang of the unknown road that could lie before them, if they faced their own deaths as they had faced the deaths they had dealt.

He did not recall falling asleep, though he must have, after that great midnight burst of Song. When he woke the next morning the yew-grove was empty but for two sprigs left in the space where the spirits had listened to his music.

"Where do you think they went?" River asked, as Ash cautiously picked up the branches.

Tamsin listened, but neither the trees nor the wind nor the earth itself held more than the rumour of passage. "I don't know," he said honestly, "but I hope they will be happier than they were here."

They left the yew-grove early, and followed the road into the heart of the encampment before the sun had crested the mountains. They were unchallenged until they met a barrier in the form of a pole mounted horizontally across the road. A guard-post flying a blue-and-gold banner stood beside it. Two elves, strangers to him, came out to question them. While Ash asked about the Tourney's organization, Tamsin considered the banner and the guards.

They considered him in return. He relaxed his posture, ensuring his hands were visible, sword and harp half-concealed under his cloak. He didn't recognize any of the elves on guard, though from the way their eyes lingered on his red and silver ribbons, they had some suspicions of his background. He smiled cheerfully, aiming for something akin to River's general demeanour, and most of the guards visibly decided he wasn't important.

They would not have lasted long, in Chirr. Kheir. Tamsin felt a small surge of protectiveness for their relative innocence. Not that they would like to hear that *he* thought them so. They wore blue-and-gold as well, chevrons, which had been the device of the King of the Free Elves.

That almost certainly meant that the current King of Elfland was indeed the same person. Tamsin sighed a little, remembering both the squalling infant of River's book of tales and the obnoxious youth he and Klara—or rather Tamsin, but he'd sometimes persuaded Klara to take his place—had failed to teach the rudiments of Song.

Later he had become the proud prince who had not *followed* Daerleon and his brothers Over the Waves (of course he had not *followed* them; he had simply chosen to lead his own subset of the people there at the same time), but who had gladly carved out a realm for himself once he had arrived. Far back from the war-fronts, naturally. Though it was also true that *someone* had to benefit from their efforts combating the Old Enemy.

From everything Tamsin had learned, the King had taken what he'd learned Over the Waves and applied it very effectively to Elfland upon his return.

The well-made road made a great deal more sense, on reflection. Once he'd conquered his way to the natural borders of the current realm, he would have had to do something with his war-restless armies. Possibly the Tourney was another such initiative, though why Daerleon was involved—

River nudged him, and Tamsin followed after her. Ash led them confidently down the main thoroughfare of the encampment, counting cross-alleys as she went. Each of the tents bore banners, many of them familiar to Tamsin from Chirr, others presumably the devices of newer lords and knights. Off to the right was an extensive cluster of red banners bearing the white-and-gold blazon of the house of Dâr.

Seeing those, Tamsin considered the situation of the Tourney again.

Daerleon was probably involved because he was both extremely competitive and for most of the war had had the largest number of people under his banner besides Sawwalith. It was only after the dragon destroyed half their northern forces that the coast-bound Prince had grown strong enough to truly rival them. After the destruction of Sawwalith and their devastating losses there—their brothers, great warriors all by then, not least—he had started to call himself the King of the Free Elves and their liege lord.

Not that *they* had ever sworn allegiance to him. Unless Tamsin throwing the Old Enemy's head at his feet counted as such.

Returned to life, with all the elves who had once marched under his banner also returned to life, Daerleon *could* have set himself up as a rival power. That he had instead taken over the Tourney ... was rather clever, actually. It gave him an extremely thorough knowledge of the individual strengths and weaknesses of the majority of the King's knights and warriors, and let him create and maintain ties with those who might cleave more towards Daerleon himself.

That was Tamsin's oldest brother, indeed. Always calculating—

"Here we are," said River, clapping her hands. Tamsin started.

They had come to a halt at a small bare patch of grass marked by a plain stake. "I'm to decorate the stake, to show my claim," Ash said, surveying the small plot with relish. "We can set up our tent here, River. There's supposed to be firewood next to the water—there's a well at every major crossroads."

"I can get the wood," Tamsin offered.

"Don't be ridiculous," River said, with a cheerful nudge and a bright smile. "Now you know where to find us, you can go find your family."

Tamsin's eyes went unwillingly to the red banners across the camp. Suddenly all he could picture was Daerleon as he lay dying, ribs crushed by the hand of the Old Enemy; as he lay dead, blood pooling from his slit throat, where Tamsin had left him. Tamsin swallowed hard, and pressed his hand against his eyes, pressing back the tears, digging his fingertips into the hollows of his temples. His new harp-calluses were rough on his skin.

Ash was so steady, so superbly solid, so good at offering a way out of the trap of memory. She said, "We'll set up, find out where to get food." A thoughtful pause. "And where we can practice."

Tamsin forced himself to answer, though he spoke from under his hand. He could not look at the bright sunlight on those old banners. He had seen too many of their owners dead. "You don't want it to be a surprise that I've been teaching you?"

"I'll let you know when you get back."

Which was a promise and a threat at once. Tamsin swallowed again at this gift, offered so freely, so easily. He blinked back the water in his eyes, the sun in his eyes. Nodded sharply. It was only mid-morning. Plenty of time to find out—what he would find out.

"I'll see you later," he said, equally a promise, and forced himself to turn away from Ash's tiny patch of grass, all potential, and the red banners flying defiantly of all that was past, and strike between them the winding laneways that would, just possibly, lead Tamsin once the Dreadful ... home.

CHAPTER TWENTY-FIVE
THE SMITH

In Forro's opinion, his existence to date fell neatly into three segments.

First, of course, had been his first life. Unlike his brothers, Forro felt little need to distinguish between his life before they had gone Over the Waves and that after. He had been a smith in Elfland before they left, making gates and hinges and tools and jewellery. Most of the time it had been jewellery, though his love had always been for tools. Going Over the Waves to war had meant, for him, finding his true art.

Not the act of war, the violence and the fight. But the tools of war —sword and shield, helm and armour—oh, when he first set his hand to the forging of a sword, then Forro had found himself.

Lost himself, some would say. But if he had, it had been in the way Tamsin had always lost himself in his music. Forro had been proud of his skill in his craft, but he had never known what it was to be an *artist* before then.

So for him it was all his First Life, when he had been a smith.

And then the second segment was the time he had been dead.

He had asked around (discreetly, of course—he was not quite so discreet as Armion could be, but he was also not nearly so loudly opinionated as some of his brothers; and though he did not like to talk to strangers, and even less to those he had known in his first life, he had very much *wanted to know*), and it was clear that in their deaths the Sons of Dâr had been as unusual as they had been in life.

Not in the moment of death, of dying. That seemed to be the same for everyone, the shocking dissolution of the bond between spirit and flesh. A pain beyond pain, disorienting in the fullest possible sense.

Everyone else that Forro had talked to had found themselves reoriented without conscious effort or choice, had regained their sense of themselves only when already at the misty Halls of Rest. There they had found themselves drifting, eddying with the shadowy, dim soul-stuff of the Halls until their discomposed spirits were able to become coherent wholes once again. And there they had stayed, sleepy and slow in remembrance, until either they had discovered themselves ready to live again—relatively few though those were, or at least few whom Forro had been able to identify—or the King of Elfland had called them out with his trumpets.

There had to be others who had not found that orientation, not heard the call to the Halls of Rest. A few said they had heard something like a horn-call, others the scent of something alluring, yet others a light or a sensation of warmth, a distant hearth-fire—but Forro could not, by definition, talk to those who had not, for they had frayed out of coherence and consciousness, dissolved their spirits into the Song of the world, and could be asked nothing.

Like his brothers, Forro had felt the shock of dying, but his spirit had been held into its shape by the great Oath he had sworn. He had felt his body dying, and then with a wrench suddenly he was no longer housed in flesh, but still, somehow, himself.

They had been bound by their Oath to their living brothers. Forro had been the second to die in Sawwalith, and so he had joined Bedellin and watched in a curious dispassion as two-thirds of their forces and three-sevenths of their brothers died.

The ghosts of Bedellin and Armion, Harlin and Harlom, and Forro himself followed behind their two living brothers as they led the sorry remnants of their people out of the haunted woods of Sawwalith. Armion was weeping inconsolably, for it was over his body that the fire-demon had caught Tamsin and broken their brother's hands with its whip.

They remembered Tamsin after he had sung the dragon to death and lost his voice in the singing. They had all been certain it was only that he could still play the harp which had kept him from throwing himself away to death.

Without their bodies, they remembered more clearly, could see what they had lost.

"They will not fail us," Forro said. And then, looking at the way Tamsin's eyes had become hollow and empty: "Daerleon will not fail us."

But it was Tamsin who survived, long past all hope; and succeeded, past all imagination.

They were unable to touch, to taste, to speak or be heard by any but the dead.

Their living brothers could not hear them. Daerleon had been grim before, honed by the long years of war into the Stonehand in truth. Little but Tamsin's music had been able to soften him, and now there was silence, and the space where the dead brothers tried to offer comfort.

Tamsin's hands healed enough to grip his sword. He could not hold pen, or harp, and barely a spoon or knife. He ate rarely, and never in any company bar Daerleon's. His silence they had become accustomed to; but now his eyes were dark and fey, and he followed behind Daerleon as if the shadow of falling death.

Their remaining followers started to call him *the Dreadful One*. On the field of battle he was unsurpassed. Off it he was almost invisible.

Forro and Armion and Bedellin followed Tamsin, as Harlin and Harlom followed Daerleon, on those rare occasions when the remaining brothers separated.

Daerleon kept fighting, grim and cold and focused. He led their remaining soldiers, fighting bitterly for every inch lost or gained.

Tamsin fought at his side, deadlier than ever, utterly silent. He was careless with his own safety, and yet seemed untouchable, as if by a cruel fate he would lose what was most important to him and be unable to throw the rest away.

The dead brothers followed behind, always behind, unable to stop crying out warnings, never heard or heeded. All the way through the last dreadful battles, until at the very last they came to the gates of the Old Enemy's fortress.

Daerleon broke down the gates, with Tamsin ever beside him. Their remaining twenty-five soldiers fought and died beside them, their spirits disappearing off to the Halls of Rest. One by one they fell, as Daerleon and Tamsin fought their way through the fortress, Daerleon opening every door, Tamsin killing everything that came in reach.

They came at last to the foot of the throne, where the Old Enemy stood with his crown made of the holy fire he had stolen, that the brothers had sworn themselves to reclaim.

Forro remembered that moment, one of the clearest between the moment of his death and the moment the chains had broken.

The Old Enemy saw them, the dead brothers bound by their own words, and he laughed.

He laughed, even as Daerleon, eyes fixed on the crown, dropped his sword; even as Tamsin, eyes fixed on the Enemy, lifted his.

The Old Enemy, laughing, chose Daerleon.

Tamsin's sword went home through the throat of the Old Enemy just as he caught Daerleon about the chest.

Daerleon was thrown across the room to crumple broken-backed upon the floor.

Tamsin's sword speared the back of the throne, straight through whatever mimicry of bone made the spine of the Old Enemy. He stood there in a spray of burning blood, frozen, his broken hands curved around his sword-hilt, eyes sliding between the crown of the fire and the last of his brothers.

The Old Enemy laughed through his bubbling blood, and his head tipped, and he whispered something into Tamsin's ear. A curse, soft and sly.

Forro heard it, where he was trying and failing to reach the crown.

Be never at rest till you gain what you seek, said the Old Enemy, with overtones and cruel implications that would not become clear for some time.

Tamsin did not seem to hear, though none of the dead brothers were able to tell what was going through his mind, behind those dark eyes, that blank countenance.

He was hesitating still, though his brothers were crying at him to lift his hand to the crown before it was too late.

Tamsin hesitated, who had not hesitated once since he first lifted his sword after Sawwalith.

Tamsin hesitated, and in that moment of his hesitation the Old Enemy lifted his own hand to his brow, and even as he died he cast the crown into one of the crevasses of fire that lined his throne room.

Tamsin opened his mouth in a cry he could not utter, but it was too late. In the very moment it might have been fulfilled, the Oath was rendered impossible.

Tamsin wrenched his sword free and with wild eyes ran to Daerleon.

Daerleon who had not seen, who was dying with his lungs punctured and everything lost.

Daerleon whispered, "Please."

Tamsin knelt beside Daerleon, sword dropped as he had dropped it for Armion. There were no fire-demons here: everything had fled but for the dead and the dying, in this throne room where the Old Enemy was still laughing in his death-throes, and Daerleon's lungs were bubbling, and Tamsin was the last.

"Please," said Daerleon.

They crowded close, the dead brothers, close behind Tamsin, who bent his head and then, silent, so silent, his eyes so dark, so dead, drew his knife and with one quick, practiced stroke slit his brother's throat.

Forro remembered the moment of his death, when some shadow-creature for which there was no name had slunk around him and sucked the blood from his veins, the marrow from his bones, the life from his body, before he'd been able to draw his sword.

None of his brothers had seen it, not even Bedellin who was already dead, caught by some cousin-monster. Forro had known Bedellin was lost, but not that he was dead, and for a moment he had not realized that he too had died.

Come, Forro, Bedellin had said, more kindly than had been possible for some years. *We must follow our living brothers.*

It took Daerleon only a moment to realize the situation.

"Oh no," he said, as they stood over the silent Tamsin, who had bent his head in anguish over Daerleon's body. It was worse than a lament would have been, to see him kneeling there, dry-eyed, the knife red in his hand.

"The crown went into the crevasse," Bedellin said, for someone had to say it.

None of them asked if Tamsin could bear this last blow. The knife was red in his hand, and they had failed. The Old Enemy's fortress was falling apart, and the exits were surely blocked. They waited.

Behind them, the Old Enemy was still wheezing.

"Oh, Tamsin," Armion said, reaching out, and failing—always failing—to touch, to be heard.

They stood close, as Tamsin knelt and shook, and then, with a sudden, strangely brisk movement, he reached out with his crippled hands and gently closed Daerleon's eyes, and kissed his brow.

"Tamsin ..." Daerleon said. But Tamsin could not hear him.

Tamsin wiped his bloody dagger clean on his brother's sleeve, and then he sheathed it. He stood, and strode to reclaim his sword. And then he looked straight into the eyes of the Old Enemy, who was still wheezing, face a horrible contorted grimace, and taking the Old Enemy's knotted hair in his left hand, with a great blow struck off his head.

The whole fortress rumbled. Tamsin turned, gory sword in one hand, severed head in the other, and strode out with his head high.

The six brothers followed him out. Tamsin walked steadily, never hesitating in his steps though the stones fell around him, and he had to thread his way through a maze of broken passages. He walked out: through the broken gates, and on down the long blighted hill where the dead lay.

He walked past the dead, ever downhill, towards the last havens of the elves on the shore. No one stopped him or spoke to him, to Tamsin Korrokaith with the Old Enemy's head in his hand. He never stopped, through the day or the night, the fumes and the mist, the slowly clearing air.

Before the King of the Free Elves, who had laughed in Daerleon's face when he had told him he would essay one final assault on the fortress, Tamsin held the head up high.

The King said nothing as the gore dripped black on the floor of his throne room. He stared, and his courtiers stared, at the bloody-handed elf, the last of the Sons of Dâr, the Dreadful.

Tamsin could not say anything, of course. He sneered at the King, and then he threw down the Old Enemy's head at his feet, and turned and strode away.

The Old Enemy's death-curse of restlessness was vicious.

The six dead brothers were soul-deep exhausted drifting along behind Tamsin. They didn't need to eat or rest themselves, and didn't even have to walk. If they dallied somewhere too long, they would find themselves back beside him without effort or choice.

Tamsin, however, had to walk, and walk he did.

He left the cities of the elves behind, for which none of them could blame him. He threw himself into fighting the remnants of the

Old Enemy's forces, fighting with the singular, terrifying focus for which he had become known. He sought out battle, following the traces and tracks of goblins and monsters with endless perseverance.

He could not stop anywhere for long. Even when he clearly intended to spend more than one night in a place, taking the time to build a more substantial shelter, he *could not* stop. He would circle his campsite, a hollowness in his eyes, a brittleness to his movements, one hand always on his sword, the other curled into his side as he paced.

One of them always stayed beside him. They couldn't do anything else, but they could do that.

They spoke to him. Tried to encourage him, tried to comfort him, tried to advise him. Told him stories of their younger days, before the wars. Sang for him, though none of them could sing as he had sung. Tried to remind him that he was more than this silent killer, that he was not alone, that he was loved.

They tried.

The land died under the Old Enemy's poison, their own warmongering, the despair of the elves who had once tended it. The waters rose, and the land fell into the sea. Those elves who had survived—almost all of them now under the banner of the King of the Free Elves—built ships and sailed away. Tamsin stood on a headland, his brothers invisible to him beside him, and watched them go.

He stayed.

He never stayed anywhere for long, but he stayed. He ranged the ravaged land, inscribing wide arcs around the place where the crown had gone into the crevasse and been lost, tethered to the holy fire as inviolably as were his brothers.

He grew thinner and harder. He sought out monsters until there was nothing more to be fought, and then he simply walked, walked, walked.

Death clarified certain things. They could see that Tamsin's silence was a burning curse in his throat and his lungs, that it was no cold nothingness as they had assumed, but an enduring, vivid pain. They could see the restlessness as a pricking, jabbing force at

Tamsin's heels, forcing him on whenever he tried to rest. They could see the bonds of the Oath tying them all, and the heavy cloak of despair that draped over Tamsin's shoulders.

They could see him buckling under the weight of it all, and yet staggering ever onwards. Nothing stopped Tamsin from taking his dagger to his own throat except for himself. But he did stop himself, no matter how thin and hollow and hard he grew.

They could do nothing. They could work none of their own arts —there were no weapons they could hold: no hammer for Forro, no chisel for Daerleon, no glass-blower's pipe for Harlin; no chalk or brush for Armion, no oven for Bedellin, no marketplace or loom for Harlom. They could not touch, and no matter what they tried Tamsin gave no evidence of ever hearing them. They could only watch as their last brother slowly withered away.

This, then, was the second part of Forro's existence.

~

The third part was coming home, and that was the hardest.

~

Unexpectedly, unrelated to anything he'd done, Tamsin found the holy fire.

There was an earthquake—a landslide—Tamsin staring at the sea where the earth and mud blossomed darkly through the water—and then as the mud settled, the light.

This time he didn't hesitate. Tamsin dove down, down and down with no care for how deep it was, all his fraying spirit and fading body straining towards the holy fire.

This time he reached it.

That was what Forro remembered: that Tamsin grabbed it, hands closing on the twisting crown that the Old Enemy had made of the flame imperishable. That when Tamsin touched it, he screamed silently, golden bubbles rising up through the water. That when

Tamsin touched it, they all felt it, their spectral hands burning, their own intangible throats screaming, their souls suddenly breaking free of the Oath's constraints.

None of them knew what happened to Tamsin, after that. They heard the music, then, finally, the call west, the call home: and wearied to the depths of their own spirits, they followed it.

Forro had perhaps lingered a moment longest, or perhaps it had been Armion, or one of the others, wishing they could tell Tamsin how proud and grateful they were.

But the call was too strong, the yearning for rest too overwhelming, and they could not tarry. Could only follow the streak of light across the sky, a shooting star carrying them with its rushing glow— could only follow, helpless, laughing, weeping, rejoicing, free.

They were free, to laugh, to weep, to rejoice, to go. *They* were. Tamsin did not come with them.

They found themselves not in the Halls of Rest, but clothed in flesh before the holy fire in their own city, before the shocked gazes of their mother and Tamsin's beloved Klara.

The six dead brothers who had failed, returned to life. Not the one who had succeeded, who had survived.

There was nothing they could do but honour Tamsin's endurance by learning again to live.

It was very, very hard, facing those they had left behind and those who had come out of the Halls before them. It was very, very hard telling their mother—telling Klara—what had happened to Tamsin. It was very, very hard rebuilding their lives without their youngest brother, knowing that he was the reason they could do it at all.

But they did it. Forro relearned the forge as he relearned his body, and he did not lose the artistry he had once found.

Perhaps it meant nothing to anyone, but to him it honoured Tamsin's memory that he sought beauty in the hammer and the iron and the steel. For each of the Tourneys Daerleon held, Forro made a weapon or a piece of armour for Tamsin. He kept them in a chest in the back of his smithy, the steel chased with silver, set with rubies, strong enough to withstand millennia of use, delicate and beautiful as the finest jewellery he had ever wrought.

It had been ... not millennia, not yet. Not in this second life, this third part of his existence. Nine Tourneys there had been, and Forro could look upon the shield he had made for Tamsin this year (who had rarely used one, but never mind that), and ...

Arguably they were still learning how to live, even long centuries after they had come home.

Forro reassured himself that those who had stayed behind had changed as well, some of them very greatly, and that they were elves. They had the time. If it took him another thousand years to be comfortable speaking to strangers, well, that was what it would take. At least Forro could say that he *did* talk to people outside his family now, even if he insisted that all commissions or enquiries go through Harlom or Harlin.

All these little choices, he thought sometimes. All those days Tamsin had decided to walk on despite the weight of everything on his shoulders, despite how much he must have yearned for rest. Thousands of years had Tamsin walked under the Old Enemy's death-curse, hopeless and yet persevering: and in the end there had been the fire after all.

Forro could go to his forge, day by day. He could try to talk to new people, now and then. He could laugh with Klara and joke with his brothers and try to pretend there was not a hole where the youngest had once had his place. He could go home and have lunch with his mother, not as if nothing had changed, but as if they had been able to bridge the great gulfs between them.

It was possible Tamsin had not fragmented and faded the instant the curses lifted from him. None of them had thought the fire could be found, and yet Tamsin had found it.

It was possible he could still come home.

CHAPTER TWENTY-SIX

RUMOURS

Klara heard the rumours first, of course, from her birds, but she paid them very little attention.

Alina had to get her news from more conventional sources, and it was much more roundabout.

Both of them were overwhelmed by the news from and of the thousands of people who had flooded to the city for the Tourney. So while Klara mentioned off-handedly that some of the birds were excited about a minstrel coming from the west, there were a lot of minstrels coming from every direction, and the birds were not always the most discriminating when it came to elvish music.

Alina had never been entirely convinced by the merits of Klara's birds. It wasn't as if Klara *needed* to know everything going on outside of the walls of the Old City. Except for a deep-seated and inveterate love of gossip that Klara would deny till she was blue in the face.

Alina had never been all that convinced by gossip, either. But perhaps that was because all her family had disappeared off across the sea and the gossip coming back had been truly awful. Now that they were home she did like to know what they were doing, and it was certain that her sons didn't tell her *everything*.

For instance: the Tourney had not yet begun, and according to her sources (in this case her good friend Certhin, a stone-carver who had been Daerleon's teacher, and had loved watching him defeat all the King's smug knights in tourneys past), along with all the usual smug knights of the King and Daerleon's various followers, there was an oddity in the form of a completely new and unknown elf-maid from the distant south.

Certhin came up for tea mid-morning of the very day the southerners arrived. Alina would have been more impressed at this speed of gossip if they hadn't had a standing date for which Certhin was late. Or if he hadn't forgotten the cakes he'd theoretically been bringing.

"I am very intrigued," Certhin said; an offering in lieu of the cakes. "I remember her grandfather from three Tourneys ago, and he had a very respectable showing indeed. Pity he didn't come with her."

Certhin had not gone Over the Waves, but he had been a faithful attendee of each of Daerleon's Tourneys and spent a good portion of the intervening decades hanging around the training grounds. He was now considered something of an expert judge of swordcraft, for all he'd never lifted a weapon himself.

"Who's her master, if she didn't come with her grandfather?" Alina asked, for she had become somewhat interested in the Tourney out of self-preservation.

Although only Daerleon and Armion of her sons actually fought in the competition, Forro was of course very busy making swords and armour both for competitors and those who fancied themselves judges of fine smithcraft, and the others maintained a solid interest in the proceedings. All of her sons had come back from Over the Waves extremely concerned with at least maintaining their skills. Somewhat worrisomely concerned at times, if Alina was honest with herself.

With the exception of Forro, they had had to relearn what had once been their primary crafts. Alina had worked not to judge Daerleon for abandoning sculpture. He was her eldest, and the one who had come closest to following her own craft, and he looked the most like her, just as Tamsin had been most like Dâr.

But Dâr was gone, and Tamsin was gone, and when he wasn't

fighting, Daerleon had taken up gardening. So had Armion, but at least plants had always been a secondary interest of his, when he needed a break from his art.

(Tamsin had never, apparently, needed a break from his music. Though from what Alina had learned from Klara, sometimes he'd needed a break from himself. Alina could not really fathom that, either.)

Certhin chuckled. "Ah, these younglings," he murmured. "She's come with friends. One of them seems to be her advisor, from what the gate-wardens say."

Alina winced. Peer advice was not necessarily a *bad* thing, but when it came to excelling in one's craft ...

Very few people were peers of the calibre that Tamsin and Klara had been, back in the youth of the world, when they had surpassed most of their potential teachers before they'd even left adolescence.

"Actually, I heard a funny rumour about the friend," Certhin said, and Alina stilled at his tone.

"What is it?" she said, forcibly casual.

"Well," her old friend said, equally casual, with equal falsity, "apparently she wears the sigils Tamsin used to, Over the Waves."

Having dropped that conversational gambit, Certhin went home, and Alina distractedly made soup. She hadn't really intended to make soup, but she had to do *something*, and she had vegetables to use up, and she was in no mood to make fiddly stuffed dumplings as she'd initially planned. So soup it was.

It was late morning. Klara would be up on her tower, listening to the gossip her birds brought. One or other of Alina's sons might show up around noon, if they were in the Old City. Alina poked at the mess of beans and broken pasta in the pot and wondered where all her skill had gone. But she dared not take up a carving knife and a block of wood, not when she felt this jittery and uncertain.

Somewhere in the mass of tents pitched for the Tourney was a young elf-maid wearing Tamsin's sigils. Elves just didn't do that, unless they had a close relationship. *No one* would do that for the Sons of Dâr, for Alina's sons, unless it was a very close relationship. Exceptionally close, even. Familial.

The idea that Tamsin could have had a child with anyone other than Klara was, frankly, inconceivable.

But.

Alina forced herself to stop adding things to the soup when she caught herself grating half a block of hard cheese into it. She took her time wrapping the rest back up in waxed linen, set that in the cool-room, pushed the soup away from the main heat of the stove, and proceeded to clean up.

She'd moved on to scrubbing the floors by the time the soup was conceivably finished. Should she make bread? But Bedellin had said he might bring a loaf, hadn't he?

Alina thought of climbing up to Klara's tower—

No. She couldn't ask Klara about this. Couldn't tell Klara *that* rumour. Not when all it was was a rumour, not when she knew nothing more than that someone had told Certhin that he'd seen someone wearing what he thought were Tamsin's sigils.

(Her sons had been infamous, Over the Waves. They were *still* infamous, this side of the sea. It was exceedingly unlikely that someone would choose to align herself with Alina's youngest son without some true connection. No one would want the Sons of Dâr swooping down on them if they didn't have the right.)

Before Alina could start rearranging all the furniture in the dining room—which included the great marble table Daerleon had made—Bedellin and Forro arrived.

Bedellin had indeed brought bread, which was just as well as Alina had no idea whether the soup was at all edible.

She was glad it was these two. Harlom and Harlin had never been as close to Tamsin, and anyway could be a bit ... well ... it hadn't been much of a surprise that those two had become ruthless merchant princes, she might say. She hadn't *expected* them to also become ruthless warlords, but then that hadn't been something anyone had expected, before the Breaking of the Lamps.

They were busy with their current mercantile fiefdoms, Harlom in the main market square of the New City, and Harlin with his glass in the central pavilion of the Tourney grounds. Alina didn't expect to see either of them before the end of the Tourney unless she made the effort to visit them herself. Which ... she might. She didn't usually attend the Tourney, having little understanding of and less relish for the nuances of violence involved, and none at all for the crowds, but she and Klara did try to watch the final matches.

Forro had clearly been in the forge; he was clean, but had missed a smudge of soot on his sleeve. Bedellin deposited his bread and a pie for later and helped her replace the chairs.

"Are we expecting someone?" he asked genially. "Armion was behind us—stopped to look at the plants Bryony's been raising this year. He's still hoping she'll part with a cutting of that yellow rose."

"*She's* still hoping he'll get the hint and ask for it as a courting-gift," Forro said.

Bedellin hummed dubiously. "He'll get there eventually. Maybe."

"Maybe we can get Daerleon to say something."

"Pity Tamsin's not here to write a song about it." Bedellin snickered at the thought.

Alina tried not to make a noise, but she had to turn around sharply to hide her reaction.

Bedellin and Forro were the only ones who could stand to talk about Tamsin at all. Harlom and Harlin had always been mystified by him—their sturdy practical crafts were miles away from Tamsin's ethereal music—but it had taken Alina quite a long time to find out why Daerleon and Armion were so sensitive about their youngest brother.

Armion's death had distracted Tamsin enough that he had been caught by some dire monster her sons called a fire-demon, which had not killed him but had taken away his ability to play the harp. (Or write, or draw, or do anything requiring fine dexterity. They all knew it was the harp that mattered.) Armion, next in age to Tamsin and closest in art, was still devastated that he'd destroyed Tamsin's last remaining tether to his.

Daerleon had begged Tamsin to kill him cleanly and quickly; and Tamsin had.

Alina had thought she had long since grieved enough for her sons, before she learned that.

Bedellin and Forro, though, had had relatively simple deaths. (That Alina could think that about her sons!) They had been close with Tamsin, when they were young. Forro had taught him his letters, once upon a time. Bedellin had been the best child-minder, second-oldest after Daerleon but much less likely to go off with friends. And of course Bedellin always had some sort of baked good to tempt elflings with.

Alina asked after their mornings: Forro in the forge, working on commissions, and Bedellin exploring the new stalls set up on the Tourney grounds.

"Actually, I had a strange moment earlier," Bedellin said, when Forro had finished describing the elaborate decoration one of the King's lords wanted for his new sword. "I was crossing back up from the tents, and thought I saw Klara coming over all friendly with strangers."

"Our Klara? Unlikely!" Forro said, laughing.

"There's not a lot of people with knee-length black hair," Bedellin protested. "Then I saw she was wearing a tunic and sword and a very boring grey cloak, and I've never seen Klara with any of those things. Her shadows are much more impressive."

"You didn't go over?"

"I was running behind—I was supposed to meet Garfol at the bakery. And she was quite a ways away from me."

"I think that's the same person Certhin told me about," Alina said slowly. "A new competitor, or perhaps a fighting-master."

Bedellin snorted. "Hardly a warrior, with hair down to her knees!"

"Quite the beauty, though, if she looks like Klara," Forro suggested.

Or Tamsin. Alina considered that she now knew for a fact what she had so long suspected, that Tamsin and Klara had occasionally switched places. Tamsin, her seventh son, had taken after his father: the only one of his brothers to have Dâr's black hair instead of Alina's copper, and to have Dâr's delicate features and slight, almost svelte form. The others had inherited her height and stocky build. A child of Tamsin's—

Oh, there was no help for it. She had to know. She gripped the dishcloth that she found in her hands. "Certhin said—asked me—is it possible Tamsin had a child?"

"You don't mean—No. You'd know better than us, surely," Bedellin said after a moment, reaching out to fold his hand over hers. "I can't imagine Klara—"

Alina licked her lips nervously. "Not with Klara."

"Not with Klara!" Forro exchanged a startled glance with Bedellin. "Impossible."

"Perhaps—" Bedellin paused, frowning. He pressed his fingers gently against her trembling hand. "It's not *impossible*."

Forro was adamant. "Tamsin never looked at anyone else. Not before we left, you know that, Dell. And not Over the Waves, either. Not through all those first centuries, before the dragon—"

"He used to go to all the festivals," Bedellin suggested. "Some of them were very ... lusty."

"He went for the music."

"He *could* have gotten drunk and slept with someone, technically." Bedellin gave her a wry, apologetic smile. (As if she didn't know her sons were adults; as if going to a *lusty* festival was in any way shameful; as if she cared anything but that something of Tamsin's— something more than a handful of songs—might yet linger to be found.)

"He wouldn't have," Forro responded sharply. "Not before the dragon, and certainly not after. He barely interacted with *us* after he lost his voice. And after Sawwalith ..."

Bedellin sighed. "We know he didn't after Sawwalith, that's true. We were with him the whole time, so we would have seen, if he had."

Constrained by their oath as they had been, once dead her sons had been bound to the remaining living ones: and the last one to live, far after the rest of them had died, had been Tamsin.

That had been another very difficult conversation. Not only the fact that six of her sons had spent an age haunting the seventh, but that they had had to watch, impotent, the gradual degradation of Tamsin's health and spirit as he endured the burden of oath and death-curses in a dying land.

"Not after Sawwalith, no," Forro said, and then he hesitated. "We don't know what happened to him, after he reclaimed the flame and released us all from the Oath. We came back here ..."

"Klara Sang us back here," his brother agreed, with the smile that always came to his face when he thought of his near-sister. All of them liked Klara for what she had done for them, and for their mutual love of Tamsin, but Bedellin seemed to consider her his own in a more particular way.

Forro always tried to be fair, even against his own opinions. "If he'd healed enough to live, but not enough to have his full memory, as we've learned was the case with some of those who have passed through the Halls, then I suppose he *could* have fallen in love with someone and had a child, and not remembered to come back here."

"So not *impossible*," Bedellin concluded. "But very unlikely."

Alina was glad their thoughts matched so well with her own memories of her youngest son. It had been so very long since she had seen him, and the others had changed so much ... though they were also themselves, just grown in unexpected directions. And indeed it was arguable that both Klara and Alina had done the same, this side of the sea.

"That's what I thought. Still, that makes it even more of a puzzle, since Certhin told me he'd heard that this elf-maid, whoever she is, was wearing Tamsin's sigils."

A silence, much more struck than Alina had expected. Bedellin and Forro frowned fiercely at each other.

"Tamsin never really had any *followers*," Bedellin explained finally. "Not the way the rest of us did. Daerleon kept him close to hand—he was too powerful to send off by himself."

"Not to mention everyone was terrified of him, and that was *before* the dragon," Forro added.

Alina might have been unable to imagine fearing Tamsin, once upon a time, but that was before she had witnessed Klara transforming the city with her Song. Alina wasn't afraid of her, exactly, but she was certainly respectful of her power.

"We can go down after lunch," Bedellin said. "I'm not busy with anything that can't wait."

"Nor me," Forro agreed, which was a good sign—he was not always particularly keen on talking to people outside of his forge.

Alina decided she'd feel better if she washed her face, and left her sons gently bickering over who was going to salvage lunch—Bedellin, of course—and who was going to see who was making a noise at the front door while she went to her room.

She was drying her hands when someone tapped on her door. Bedellin opened it when she called him to enter. His expression was very strange.

"What is it?" she asked, searching his face. All she could think of was—"Has she come? The—the girl?"

Her granddaughter, she barely dared think to herself. But imagine, imagine, if Tamsin *had* ...

"Not a girl," said Bedellin. Wonder crept over his face, and a kind of fearful awe. "It's Tamsin. Tamsin himself. He's home."

"Oh," said Alina, and sat there with the cloth in her hands, remembering that moment when she had realized six of her sons were back from the dead, but the seventh was lost.

Tamsin. Not Tamsin's child. *Tamsin.*

Have we not grieved enough? she had once asked Klara, in the depth of Klara's winter.

Tamsin was the one who sang spring, Klara had replied, and, *If we had exchanged these places, he would have hope.*

Alina wasn't certain she had enough left to bear her from bedchamber to kitchen.

"Come," Bedellin said, and gently pulled her upright. "Come and see for yourself."

CHAPTER TWENTY-SEVEN
THE UNFORGOTTEN

Tamsin walked slowly but without stopping through the sea of tents. The whole thing was very strange: not so very dissimilar to the many army encampments he'd known Over the Waves, and yet also so different in feel. There was no desperation, no deprivation, no true fear. Only excitement and anxiety and the gleeful anticipation of winners and losers.

He kept half-recognizing faces and voices, but he tried his best not to turn his head, not meet any eyes. He did not want to be recognized, not yet.

Rather than put up his hair into the crown of braids he'd worn for war, that morning he had left his hair down, mostly loose but for a netting of braids coming from his temples to join into one long plait, to hold the hair off his face and be a place for the ribbons and his new ornaments (and that old, mysterious comb). He was still wearing his old tunic, but it was a warm day, and he'd folded the cloak over his arm, half-hiding his harp and his sword.

He didn't look like Tamsin Korrokaith, who had stalked balefully through the army camps at the end of the wars.

No one flinched back from him, no one blanched when they caught his eye.

No one knew him. Any moments of confused half-recognition faded swiftly.

Tamsin son of Dâr was a ghost, a bogeyman, a legend, a rumour. Not someone any of these elves expected to see come round a corner with a harp on his back, a sword at his side, hair down to his knees.

The Scourge of Chirrkal, the Blade of the Firnoi, the Butcher of Hinnúrin.

The Oath-bound, the Thrice-Accursed, the Dreadful.

The Golden-Voiced, the Dragon-Slayer, the Death-Singer.

He could have crowned himself with moonlight and blood. Could have lifted up his sword and his voice. Could have cried out one note and knocked down every tent and banner and warrior in this camp.

It had been a long, long time. Never had he been so grateful for that.

The path through the tents led him eventually to a series of more permanent buildings at the edge of the city. Tamsin noted that these seemed to be mostly devoted to the business of war—or at least tournaments. He could hear the familiar noises of smithies off to one side, and in front of him were shops selling small finished items such as straps, belts, under-armour padding, whetstones, daggers, sheaths, polishing creams and cloths.

He passed through them, glad—so very glad!—he needed none of it. Albeit Ash had no armour ... Tamsin considered the matter as he picked a street that appeared to lead towards the old city. Once she got past the initial stages of the Tourney and her skill became clear, Ash would probably start being challenged outside of the formal lists, and that would give her the opportunity to win arms as well as money. But before then ...

Ash didn't have any family here to supply her, and she was attached to no lordly house. Except insofar as she and River had informally adopted Tamsin ... he was her teacher ... in some ways Tamsin could—indeed, arguably *ought to*—stand as her patron. Ash wouldn't want to wear his colours, he imagined, but she could honourably bear any gifts of armour he offered her.

He had very little of anything but the harp on his back and his skill. And his reputation, of course.

(All the layers of that. The Death-Singer, the Dawn-Singer, the greatest bard and the most feared warrior of the Firnoi. *Would* anyone stay to hear him put hands to harp if they knew who he was? Or would they remember only the battles where his voice had called down death?)

And—possibly—there was his family. Forro had been—was again?—one of the greatest smiths of the Firnoi ... That would be armour worthy of Ash, if Forro was willing to craft it. If Forro was ... was here.

If Tamsin's family was willing to welcome him, to acknowledge him, to let him make his apologies and express his regrets. Daerleon had been fell and fierce but *he* was not the Butcher of Hinnúrin, not the one who had sung all the inhabitants of Dumloth into a sleep so deep they had never woken. He had ordered Tamsin to take the cities, but Tamsin was the one who had decided how.

Tamsin had to find out what had happened to his family, first. Had to see if they would accept him. Had to ... had to see for himself whether they were alive.

There was a lot he would give, simply to know they were not lost to the Eternal Night to which they had sworn themselves. Tamsin had endured long enough to grasp the holy fire, to be burned again by it, but had that been *enough*?

Daerleon was here, he reminded himself. (Someone who called himself Daerleon was here, a more cynical part of himself answered.) But if Daerleon, then why not the others—

Tamsin was here, however impossibly.

He clenched his hands into fists. He was here, here, and healed enough to play, to sing, to reach first for harp and not for sword. He took a deep breath. He had endured long enough to reach this point. He could endure long enough to cross the last half-mile between the new city he did not know and the old one he once had.

He had faced the dragon, the Old Enemy, all those goblins. He had faced the loss of all he loved, the long solitude, what he had become. He had started to sing himself into a new person, one that might fit into this new Elfland under the Sun.

He could face his mother, surely, and offer her that.

He reached the pale stone wall marking the boundary between new city and old. A hummed enquiry told him the main entrance was to his right, so he turned to follow the narrow laneway at the base of the wall. The wall sang softly back to him, telling him of its history. Built by the new King, the King-outside-the-Walls, but the line of its foundation had been chosen by the Singer-Within.

Tamsin knew the voice of the Singer-Within as well as he knew his own. Klara, Klara, his heart cried. He brushed his hand along the stone. Golden light gathered under his fingertips, trailing behind him like a shooting-star's tail. Klara, Klara.

The old city sang to him.

It knew him the instant his feet crossed under the archway where the gates stood wide. Tamsin stepped through and stopped, struck by music.

He'd done it to so many. Caught them with his song, his voice, his hands on his harp. Netted them with beauty, snared them with it. No one had been spared, but for himself.

He stood now, caught, still as one of his brother's statues. His hair wafted around him in the light breeze coming down from that mountain that had not been there, the last time he stood on this ground. The great enclosing wall had not been there; these paving-stones were new (ancient, but new); these buildings were half of them ones he knew, but moved, shifted, rearranged, as easily as the standing stones he and Klara had once sung to dancing.

The city sang to him. The city, the old city, *his* city. Klara's voice was in every stone, every shadow, every spray of water from the fountains and waterways that were everywhere—and yet his voice was there too, Tamsin's own voice, echoing back to him in the light reflecting off glass and crystal and silver sculptures he had never seen before.

Tamsin! Tamsin! sang the stones, greeting him, and the waters cried back, *Tamsin! Tamsin!*

He had thought the mountains remembered him, as he remembered them: white-browed Dilirat, broad-shouldered Auquiel, the curving cliffs of Irzond. They had heard him singing their names, heard his voice running through the earth, in the winds.

They had not named him in return.

Tamsin! Tamsin! murmured these houses, and all the reflected and glimmering light gathered around him, singing greetings. *Tamsin! Tamsin!*

He had never seen this city under sunlight. Only under starlight, under the soft coloured glow of the Lamps.

It was beautiful, under the sun.

There were people here, he realized slowly, catching movement, like flowers opening, turning towards him. They were dressed in gorgeous clothing, far more brilliant than he'd seen out of the corners of his eyes in the newer city. Great sweeping gowns and robes of blue and orange and starry midnight, or the delicate hues of clouds catching the sun, or something that reminded him of the pale gold of a foggy dawn. A few elves had been on the streets, tending their gardens or going about their own business; others had been drawn to their doorways and windows when the bells began ringing, the stones singing.

They were all looking at him.

No one had looked at him like that in so long.

No one had *seen* him.

He knew these people, most of them. They were *his*, the way no one else had ever been.

These had been his neighbours, his brothers' fellows, his mother's colleagues, his father's friends. They had heard him and Klara learning how to play; had given Tamsin cakes and fruit, encouragement and admonitions, scraps of fabric or minor jewels or punnets of vegetables for his efforts. They had heard all his songs.

They would know what he had become, Over the Waves. That Tamsin Tammorath had become the Oathbound, the Thrice-Accursed, the Dreadful, most feared of all his fearsome brothers.

They might have grieved for him, these people.

Tamsin lifted his head. He had faced his dead on that dreadful bridge. He had wrought himself a new harp out of bones and hair and hope. He could face those who had once cared for him.

He said nothing, but he met their eyes. Names drifted into his mind, settling down like falling petals, falling snow. Rashel ... Verilian ... Morva ... Certhin ...

Certhin, Tamsin's mother's dear friend, Daerleon's carving-master. Once he had carved a tiny version of the great Lamp of Gold out of golden alabaster, and Tamsin had spent years learning how to sing light to settle in it.

Certhin was the one wearing a robe like a foggy dawn. He met Tamsin's eyes fearlessly, his own wide, astonished, and then he walked slowly towards him. Tamsin stood where he was, caught now not by the welcoming music of the city but by the grip of all those attentive eyes, minds, hearts. His own heart was hammering. Certhin did not look away, not once, all the long way across the open space in front of the gate.

Certhin stopped right before him. Tamsin stared at his mother's old friend, his honorary uncle. He was trembling, unable to move, unable to speak. This was not the death-curse of the dragon, the Old Enemy, his own father's Oath. There was nothing holding him but himself.

"Oh, Tamsin, it's *you*," breathed Certhin. His voice was so unutterably familiar.

He was the first person who had recognized Tamsin on sight since the fall of the Old Enemy.

Certhin cupped Tamsin's face with cool callused hands. His robes whispered softly, like the wind in distant trees. They were such a beautiful colour, soft as one of Armion's chalk sketches. "Tamsin," he said. "Tamsin."

Tamsin, Tamsin, sang the stones, the fountains, the earth beneath them. *Tamsin, Tamsin.*

Tamsin felt Certhin's thumbs brush against his cheekbones, tracing out the lines of his face. The old elf—older even than he!—had luminous grey-green eyes, brilliant in the sunlight. He held Tamsin's gaze easily, as if there was nothing between them but a long absence.

"Certhin," said Tamsin. His voice rang in the sunlight, the singing stones, the friendly wind.

There had been no sunlight, the last time Tamsin had been here. He had sung light with that song he had learned for Certhin's lamp; and then he had sung away half the city to follow his father to death. Tamsin swallowed, feeling his throat move against Certhin's gentle hold.

"Oh, Tamsin," his mother's friend said, unsmiling, intent. Tamsin braced himself. Certhin leaned down and kissed him on the forehead. "Welcome home."

Tamsin, Tamsin, sang the city that had once been his.

Welcome home, said the people he had left behind or led to war. *Welcome home.*

Tamsin knew the buildings, but not the streets.

And yet he did know the streets, from the strange dark dreams he'd had when he'd first gone Over the Waves. He had dreamed of all the colour and warmth leached out of the city, his city, that it had become plunged into an endless winter, an endless night. He had never dreamed of it in the sunlight, not until those long years in which his mind had started to fray.

He had dreamed of the shadow-garlanded houses sprouting icy

feet and walking to new foundations. He had dreamed of a silence as bitterly cold as the dragon's curse had been fiery, in which strange coiling winds drew hoarfrost across every surface. He had dreamed of the land arching its back under his feet, lifting up its head into the starry night sky.

After the death of the dragon, he had dreamed, sometimes, that he sang in Klara's voice. But all had been different: no life flowered then, just strange birds of shadow and twisting spires of ice.

It was different now. At each footfall light ran through the paving-stones, as if he walked on the sand at the edge of the sea and water rippled underfoot.

He should have lifted his voice, should have sung some greeting back to the city. He could not. He could feel the song in his throat, rising up from his heart, but he could not open his mouth. He did not know how to receive this.

Klara, Klara, he thought. She was everywhere and nowhere, her voice echoing behind the bells, the shadows, the sunlight splashing at every corner's silver rain-chain.

Tamsin, Tamsin, sang the city.

They let him go home, the people at the gate, those along his road. No one else came up to him, no one stopped him. They met his eyes, stern, smiling, unafraid, in their gorgeous clothes all the colours of the sky. They stood in their gardens, the flowers twining around sculptures of silver and marble and crystal; and everywhere there were birds, white and black and starry-bright.

All those frigid nights. All those silent, empty streets, the houses bound in shadows and icicles. All those songs Tamsin had tried to sing in Klara's voice when his own had been lost.

(All those times he had imagined her voice in his ear, in a cool and comforting thread of shadow, in his throat when he could not himself utter a sound.)

(All those times he'd imagined his brothers singing to him, telling him stories, urging him to hold on, to live.)

(All those dreams and hallucinations that had enabled him to endure.)

He walked under a many-pillared colonnade, deceptively simple. The vaulted roof was covered with verdigrised copper, set with traceries of untarnished gold in the form of great fern leaves unfurling overhead.

He could not sing, perhaps. But he stopped in the middle of the colonnade, where a cross-path led to a stair half of marble, half of leaping water, carved swans and living fish cavorting amongst copper and amethyst lotuses. He could not sing, perhaps, with this much in his heart. But he could unfold his cloak and unship his harp.

There was a stone bench there, simple and elegant as the silver hair-comb. Certhin's work, if Tamsin had not forgotten everything he had once known.

Perhaps he had. Perhaps Certhin had had a dozen apprentices, each more skilled than Daerleon had ever been at the craft, and this was one of their works. Perhaps Tamsin didn't remember anything at all.

Tamsin, Tamsin, sang the water as it leaped gaily down the stairs.

Tamsin sat down with his harp. For a few moments he simply sat there, staring out over the city, running his hand up and down the glossy smoothness of the pillar, around and around the gentle spiral.

Tamsin, Tamsin, sang the columns, picking it up from their plinths, which had known him when they had been the stones of Forro's first smithy.

The city was *old*, and much of it was made of what had gone before.

He looked down the fall of water, down into a small valley that had not been there before. The valley was a garden, green grass and silver trees and great round lily-pools. In the centre was a stone basin in which burned the memory of an ancient light.

The silver trees were full of white doves. They looked at him with dark eyes; they did not sing.

Tamsin bent his head over the bone harp and could think of nothing to play but the lament for his father. But that did not fit the sunlight, the laughing water, the city crying out his name, the flame imperishable returned beyond hope or reason to its heart.

Eventually he stood and walked with the harp in his hand to the end of the colonnade, where he knew stood his mother's house.

Tamsin, Tamsin, sang the stones, the tiles of the roof, the silver-and-copper rain-chains. *Tamsin, Tamsin,* sang the intricate wooden shutters, the door carved with the flame over the Mountain. *Tamsin, Tamsin,* sang the courtyard gate, the stone lion lounging along one wall, the glass bells strung overhead.

He walked as in a dream. There had been shadows last time he'd seen this house: shadows cast by the lights Tamsin had sung up, which had faded when he followed his father Over the Waves.

There was a red-haired elf at the door. Tall, in a cloud-white tunic, saffron-yellow robes slipping off his broad shoulders, trying to brace what seemed to be a large lemon tree in a terracotta pot so he could reach the handle. Tamsin drew slowly nearer, hardly daring to breathe. Red hair more truly a dark auburn, curly tendrils escaping a simple high braid, a gold ribbon wound through the plait.

Certhin had never died. If Tamsin had dared think of who might linger in the city, his name would have been one of the first to come to mind.

Armion had gone Over the Waves, and died there.

Tamsin had *watched* his brother die. Armion had been speared by a fire-demon, spitted like a boar. Tamsin's palms burned with the memory of the whip he had caught barehanded rather than let it defile his brother's corpse further. Not that it had helped.

This was Armion alive again. Armion in yellow and white, no weapons visible, a smudge of charcoal on his cheek, blue ink on his fingers where they were scrabbling on the rim of the pot.

Oh it was true, those old legends. The dead *could* return to life. They could. They could.

"Klara, could you get the door for me?" Armion said, mildly exasperated. Tamsin stopped at the sound. His brother's voice was light, pleasant, the old Firnoian accent with a bit of the Chirrtal overlay. So Tamsin sounded, talking to River in his mother-tongue.

Tamsin was drowning again, the fire in his hands, in his eyes, in his mouth.

Armion nudged aside a branch with his chin and grinned over his shoulder at him. "Please?"

Tamsin said, "Armion," and Armion dropped the tree on his foot.

CHAPTER TWENTY-EIGHT
THE LEMON TREE

Even as Bedellin began laying out food in the kitchen, and their mother went to her room, there was a loud crash out front. Forro hesitated a moment, then opened the door, preparing to gently rib his brother.

Rather: he opened the door, and noticed three things simultaneously.

An overpowering scent of bruised lemon, a mouthful of leaves, and the commingled sounds of Armion laughing hysterically and Klara half-laughing, half-swearing ferociously in a language Forro had not realized she knew. She was bent over, her long hair falling everywhere, the ends dragging in dirt and broken potsherds.

Forro looked again. Evidently Armion had been carrying a potted lemon tree, and had for some reason dropped it on Klara's foot, where the pot had broken.

He made to help Klara upright and into the house, but stopped when he saw that her hair was not wholly loose as she usually wore it. The top layer was braided intricately with crimson and silver ribbons, a whole string of tiny silver bells chiming softly in counterpoint to her swearing, and tucked in was—

That was the comb that Forro had made for their mother when Tamsin was born.

Forro stared at the silver comb. It had been one of the first items of jewellery he'd designed and made entirely by himself, and he had been so proud to give it to his mother. She'd been in bed when he'd brought it to her, and he remembered how disappointed he had been that his newborn baby brother hadn't tried to grab it.

Tamsin had been so tiny, his tuft of dark hair different from the rest of his brothers from the beginning.

His mother had kept the comb until after their return from Over the Waves.

When they'd talked to Klara and their mother about what had happened, Alina had explained how a great raven had come out of the west with news that Tamsin had gone to his rest. She'd given the raven the comb to lay wherever Tamsin was, if he could be said to be anywhere in death, and Klara had said she'd enchanted it with that portion of Tamsin's voice she'd been keeping safe for him.

Forro had made many enchanted things—swords and spears and shields, necklaces and rings and coronets and earrings and brooches— but he did not understand in the least what Klara had meant. Except that it had been a gift, and a promise, and a hope. He had understood that.

Klara had also talked about how she and Tamsin used to sing in each other's voices, back when they and the world were young.

And there was, the rumour had it, a girl come to the Tourney that morning who looked like Tamsin.

A hank of hair slid over the elf's shoulders, and Forro saw the strange greenish-grey colour of the tunic she—*he*—was wearing.

He had not heard that voice for thousands of years, but he had spent most of those thousands of years staring at that tunic and listening to Harlom move from disparagement of its cut, colour, and fit to reluctant awe at its longevity.

Not someone who *looked* like Tamsin. Not a child Tamsin had somehow sired, daughter or son. Not someone taking on sigils to which they had no right. Not a stranger at all.

He meant to say *Tamsin*, but what he said was, "How are you *still* wearing that same tunic?"

And then he reached out, because for so, so long they could look and speak but not touch, not be heard. He moved slowly—Tamsin's reflexes had been violently defensive for so very long—his hands trembling as he brushed the silky black hair away from his youngest brother's face.

Tamsin straightened up equally slowly, though without any evidence of pain or stiffness, and he met Forro's searching gaze with his own. His eyes had been so dark and empty, last time Forro had looked at them. So flat, somehow more deadened than the spectral eyes of the actually dead.

They were still dark, heavy with all Tamsin's lonely years, but they were bright as well, alert and alive. Alert, alive, and *seeing* him.

No matter what they had done, no matter how they had tried to convince him they were real, for all those thousands of years Tamsin had looked straight through them.

Forro dropped his hands to Tamsin's shoulders, and stared. He found himself unable to do anything else. "Tamsin," he said. "*Tamsin*."

Tamsin's face was softer than it had been, gentler. When Forro had last seen him properly he had been whipcord-thin, hard as petrified wood. Everything had been stripped away but for the singular goal of endurance.

The last time Forro had seen any expression at all on Tamsin's face had been when Tamsin had found a natural hot spring and allowed himself to relax.

(He'd nearly smiled, floating there in the hot water, staring up at the stars above him. It was the first time since Sawwalith that Forro had seen him visibly appreciative of something beautiful. It had nearly been the last time, too, but for the fact that even in that moment of unexpected comfort Tamsin had never let himself float out of reach of his sword. It had seemed such a grievous pity that he could not forget even for a moment. But then the goblins had come.)

With his hair half-down, waving tendrils framed his face, softening the hard lines of his cheekbones and jaw, the winged arch of his eyebrows. His long lashes had always been incongruous and probably the feature that had most let him pass as an elf-maid when he wished, that and the general delicacy of his build.

He did not really look that much like Klara. But neither did he look that much like the bitter killer he had become.

"Forro," Tamsin said, tilting his head up slightly to look directly at him. He was not quite smiling; his dark eyes were searching, looking for something.

His voice—ah, his voice! It was *his*, and he was speaking—

"Tamsin," Forro said again. His hands closed on Tamsin's shoulders. He felt hard muscle, lean rather than bulky.

It had been a thousand years since Forro himself had returned to life. It should not seem so utterly impossible that Tamsin was flesh-and-blood, warm under his hands, *alive*.

"You're *speaking*," Armion said, and they both looked at him. He had his hands full of the lemon tree, as if it gave him stability, though given that it had spilled the majority of its soil and lost its pot, that seemed over-ambitious. His eyes were wild, dazed, and he too was staring at Tamsin.

"You're *alive*," Tamsin returned, almost as dazedly, his face incredulous, blank in his shock. "I thought—I heard—they said Daerleon was running a Tourney—but I didn't know—I wasn't sure—I—" He stared beseechingly at them. "I'm sorry, I'm sorry, I'm sorry."

Forro should have had words, but he did not. He pulled Tamsin forward, stepping to meet him, and carefully embraced him instead.

Tamsin was the smallest of the brothers, and Forro the tallest. He'd always liked how Tamsin's head fit under his chin. Not that Tamsin had let him do that after they'd gone Over the Waves.

Tamsin had borne pressures that none of the rest of them had survived.

He let Forro hold him now. They stood there for a long time, neither speaking. Forro stroked Tamsin's head, careful not to tug on the braids, amused at the small vanity of new ribbons and ornaments when Tamsin truly was wearing the same tunic he'd worn for thousands of years. Armion quietly stood the lemon tree against the wall, kicked the potsherds out of the way, and then joined the embrace.

At last they felt Tamsin stir, and released him gently.

"Don't be sorry," Forro murmured to him, stepping back but keeping one hand on his shoulder. He did not want to stop touching him, wanted that tangible reminder that he was not a ghost, that Tamsin was there, real, alive, and so was he. "You're here, that's all that matters."

"You succeeded where we all failed," Armion said, reaching out for Tamsin's hand. He turned it over so they could see the wide bands of scarring across the palm and fingers.

The dead did not bear the scars they had earned in life on their bodies; only on their souls. That had been a hard thing, to re-learn their bodies, rebuild all their muscles, regain all their calluses. Forro still caught himself running his fingers along his forearm where once there had been a scar from a goblin's blade. He had it no longer; but Tamsin had his.

"It is I who am sorry," Armion went on, tentatively running his finger across the scar. Tamsin curled his hand reflexively, but they had watched him long enough to know that the movement *was* reflex. There was none of the stiffness and pain that had been so obvious, no matter that Tamsin had never shown it on his face.

Tamsin frowned, lifting his gaze from his own hand to Armion's face. "Did—did Daerleon tell you it was your fault? It wasn't! I was a fool, and made a foolish mistake." He made a wry, resigned grimace. "Hardly the first time, nor the last."

Forro had just seen more expression from Tamsin than he had from the point the dragon took his voice to the recovery of the holy fire. He swallowed. Tamsin had turned so far inward, letting nothing out but the sharp point of his blade.

(An hour spent floating in a hot spring, staring at the stars above him. A few moments here and there, when Tamsin paused to look at a sunrise or sunset, a tree or a bird: perhaps in enjoyment, or perhaps to consider his direction or the possibility of danger. A handful of days when Tamsin had carefully stacked stones into cairns, moving slowly with his damaged hands, and then sat there staring at them, face blank, eyes empty. He always made seven, cairns or stacks of stones or wooden markers or circles of acorns. Six together, and one a little apart. They had never been sure whether or not they should stand in front of what were clearly intended as memorials to them and their father, who was not and could not be there. Dâr's Oath had not bound him more than the bargain he'd already made of his soul to the gods on their mountain.)

All those thousands of years with nothing to do but bicker amongst themselves as they watched the curse-driven Tamsin wander. Forro knew his other brothers so intimately, and Tamsin not at all.

"Daerleon—no," said Armion, and now it was his time to look beseechingly at Forro. "I—I saw—we saw—Tamsin—"

Tamsin did not know that they had haunted him. He had never known it.

"Let's go inside," Forro said, and took his brother's hand. Tamsin let him with a somewhat bemused expression, though he shifted the position of whatever he was holding in his other hand. Armion caught his slipping cloak—also, impossibly, the same one they'd grown so familiar with over their years beside him—and revealed both Tamsin's same old sword at his hip and what looked like a very new harp in his hand.

"You have a harp," Armion said, his voice fierce, demanding. "You can play."

"Yes," said Tamsin, and now at last he smiled, brilliant and warm as the sun. "I can."

Inside, Bedellin was laying out a meal, singing to himself as he sliced a cucumber. Tamsin tilted his head, listening, as they came into the room. His hand was trembling in Forro's clasp.

The kitchen was large, the centre of the house. Forro and Armion led Tamsin there, stopping before the table where Bedellin was stationed, the inglenook with fireplace and comfortable couches behind them. Platters of beautifully arranged vegetables were laid before them. Tamsin stared at the food in wonderment. Bedellin sang a little louder as he heard them come in.

Tamsin tore his gaze from the food. "That's one of mine," he said, with an almost convincing lightness.

"No, it's Tamsin's," Bedellin corrected, barely glancing up. He made no strong reaction; had obviously seen what he'd expected to see. Forro, Armion, and ... Klara.

Tamsin glanced sidelong at Forro, his eyebrows quirking up, a sudden gleam in his eye, delight in his face. "Are you certain?"

That was Klara's timbre, her tone of friendly challenge edged with a purring hint of danger. If Forro hadn't known this was Tamsin (*Tamsin!*), only heard the words, he probably would have refused to believe it wasn't her.

But—but it *was* Tamsin. Tamsin not as he had been, wandering lonely and haunted; nor as he had been before then, silent and deadly; nor as he had been before *then*, bright and burning as the Sun with his song; but as he had been as a young and proud elf in the youth of the world.

Beside him, Armion sucked in a sharp breath. Forro felt dizzy with a sudden onslaught of memory.

Tamsin Tammorath had dressed in silks and jewels and gold, those wide expressive eyes outlined with kohl and brilliant powders, song swirling around him like the perfume he'd once loved. He'd layered glamours over himself, not to hide or conceal (they had *thought* not to hide or conceal) but to accentuate and delight. They had all done it in those days, especially those in the circles of art and fashion; and Tamsin and Klara had been foremost in both.

Forro himself had spent his energies enchanting the jewellery he designed and made for others, jewels to bring forth all the qualities of beauty in the jewels themselves and in those who wore them. Tamsin had been powerful and talented enough to do it with his voice even in the midst of a performance, and he had moved in eddies of soft light and fragrant airs, golden and glorious as his voice. He'd not had to *work* for it, seemingly, as evidenced by the way he'd wafted through his days in the kind of outfits that everyone else kept for special occasions.

Everyone else but Klara, who was his dearest rival, and wore silver to Tamsin's gold.

Forro glanced down at Tamsin beside him. His brother shrugged as he met his glance, sly and shy and delighted all at once, sharp eyes aware that this was an admission he'd never made.

The brilliance of it floored him. All Klara and Tamsin had had to do was switch their colours, adjust their voices—Klara drop hers a trifle, Tamsin lift his—and expectations would do the rest.

Armion covered his mouth to hide the snickers clearly starting to bubble up. Forro shook his head in mock remonstrance. Tamsin quivered with stifled laughter.

(True laughter was another long-lost thought. The Oath and the wars had taken that from Tamsin, from all of them, long before he'd lost his voice.)

"Yes," Bedellin said, keeping his attention on the cucumbers, though he was smiling. Part fondness for the memory, part enjoyment for needling Klara a touch. "I am quite certain that was one of Tamsin's. He composed it on the spot in my bakery once in exchange for a loaf of bread."

When she'd finally admitted to switching places with Tamsin, Klara had told them that those exchanges had indeed almost always been Tamsin. He'd been the one who would compose a tune for a bun or a cake or a hairpin or a ribbon or a pot of jam. She'd always either offered her songs entirely free or for proper recompense, and had never thought of her songs as *trifles*.

Both of them had written songs of astonishing beauty and power. But Tamsin's little ditties had made their way into the common culture of the city, the melodic heritage of every later minstrel who balked at the great Songs of the bards. They never believed that the same bard who had written the Dawnsong had composed them.

"That's true," Tamsin said easily, his grin now wide and unreserved.

If this was the healing of the Halls of Rest, Forro could not in the least regret the long mourning and sorrow for Tamsin's absence.

Except that Tamsin bore his scars. Wherever he'd been, he seemingly hadn't died.

"If you agree with me, why are you—" Bedellin looked up as he spoke, and at that moment recognized him. The knife clattered onto the worktable, scattering cucumber slices and chiffonades of mint leaves. Bedellin gripped the edge of the table. "*Tamsin.*"

Tamsin tugged free of Forro's hand to perform a bow of the sort no one had bothered with since before the rising of the Sun. "The very same."

Bedellin stared, taking in the old tunic and the new harp, the bright ribbons and untarnished silver, the long wavy hair, the very old cloak and the even older sword. The scarred hands, and the open face.

The very same, and yet entirely different. But then they all were.

Tamsin gestured at the platters. He might have been nervous; there was something anxious in his eyes. (*I'm sorry, I'm sorry, I'm sorry* had been nearly his first words to his brothers after two ages. What did he think he needed to apologize *for*?) "Do I need to come up with a song for lunch? I've been playing for all the villagers betwixt here and the Downs, so I'm not as much out of practice as you might expect."

That was almost too much for Forro; it was too much for Bedellin. "I'll just—" he said, gesturing incomprehensibly, and fled the room.

Tamsin flinched.

CHAPTER TWENTY-NINE

THE HAUNTED

Tamsin was bracketed between his brothers, trapped in the middle of the kitchen, the middle of the house. He could not *go* anywhere. He had to face this.

He clenched his fists.

He *could* clench his fists. Remember that. He was no longer voiceless, silenced, lost. Forro and Armion and Bedellin were alive. Daerleon was alive. Harlom and Harlin were alive. Klara was alive. His mother was alive. *He* was alive.

The scent of mint and cucumber was very strong, cool and invigorating, foreign. The plates of food Bedellin had been setting out were beautiful, fresh and preserved vegetables laid out in gorgeous colours, elaborate patterns. The utter *unnecessariness* of it dizzied him. The very idea that one might have the leisure and luxury to carve radishes into roses! To make a rainbow of last summer's preserved roasted peppers, each sliver uniform! To have half a dozen cheeses to choose from!

Tamsin clenched his fists, feeling the pull of the scars. He pressed his elbows close to his side, clutching the harp close. The door slammed shut behind Bedellin. He flinched again.

He had known this might happen. He had *earned* this.

He had never raised his voice against his brothers. But that wasn't enough, was it? He was Tamsin Korrokaith. The Thrice-Accursed. The Death-Singer.

(His brothers had been Oathbound also, but they had not been cursed as Tamsin had been cursed. He bore the death-curses of the dragon and the Old Enemy and the whole city of Hinnúrin upon him, their blood on his hands.)

"Tamsin?" Forro said hesitantly.

Tamsin forced himself to look up.

Forro was looking down at him, frowning, heavy brows pulled together. His eyes were brilliant. It took Tamsin several moments to realize that it was tears in Forro's eyes, not condemnation. Tamsin tried to breathe through his nose but his breath caught, shuddering in the top part of his ribcage.

He wanted to weep, but he could not. He was thinking of too many things—the rainbow of vegetables on the plate, the ribbons the Linwairi villagers had given him, Armion dying—the fire-demon's whip coming down—the crown of holy fire spinning into the chasm when Tamsin looked instead at Daerleon—

Ash nudging him and saying, *You're not actually very frightening, you know.*

But she and River had never seen him kill anything larger than a rabbit or a grouse. They had seen the armies of the dead marching towards him, past him, ghostly eyes on him, but they did not know what it *meant*.

Bedellin and Forro and Armion knew. They had been great warriors themselves, great lords under Daerleon's rule, commanding many soldiers under them. They knew that Tamsin had never been trusted with command. He had been the Blade of the Firnoi, the greatest weapon the elves from Over the Sea had possessed. He had been the tool, not the wielder.

(But he was not a tool. He was a person. *He* had chosen to lift his voice in those songs of death, to raise his sword when his voice failed, to keep raising his sword even when his hands were broken and all the heart was gone from him.)

Armion gently took the harp from his hand, and Tamsin let him.

Forro's face suddenly shifted, and he stepped forward and engulfed Tamsin in another embrace.

Tamsin held very still. He could still smell the cucumber, the mint, the more pungent vinegar of the roasted peppers, all washed over with the heavy iron-and-fire scent that had always said *Forro* to him.

He had spent a great deal of time in the forges as an elfling, watching his brother turn fire and metal into beauty. Harlin had been impatient with Tamsin's questions, but Forro had never minded. So long as Tamsin had been willing to work the bellows, he had always been willing to explain all the whys and wherefores Tamsin could ask of him. Later he had let Tamsin practice singing, even when he sometimes ruined the metal with uncontrolled power.

It had rarely been their parents Tamsin had gone to, but Forro, Bedellin, Armion. Bedellin for advice, Armion for companionship, Forro for comfort.

"I don't want to be the Dreadful any more," Tamsin said into Forro's broad chest, the heavy linen of his tunic. His brother's arms tightened around him.

"You must be so tired," Forro murmured back, his breath stirring the hair on the top of his head. Tamsin had not felt *small* in a long, long time. He shuddered. "Oh, Tamsin, I know. I know."

The Silver Hammer, Forro had been called. Fierce, feared, yes, but admired to the end for his smithcraft. No one had ever fled him except on a battlefield.

Another hand came onto Tamsin's back, rubbing between his shoulderblades. As if that was the release, suddenly he was weeping, the tears rolling hot and hard down his face, off his chin. He buried his face into Forro's tunic, shame flooding through him.

He had gone singing Over the Waves, bright and glorious as the new Sun overhead, leading them all to ruin.

(Tamsin had followed his father and his brothers, but the people had followed him, their bard singing of glory and fame and great deeds, of vengeance and courage and honour. And they had died, all of them, *all of them*, his father, his brothers, all those people who learned so quickly to fear his voice. All of them but him.)

Forro moved, and Tamsin could not bear to look at them, his family returned from the dead, his mother who had refused to come, who had told him he would destroy his art if he went—

Forro moved, and so Tamsin moved with him. He found himself tipping back, half-falling onto a soft surface, his sword (for once forgotten) twisting up under him, the belt catching on his tunic.

"Let me," Bedellin said, soft as if to a nervy horse, and Tamsin nodded, head bent, eyes screwed shut. Bedellin unfastened the belt before tugging the whole thing off from around him, scabbard and sword and belt suddenly gone. A swift sharp pain as it tangled in his hair, tearing out a handful of strands.

It was not the first time since he had woken in that iris- and rowan-girdled mound that Tamsin had removed his sword. He had washed in some of those cold streams on the high Downs, and when they had reached the villages he had bathed there.

He had thought he was doing better; that he no longer *needed* the sword immediately in reach to feel himself.

Harp taken by one brother, sword by another, held firmly by a third, Tamsin felt—he did not know. At once vulnerable and ... he did not know. As if they thought him a rabid animal, and needed to disarm him. And yet he did want to be held.

Oh, how he wanted to be held.

"Tamsin," said a voice like honeyed cream, cool and smooth and sweet, unforgettable. (So long forgotten.) His mother's.

Alina smelled like cedar and lemon with undertones of lemon-flower and something else he did not know. His imagination had grown so impoverished, Over the Waves. He had forgotten so much, everything but the endless narrow path in front of him. All he could do was curl his broken hands around his sword, tuck them into his sword belt, bend his head into the wind, trudge on.

A cool cloth touched his face, pleasantly rough on his hot skin, breaking into the lurking memory.

He was not voiceless, broken, lost. He had healed enough that his voice could sing forth beauty, laughter, life. No longer did his throat bleed, the grass burn, when he sang. The bone harp exulted in merriment, in dancing-music, in joy. He had made friends with River and Ash, elf-maids of the new Elfland, young and fearless and so full of life. He had played for the villagers, and they had not fled his singing.

He had faced his dead. He must remember that. He had walked across that bridge, seeking life. He had endured past the end of all thought and hope, when spite and determination alone kept him still putting one foot in front of another, refusing always to let the Old Enemy win in the end. He could keep putting one foot in front of another when it came to living.

He had faced all those goblins, Over the Waves, who had sought his death, and died to none of them. He could face all the elves, this side of the sea, whom he had killed, and learn to live with them.

He could teach them his music was no longer death to hear.

He pulled his arm free of Forro's hold and drew the damp cloth down his face. And then he opened his eyes to see his mother, who was kneeling in front of him.

She'd cut her hair, he thought foolishly, seeing that her messy braid fell not far past her shoulder. It used to fall past her waist, a waterfall of deep copper shot with gold.

She was wearing jewellery of copper and gold set with malachite, earrings and necklace and bracelets that must have been Forro's work, the lines were so familiar, and a pale grey dress that glimmered like mist.

She had tears running down her face, but she was smiling. She was smiling. She reached forward and he flinched back instinctively, waiting for the smile to twist into horror when she remembered what he'd done, what he'd become, what he *was*—but she took his hands in her own, and simply held them close, smiling at him.

Tamsin blinked, and blinked again. The tears were hot in his eyes, his nose, his throat. He looked helplessly from his mother (*his mother!*) to Armion, who was cradling the bone harp to his chest, and to Bedellin on the other side, who was kneeling beside her, beside Tamsin, Tamsin's sword on the floor in easy reach.

They were squeezed on a padded bench pushed back into the inglenook. It was astonishingly soft. He could not think the last time he'd sat on a cushioned seat. It was as unfathomable as Bedellin's beautiful plates of food.

His mother's hands were soft, too, warm as she worked her fingers between his. Tamsin looked at her dark, brilliant eyes—for all he looked more like his father, everyone used to say he had his mother's eyes, dark rather than bright grey—and could not bear the welcome shining there.

Surely she knew what he'd done. Surely she'd heard.

He looked down, away from her, at the sword in its battered scabbard at his feet. His hair fell about him like shadows, and for a wild moment he wanted to sing up the shadows to hide him away. He was distantly aware he was shaking. He tried to clench his hands, to anchor himself, but he could not, not with his mother's fingers interleaved with his own.

There were too many things he had not felt for so long. His brothers were dead, dead, dead, they had been memories, hallucinations, ghosts called up by his own longing. They could not be here, Forro with his arm over Tamsin's shoulders, Armion and Bedellin looking at him.

The scents of mint and vinegar and roasted peppers was strong in his nose. He dragged in the air until he could taste it in the back of his throat. Mint he had found fairly often, in his wanderings. Vinegar ... sometimes he had come across the vinegary remnants of rotten fruit. But roasted peppers never.

He could not bear this silence. Not when his throat and lungs no longer burned with the dragon's last fire. Not when he *could* speak. Must speak. "I'm sorry," he said, meaning ... everything.

I'm sorry I left. I'm sorry I stayed away. I'm sorry I became a monster. I'm sorry I hesitated and let the Old Enemy throw the fire into the earth. I'm sorry I lost my voice. I'm sorry I lost my way. I'm sorry that even now I cannot bear to have my sword out of reach. I'm sorry. I'm sorry. I'm sorry.

His mother gripped his hands until he looked at her. "Tamsin," she said simply when he did, the tears still in her eyes, his name soft in her mouth. "My love. We thought we'd lost you."

"You did," he said: the truth. Now there was horror in her eyes, or ... grief? "I lost myself," he went on, more quietly. Uncertainly, not for the truth of the thought, but because he could not tell what the expression in her face betokened.

She lifted their joined hands to her lips, and kissed his cold fingers. He was still shivering. Forro shifted position, drawing his arm more tightly around Tamsin, squeezing. Tamsin's hair was caught but what did that matter when this was real, solid, true?

"Can you tell us about it?" his mother asked. "Your brothers have told me what they could. But after ..."

Tamsin swallowed hard, Daerleon's death vivid in his mind's eye. (Daerleon's banners were flying in the Tourney. Daerleon was down there somewhere, red hair shining—)

"How does Daerleon wear his hair now?" he asked abruptly.

He sounded desperate, fearful, foolish, but Bedellin's eyes were full of understanding. "Long—not so long as yours. Past his middle back when it's wet. Usually it's a tangled mess, of course."

Tamsin nodded numbly. He couldn't make sense of the *of course*. (From being under a helmet?) He found he was trying to make fists again, to remind himself he could. All those weeks with River and Ash—

The thought of the two young elf-maids steadied him.

You're really not that frightening, you know. They had no idea.

This time his mother let go of his hands. Her eyes were steady, shining, compassionate. She put her hand on his knee instead.

They were all touching him so much. As if he were the ghost. He didn't want them to stop. Tamsin found the damp cloth on his lap and wrung it between his hands, the rough flannel right to the touch. "After Daerleon—after Daerleon and I attacked the Old Enemy," he began, "I ... I ... I didn't manage to get the crown, he'd gone for Daerleon and I went for the killing blow—"

He stopped there, the one moment of satisfaction at striking that blow ringing through his body. One moment only, for in the next he'd seen Daerleon crumple in mortal injury, and Tamsin had been torn between brother and Oath, and—

"I went after Daerleon," he got out, staring at the sword by his feet, clean and plain in its old scabbard. He hesitated a long moment before he could manage any more words. Finally he looked up at Bedellin; he could not look his mother in the eye. She had not sworn the Oath; did not know the way it had felt, how it had chained their spirits, scorched their hearts, rubbed away all the good until attacking an elven city for its strategic location seemed a perfectly reasonable tactic in the war against the Old Enemy.

She did not know what it meant, that Tamsin had gone after Daerleon instead.

He did not know what it meant, except that if he'd been able to break the Oath *then*, with the holy fire directly in front of him, that meant he *could* have broken it before. But he hadn't: and so if he had become the Butcher of Hinnúrin, the Blade of the Firnoi, *the Dreadful*, it was because that was something he *was*, inside.

He breathed in deeply, cataloguing the scents. Lemon, mint, vinegar, peppers, iron, earth. Softness under him, the cushions. The sturdy warmth of Forro at his back, his strong arm holding Tamsin firmly. The damp flannel pulled tight on his fingers. It was probably cutting off his circulation. He eased up the pressure for a moment, watching the blood flush back into his fingertips.

Bedellin nodded at him, grave, without condemnation. He did not look afraid after all. Merely ... sad.

River had looked sad, when Tamsin lifted his sword to her throat. Child of the sunlit Elfland as she was, she had not seemed to understand fear.

Tamsin picked his words carefully. He was so terribly out of practice with speaking, still. He'd not tried to articulate anything like this in modern Firnish to River and Ash; the old Firnoian wavered in his mouth. "The Old Enemy threw the crown into a crack in the earth. I beheaded him afterwards but I didn't get the fire. I'm so sorry."

His brothers looked at each other, Armion and Bedellin behind their mother's back, then over Tamsin's head to see what expression on Forro's face he didn't know. But Forro squeezed him again, pressing Tamsin back against his chest.

"From what I understand, you were the one who paid the greatest price," his mother said. She gently took the cloth from his hands. He looked from her face down to her hands, unsure. She reached up and brushed at the tears under his eyes.

(When had he started weeping again? Had he ever stopped?)

She smiled, sad but with a glimmer of humour. "I understand you threw the Old Enemy's head at the feet of the King."

Forro's chest rumbled against Tamsin's back. Laughing, he identified after a moment. (Forro, laughing! Forro!)

"I did," Tamsin admitted. "And then ..." He shook his head, helpless to describe the long years that had followed. "I wandered," he settled on. "It was ... tedious."

"Gruelling, from what your brothers have said."

He stared at her, and then at Armion and Bedellin, who looked ... guilty? Tamsin tried to make sense of their expressions and could not. "I don't—what do you mean?"

Now his mother's expression changed, flickered with surprise, quickly becoming appalled shock, grief, other emotions Tamsin could no longer name. "Dell?" she said, shuffling over so he could come closer.

Bedellin moved Tamsin's sword out of the way, though not entirely out of reach—if he lunged forward from the couch, he could easily break Forro's hold and grab the hilt as he rolled to his feet—

Which he would not need to do.

Bedellin took Tamsin's hand in his, because apparently he also felt the need to be in constant touch. Tamsin's skin was crawling with their proximity but yet—but yet—he did not want to move, to let go, to be let go of.

He was distantly grateful that River and Ash had taken his arm, from time to time. He would not have been able to stand this amount of touch without that practice and familiarity.

"We were bound by the Oath," Bedellin said. His eyes were intent.

That had been the basic fact of their lives Over the Waves. "Yes."

"When we died," Bedellin said, very carefully, "we were still bound."

"Yes." That had been a fact Tamsin alone had lived with, the bitter reflux forever curdled in his stomach. Wherever they had gone after death, *his brothers were still bound,* because Tamsin hadn't seized the holy fire when it was there in front of him.

He said it again, "Yes." And then, because Bedellin was still staring at him, intent, so very intent, he added: "Were you—were you in the Eternal Night?"

Bedellin closed his eyes for a moment. When he opened them Tamsin wanted to reach out to comfort him, so sorrowful and pained did he appear. But Forro was gripping him too tightly to move.

"No more than you were, alive," Bedellin said.

Tamsin shook his head. His head was spinning. "I don't understand."

"We were—with you," Armion said.

The bone harp gleamed in the sunlight coming in through the windows beside his brother, catching Armion's auburn hair into ember-brightness.

"We were bound to you," Armion went on. "We ... haunted you, is probably the word."

Tamsin felt all the blood drain from his head, or into it—he couldn't tell through the rushing in his ears. Forro's arm held him upright, otherwise he—he—Tamsin forced his thoughts to hold still.

His brothers had *haunted* him.

"We know you didn't know," Bedellin said gently. "But we were there, the whole time. We ... tried to keep you company, as best we could."

All those times he had seen their bloody forms looming over him, condemning him—

No.

Forro was holding him as if to anchor him to life. Armion was cradling the bone harp tenderly, as if it were a newborn babe. Bedellin was kneeling at his feet, carefully not blocking Tamsin's access to his sword.

All those times they had sung to him, told him stories, talked to him, reminded him of what it had been like when they were a family. Warned him, cheered him, comforted him, reassured him, encouraged him, cheered him on.

All those times they had chattered to each other behind him, beside him, over his head, teasing and laughing and quarrelling and simply *being* his brothers, as if death had released them from the constraints of the Oath and all the narrowing and diminishing of their years at war.

He had thought they could not be real, because of that. Because the way they had been at the end had had no laughter or love in it. Because the longer the long years went on the more they were the way he remembered them as being, before; and he had known his mind and memory were fraying, fading, breaking, and dared not let himself treat them as real for fear it would hasten the decline.

Armion said, awkwardly sincere, "We know you couldn't see or hear us."

"Oh," Tamsin said, reeling. Forro's hand was solid on his shoulder. (*He* was solid to Forro.) His heart was beating so fast. "But I did."

CHAPTER THIRTY

PAINTER AND PORTRAIT

Armion remembered his own death vividly. Everyone who had died did.

His last living sight had been of Tamsin's face, the moment before Tamsin realized Armion had been struck with a mortal blow and was still trying instinctively to shout a warning, though by then he had been voiceless for decades.

Armion's first sight after dying—the first thing he could hold in his mind after the realization that he was dead but not *gone*—was the moment Tamsin's face shut down into the blankness that would thereafter characterize him. The moment, he thought later, when Tamsin had gone from *Accursed* to *Dreadful*.

What passed between those two moments—the silent scream, the blank silence—he could piece together from what Bedellin and Forro told him, from what Daerleon murmured aloud when he tended Tamsin's broken hands. Tamsin had dropped his sword and lifted his hands to stop the fire-demon's whip from cracking down over Armion's body, and ... that had been the end of Tamsin, in many ways.

The dead brothers bore uneasy witness to the way Daerleon grew ever more stony-hearted and grim, his attention only focused on the hopeless war against the Old Enemy. Tamsin followed behind him, doing whatever Daerleon told him to do, no longer anything but a killer.

It had taken Daerleon a long time to soften after he had died at Tamsin's hand, as they watched Tamsin wander in endless silent loneliness. But they had had that time, all that long time Tamsin endured, and somehow they had slowly found healing.

Come back to life after Tamsin had inexplicably stumbled on the holy fire, Armion had tried to reclaim his own art. He could still draw, after all—he'd been making maps and sketching fortifications all their time Over the Waves—and slowly, excruciatingly slowly, he'd taught himself to look at the small overlooked beauties again.

He'd drawn sketch after sketch of Tamsin in the wilderness. His crippled hands, never far from his sword. The simple mourning braids he wore in his hair, the sole element of personal decoration he attempted. His expression, impassive and remote no matter what he was doing, what surrounded him.

Tamsin fighting goblins, like a flash of lightning caught in elven form. Tamsin sitting beside a small campfire, staring into its flames, thoughts utterly unfathomable. Tamsin building memorials for them, stones piled on mountaintops, in valleys, on the shore.

Tamsin always silent. Always, always, *always* silent. He could have made noise with his feet, at the very least, but even as the years unfurled after the last of the goblins were gone, endless years of an even more futile and desperate exile, he had never sought to make sound. He walked silent and self-contained, nothing like the wild, exuberant, ever-noisy Tamsin Tammorath, who had made music with sticks and rocks and reed-pipes if he had nothing else to hand.

Armion had wondered—they had all wondered, eventually— whether he had ceased to want to, or whether the curse burning his throat and lungs prevented him from clicking his tongue or whistling.

Perhaps they had talked, sung, chattered all the more loudly because of his silence. Nothing could hear them but themselves— very rarely Tamsin would respond, excruciatingly slowly, to their exhortations, but they could never tell if their words were ever more than an echoing whisper to him. Eventually getting up after falling, eating after long fasting, building a fire against the cold, moving away from a dangerously high riverbank—all those were things Tamsin might well have decided to do on his own.

All those sketches, a thousand years of trying to make sense of an existence that had been at once theirs and not theirs—for though they had wandered, they had not been alone; they had not hungered, thirsted, fought; they had been bound by the Oath, tethered by and to it, but no longer was it their burden to carry—

All those sketches, and when Tamsin himself showed up at his side, Armion did not immediately recognize him.

It was Tamsin's eyes, he realized when they were inside. Over the Waves they had been so dead, dreadful indeed, the light gone from them. They were still large and dark, still framed by those long eyelashes, those winged eyebrows; Armion's sketches had not misled his memory. But now they were full of sparkling light, brilliant as a starry night.

Tamsin was not very like Klara, whose dark eyes were black pools, silver-sheened, except that Armion had only been half-looking over his shoulder and seen the pale face, the long dark hair.

Inside, Tamsin let himself be tugged to a seat by Forro, let Armion take his harp, let Bedellin unfasten his sword-belt before he got himself entirely twisted up in hair and scabbard. Armion held the beautiful harp in his hands, already wanting to sketch it (to draw *Tamsin playing it*), and watched the momentary panic bloom across Tamsin's face as his weapons were taken from him.

They had witnessed Tamsin destroy thousands of goblins. They knew full well that if he'd wanted to, he could have seized his sword and killed them all in one of those thunderbursts of deadly violence for which he was still renowned. Armion watched as his little brother tracked Bedellin's movements, the location of his sword, the way that Bedellin deliberately set it with its hilt facing Tamsin, belt neatly wrapped around the scabbard out of the way, belt-knife tucked close by, no one between Tamsin and his sword.

Their mother, thankfully, let Bedellin's discreet nudge guide her to one side. Armion was privately surprised that Tamsin let Forro keep him firmly in his embrace, their mother holding his hands. Answering questions.

They were impossible questions, with impossible answers.

"I wandered," Tamsin said, when they came at last to the topic of his lonely exile. His face was remote, the tears running down his face catching the sunlight through the window like drops of molten gold. He seemed to search for the words. "It was ... tedious."

Tedious?

Armion exchanged an incredulous look with Forro, who seemed torn between laughter and tears. The word Tamsin came up with to describe his horrible exile was *tedious*?

"Gruelling, from what your brothers have said," their mother murmured gently, encouragingly.

Tamsin's remoteness dissolved into honest confusion. He looked searchingly at them. "I don't—what do you mean?"

Bedellin moved forward, careful to move Tamsin's sword out of his way but not out of Tamsin's sight or reach. Tamsin watched him, hands twitching, brows drawn together, always aware of where his sword was. But yet he let Bedellin take his hands. Armion found that gesture of trust almost unfathomable. He looked again at Tamsin's face, the way he'd braided his hair back with ribbons—scarlet and silver, his old colours—and a long chain of silver bells—how his face was softer, less gaunt. How overall he was less ... hollow.

Something had happened to him, to let him heal, all those long years after they had come home without him.

Tamsin said, "I don't understand," his voice cracking. Armion could not take Bedellin's circuitry. "We were—with you."

Tamsin lifted his gaze to stare searchingly at him. So different than all those sketches; than all those years staring through them. It was unnerving.

Armion forced himself to continue speaking. "We were bound to you. We ... haunted you, is probably the word."

Tamsin went completely white. Forro leaned forward, gripping him hard, when he swayed. They waited until his breathing evened out and he seemed to be listening again.

"We know you didn't know," Bedellin said gently. "But we were there, the whole time. We ... tried to keep you company, as best we could."

Tamsin's face turned alarmingly inward, bleached and blank as driftwood. Armion had not spent much time by the sea, until those long centuries when Tamsin had paced the shorelines of Kheir, following the scalloped edges of the waves until he had circumambulated the entire continent.

Armion girded his loins. This was his brother, their brother, the one who had endured the unendurable for their sake. The one who had somehow passed through life into ... this. "We know you couldn't see or hear us."

"Oh," Tamsin said, leaning into Forro's grip. Now he looked like the endless sketches. Armion didn't like it. "But I did."

The moment after Tamsin said that felt suspended, like something caught on an edge, a pivot-point, a balance—and then Tamsin's face changed, from blankness through bewilderment to astonishment to, unexpectedly, a smile like the first dawn.

(Armion knew the full weight of that metaphor. They had all *seen* the first dawn, the first sunrise, that light filling the sky after the darkness, changing the sky from violet to blue—and they had all heard, so many times had they heard, Tamsin's glorious ode to its beauty and power. The Dawnsong *resonated*.)

"Thank you," said Tamsin, and the sun was in his eyes, in the tears beading his eyelashes, streaking his face. Once he'd sung golden light around him, a glow and a gleam, a glimmer like the shimmer of heat above a fire, fey and wild and beautiful in the way that none of the rest of them had been.

Armion had never been particularly interested in portraits, before. The years of sketching his memories of Tamsin had led him outwards to his other brothers, and then their mother, and Klara ... He imagined a chalk-pastel portrait of Tamsin as he was now, the sun in his eyes, silver and scarlet in his hair, an incongruous smile on his face. His face was more open than it had ever been, Over the Waves or before, when he'd layered those veils of light and magic and performance between himself and the world.

Tamsin looked down at their mother, who was still kneeling before him. "I didn't know," he told her. "I ... was afraid. I could feel that I was starting to slip ... The more I could see and hear them the more I ..." He shrugged, wry, amused, sunlit. Met Armion's gaze. "You probably know what happened better than I do. My memory of the end is ... unclear."

"There was an earthquake, and a cliff slid into the sea," Bedellin said.

Tamsin frowned thoughtfully, his face going distant as he delved into his memory. "Was the water ... I seem to remember the fire was ... Was it under the water?" His voice trailed off, uncertain. "I think I took the fire in my hands. You were all there, then ..."

Forro cleared his throat. "Klara said that you dove—"

Tamsin burst out laughing, merry and unexpected as anything Armion had ever encountered. "Klara! What has she to do with it?"

Forro's expression was uncomfortable, if unseen by Tamsin. "She ... she told us she had some sort of vision or dream of you ..."

Tamsin sat for a moment, not quite shocked, not quite disbelieving. Considering, Armion realized slowly. (It was so strange to see this range of expression on Tamsin's face; to see this evidence that *Tamsin* was indeed there, alive, aware, inside himself.) Slowly, he said, "Mum, was there a period in which the city—this city—was ... frozen?"

"Yes," said their mother after a beat, though whether the hesitation was due to the strange question or Tamsin's use of *Mum* was unclear.

Tamsin's face cleared, and he smiled with a private sort of amusement, sly and delighted and wondering and a little sharp. He hummed, a few bars of something Armion didn't recognize. "How good to know that wasn't entirely in my own head, either," he murmured. "Do go on, Forro. Klara said—?"

Forro could not see Tamsin's expression, and his own face was troubled, looking down on the top of Tamsin's head. His voice was even enough, speaking. "Klara said you dove down for the fire, and she sang ..."

Tamsin hummed another few bars, and this time Armion did recognize the music. He shuddered involuntarily at the memory of that ineluctable *call*, where the horns calling them to the Halls of Rest had entwined with Klara's song calling the holy fire home, and they had followed the fire, as they had for so long followed the fire.

And he shuddered, too, with something between awe and joy, for that was music coming from Tamsin's throat, at last, at last.

"Yes," Forro said hoarsely. "That song. Called us home."

Tamsin smiled, a very private sort of smile. "Did it now?" But he said nothing more, twisting in his spot to look up at Forro with steady interest instead.

"And—that's all we know," Forro went on. "We came home. You ... didn't."

"And Klara hasn't had any further ... visions, I take it."

"No," Alina said, and Tamsin glanced again at her. Whatever was in her face stilled the burgeoning amusement. (If amusement it was; certainly something had struck Tamsin, in the song or the story.) "We have had nothing. Save that a great black raven came out of the west and told us you had gone to your rest, and would not come home until you were ready." Her hand reached up to the silver comb Tamsin wore in his hair, and she brushed his cheek with her thumb. "I gave the raven that comb, to give to you, to leave with you, if there was anywhere you ... were."

Not drowned Over the Waves and forever lost, a houseless shade wandering a dead continent, that meant. But they had all, in their own ways, tried to have faith in the raven's promise, that wherever Tamsin was he was at rest.

"I don't know what happened," Tamsin said, with a kind of tranquility that suggested he'd come to terms with it. "I more or less remember the fire and the water and the song ... and then I was dreaming, probably, but of nothing in particular ... and then I woke up."

He said *that* as if it were a holy mystery, the way their father had spoken of reaching the peak of the mountain of the gods and finding the flame imperishable burning there.

"And then I woke up," he repeated, wonderingly, tugging his hands free so he could flex his fingers, holding them palm out so that the red scars were plain to see. "I woke up, and my hands didn't hurt, and I could *speak* ..."

And sing? *Sing*?

The question they dared not ask hung there. *Could* Tamsin sing? Could he Sing?

Tamsin was staring vaguely into space, smiling, twirling his hair around his hands. "And I had so much hair," he went on, laughing a little. "So impractical! And yet ..."

And yet he was not the Dreadful; did not *want* to be the Dreadful any longer, he who had fallen ever deeper into violence and death. What had Bedellin said? That anyone with knee-length hair was hardly a warrior?

He could braid it up, obviously. But the fact that he had not immediately cut it off—that he had, instead, taken care of it, found ribbons somewhere to braid into it; that it fell around him in healthy waves: all of that said that he had chosen a new path than the one that had constrained him for so long.

"I wasn't expecting to wake up, let alone home in Elfland," he murmured. "But then I did."

Armion could not look at him. He ran his fingers lightly along the smooth curve of Tamsin's harp, wondering at its materials. Bone and antler, seemingly, strung with ... braided threads?

Armion eyed Tamsin's dark hair, and looked back down to the dark strings on the harp. He plucked one, gently; the string was springy, and sounded with a clear, brilliant sound. Tamsin's eyes cut to him immediately, and his smile widened. "Do you want to learn?" he asked eagerly. "I could teach you!"

Tamsin had *never* been inclined to teach; he had been rather jealous of his skill, and after a certain point had not even liked anyone watching him practice. "I ... could show you how to draw, in return?" Armion returned tentatively, looking at Tamsin's scarred hands. The harp kept vibrating even after the sound had faded from audibility.

"That would be very helpful, I expect," Tamsin agreed, running his fingers through the tangles he'd made of his hair. "Carving the harp—" He turned to Alina, face lit with sudden mischief. "Rather, carving a comb—or two—or three—I might have broken a few early attempts—the carving helped me regain some of the dexterity in my hands. Not to mention all the polishing."

He sighed, then laughed, bright and merry and full of true good humour. Armion wished he could see their mother's expression. But he knew it would be, must be, full of wonder, that Tamsin had come home past all imagination healed enough to laugh at himself.

"Playing too, of course, once the harp was finished, which was only—a fortnight ago? Perhaps three weeks. At the edge of the Downs. But I haven't had much opportunity for anything like writing ..."

Alina said, "Where did you wake up? And ... when?"

Tamsin shifted position, pulling the plaited part of his hair from where it had caught between him and Forro. His face was so alive: Armion could not stop marvelling at it. "West of the river, but far south of the bridge over the Swanlands. As to when ... two months ago, perhaps? Three? We must have been a month coming north to the bridge ... not that we were going very quickly!" He smiled at them, suddenly, a flash of a wry, winsome smile. "So many rest-halts and stops to look at the view ... It was good for me."

Tamsin-that-was had rarely halted longer than the minimum, the pricking, goading curse forever rendering him restless.

"We?" Bedellin said delicately, and looked at Forro. "We heard that someone wearing your sigils had come with two southern elf-maids for the Tourney ..."

"They described *three* southern elf-maids, I expect," Tamsin agreed easily. "River and Ash. Ash is here for the Tourney. River wants to write a history of the ... what did she call it, the Shadowed Age. They were not expecting to run into Tamsin Korrokaith on the riverbank, nor was I expecting to encounter them, but they have been very good company. And excellent students." He turned a beaming smile onto Armion. "I cannot imagine why I was ever so unwilling to teach before! It is a splendid thing, sharing knowledge and skill."

Armion *had* always liked to teach, before. He'd had students, many of them. Tamsin had always scoffed and flitted off after Klara.

"What have you been teaching them?" Forro asked, eyes suddenly narrowing with speculation. "Not ... fighting?"

The betting for the Tourney was always fierce, and though Forro made Bedellin place any bets he might want to lay, he followed the various contests and competitors with keen interest.

"Fencing, rather. Ash is very good," he said simply. "You'd want me if it were a matter of life or death, of course, but otherwise ..."

"Will she beat Daerleon?" Armion asked, which was an absurd question except for the way that Tamsin looked—

"I haven't seen him spar," Tamsin demurred. He grinned at their mother, bright-eyed and cheerful. "I've been teaching River to sing, a little. Can you believe that she didn't know *any* Songs? Not even how to shoo away insects! She wants to be an historian more than a musician, alas. Her voice is decent and she *could* be good, if she was willing to practice."

"*You* can sing?" Armion asked, unable to wait any longer.

He nodded, and the length of tiny silver bells—snowdrops, Armion saw now, looking more closely at them—the snowdrops chimed delicately. One hand went up, curling into the long ribbon-woven plait.

"I'm working on it," Tamsin said, but he was smiling, sly and shy and brilliant again, and this time when his hands twitched he was looking at his harp, and not his sword.

"You'll be Tammorath again," Forro said, deep and intent above Tamsin's head,

Tamsin looked at their mother, but he spoke to all of them, steady with some footing he had gained from his long rest, his recent journey, the young elves he had taught and travelled with: "Yes."

CHAPTER THIRTY-ONE
SINGING THE SUMMER IN

Bedellin stood eventually, returning to his food preparation. Tamsin leaned back against Forro as if he were young, watching.

"Will you—that is, are your hands healed enough for eating this?" Bedellin asked him, gesturing at the array of platters. "There's some soup, if that's easier."

Tamsin rubbed the scars of his left hand with his right thumb. It seemed strange to him to speak of such things. But his brothers had watched him all those straitened years when he could hardly do more than tear at a rabbit with his teeth.

"I think I can manage," he said, though even as he spoke his eyes dropped down to his sword and belt-knife. He forced his eyes back up after he'd reassured himself they were still where they had been, not far from his feet.

"I am glad to hear that," Bedellin said, moving to a loaf of bread and beginning to slice it. Tamsin watched, mesmerized.

"There's so much food," he murmured.

Forro's arm tightened around his shoulders. "There's a gracious plenty of everything, Tamsin."

"River and Ash had cinnamon," he said dreamily, remembering that first morning. "I had forgotten it existed ..."

"You're home now," Alina said, patting him on the knee as she stood. She looked down at him for a moment, her eyes very soft. "Tamsin."

He looked up at her, at the way her hair was coming out of its braid, the depths in her eyes. She, too, had lived all these long years.

"You weren't alone?" he asked, suddenly urgent. "Certhin is here, I saw him as I came into the city ..."

"Certhin, yes, and Klara. I was not alone as you were alone, Tamsin."

He dared not say aloud that he hoped she had not been haunted as he had been haunted. She could not have been—his brothers had followed him—and yet how could she not have been, with her husband dead beyond all possibility of return and her sons lost Over the Waves?

"Come and eat," Bedellin said into the silence. "Perhaps—"

He stopped, and they looked over at him.

"Perhaps you can play for us after, Tamsin," his brother said, and there was no fear in his face as he spoke.

Tamsin was aware that even if his hands were no longer crippled that his table manners were woefully out of practice. Neither their camp-sites nor the village inns where they had eaten plain country fare had required more of him than remembering to take small bites and chew with his mouth closed.

He was fairly certain that wearing a sword to his family table was wholly impolite, but when he hesitated on standing, not quite able to leave his sword behind him on the floor, Armion held it up to him.

"There's no shame in needing to wear it still," Armion said gently.

"I don't need to," Tamsin replied, even as he reached for it. "There's no danger here."

No enemies. No goblins. No monsters. Nothing but his brothers, his mother, and them he would not harm.

"Not for use," Forro agreed, taking the sword and unwrapping the belt from around the scabbard. "That your heart needs it to feel safe ..."

Alina turned around to regard them, a faint frown drawing her brows together. Tamsin looked down in shame, his face and ears burning.

Forro belted the sword on, settling it just where Tamsin had so long worn it, though his hands lingered a moment on the discovery that Tamsin had put on enough weight since his awakening that the buckle had gone several holes out from where it had obviously been for so long.

"You needed it for a long time," Armion said. "We watched you, Tamsin. You *needed* it, to survive."

He hesitated again. "I don't need it to live."

"You won't, perhaps. Give it time," Alina said, and this time when Tamsin looked at her, she smiled at him. Sadly, but with candid care. "It took your brothers a long time to set down their weapons once they could take them up again, and they had been long unhoused."

That was a reassurance. Tamsin nodded shortly, and let Forro draw him over to the great stone table Daerleon had made some time before he was born. The seats were wood and were new. Newer. Each chair-back was carved by their mother's hands in the sigils they had used Over the Waves.

Tamsin traced his hand over his silver star.

"We never stopped hoping you would come home," Forro said.

Tamsin had stopped hoping he would ever see them again, a long time ago. "I could not keep such hope alive."

Forro laughed, incredulous. "Tamsin, you cannot mean that. You kept going."

"That wasn't hope," Tamsin said, tracing the star again, trying not to remember those bleak wastelands, those barren mountains, those desert shores.

(They had been true, his visions, he reminded himself. Not the bloody, vindictive shades of his guilt; but when he had imagined that there was always one of his brothers walking at his side, keeping pace with his relentless movement, that had been true.)

"What would you call it?"

He shrugged, but he found a smile tugging at his mouth. "Stubbornness. Spite. I found myself incapable of letting the Old Enemy *win*."

"Oh, is *that* what it was!" Armion laughed, tugging at the end of Tamsin's braid as he went to his seat. "We stand corrected!"

The food was as good as he had imagined it. Tamsin ate self-consciously, slow with the utensils, grateful for the bread. Grateful, too, that his mother did not stare too much at his clumsy handling of fork and knife. His brothers had already seen him at his worst. They would not be surprised now if he took a mouthful of the roasted peppers and then sat there with his eyes full of tears at the layered flavours.

Afterwards he tried to help clean up, vague memories of their youth stirring, but was pushed back to the padded bench in the inglenook where Armion had left his harp.

He looked at Forro, who was the one to have so pushed him. "You're not afraid?" Tamsin asked, searching his brother's face anxiously. "I—I won't play if you—"

Forro gathered him into his arms once again. Tamsin bowed his head, unable to pull away from this touch. They had not touched so, not all the time Over the Waves, not even when meeting after a parting of years or decades. After Tamsin lost his voice Forro had tried, but Tamsin had not been able to bear pity, not then.

"We have missed your playing," Forro told him fiercely. "We have missed your singing. We are not afraid of you."

Everyone had been afraid of him. Tamsin remembered the way the hardened soldiers of their armies had shrunk back from him, scattered when he raised his harp, fled when he lifted his voice.

He had stopped singing in public outside of battle after the skirmishes in the marshes of Halen. By the time he took Dumloth he had stopped singing in private either. By then he had ceased to be *able* to sing anything but destruction.

He remembered the reflection of himself in the dragon's burning eyes. He had looked utterly mad, burning with power, searing out his own throat with his Song.

His brothers had been roughly comforting, in those months of convalescence when his sight gradually returned to him and his voice never did.

"Thank you," he said, and bent his head to tune his harp.

Not a song of battle, whether weapon or record. No laments—they had all mourned enough. Been grieved enough. Not a song of glory, either, when they knew how empty the triumphs had been, were, in the end.

Bedellin and Armion clattered in the kitchen, putting away the leftover food, washing the dishes. (How astonishing that there could be leftovers; that there was hot water for the washing, and a sink, and dishes.) Forro hovered a moment, then sat down beside their mother at the table. Alina took Forro's hand, and they sat there looking at him, smiling.

Tamsin played a scale, loosening his hands, listening to the way the room seemed to waver between ages. If he did not look too closely at the things that had changed it could have been any moment of his youth before the Breaking of the Lamps.

It had been much easier, singing for River and Ash, when they had known nothing about him. He had not had to play to their imagination or expectation of what the greatest bard of the Firnoi should sound like.

His mother and brothers did not have to imagine anything. They could walk in their own memories of what he had sounded like, in the youth of the world. They had had Klara to remind them over and over again of what he had been, what he had lost, what he had not yet regained. What he might never regain.

A movement caught his eye, and he looked up to see that Bedellin had put his hand on Armion's shoulder, holding him back. Armion met Tamsin's eyes, sober and still.

"It took me years to be able to show anyone my drawings," Armion said. "If you're not ready, we understand."

"I've been playing in villages for the past fortnight," Tamsin said, and shook his head violently. They hadn't mattered, not the same way. They had thought him Tamsin Tammorath's unknown and unacknowledged child, not Tamsin Tammorath himself.

He played another scale, knowing his hands were still fumbling and awkward where once they had flashed across the strings. A flurry of arpeggios, halfway to the rhythm of one of the Linwairi songs he'd played for the shepherds of Underdown and Sticklebrush.

Perhaps that was the way into it.

He let the music take him, the melody unwinding as he plucked the complex rhythms of the dancing-song, his voice weaving through the notes without effort or thought.

One song flowed into another once he started. He followed the Linwair upriver, song by song, until he came to the headwaters and the songs he had played in Underdown and Sticklebrush to welcome the summer in.

That led at last into one of his own songs, a short thing and simple, but a new one. This echoed the skylarks that had sung when he first strung his harp, that first early lark out before the dawn had crested the sky.

Tamsin stopped there, a moment before the light came, holding the last note until the harp-song faded. A motion to his side caught his attention, and he turned to see that Daerleon had come in.

Daerleon.

Tamsin stared at his eldest brother, but it was Daerleon who looked as if he'd seen a ghost.

Daerleon stood straight and tall, his hair in a careless sort of topknot. He wore plain clothes, tunic and leggings in undyed linen, a linen coat in a faded red carelessly open overtop. He wore no jewels and bore no weapons, and that was the strangest thing to Tamsin's eyes.

That, and the way that Daerleon's grey eyes were cool and clear, without the false brightness of his madness at the end.

There was no scar at his throat. Nothing to show where Tamsin had sliced across with the blade that was even now at his hip.

"No," Daerleon said, still in the doorway where he'd stopped. "It —it can't be true—I don't believe it—I don't—it *can't* be you."

Tamsin's hands curled tight around his harp. All the song had died in his throat. He could not bear to look at anyone. All he could see was the way that Daerleon's blood had spilled out, scarlet as their banners; all he could hear was the horrible bubbling laughter of the Old Enemy dying behind him.

They had been standing around him, his dead brothers, when Tamsin had turned away from the holy fire to his last living brother, and failed them all.

Slowly, he looked up, and met Daerleon's cool grey eyes, so very much like their father's. He had faced his dead on that terrible bridge. He had faced the shades of all those goblins; of the Old Enemy and the great dragon; and of the Elves, one by one and in companies until the last was the shade of his brother, the smiling, shining Leon of his childhood, brilliant and fair.

He had faced his dead, the guilt and the grief of them. He had taken that guilt and that grief, the heavy self-inflicted burdens he had carried for so long, and he had dropped them like pebbles of chalk on the white road home.

Daerleon had been dying, all his chest crushed by the hand of the Old Enemy. Nothing could have saved him but a miracle, and Tamsin had had none of those—

Except one, perhaps. The unlooked-for grace of the flame imperishable reappearing long after he'd lost all hope; and whatever miracle had brought him from that overwhelming sea to the iris-girdled mound where he'd awoken to life.

He had had none when Daerleon had looked at him with his eyes bright as the dragon's and asked for death.

No miracles then; but grace since.

Tamsin breathed in carefully, and then he set his harp down, rose to his feet, and crossed the room to the doorway where Daerleon stood struck speechless.

Tamsin tilted his head back to look at Daerleon, who was not as tall as Forro but was taller than he. This close he could see the way his fierce and ruthless brother was trembling, every muscle locked, his lips pressed firmly together.

Daerleon had asked for death, and Tamsin had given it to him.

Daerleon had ordered him to kill; to take cities; to fight in battle after battle; and Tamsin had.

Daerleon had also ordered him to eat, to rest, to bathe. Sometimes he tried to give him other things to do, things to remind him that he was not only the Sword of the Firnoi, not only a weapon, not only a tool—that he was an Elf, and his brother, and that he had loved and been loved, once.

Tamsin had followed him all the way to the end, and once the end was reached, had kept going anyway, step after relentless step. Haunted by his grief and his guilt and his shame; and by his brothers who whispered words of love and encouragement and hope to him who had thought he had none.

They stared at each other, Daerleon and Tamsin, oldest and youngest of seven: the warlord and the bard who had between them led their people to ruination.

And yet here they were, this side of the sea, this side of death, and somewhere not far from here the flame imperishable burned once more.

Tamsin reached out with his hands wide, his palms up so that Daerleon could see the scars, fingers outstretched so he could see that they no longer bound and burned him. He moved slowly, so that Daerleon could brace himself if he needed to.

Forro had embraced him. Armion had embraced him. Bedellin had embraced him. His mother had embraced him.

River and Ash had walked with him across that bridge, and on the long road that led on from it.

Daerleon's hands were braced on the door-jamb, his arms rigid, all his muscles bunched. Tamsin reached up and cupped his brother's face in his palms, guiding him to meet his eyes. He recognized the shame and grief and guilt in Daerleon's—and at last this was something Tamsin *could* answer, a gift he could give. So many gifts had he himself been given! So many small miracles. So unanticipated and unexpected a grace!

"Daerleon," he said, "I am sorry it came to it, but I am glad you asked me to help you, when you needed it."

Tamsin thought again of that smiling young Elf with his hair a waving banner, sauntering gladly down the bridge between life and death. He thought of how River had been sad, not afraid, when he went automatically for his sword; how his family were sad, but understanding, when he could not bear to be unarmed even in his mother's house. And he thought, as well, of how much he had needed his brothers to tell him he was forgiven for not claiming the Old Enemy's crown when it was right in front of him.

"Daerleon," he said, staring very intently into his brother's eyes, which were not like the dragon's now; which were cool and clear and shining. Daerleon trembled under his hands, and now it was Tamsin's turn to run his thumbs under someone's eyes and brush away their tears. "I forgive you for asking me to kill you. For leaving me the last to bear the Oath. For ... all the other orders."

He stopped, for his voice was shaking. But he had promised himself, had he not? He had walked across the bridge of the dead: and he had walked the road to the city of the living.

"And I thank you," he said more softly, "for never forgetting that I was something more than the Thrice-Accursed and the Dreadful, and not letting me forget either, for all I never showed you I listened; and for all the time that you and our brothers spent at my side when I thought I was alone and only dreaming that I was not."

"We never left you," Daerleon whispered. "Even if we could have, we wouldn't have left you alone—not like that!" And it was as if his words were a release, for suddenly Tamsin was half-engulfed in brothers, with Daerleon sobbing upon his shoulder and Forro once again at his back, holding him safe and sound and *home*.

Home, home, home: the word rang in his mind like the bells chiming in the city when he had walked through its gates. And yet—and yet—

He had never been particularly close to Harlin and Harlom, and would see them in good time.

There was another whose name rang through the city, through his memory, through his heart.

Klara, Klara, he thought, and when they had all finished weeping for the time being, he took up his harp and slipped out of the house.

The streets led him directly to the garden he had seen from above. If he looked up he could see the bench where he had sat with the harp silent in his hands, the stream leaping between the bronze and amethyst lotuses.

The garden was very beautiful, and all Klara's. He knew it from a hundred dreams, when it had been cold and dark, all frost-rimmed shadows. It was still full of shadows, but now they were the warm dancing ones cast by the flame imperishable.

Tamsin walked the small enclosure, dreams and memories of dreams overlaying the silver-boled trees, the smooth green lawn, the white and black birds with all their long ages of gestation. He caressed the glossy leaves of hollies that had once been shadows, their prickles ice; ran his fingers lightly over the smooth warm bark of the silver trees, watching how golden light chased after his touch.

Klara had been full of silence when she laid down the first layers of this garden. Silence and grief and rage that had hardened into ice, the opposite and match of his Song and grief and the rage that had burned so fiercely until it had charred out his very heart.

But a winter's night gave way in its time to spring, and where the fire had blazed the ashes gave strength to the new growth that came after.

Tamsin sat down on the crystal bench he had seen so often in his dreams, and he set the bone harp on his knee. His heart was full of Klara's shadows, his eyes full of the light for which he wrought such woe, and when he tipped his head up he could see a dark figure standing at the very highest peak of that shining crystal tower rising above him.

He smiled as he bent his head over the harp and began once again with that old Linwairi song to sing the summer in.

CHAPTER THIRTY-TWO

TWO EAGLES, FLYING

Klara heard the rumours from her birds, of course, but did not believe them.

There were so many people coming from the outflying regions of Elfland to the Tourney that the birds were confused, and brought her such an overabundance of information, fact and rumour and whisper and observation all tangled together, that Klara was used to disregarding most of it.

The birds that had flown farthest told her of a great mist falling over the Swanlands, hiding the bridge, a mist that roiled with silent death: but such a thing had happened before, and would again, and it meant little without any other phenomena to bolster the case of one possible cause over another.

Then, too, the far-flying birds least understood what Klara was interested in: they told her what they found notable. They told her of the overlapping concerns of swans and swan-maids, whose voices rose up in raucous clamour until the mist swept down the bridge and silenced them.

Klara took this as a possible omen, and set it aside.

The birds that flew over the wide Downs were for the most part wild. They shared news freely with Klara's birds, the white crows that explored the nooks and crannies of Elfland on their own concerns before returning from time to time to tell her what they'd seen. Most of their news was of sheep and shepherd, eagle and fox, wolf and hare; sometimes they spoke of spirits, or the people that were neither elves nor animals, but lived in the close embrace of magic.

They told her of three travellers coming east along the Road, and they described the flash and clash of metal once, twice, thrice a day, sometimes more. Klara understood that they were competitors coming for the Tourney, and set that news aside also.

They told her of the music at night, the music that sounded of joy in death, but the white crows flew in the day, and had filtered the news they had in turn received from the owls. Thus they described it in the terms they understood: to the owls, to the crows, the music was white as bone, black as death, sharp as the talons closing on prey, as the sun rising over the grass.

They told her the music lingered after the minstrel passed on, that the villagers danced and sang and were somehow *different*.

Klara should not have disregarded this news, but the birds had tales of minstrels coming from every direction, and those from the sea seemed, that year, more intriguing. And in a Tourney year there were always more festivals and dancing and singing than usual.

Besides she was busy, in her own way. Had ensured she was too busy to think too much about such things.

Tourney years made everyone who remembered him think a great deal more of Tamsin than usual. Klara was no exception; though it irritated her, to have her private grief and hope and longing every-where around her. She could hardly deny the emotions to his broth-ers, who had adopted her as their sister, but it nevertheless was the case that her careful balance of grief and hope and longing was canted all out of proportion.

There were too many people singing Tamsin's songs from Over the Waves. A minstrel singing *other* songs from Over the Waves did not register as it ought.

She could not possibly have missed the greeting the Old City gave its long-lost bard.

Klara stood at the top of her high tower with the spray catching the sunlight behind her, and listened.

At first she did not hear anything strange. Nothing to note, not in particular, except to think, *The city sounds fine today.*

The song rippled towards her in stages, soft as mist turning to rain; or the sun rising. It was already sounding forth in the bells when Klara realized what it could be, what it must be, what it *was.*

Who it was.

Her tower was high, spray-dazzled, glittering in the sunlight. (The sun was high: this was another sort of sunrise, another sort of dawn, another sort of light altogether.) Klara stood there with her white birds circling around her, all the white doves of the city flashing, fulgurations of white wings, the thunderclaps of their wings clattering against the stones.

The stones hummed under her feet. Klara was barefoot, this fine spring day, the water and the light washing over her feet, the cool stone vibrating into her bones, her blood, up her spine, into her heart.

The bells rang, the silver-lipped bells Alina had made; the great bronze bells that were older than the sun or the moon; the tiny crystal and glass bells that had been strung on long lines throughout the city, tongueless and mute in honour of that one whose voice had been lost.

(Tamsin's brother Harlin had blown them, bell after bell, relearning his craft. Each one a perfect gradient, white through all the blues to violet, to red, to orange, to yellow, to green, to dazzling diamond-clarity.)

The bells were singing now, their voices freed at last, each tone as flawless as its colour.

Klara gripped the stone parapet, where the water fell down upon her in the finest droplets.

The birds circled; the bells rang; her heart whispered. *Tamsin, Tamsin.*

She traced the path he walked by the way the Song unfurled around him. Under his footfalls the stones resonated, power coalescing under each step, vining outward in tendrils that budded and blossomed in light and song.

All those tongueless bells, singing forth. All those silver trees, blooming gold. All Klara's shadows, pouring towards him like the waters rushing down a cataract.

The road curved, the stairs opened up, the colonnades shifted, and Tamsin walked home.

Klara stood on her high tower, a Song of greeting in her throat, her hands on the stone parapet, the water running down her face, listening.

He did not sing. Not then. Nor did she. But the city did.

She did not go down; not at first.

She stood on her tower, the world whirling about her, the birds hanging in the air, still as painted images, as memories. She stood silent in the midst of song; stood transfixed by hope and fear, so perfectly balanced.

Tamsin, Tamsin, cried her heart.

Tamsin, Tamsin sang the city, her city, his city.

Later—how much later she did not know, could not tell; there was too much light in her eyes, too much Song in her ears, too much time thickened around her, heavy as grief and yet sweeter than honey, than love—later, later, she heard his voice.

The harp-music came first, a trickle of notes winding their way up to her eyrie, her high perch, climbing up the scintillating water-drops that had once been ice, once been tears, once long ago been hope. It was not the music *of* her water-fountain, her crystal spire, her shadows and her ice and her birds: but each note twined with each of hers, matching leap and whirl and poise—

Once Klara and Tamsin had wheeled and whirled around each other, their voices raised in challenge and delight, two eagles soaring ever higher until they could lock their claws together and tumble down and down and down all the footless halls of the sky.

Klara stood frozen at the top of her tower as the harp-music rose about her, note by note building a city of memory.

It was not the perfect, flawless, faultless playing of her memory. This was the music of one whose hands remembered pain and death, who had been broken, who had fallen and faltered and failed.

Who had stood up, each time he had fallen; who had tried again, each time he had failed; who had put one foot in front of another long after he had drained every last drop that could possibly have been squeezed out of his heart of hope. Who had walked and walked and walked, silent, silenced, dark-eyed, stony-hearted, until out of nowhere there had been the light to which he had so long been bound, which he had so long sought, and with all the bonds broken, he had dived down into the murky water and grasped it at last.

She knew the halls of his memory: the soft light of the Lamp of Day, brilliant without the edge of the bright Sun; the softer-yet light of the Lamps of Night, bronze here in the City of the Firnoi, casting everyone into sepia hues but for Klara in her silver and Tamsin in his gold.

The harpist built the city as it was long ago, so long ago her memory had almost lost it; so long ago his memory had burnished it smooth and sweet as a river-worn stone.

Klara gripped the stone parapet, the water beating on her shoulders, each drop beading in her hair, netting it with silver and crystal spangles. She could feel the city listening through the stone, through her hands, the resonant memory, slow and deep, rising in the stones (in the queen who had slumbered in her moat all these thousands upon thousands of years; in the old king who had sunk deep into his own palace); in Klara, who held this city as it was in her heart.

She opened her mouth to take the song back, to claim the city for her own, to reclaim all the years the harp-music did not—

And then he began to sing.

Tamsin Tammorath, whose voice had heralded the new-risen Sun. Tamsin Indorath, whose voice had summoned and strengthened armies. Tamsin Korrokaith, who slew cities; who had slain the great Dragon; who had struck off the head of the Old Enemy upon his throne.

Tamsin the seventh son of Dâr and Alina, whom Klara loved.

Tamsin sang.

No. Tamsin *Sang*.

His voice wove through the city's voices, all those sweet-sounding bells, those resonant stones, those curious hearts and souls of his family and his people. He sang of the youth of the world—

No. He sang of the youth *in* the world, the spring come again after the long winter, the sun rising after darkness.

He sang of safe shadows, kind strangers, forgivable mistakes.

He sang of waking after a sleep that might have been death or might have been enchantment but was, whatever else it was, rest.

Waking to birdsong and sunlight and the wind in the leaves, waking to health and painless scars and *a voice*.

He sang of a road, where there had never been a road before, passing from death into life. Of walking that road, facing all his dead, all the fearsome ranks of his dead—all the midges and gnats and game-birds and rabbits and fish and deer and goblins and monsters and *elves*—

The grief of the elves dead at his hand, at his voice, *this* voice, which had been a weapon and was now a gift, a glory, something splendid.

He delved deeper and deeper into the Song, quarrying the stone that his heart had become, cracking open the rough lump and finding within the glittering crystals of something ... lovely.

He sang of the bridge between death and life: how joy and hope and pragmatic sense had held him to his course, had guided him even past the elves, past the Dragon, past the Old Enemy, past all the dead dross of himself.

He sang of the friendly strangers who chose to become friends, who looked on the most feared warrior of the Shadowed Age and saw instead someone who needed a kind and helping hand, and offered it.

He sang of the flowers and the grass of the Downs, the high clear air, the wind blowing sweet and warm, the cold water running over the white chalk. The fires of an evening, comfort and company after so long alone.

(Always, echoing back and forth, the dark shadows that had not been safe, the strangers that had been enemies, the mistakes that had broken himself and his family and his people and the world; the loneliness and the dread that had swallowed him, as once Klara herself had seen the self-inflicted curse of the Oath stretching its jaws wide to swallow him.)

Tamsin sang of this new Elfland under the Sun, new to no one but him and the children born that year, and step by step how he had found his way home.

Step by step, Klara followed the music down.

Two eagles they had been, spiralling ever higher, daring each other to heights beyond anyone else's imagination. Tamsin had sung himself into the instrument of death—into Death itself, as the song that had come to be sung of him had it, that Death who came crowned in moonlight and blood.

He had sung himself into Death, had Tamsin Tammorath, but he had once been the poet of spring, the bard of spring, and now he sang the seed of himself out of death once more into life.

Klara had sung herself into shadows and ice, and sung herself out of her winter into spring.

It was the spring of her imagination that held the city now, that welcomed him home.

Two eagles had they been, spiralling ever higher, always putting off the moment when they would lock their claws and tumble down the footless halls of the sky.

The exquisite harp, the flawed harping; the flawless voice, the broken heart.

The city of ancient memory, hazy with the antique glimmer of the Lamps, given to a new shape, a new life under the Sun.

Two eagles had they been, spiralling ever higher.

Step by step, Klara followed the music; and step by step, her feet ringing heartbeats and chimes from her crystal spire, her glittering fountain, her silver trees and singing birds, hardly aware of her voice at first, she began herself to sing.

She sang of the two superlative singers, peerless but for themselves, their voices shaping the world, too proud to realize how they shaped themselves. She sang of their glory and their folly, their strength and their skill, their pride and their joy.

Tamsin sang of flowers and sheep, shepherds dancing on the green, the prickle of teasel seedheads in his hands, the country she had once loved and left behind.

Klara sang of the crowns of flowers and of jewels, the crafts of his brothers' hands, the storms and sky-colours woven into cloth, the arts of the Old City as it was now, a brilliant jewel set in the white stone of the encircling wall, the verdant plains.

Tamsin sang of the tournament that was for strength and courage and skill, and not for death: of the banners of the once-dead flying proudly: of the city full of faces he knew, and whom he loved.

Klara sang of the river and its otters, its kingfishers and its swans, and the great wide marshes Tamsin had known Over the Waves and which she had seen in her dreams. Tamsin sang back the city of shadows and ice, the deadly beauty of the deepest winter, the slow yearning for spring.

Spring was all around them, in the flowers foaming over walls, the leaves bursting forth in all their shades of green and red and gold, in the birds flying in Klara's wake, her midnight gown caught into iridescence.

Down she went and down, her voice rising up, twining with his, gold and silver as the sun and the moon, their voices mingling like starlight reflected on a still pool.

He was sitting on her crystal bench in her garden of shadows, which was now a garden of light, for the flame imperishable burned again in the stone basin.

A white harp was in his hands, bright as moonlight, strung with shadows. His hands were scarred, but they were deft on the strings; his dark hair was woven, as in all the stories, with scarlet and silver.

He looked at her with his dark eyes, his long lashes, his solemn face, the song pouring forth from him like the light from the sun.

Death came crowned in moonlight and blood, Klara thought; but *Golden-voiced Summer called to Silver-voiced Winter* was what she sang.

Tamsin smiled. Klara had never seen anything so beautiful. She smiled back; and then she had never heard anything so beautiful as the splendour in that splendid voice.

(They had been peerless, in the youth of the world, before they knew anything. They were peerless still, Klara and Tamsin, no longer young, no longer innocent; their voices held depths that they had never known to reach out of—or for.)

They sang to each other, winter and summer, two eagles spinning around and around, wheeling and whirling in the halls of the sky, handing off the part of spring as they had ever handed off their parts, until Klara was singing Tamsin's summer-voiced joy and Tamsin sang Klara's wintry repose, and the birds and the bells and the holy fire whirled around them.

Dizzy, dazzled, drowning in light and song, they let the song of spring unfurl into blossoming summer.

Tamsin's hands stilled on his harp, the strings folding into the air instead of fading, their voices gathered by the shadows and the sunlight into the leaves and branches and stones and bells of the city.

They stood there, Tamsin and Klara, facing each other over the stone basin, the flame imperishable dancing over the crystals.

Tamsin looked exactly the same, and entirely different, and Klara had never wanted him more than with that bone-white harp humming on his knee and the flame for which he had destroyed himself burning merrily before them.

Tamsin, Tamsin sang the city around them, in full riotous bloom, summer over their shoulders and in their hair and their hands and oh, his eyes, his mouth, his heart.

Oh, it was their city, it was his, it was hers, hers, hers, and how she had *missed* him.

Tamsin met her gaze, solemn and sunlit and alive, and then he said, "Klara."

He said nothing more. But then they had rarely needed to *speak*, back when they and the world were young. Klara smiled, slow and perhaps a little sly, and she said, "Tamsin," and felt nothing else needed to be said by her, either, just then, when there was all the sky around them.

They came back hand-in hand, Tamsin Tammorath and Klara Kanorath, their eyes full of light and their voices full of song. Tamsin's harp was on his shoulder and his sword was at his hip, and Klara's shadow-birds followed her in their coveys and congregations, for they were not now who they had been, in the youth of the world.

They walked through the city long that day, wending the streets that were not the paths Tamsin had grown up running, but which ran through his dreams. They walked hand-in-hand, heads bent as they spoke together, their long dark hair mingling over Klara's gown of midnight and Tamsin's ancient tunic like the welcome dimness of a midsummer eve.

Throughout all the Old City the bells pealed. Outside its pale walls the song of the summer tumbled down with the afternoon sunlight, heavy and heady as honey, as love returned manifold, as peace.

Down in the Tourney grounds, Ash turned to River, and, pleased, said, "He's home."

AUTHOR'S NOTE

The Bone Harp stands by itself amongst my works: the Fairyland one might reach from the Nine Worlds is not, exactly, this Elfland; it knows neither sun nor moon, nor a history such as Tamsin's and Klara's.

To follow on from here to my other books, I would suggest *The Bride of the Blue Veil*, which takes up the fairytale motifs and style, or *Portrait of a Wide Seas Islander* for an introduction to the main current of Nine Worlds stories.

I expect there will one day be a sequel to *The Bone Harp*. To stay abreast of any news, please visit my website, where you can also join my newsletter.

www.victoriagoddard.ca

ACKNOWLEDGMENTS

Thanks so much to Wesley for suggesting this story in the first place (and for ongoing support through the writing of it), and to the wonderful moderators of the HOTE Support Group Discord server, particularly Jenny and Bread, for their splendid encouragement, cheerleading, and reading of the early draft.

I'd also like to thank Alex G. for her thoughts on just what sort of people decide to go adventuring with a total stranger (and for the strangely beguiling idea that the immortality of elves might be a bit like that of lobsters, which I'm sorry didn't otherwise make it into the text), and Alice Degan for her excellent and timely copyediting even after I'd missed several deadlines.

www.ingramcontent.com/pod-product-compliance
Lightning Source LLC
Chambersburg PA
CBHW022016310726

48972CB00006B/1671